PALEOL
Elegy of Dirt a
Book C

S.A. Adams

This is a work of fiction, all people, places and the events surrounding them are products of the author's imagination. Any resemblance to actual persons, living or dead, or actual events are purely coincidental.

Preface

When our African ancestors first crossed the Sinai and made their way north into Eurasia, it was a different world. A receding ice age kept Northern Europe under large glaciers, and the climate was cold and dry. Along with the changing temperatures and landscape, the human migrants would have hunted and competed against Pleistocene megafauna such as mammoths, straight-tusked elephants, woolly rhinos, cave bears, lions, hyenas, and sabre-cats, all of which were larger than their modern versions.

These first travelers and colonizers did not cross into Eurasia once, but in successive waves. Each new wave out of Africa brought humans slightly different from their forbearers, with cultures and technology that varied from that outside the continent. As the newcomers made their way north, they must have soon discovered that they were not the only people living in the area.

For most of human history, Homo sapiens shared this earth with other human species. However, all the other species went extinct before written history began. Neanderthals, Denisovans, and Homo Floresiensis are just three examples of other human species that once shared this planet with us. Neanderthals had been living in Europe and the Middle East at least 250,000 years earlier than Homo sapiens.

This means Neanderthals had occupied Eurasia for a longer time than modern humans have occupied the entire world up to the present. They were one of the most successful hominid species in the world and most recently to have gone extinct. While they are closely related to us, they are, in fact, a distinct species, descended from a common hominid ancestor. Neanderthals had brains that were on average larger than that of humans, but their brain lobes were smaller in certain sections. They were more robust, considerably stronger, and their shorter and stockier stature allowed them to conserve heat more efficiently in the cold climate. New scientific evidence has shattered the old stereotype of the dim-witted brute.

Neanderthal burial sites, cave art, and stone tools lead anthropologists to theorize that they were a highly intelligent species with technology that rivalled that of Homo sapiens. However, they had evolved almost exclusively in ice age Europe while Homo sapiens evolved in Africa. Most interestingly, DNA research has shown that all modern humans who do not originate from Africa carry up to 4% Neanderthal DNA, proving that Neanderthals and Homo sapiens did, in fact, breed together. This is central to our story.

As successful as the Neanderthals were, however, 40,000 years ago, their fossil record mysteriously ends. Whether their extinction was related to climate change, competition with modern humans, or a mix of both is still a mystery. However, I don't believe it is a coincidence that these successful evolutionary cousins who lived throughout the ice age with its many temperature fluctuations went extinct a few thousand years after the arrival of modern humans.

Homo sapiens continue to drive thousands of species on earth to extinction every year; the Neanderthals could possibly be humanity's first sin. The wonder, fear, and ensuing drama that must have played out when humans first encountered Neanderthals is a fascinating idea to imagine. This is a fictionalized version of their story. A story that could only be written with any scientific accuracy because of the amazing discoveries that have recently developed over the past   fifteen   years.

Prologue

Time fogged traumatic visions of childhood, but the feeling of terror remained just as distinct as the day it happened. Memories of tall men yelling with anger, their words incomprehensible. His memory includes the feeling of a hard kick to his back and being thrown to the earthen ground, followed by the sounds of crying and confusion.

A woman is being dragged by her long hair, her protruded face and large brow contorted with pain and anger. The woman looks at the young boy, and her face is familiar. Her eyes are staring at him with maternal sympathy as they dragged him away.

A dark-skinned man is being held by other men. The screams from the woman suddenly stop. The man being held falls on the floor with cries of anguish. The boy feels another kick, then more pain and darkness.

He must cover his eyes when opens them again. *So bright!* The boy feels the bite of icy wind and freezing snow against his skin. Coldness, hunger.

He is alone and cannot stop shivering. He tries to get up and walk, but the snow burns his bare feet, so he returns to the small fur from which he came. It offers little cover and warmth, so he curls up, his tears freezing onto his face.

He whimpers out his mother's name, over and over, until a shadow looms over him. A short and stocky long-haired figure is smiling gently at him. He remembers the brutish grunts that are scary at first but over time become the familiar sounds of reassurance and safety. Strong arms pick him up out of the cold. He is being carried away in those powerful arms. They give him water and food. Soon, a feeling of protection surrounds him. The boy is going home.

PART I - Tribe's Apart

Chapter 1

Sira hobbled her way through the uneven ground of the trail. She seemed unbothered by the slick mud as she limped forward, pretending that each step was a laboured effort. She put a great weight upon the walking stick in her right hand, demonstrating she was crippled or old–easy prey. Animal pelts were wrapped around her entire body so that only her eyes were showing. The eyes were bright brown and energetic as they darted back and forth, accustomed to life in the wild.

With every step, Sira's sense of nervousness grew, and her hand quivered upon the stick. She steadied herself, then resumed forward. She felt a strong desire for recognition, a desire for respect. The desire was strong enough for her to overlook the high risk of this endeavour.

She inhaled and focused on her breathing, ignoring the sound of the stream as it trickled over the smooth river stones. The valley stream cut a gorge through the dry hills, creating a lush forest on either side. A chilly breeze ran upstream, nipping her face and rustling the leaves of the canopy overhead, but she ignored that too. The valley was deceptively calm and peaceful, but she knew otherwise. There was death here. She could not hear it or see it, but could catch its occasional dank scent. A lifetime of hunting and living with nature had moulded her senses so that she could feel its presence. A predator stalked her.

The unmistakable whistle of the bluebird sounded ahead. In one deft movement, she chucked the furs. Before they had even hit the ground, she was already in full sprint. She had transformed from the old cripple to a young athletic hunter. Her bare feet thumped and pounded the ground as she flung up leaves and mud. Her dark legs strained with hard, lean muscle as vegetation cracked upon impact with them. Exposed tree roots caused her to skip and jump from side to side. She had to duck under a giant fallen tree covered with moss and flat fungi. The cold air took on a life of its own as it bit at her naked breasts and exposed legs. A muffled patter in the mud behind her grew louder. It was closing in at an inhuman speed, but she didn't dare look back.

Sira knew a mature predator might have been more cautious and not fallen for the ruse, but this one was young. It had been stalking what it thought would be easy prey, and now the sight of its fleeing quarry triggered its evolutionary instinct. The chase was on. It abandoned all caution and sprinted forward at full speed, the slopping of its enormous paws in the mud and the snapping of vegetation becoming louder as it gained velocity, now opting for speed rather than stealth.

Sira could hear the grunting of the creature's breath behind her. Her throat constricted with fear, and each breath now burned her lungs. *Had this been a mistake? Maybe she miscalculated the distance? Did she not react quickly enough?* Doubts swirled her mind as the feline breath sounded as if it was only a few steps behind her. Terror filled her, and she fought the urge to look over her shoulder. To her relief, the spot she had marked earlier suddenly came into sight, a mud depression in the trail surrounded by rocks and bushes. The perfect spot for an ambush if she could make it in time. She gave one last push with all her strength as she dived belly down into the watery black mud, bracing herself for the pain of teeth and claws.

* * *

Tonik sat crouched behind the bushes and heard the bluebird call. Kadam could imitate the sounds of the birds so well he almost couldn't tell the difference. The bluebird sound was one of the many his tribe used for signals, and he knew this one meant the cat had been spotted.

A few short moments later, he heard the patter of Sira's feet. He could see the whites of her eyes, and her frantic breathing revealed the terror which had gripped her. Tonik's heart skipped a beat. The brown cat was closing in on Sira, manoeuvring to pounce. *It is too close!*

He crouched in anticipation, tightening the grip on his spear, his palms wet with perspiration. This wasn't just any girl, it was his Sira.

Sira dived for the mud, and he did not wait for the impact. He burst out of the bushes, spear at the ready. As Sira's body hit the mud with a splatter, he met the cat in mid-air as it pounced for her.

The original plan involved him planting the back of his spear into the ground and letting gravity do the work for him. But he had been too hasty and could not get the butt of the spear down quick enough.

Caught by surprise at the sight of him, the cat jerked its head up, and they crashed together. The cat's nose and flat sides of its two large fangs hit Tonik squarely in his chest, and they crashed backwards together. "Uuuugh," Tonik gasped as pain shot through into his chest. His flint-tipped wooden spear had missed its mark and punctured the big cat under the skin of its front limb.

He hit the slick mud with the weight of the cat upon him. The wind was knocked out of his lungs, and his vision blurred as he contacted the ground. The animal let out a terrible roar and tore its claws across Tonik's shoulder. This fresh shot of pain cleared his vision, and he looked up, straight into the mouth of a sabre-toothed cat, its eyes filled with fury.

He tried to move into a defensive position, but the mud was too slippery. His arms and legs flailed uselessly as the cat's jaws opened, angling to sink its massive canines into Tonik's head. The breath of the cat was hot on his face, and its weight on his chest made it impossible to breathe. Then he heard an awful hiss, followed by choking, and looked up to see blood spewing from its mouth. It spattered onto Tonik's face and stung his eyes.

The great cat coughed and heaved another few final breaths that smelled of foul meat. It went limp, and the full weight of it sagged onto him. After a few attempts to struggle free, Tonik thought he might suffocate under the animal but soon felt it being slowly dragged off his body. He wheezed, coughing as a rush of cool air filled his lungs.

Moments later, he heard a chuckling sound, followed by a high-pitched giggle. He wiped his eyes free of mud and blood and came up to his elbows. Two other men were standing over him with huge smiles. Another round of laughter came from them.

He glanced at the cat, which now lay still, two spears lodged deep inside of it. Tonik gave a last sigh of relief and fell back into the mud. The two men's skills would normally cause Tonik jealousy, but right now he was just grateful to be alive. Kadam and Rooti were always chosen as hunt leaders, and this showed why. The two men had burst upon the cat in perfect timing, both spears hitting their mark. Either of the men's hits would have been enough to neutralise the creature, but they were survivalist hunters, and they took no extra chances when dealing with such a dangerous creature.

"Tonik, stop big tooth with his chest," Kadam said mockingly as he beat his own chest and pointed to the dead cat. "I don't know this way to hunt big tooth, I will call this Tonik's way," he teased. He turned to his fellow hunter and asked, "Rooti, you want to hunt a big tooth next time, like Tonik?"

Rooti shook his head disapprovingly. "No, that way looks like it hurts," he said, smiling and pounding his chest, followed by another giggle.

"Rooti, you kill a big tooth, but you still laugh like a girl," Tonik jousted back. Now he extended his arms, signalling the two to help him to his feet.

Sira stood up from the mud, her face and chest dripping with black goo. She made a giggling sound, imitating Rooti's laugh. Her white teeth and bright eyes were the only thing visible underneath the mud. "We killed him!" she exclaimed and hopped over to the cat with fascination.

"*We* killed *her*," Kadam corrected, signalling to himself and Rooti. "It is a girl big tooth, and she is not yet grown. She may be with her mother still. Let's move it up the hill, this place to easy for her to make ambush on us. I don't think Tonik's chest can take another hunt," he chuckled.

Rooti and Kadam turned to where they had stashed their stone hand axes while Sira and Tonik went to the stream to wash.

From behind them, Kadam and Rooti's voices could be heard reciting the hymn of the hunt. "From dirt our bones, and our bones to dirt."

Sira gazed at Tonik with affection. "Are you hurt Tonik?"

"No!" he said with pride as he hobbled over. "But ugh... I don't think I can run," he said, probing his chest delicately with his finger.

They waded out into waist-deep water together. Tonik was quivering from adrenaline, but he shivered even more and made a whooshing sound as the freezing water washed over his waist.

Sira laughed at his reaction and splashed water on him. She approached him affectionately, cupping water in her hands and washing away the mud from the cut on his shoulder. It was not deep; the cat did not have a chance to dig in before Kadam had paralyzed it. There would be no worry about him getting the fever, but it would leave a nasty scar.

He grimaced as she cleaned the cuts, delicately

moving her hand over his chiselled muscle. Tonik looked down. Her smooth dark skin shone in the glimmer and reflection of the stream. She was tall for a woman of their tribe, taller than many men. Her body hardened by all the years growing up and hunting with men. Her hair hung down to her shoulders in thick, matted ropes. She was also shivering from the cold water, and tiny bumps appeared on her arms, which only accentuated the firm suppleness of her skin. He watched as the mud rolled down the cleavage of her breasts, then over the slight bumps of her abdomen muscles.

Tonik felt proud of her, although he didn't express it. Their gazes met, and her dark brown eyes lit up, making him stir. She gave him a mischievous looking half smile, then pushed him back and whipped her head, purposefully hitting his cut shoulder with her wet locks. He flinched slightly at this, and it made her half smile grow full. She splashed him again and yelled, "Tonik the mighty hunter! He hunts with his chest and not his spear!" She held an imaginary spear at her waist and thrust her hips forward in a way that insinuated something else.

Kadam and Rooti roared with laughter at the display.

Rooti stood up, his hands already completely covered in cat guts. "Kadam, Kadam, look at me," he cried in a woman's voice. "Look, look, I'm Sira! The baby cat is going to catch me!" He mockingly ran and imitated the look of fear on her face during the chase.

Kadam growled with pleasure.

Tonik, still enchanted by Sira's beauty, replied, "Sira, you ran well. But your face..." He imitated her face, unable to finish his sentence before laughing. With that, the three men went into a fit of laughter together. It was the best kind of laugh, the elation one only feels when faced with danger and survives to feel the rush. Their survival depended on their collaboration. These moments bonded them as one, something bigger and stronger than any of them could be as an individual. For a brief moment, they felt free from all the dangers of the world.

Kadam finally broke the moment of jubilation. "Hurry and help us clean this cat before the hyenas catch the smell!"

Disappointment struck her. She felt she earned and deserved more recognition for her part in the hunt. The respect she craved from them was being denied. She felt cheated in her well-earned glory. Baiting the cat was her idea, after all.

***

Sira had always been a deep thinker, spending a fair amount of time daydreaming about the future. Most members of the tribe thought her a curious creature. Her father, Raam, would joke and say that she must have clouds stuck in her head, and that was why she was always staring up at them.

Tonik was the only person who understood her, at least the only one who had the patience to listen. She would sneak over to his sleeping fur at night and talk to him about her ideas until the moon was high in the sky. Most of the time, she knew he didn't understand, but he smiled and politely made the head gesture of agreement.

The idea of baiting the sabre-cat by pretending to be old and crippled was another one of her ideas. It took almost the entire morning to convince the other three men. Killing the cat was a revenge hunt for them, dangerous and ill-advised by the elders of the tribe. Two of their fellow tribe members had been killed recently by a sabre-cat, both victims elderly and frail.

The first victim was an elder man named Soot. He had gone searching for the dream mushrooms near the stream several days ago, but never returned. The other was an elderly woman who strayed too far from the fire to relieve herself at night. Only her bloody fur blanket, feces, and paw prints remained.

Once one of these cats had the taste of people, it would continue to hunt them. Although the tribe had been under severe hardship recently, the honour of hunting and killing such a creature was irresistible. The group of hunters led by Kadam had tracked the cat for several days, but sabre-cats were cunning and elusive. The cat's spoor led them in a giant circle, through the valley and hills until ended up close to where they had started.

They had finally agreed to Sira's baiting tactic for lack of a better idea.

Success at killing the cat gave them renewed energy as they imagined the fresh meat. The story around the fire of a big tooth kill would enthral the entire tribe. But Sira knew that Kadam and Rooti would take all the credit for themselves. The two older and bigger men would playfully mock her and Tonik in front of the tribe as they did now. Everyone would celebrate the two men's victory. Kadam and Rooti would each get to keep one of the cat's long canines, a powerful and coveted trophy among their tribe.

As the men finished gutting and cleaning the carcass, Sira walked back down the trail to collect the fur she had dropped during the chase. From a distance, she could hear Kadam's voice barking at Tonik, chiding him for jumping out of the bush too early and almost spoiling the kill.

"You are too worried about Sira. You keep your eyes on her instead of the big tooth, then you missed!" he snapped.

Sira smiled to herself. It gave her a strange pleasure to know that sometimes Tonik could not hide his love for her.

Kadam carried on with his chiding. "Don't

think because of that small cut, that you won't take turns carrying," he warned.

Sira thought about the long walk back to their camp. Each of them would have to take equal turns in carrying the carcass. Women would often hunt alongside the men in their tribe. However, they were expected to perform their share of the workload or risk not being invited back again. The pressure for a woman hunter to perform was very high from the start, and many lacked the confidence to try.

Now that she was out of sight from the others, she dropped her shoulders in weariness and bent down for the fur. A chilly breeze whipped through the trees again, this time from a different direction. A strange sensation came over her, and she felt another shiver. An ominous sixth sense struck her. A feeling one gained from living their entire life in the wild. Something was watching her.

She jerked up and peered into the line of trees. A quick fear hit her again when she remembered the comment about the big tooth's mother. But the breeze carried a mysterious and unfamiliar scent, not the scent of a big tooth. Her eyes darted to a shadowy movement of limbs. She strained to see between the trunks of the cedar trees, but all she saw now were the flickering shades of green and brown from the sun's rays catching the leaves overhead. The scent abruptly vanished, her fear fading with it.

Sira huffed and turned back, angry with herself. At her age, she should not be afraid of forest shadows.

Chapter 2

Jubilation filled the tribe as the four weary hunters entered the camp. Relatives and friends that had spent the last few nights in anxious anticipation now rushed forth with cheers of triumph. The sight of the slain sabre-cat was a spectacle that no one could ignore. Not only had they returned without serious injuries, but they had also killed a dangerous animal of the area, eliminating at least one worry from their minds.

Adults around the camp were busy performing various tasks, such as grinding edible tubers or collecting wood for the night's fire. A group of dirty-looking children had lumps of charcoal in their hands. They had mixed it with saliva and were using it to draw outlines of their hands on the rock wall. Once they caught sight of the hunters, the coal fell from their little hands with disinterest. Skipping to the hunters with wide-eyed expressions, they danced around the sabre-cat in fascination. It was a rare and morbid curiosity to see such a shy and elusive creature up close.

A wrinkled old man sat on a rock etching holes into a hollowed vulture bone. Upon sight of the hunting party, he blew through one end, trying to play the bluebird-inspired tune of their tribe. He shook his head in frustration, as the sound was not yet right. The sight of the cat made him drop his makeshift flute to the floor and ease off his rock.

This rag-tag clan did not have any fancy name or unique symbol to represent themselves as other, larger tribes did. After their separation from the great Auroch tribe many seasons ago, the wise and charismatic middle-aged Raam had formed his own clan, comprising his closest family and allies. To the neighboring tribes, they came to be known simply as "Raam's tribe." They were peaceful, keeping to themselves and using Raam's skill at trading and negotiation to keep them out of conflicts. They made their home among the bountiful plains and thick forests that lay between the coast and the mountains. Being semi-nomadic, they followed the migrating auroch herds and mammoth families. They were brave hunters of the megafauna, and their tribe took great honor in hunting the large creatures.

Raam had been in a circle with a group of young boys practicing knapping stones. They used a large stone anvil which sat half-buried in the earth. Using this as a base, they practiced chipping off flakes from a core piece of rock using another, harder rock as a hammer. They fashioned all their stone tools in this manner. Knapping was an art form that required practice from a young age. One could go through hundreds of cracked and irregular designs before attaining the skill required to make a tool worthy of use. They passed these skills and techniques down from generation to generation.

Raam seemed to have endless patience for teaching, and he spent hours a day knapping. He created hand axes of various sizes and weights, and spear tips he would fix to wooden shafts with tree resin and plant fiber. He gladly shared his tools throughout the tribe for the benefit of all.

At the sight of his daughter, he called for Sira's mother, Tikara, who had been cutting and fashioning deer hide skirts. The three of them rushed together and embraced.

Raam looked with pride at his daughter and the slain cat. His dark eyes squinted with concern when he saw the cut on Tonik's shoulder, and he was eager for details.

Sira's eyes darted around the camp, searching for anything amiss. "Has there been any sign of the Red Feathers?"

Raam swept away a gray-haired lock from his face. "No, and Pliny and Jin are still scouting for them. We cannot stay here much longer. They will track us here soon."

* * *

Raam's tribe was taking temporary refuge in this shallow overhang. It sat in a ravine along a shallow-moving stream. While it was an effective hideout, it was infested with buzzing insects. They used the insect-repelling quince leaves under their furs to make their beds, but the leaves had become dry after many days, and their legs showed red welts.

Despite the insects, the cave overhang provided stealth for the tribe's fires at night. They had been on the run for many days. Only thirty members remained from a clan that was once seventy-five strong. Three moon cycles had passed since they had engaged in a conflict with another, larger tribe. They had termed their attackers the "Red Feathers" because of their warriors donning a large black and red feather braided into their hair.

Old Soot claimed the invaders came from a faraway land, where all people once came, along an endless river and forests so thick one could not walk through them. But Soot was an old shaman who ate dream mushrooms so often one could not rely on the stories he told.

The Red Feathers' way of battle did not follow that of normal tribes, where small violent conflicts quickly ended in a negotiation or bargain. The Red Feathers seemed to be as many as the great auroch herds, and they attacked without warning or provocation, making it difficult for the local tribes to defend against them. The Red Feather's territory expanded faster than the tribes could react, and they captured or killed anyone who stood in their way.

They had hit Raam's tribe in an ambush one evening. Many men died in the tribe's defence. They took others captive. Although the kidnapping of young females between tribes was a known practice, the large-scale capture of people was alien to them.

Shattered and beaten, Raam's tribe lay in ruins, refugees in their own land. Evenings by the fire usually brought fresh tears and cries of those missing their loved ones.

But today, their spirits were slightly raised at the sight of the fresh kill. The meat was much like that of the savory wild boar, and they ate until their bellies were bloated, causing them to plop down on the nearest bed of grass near the warmth of the fire.

Kadam captured their imagination with the story of the hunt. He was not an eloquent storyteller, but his physical presence had a charisma of its own. Younger boys looked up to him, while young girls watched with dreamy eyes. Kadam was blunt, loud, and obnoxious. It was perhaps why, at his age; he was still without a permanent woman or child. But his incredible bravery and strength gave him a high status in the tribe. He had single-handedly killed at least five of the Red Feathers during their attack, allowing time for many of them to escape. Even though he was the biggest and strongest man, Kadam seemed to lack the ability to predict and plan for tomorrow, a skill highly valued among their people, so the tribe still heavily relied on Raam for direction.

After Kadam had enacted the story of the day three times, each time exaggerating further his personal exploit, some tribe members shouted for a new story.

Evening stories by the fire played a pivotal role in handing down knowledge and lessons from one generation to the next. There were countless stories in their collection. Tales of their daily dramas, battles, family histories, exciting hunts, and tribal myths. They passed some myths down from an ancient time that no longer existed, about places they could no longer see. Other myths were complete fantasy told for pure entertainment or to scare children into doing as the elders wished.

As the darkness of night set in, the rocky overhang glowed orange with the flicker of firelights. Smoke billowed up and filled the top of the roof, then slowly dissipated out into the night air. Tribe members shout out requests for their favorite stories to be told before Sira stood up. "Father, tell us the story about the Others."

A sudden silence fell over them. Even the boys' knapping had stopped. It was so quiet the high-pitched squeaks of bats were audible as they flew around the top of the overhang, gorging on insects escaping the smoke.

A young boy of three years got up to join the circle, but his mother shooed him to return to his bed. He gave a few cries of protest before sitting back down. His brother, who was six, lay knackered out on the grass bed after a long day of hunting small game and chasing girls.

Kadam stood up, waving his arms. "No! No! We hear this story too much. I don't see the picture of this story because it is not true!"

But everyone made the hushing sound to him, so Kadam sat reluctantly, his face clearly unhappy.

Raam moved to sit in the center of the group, looked around at everyone, and cleared his throat. Tikara settled next to him, handing him a hollow end of an auroch's horn. It was filled with water, broken pine needles, and wild ginger. It had been heated by placing hot stones inside it, so Raam cradled it and sipped it slowly, clearing his throat.

The little three-year-old boy had returned to the circle around the fire. His mother was about to chastise him, but his father noticed the boy and picked him up, sitting him on his lap. The boy clapped his hands together in joy, and the father gave him a playful nudge on the shoulder. The boy's mother sighed and gave in.

"When I was a young boy, my father's father was still alive and healthy," Raam started.

"Waaa, he mussst have been old!" screeched a girl with a dirty face who was missing two front teeth.

"Yes, he was old. Not everyone knows their father's father, but mine was still strong," Raam went on. "He told me the story about the Others." Raam now gained momentum as his memory came back. "He said when he was a boy, his father and uncles took him on his first hunt. They lived at the bottom of a great mountain range and forest near to where we are now. That day, there were no animals in sight. Even the ground had no signs. So, they went farther into the rocky forest. It was there he saw the Others."

"What did they look like? Were they giants?" another young boy asked.

"No," replied Raam. "My father's father said he saw them from afar. They were on a ridge at a great distance, but he could see that they were small." Raam held his hand up to his shoulder, indicating height. "But they were big!" he added, holding his hands to his sides, showing width. "They had strange black rocks on their spears, a kind my father's father had never seen and never saw ever again. There were four of them standing around a mammoth that was lying on the ground." Raam stood up now and mimicked the positions. The fire projected a massive shadow onto the back of the overhang, heightening the suspense.

Kadam suddenly interrupted, "Four hunters only to kill a mammoth!?" He laughed at the thought and looked to his fellow tribe members for affirmation, but they ignored him as they were now captivated by Raam.

"No," said Raam. "I told you before, they were not killing the mammoth." He pointed his finger up to emphasize this point. "My father's father watched as three of the Others went in close to the mammoth's head. They raised their hands very close to the tusks and were making a noise like this." Raam hummed loudly with his mouth closed, then continued, "Then the mammoth listened to them and it became still. Then the other did something my father's father said he didn't understand. He went to the back of the mammoth, and he placed both his hands inside!" Raam exclaimed this part while opening his legs and gesturing both hands to his genitals.

Some of the younger tribe members strained their faces to understand what Raam meant, so he added, "The Other put his hands inside the part where babies come out!"

With that, the young ones giggled, and adults murmured with the sounds of disbelief.

Raam continued, "After a short time, the mammoth made the call of its kind with his long nose." He made a trumpeting sound, gesturing his hand as if it was a trunk. "Then from behind, the others pulled out a baby mammoth from inside the mother!"

Tikara interjected as she always did at this point in the story. "Sometimes we people come out the wrong way. It causes great pain to the mother, and you must help pull out the baby."

"Yes, that is right," said Raam.

"But why would the Others do that? Did they plan on killing it after?" asked Sira.

A few more joined in the questioning, trying to understand the logic of it.

"I asked this question to my father's father when he told me the story. So, I will tell you what he told me." He lifted his head up and inhaled deeply, collecting his thoughts as if he was about to say something very important. Then he shrugged his shoulders, smiling. "How in all the fires should I know?" He laughed. "The Others differ from us, and they do things we do not understand. Maybe they thought killing a mammoth while having a baby would be dishonorable," he added, clearly happy he had left his audience on the edge.

One of the younger girls asked in a frightened voice, "Is it true they come at night and eat young ones?"

Tonik added, "I heard they can control the winds, and that is why you can never catch their scent."

"I don't know what kind of person can control the wind," replied Raam, "But I'm pretty sure they don't eat young ones. I don't think the Others wish us harm, and they stay far away from us."

"They had an entire mammoth with a young one and they didn't kill it?" Kadam questioned with disbelief. This point of the story seemed to cause him the most skepticism. "What kind of people would not take a mammoth for its meat? And too afraid to show themselves? If they are afraid, then they are not brave!" Kadam said confidently, and some men responding in agreement.

"Why don't they ever show themselves, Father?" Sira asked.

Kadam answered quickly, "Because Rooti and I would kill them if they tried! I am not afraid of these *Others* who do not exist!" Kadam was on his feet with braggadocio.

Raam turned to Sira while pointing at Kadam. "That is why the others do not show themselves," he said solemnly.

"Ha! Like Kadam said, scared people." Rooti repeated.

Raam quickly countered, "Do you not also run and fear the Red Feathers?"

The two men huffed and backed down at this. After several quiet moments, the once festive and cheerful mood had shifted. Talk of the Red Feathers and the Others always left them with many thoughts and fears. There were many things to be afraid of in this world, but none were more powerful than the fear of the unknown.

Kadam lept to his feet, his great arms punching the air. "Alright, who wants to hear the story again of the big tooth!"

he boasted, holding up the large canine of the slain creature.

There was a roar of approval. The people were content to change the subject.

As Kadam's antics continued, Sira scooted over to her father. "If the Others are such big and strong hunters, why are they so afraid of us?"

"I don't know, my child. They are different, not like us," he said, responding exactly as he always did.

"Do you think we will ever see one? Maybe they are in the mountains we are heading to?"

"You will never see the Others, my child. You cannot see the things that do not wish to be seen. But I will tell you something my father's father told me, but you must promise not to speak of this, or it will frighten them," Raam whispered and gestured to the rest of the tribe.

Sira's eyes now lit up in the firelight as she came to her knees in anticipation of some new and exclusive information.

Raam leaned close to her ear, his expression no longer held the cheeriness of his story-telling face, and he used a tone that made the back on the back of Sira's neck stand up. "The Others are always watching us."

* * *

When the people had heard enough stories and the whispers of private conversations were replaced by snores, Sira got up from her bed of grass and snuck over to Tonik. He grunted slightly in pain and held his chest when she slid her body against his. He put his arm around her neck, and she rested her head upon it.

Sira had always wanted to be a hunter, and her personality had hardened over her lifetime of having to compete with maturing boys. Yet she hadn't lost her feminine wiles, exposing them rarely but effectively. She did so now, as she turned her lips into a half-smile and batted her long eyelashes. They were barely visible under the fading lights of the campfires.

"Tonik, do you think—"

Tonik judged her look, anticipating the question. "No, I find it hard to think when you are close."

She continued despite his complemental rebuke. "Do you think about what is in those mountains far from here? The ones we can see when the air is clear? I wonder what is over there. I wish to go there and see. Do you think we will see it someday soon?" Sira asked in one breath.

Tonik responded with slight annoyance, "When we were downstream, you wanted to see what was farther up the stream. When we were up the stream, you wanted to see what was in the hills. Now you want to see what is in the mountains. Tomorrow you will want to see what is past the mountains."

She huffed with frustration. "Don't you also wish to see and to know?"

"I only want what I can have for the day. I want to be a stronger hunter like Kadam and Rooti. I want to be far from the Red Feathers. I want to hunt meat to feed the younger ones. I want me and you... to have a young one as well," he said affectionately, pulling her closer and kissing her head.

"Tonik, I..." She sighed, words failing her. She was not ready to have a child with him, especially not now with the current threat looming over them. If she was honest with herself, she wasn't even sure she wanted one with him at all. Sure, she had feelings for him, but how strong? Strong enough to make a life bond? He was the most eligible man in their small clan, if not him, then who else? Maybe she just needed more time. "I need more time," she replied to him. She brought her face up to his, then kissed him gently.

His breathing rose, and he tried to squeeze her tighter, but she wriggled out of his arms like a mongoose caught in the grip of a snake. She snuck back to her bed without making a sound.

Tonik squeezed his hands in frustration and cursed himself as the warmth of her body was now gone. He should have known better than to broach the subject so abruptly.

* * *

That night, a multitude of stars and the milky stripe lit up the night sky. The night always brought sounds of yelping hyenas and the roaring of cave lions as the two enemies sounded their territories to one another. Some nights, wolves howled, mammoths trumpeted, insects buzzed, and small mammals cried out in pain. Rarely was there a night devoid of the sounds of life, and the people understood they were a part of it, caught in a never-ending game of survival. This night, while the tribe slept safely around the fires, a distinct cry reverberated through the valley. The cries of a feline mother, desperately searching for her cub and hearing no response.

Chapter 3

The crazed expression of a wild-eyed warrior filled Sira's vision, screaming that horrible tribal battle cry. Tonik appeared, shoulder-charged at the man and knocked him down. Taking her by the arm, they turned to run. Violence was all around them, a grisly scene of murderous rampage. The Red Feathers ambushed them in the night! Tonik and Sira fled the camp, meeting with other survivors that cold night, that terrible night that had changed their lives forever. The nightmare of it had returned to her ever since.

Sira awoke. The soothing songs of morning birds echoed against the rock face as she focused her eyes. Despite the coolness of the morning air, her head perspired. Sunlight poured into the overhang, and members of her tribe yawned and stretched as they arose from their beds. The fires were only embers now, and they billowed up thin wisps of smoke.

At the entrance, a small group of people, including her parents, Raam and Tikara, were speaking with the twin scouts, Pliny and Jin. The tense body language and concerned expressions hinted at trouble. She roused herself up and went to wake Tonik. It took some effort. A giant bruise had appeared on his chest overnight, and he winced as he probed it with his finger.

"Don't behave like a child. That bruise will be gone by the next full moon," she scolded, then helped him up.

"Humpf, well, I don't have big soft spots as you do," he responded, poking at one of her perky breasts. It earned him a slap to his wrist.

They walked over to Raam and were joined by Kadam, Rooti, and a few other hunters.

Raam was tight-lipped, and his eyes held a stern gaze toward the distance. His long black and gray locks shined in the sunlight, and he turned to look at the small group through wrinkled eyes. "It is time to move. Last night, the twins spotted fires in the distance. It is the Red Feathers, and they are still hunting us."

"We know it's them. They always make large fires," Pliny said.

"And they always come from the same direction," added Jin, pointing south.

"Yes, and we have been going in the opposite way," replied Raam, pointing north. "I remember traveling here as a boy. The stream we follow meets another. This new river splits in two directions. One goes toward the Great Sea, the other comes from the mountains. We must decide which way we should go."

"We must keep following the auroch herd so we can hunt and have meat," Kadam responded.

They had been moving behind the great herd for several days, and it had been a reliable food source.

"Yes, the herd will provide meat for as long as we follow, but..." Raam paused for a moment and looked at Sira, giving her the signal and opportunity to speak.

She took the cue. "But the Red Feathers will know we follow the auroch, and on this ground, we make tracks that are easy for them to follow."

"Yes," Raam proudly affirmed. "But the ground that goes toward the mountains turns to rock. It will be more difficult for the Red Feathers to follow, with plenty of places to hide."

Kadam huffed in displeasure. "And what will we roast in your rocky land? That way lies nothing, no meat, just worms to feed our bellies. Hiding is not what brave hunters do."

Sira had a flash of insight as a picture formed in her mind. "Do we know which way the auroch will move?"

"Of course, they will follow the water toward the sea for a few days before crossing and heading into the mammoth grasslands," Kadam replied, pointing northwest.

"Well, if we stay ahead of the auroch, they will walk over our tracks. The Red Feathers will not know which way we went," Sira said thoughtfully.

"I can see what you speak," said her mother, Tikara.

"Hmm, yes. If we can stay ahead, we can still hunt the auroch from the front," Kadam agreed.

Raam nodded in agreement. "Yes, I can see this. But the Red Feathers are cunning. They will still know to follow the auroch. A group of us must lead them away. This group must be small and fast. Able to lead the Red Feathers into the mountains. The rest of us will follow ahead of the auroch. The smaller group will mislead the Red Feathers in the mountains, then circle around and find us where the water meets the mammoth grasslands. Near the sea, there is a people known as the Fishtooth."

"The fish... teeth?" asked Tonik.

"Yes." Raam picked up his intricate necklace, singling out a long-rounded tooth. "They used to wear the teeth of a great fish around their necks like this one. They are fishermen from the Great Sea. Our tribe used to trade with them when I was a small boy. They have a large village that never moves. We must join with them or we will not last through the winter. If the Red Feathers keep coming, at least we can fight them together with the Fishtooth. Our hunters will slow the Red Feathers in the mountains to allow us time to reach the grasslands."

They looked at each other in consternation. Being separated and leaving their families alone was an enormous risk, but they agreed it was a good plan. They had felt the days becoming shorter and colder and every year, the winters lasting longer. The realities of winter were harsh on any tribe. With their small numbers, it could mean the end of them.

* * *

Raam selected the eight members who would lead the Red Feathers into the mountains. He emphasized their names so the entire tribe could cheer with admiration and gratefulness. Among the chosen were Kadam, Rooti, Tonik, and the brothers, Marka and Rakka. Also, the young twins, Pliny and Jin. Although the twins had only passed fourteen winters and did not have the hearts for fighting, they had proven their worth as scouts. They had eagles' eyes and could creep through the forest as quiet as the big-tooth cats.

Sira looked at her father, ready to explode with anticipation. Finally, he announced, "This group needs a leader who does not just have strength in the arms and legs. They need a leader who can see tomorrow." Raam pointed to Sira. She did her best to hide her blushing, straightening her spine and looking at her father confidently, then bowing her head in acceptance. A female leading a group of male hunters was a rare occurrence, and murmurs of consternation sounded through the tribe.

"I will follow her!" yelled Tonik.

The rest of the hunters huffed but accepted the nomination.

* * *

The clan began preparations for their migration, wasting no time in wrapping their belongings into travel mode. Thoughts of meeting the Red Feather warriors caused no hesitation. The only items left in the cave would be a few unusable bones of the sabre-cat, broken flint knapping, and the charcoal drawings on the rock wall.

When the rains came, the stream would rise and fill the overhang with thick mud, burying its contents forever.

Raam had outfitted the eight hunters with his finest spears and gave them each a small, pointed flint knife that had a handle wrapped with fiber. The flint knives were sharp enough to slice through flesh and puncture muscle tissue. The knife had a leather sheath that cleverly tied around their thighs, courtesy of Tikara. The tender back strap of the sabre-cat had been smoking over the fire, and they wrapped it in deer hide to be eaten along the way.

Their route along the stream crept through hills of low standing brush. Patches of young spruce and cedar trees dotted along the shore. The area contained a plethora of wild edible plants and tubers, and the women collected them as they travelled. Their gathering was so efficient, it didn't even slow the tribe's pace as they moved. The ground was a soggy mix of mud and grass, dank with the smell of the dangerous and territorial auroch.

It only took several hours at a brisk pace to get ahead of the auroch herd, which was moving sluggishly on the opposite side of the stream. The great bovine beasts were lethargic, with bloated bellies gorged from the grazing of fresh river grass. They only grunted in slight annoyance at the smell of the humanity. The auroch were in migration mode, focusing on the path ahead of them. Cave lions and hyenas would follow behind the herd as well, preying on the weaker individuals, but the people paid no mind to this. In the daylight, they were the masters of the land. No creature in the world was a match for people when they worked together, and even the great mammoths instinctively steered clear of people in groups.

The sun was high when they reached the T-junction in the river. Here the waters mixed, becoming wider and faster. The tribe sloshed down into the ice-cold water to refill their water gourds and soak their feet while the auroch herd lingered a safe distance behind them. Pliny and Jin ran up to a giant tree on the hill as a lookout point.

It was an opportunity for the old and young to rest. A few mothers unfolded their babies out of the soft fur skins they had wrapped around their chests. Some were large enough to stand on their own and stumbled around the edge of the stream under close supervision. It was here the tribe would separate.

Raam turned to Sira to remind her, "It will take today and tomorrow to reach the great mountains." Raam pointed in the distance to the rocky peaks half-covered in clouds that stood out over the hills. "Try to make as many tracks as possible. If they see there are only eight of you, they could know it is a trick. And keep your fire low and out of sight-"

"Father, stop, I know all this," Sira interrupted.

They embraced each other once more. There was no word for love in their language, but none was needed. They found other ways to express the emotion. It ran through every fibre of their being. Love was the cohesion that kept the clan together, kept them unified.

"The Red Feathers are coming!" Pliny and Jin said in unison. The twins had appeared out of nowhere, and Raam and Sira jumped with fright.

"By my bones, you two will make my heart stop one

day!" Raam chided.

With news of the Red Feathers, they hastily said their farewells. They tried to trick the children by reassuring them their fathers were on a routine hunt, but the tension was easily read, and a few were crying as their fathers embraced them.

The hunters' mood was somber at the idea of leaving their families alone. They would love nothing more than to continue to follow the auroch herd, hunting and eating meat with the tribe at night. However, they had faced the Red Feathers' savagery before, and the love for their families took precedence overall. So strong was their bond together, a true hunter would easily sacrifice themself for the survival of the clan.

Rooti playfully punched his son on his shoulder as he left, and the young boy watched his father in reverence.

Once they were out of sight from the rest of the tribe, Sira stopped and looked in the distance. She could see the land rise quickly, and water fell in several places as the river descended in elevation. The hills ahead were rocky and thick with trees, dark and inhospitable. Without her father, leading these men seemed daunting. This was the moment she had been waiting for all her life – the chance to prove herself as a leader. Now that the moment was here, she felt unprepared and somehow undeserving.

Tonik interrupted her thoughts, playfully bumping her shoulder as he passed by. "Let's go, fearless leader!"

"Ugh, don't call me that."

* * *

At the abandoned overhang, a group of warriors slowed the gait of their stalking strut. They wore short pieces of animal skins around their waists and thick hide bracers around their wrists and forearms. The leading scout stopped and investigated the empty camp. He took a quick sniff, then turned his head towards his followers. The black and red-tipped feather braided in his hair hung down to his shoulder. Scars in ritualistic, circular patterns were etched into his cheek, and a small porcupine quiver pierced his nose. He gave the other men a wide, devilish grin, and he licked his upper lip.

The other men grinned with excitement. This region had never seen hunters like them. They moved and acted with one purpose, to bring tribute to their leader, who they called Father, to which everything in this world belonged - man and beast. They were on a never-ending quest to bring back the Father's possessions. This made them fearless and obsessed.

They hunted not only out of necessity; for them, it was as much for sport as it was survival. They hunted men and women as much as they hunted animals, raiding other tribes, killing and raping or taking captives along the way. For them, no hunt was as thrilling as hunting other men. They were on the trail now and knew they were gaining ground.

Their fires behind them moved slower than their war party, giving their prey a perception that they were still far behind.

Parallel to them, along the other side of the stream, staying hidden among rocks and trees, another creature also followed. The pain and confusion of losing it's cub was still present. It also followed the scent of the people it hunted. It was an angry creature now, driven by a mother's rage.

Chapter 4

The group of eight hiked their way into the mountain range that steepened over the second day of travel. They made their first night's camp on a slope surrounded by rocks and shoulder-high thorn bushes.

By the second afternoon, their progress was reduced to climbs up steep, loose rock, sometimes on all fours. By sundown, they had reached a great plateau. The vast yellow plains stood out before them, broken by the green dots of distant treetops.

To their relief, they could see the fires of their pursuers following them instead of the rest of the clan. The first part of their plan had worked.

The air was cool and calm on the plateau. The thick cedar forest was pristine, with no signs of a recent human settlement. At sundown, they made camp behind a small ridge. Tonik removed an auroch horn which was tied around his shoulder with a tendon chord. Inside the horn lay a hot ember, kept alive with ash and dry dung. Now, all he would have to do is empty the ember into a new pile of kindling to get a fresh campfire started. He blew into the flames until it reached a sufficient height. The eight of them gathered around, close to each other.

"Tomorrow, we must return to the rocks and hide our tracks. We will first walk in this direction," Sira finally said, pointing north. "After we fool our tracks, we must turn west to find the water that will lead us back to the grasslands."

"The baboon that doesn't cover his tracks gets eaten by the leopard," Rooti said, reciting a proverb.

"We can use the water to hide our footprints. Also, along the river lies tall grass," Jin added.

"If the nose horns don't trample us!" Pliny complained.

"We are only eight. We can sneak through the nose horns, but the Red feathers will have a more difficult time doing so," said Jin.

Kadam spit out a piece of grub worm he had been roasting. "Blah! I told you there is nothing to eat in this place but worms. Nose horns or not, I will be glad to be gone." He tried to grab another grub worm off his roasting stick, but it fell out of his clumsy fingers and into the fire. "Blah!"

The rocky ground had been devoid of game, but Pliny had found a rich cache of grubs under some rotten logs. The meal was enough to stave off hunger, but not enough to stop their bellies from rumbling. The idea of heading back into the grasslands was well received.

Tonik looked up from roasting his fat grub. "Do you think Raam has met the Fishtooth?"

"I don't know. But if the Fishtooth tribe is out there, my father will find them and convince them to join us," Sira said.

Rakka chimed in. "The Red Feathers will keep coming for us. With or without these Fishtooth, we will battle them again."

"I, for one, hope that battle never comes. I wish to spend the rest of my days in peace teaching my boy how to hunt. He is almost ready, and I will see him become the strongest hunter in the tribe," Rooti said.

"I can see this!" Sira smiled, grabbing his shoulder.

"My boy is of the same age. He will hunt with Rooti's boy. They will bring meat for us one day when we are too old to run," Marka said cheerfully.

"Ha! Now this I can see, me still hunting while you two roll around together in a cave," said Kadam. "I will battle the Red Feathers. I will see this day soon. I will kill their brothers as they killed ours. Their bodies are like small sticks, and Kadam will break them!" He broke his roasting stick in half.

"Yes, but when we battle them, we must make sure all our families are safe and far away," Sira said.

They all nodded in agreement. Rooti and Marka never had enough words when speaking about their children and their aspirations for them. They were hard men, forged in a world where one mistake could end their life. A world where many did not live to see their children grow into adulthood. Speaking about one's children could bring tears to the eyes of even the toughest man.

Rakka looked up to Sira. "Sira, you are a powerful

hunter. We have seen you these days. We are all waiting for you to make a young one. Rooti and Marka eat a lot, and it will take many young hunters to feed them while they roll around in the cave," he said, chuckling.

"Tonik, does your snake not beat the bush deep enough to give her a young one?" Marka teased.

Sira came to Tonik's defense. "His snake slithers just fine." She looked at Tonik with a naughty smile.

The group laughed and lifted their fists toward Tonik in honor as he smiled uncomfortably. Sira wearied from this type of conversation over the past two days; however, she played along, knowing it was important to keep the men's spirits up.

As the night grew darker and the conversation died down, Pliny and Jin stood up.

"We are going now to keep watch," Jin said.

"We give thanks to you two. Please keep your eyes and ears open wide. In this forest, one cannot see far, and it would be easy for the Red Feathers to sneak up on us," Sira said to them.

"No one sneaks up on us," replied Pliny in his feminine voice.

"We sneak up on them," they both said at the same time.

The twins climbed up to the ridge and back to where the ground dropped off for a better vantage point. Over the night, they would hold each other for warmth and take turns at watch.

Pliny and Jin were not twins because they were from the same mother, but because they had been inseparable from childhood. They had never shown an interest in the opposite sex. Instead, they shared their nights together. It was a rare but accepted occurrence. Twin souls' was the name the tribe gave it, twins for short. Their family's death at the hands of the Red Feathers had brought the two teenagers closer now. Despite many young women being frustrated at their ignored advances and being teased by the men, no one ever questioned the twins' value in scouting. They had learned from Jin's late father, who had been the clan's greatest hunter and tracker.

The night quickly grew colder, and Sira held Tonik close near the fire. The danger and adventure had awakened something in her, and she suddenly felt an attraction. But they were both exhausted, and Sira never enjoyed partaking in physical pleasure with other men so close by.

Through their teenage years, Sira kept their playful sexual encounters to a bare minimum, just enough so he didn't lose interest and chose another woman. Now that they had passed through seventeen winters together, the clan thought it strange she had not yet conceived. She could not keep up this selfish game for long. She would have to let him go or claim him forever. Tonik was a very simple soul, quiet yet dutiful to the tribe. She knew he truly loved her, and he had remained patient as they matured, waiting for her to accept him in her own time. After the death of his parents at the hands of the Red Feathers, he felt an urgency to create his own family. He was handsome and strong, and all the other young women vied for his attention, but Sira had no time for thoughts of jealousy. Her dreams and aspirations were to one day lead the tribe like her father. She promised herself she would decide about Tonik once they were safe.

* * *

The previous afternoon, not long after the split between Raam and Sira, the war party leader of Gondo-Var, known as *Master*, came upon the T-junction of the river. He wore two black and red feathers braided on each side of his hair. Stripes of red ochre and black charcoal painted his body, and black dust circled his eyes. Tied on his waist was a thin, smooth wooden club with a weighted bulge at one end.

The Gondo-Var warrior with circular scars on his cheeks had been waiting anxiously with his tracking party at the junction. He was excited to see Master and report his good news.

Master approached calmly, scanning the area as he walked. His stride had a confident and dangerous presence surrounding it, and other warriors instinctively walked out clear of his path.

The Gondo-Var tribe was more complex and hierarchical than the small clans of the region. There were a variety of ranks and social positions, as well as entire war parties that acted almost independently. But all were united under Father and their common banner—the great black bird that they worshipped. Master had not gained his tribal status through parental lineage. He had never even known his parents. He had gained his position through sheer tenacity and brute force. As far as fighting was concerned, he was unmatched among the Gondo-Var. He had fought, killed, and schemed his way to the top and now answered only to Father. His feats were legendary among the Gondo-Var warriors, and his presence drew awe and respect.

He stood up close to the one with the circle scars and stared down at him. Circle Scars judged the tension and nervously blurted out, "Master, the tribe has taken to the mountains. Their tracks lead up and we are ready to run them-" Circle Scars felt a sharp slap against his face before he could finish.

Master stood over him with his hand raised. "You fool. Can't you see what they have done? If these filthy people are more cunning than my best tracker, then you are no longer are my best tracker. They have split and sent the women and children ahead of the auroch herd."

Circle Scars looked down the river, clearly bewildered.

"No matter, Father has requested more men, so leave the women for now. We will attempt to capture their hunters alive first, and if they refuse to surrender, they will die. Also, in those mountains, perhaps we may spot one of..." Master paused and looked up at the peaks, "... the Others," he said with a delicious smile.

"Yes, yes, the Others. Master will find one and bring it back to Father," Circle Scar said.

Of all the Father's possessions, one of the Others was what Father coveted most, and he had become increasingly impatient in his demand. But they had not spotted one of the mysterious people in many years, and the inability to find one had become a thorn in Master's side.

"Bring me the carriers!" Master commanded.

Two dozen enormous men came forward. They wore leather around their shoulders and waists in a system of straps. A group of smaller, leaner men hurried over and strapped their legs onto their backs. The big men would take turns carrying them up the mountain, and when they arrived at the top, the riders would dismount. With fresh legs, the riders would quickly run down their prey.

As Master strapped onto the back of one of the big men, he turned and spoke to Circle Scars. "We will sneak in to get closer under the cover of darkness. You gather a group to track the auroch. Find out where the rest of the tribe is going, but do not engage them until I return. From now on, your name will be Last Chance, and that is what everyone shall call you. If you fail again, you will not have a name."

Chapter 5

It did not feel like Sira had been sleeping for very long when she felt the gentle hand brush her shoulder. Exhausted from the journey, she ignored it at first, but it squeezed and shook her, gesturing her to wake up. She opened her eyes and saw Pliny looking over her with a hand over his mouth, signaling to stay quiet.

Pliny awoke the other men in this manner, and Rooti quickly got up and poured soft dirt over the fire embers. In the dim morning light, they could see vapors of steam rising from their breaths. Fog covered the ground in a thick blanket.

Pliny opened his arms wide and squatted, gesturing for them to come close into a huddle so he could whisper. "The Red Feathers have almost made it to the top of the ridge. They used the fog to hide their movement. There are many of them, and they will be upon us soon. You all must go quickly and quietly, and do not stop for anything!"

"Wait, where is Jin? Are you not coming?" Sira asked.

"Jin and I should have seen the Red Feathers approach. It is our fault and now it is too late. You will not make it out of the mountains fast enough unless Jin and I slow them down and lead them away. We have decided this, and it will be so." Pliny said proudly.

Sira protested. "Pliny, no, that is too dangerous. We cannot split up"

Kadam held up his hand to interrupt. "They are good hunters, and they make us proud. We will tell the others their bravery."

Sira could see that Pliny had made up his mind. The men of her tribe were proud, and acts of courage were honored and sacred to them. If Sira forbade the action, she would rob them of that honor. If they made it out, their story would be told at night by the fires.

She grabbed his soft face and kissed his head. "Go well, little brother. If anyone can slip through them, it is you two." She held back the tears in her eyes as he stood and turned back up the ridge. The rest of them gathered their things and quickly strode out of the ridge in silent consternation. They had little hope that they would ever see the twins again.

The six of them ran with their heads low. Their only hope now was a quick escape to the river where they could throw off their tracks. They zigzagged through the old dark timber of the ancient forest at a light run. They reckoned they could easily keep ahead of their pursuers, as the Red Feathers would be worn out from the difficult overnight climb.

Soon, the morning light shone through the trees and broke up the fog. The forest came alive again with the sounds of birds and insects, and the smell of pine filled the air.

Rooti stopped running and held up his hand, gesturing for the others to halt. He turned his head to listen. In the distance, faint shouts echoed behind them.

"How could they be so close already? Do these men not tire?" Sira lamented.

Kadam and Rooti looked at each other gravely, but said nothing as they turned to keep moving, this time with more urgency. After several more minutes of hard running, the area ahead of them opened and they could see the sky through the trees. Rooti and Marka were a few paces ahead when they both came to an abrupt stop at the end of the tree line.

"What is it?" Sira asked, approaching with apprehension. She gasped in horror at what lay ahead of them. A massive grey cliff dropped straight down into the raging white river below. The dizzying height made Sira stumble back.

Kadam did not approach; his lifelong fear of heights forced him to stay a few arms' lengths from the edge.

Sira tried to see where the cliff ended to her right, but the edge curved around and her vision was obstructed. Echoes from the Red Feather warriors' voices became louder. They looked at each other in panic as they realized it could trap them.

"Follow me! Along the ridge!" Sira ordered.

They dashed along the edge, hoping that the cliff would

drop off to a shallow point somewhere ahead before their pursuers caught up to them.

Rooti gasped between breaths, "Sira, Tonik, you must lead up front. Whatever happens to us... you must keep moving. Do not stop!"

"It looks like Kadam will get his wish sooner than we thought," gasped Marka. The four men dropped back and to the right, covering Sira and Tonik. Echoes of shouts from their pursuers bounced off the terrain and seemed to come in all directions now.

"They are trying to surround us!" Kadam panted.

They ran hard for several minutes until the echoes stopped. A group of five warriors had appeared through the trees to their right. Once they had acquired their quarry, their hoots and shouts had abated. The four men veered in their direction while Sira and Tonik continued running forward.

The Red Feather men were thinly built; their bodies developed for long distances on open plains instead of brute strength. They let out a high-pitched war cry as they rushed forward. The four men fully expected a volley of spears to be thrown. However, the warriors had been travelling light and only held small wooden clubs. Marka, Rakka, and Rooti waited for them to come close enough, then let loose with their atlatl spear throwers.

The Red Feathers had not expected the accuracy of men's throws, and both spears hit their mark, high on the men's chests. They quickly rushed and removed the spears from the two men who were writhing and dying on the ground. Kadam engaged two other men alone in close combat. The first warrior swung his club wildly at Kadam's head, but he easily dodged and thrust his spear deep into the man's ribs.

"That was for Juro!" he cried as he broke off the spear and kicked the man to the ground. The second attacker came at him. The club raised high for an overhead swing, but Kadam was too fast. He rushed in and grabbed the man's hands before he could swing down and plunged his flint knife straight up under the chin of the screaming warrior. The knife went through the top of his mouth and into his head. Kadam pulled the man close and looked into the man's terrified, open eyes. "That one was for my younger brother Rakan!"

"More are coming!" cried Rooti.

"These little men are too easy to kill!" Kadam yelled, pulling out his flint knife from under the man's head.

"They come to us with clubs and not spears?" Rooti yelled, bewildered.

Another group of six warriors had appeared, again heading toward them. But this new group had seen the folly of the overconfident scouts and approached more carefully.

Sira and Tonik stopped and turned to watch from afar. She saw this new group take out a long, curved stick with a chord attached. In leather pouches, the warriors carried small, spindly looking spears with feathers attached to one end.

"Ha! Come, little ones, what will you do with those? Do you wish to pick Kadam's teeth?" he yelled in defiance. This new group moved cautiously, as if they were judging their distance. Marka and Rooti laughed and hit their chests, shaking their spears at the Red Feather men now fumbling with their strange, curved sticks.

"Ha! Little stick men afraid now!" Kadam laughed.

Something about these men and the way they handled these strange weapons gave Sira an awful premonition. "Kadam! Rooti! Run! Move away!" Sira yelled.

The Red Feathers held up the curved sticks in unison and pulled back on the chord with their other hand. Kadam caught a flash as something whizzed by his head, too quickly for him to react. There was a thump in the tree behind him. He looked back and saw the arrow lodged horizontally into a tree.

"How?" Kadam asked, confused. Then he looked toward Rooti, who stood in shock, looking down at his chest. An arrow was sticking out through the middle of him.

"Rooti!" Kadam yelled and rushed over to him. Rooti's legs gave out, and Kadam dropped to his knees, holding Rooti in his arms.

"Kadam," Rooti said as he coughed up blood. Choking,

he fought to speak his last words. "My boy. Take care... my boy..." His head fell back, and his eyes stared blankly into the sky. Kadam closed his eyes. "From dirt our bones, and our bones to dirt," he said, then laid Rooti onto the ground.

The arrows had not hit Marka and Rakka and they rushed to the warriors, stabbing two with their flint knives before they could reload. However, the other four archers had already nocked their bows and let loose at near point-blank range. Arrows hit the two men in the torso, Marka went down immediately, but Rakka could still stab another archer through the neck before falling to the ground with an arrow lodged through his lung.

The Red Feather warriors stabbed their downed bodies with spears, shouting in revenge. More men came in through the trees and several broke off from the group to follow Sira and Tonik. Kadam let Rooti's body rest gently on the ground and brushed his hand over his eyelids to close them. He stood up slowly and clenched his fists in fury as the Red Feathers surrounded him.

* * *

Tonik and Sira sprinted wildly over the rocky ground as the terrain descended, but their lungs grew winded. Tonik glanced back to find a group of warriors slowly gaining pace with them. Although they were slower, the warriors looked built for stamina. Whether their prey was man or beast, they wore them down, much like the wild dog packs of the savannah. Tonik tried to judge how long it would take before they caught up. He looked to Sira, then made a decision. He veered to the left and let Sira continue down the slope. "Go, Sira, I will meet you back on the grasslands!" he assured her.

"Tonik, no! Don't leave me!" she screamed.

"We won't make it, Sira. Do as I say, please. Make it back! You must!" he yelled without stopping. "I will find you again, Sira. I will get back to you!"

"Tonik, no! No!" she sobbed in frustration. She had no choice but to keep running.

Tonik gained the attention of the Red Feathers, buying

Sira a few precious moments. He tried to double back along the ridge, but they had expected this. The four men soon surrounded him, and now Tonik had his back to the cliff. He backed up to the edge and looked down. Although it was not as high as previously, it was still too far to jump. The water raged below, and it was impossible to know how deep the river was. A large chunk of stone broke off the ledge by his foot. It fell, smashing spectacularly into a hundred pieces in the rocks below.

The warriors approached closer, laughing. He swung his spear in a semi-circle, trying to keep them at bay. Tonik was a brave warrior, but he lacked the power of Kadam or Rooti. He stood no chance against four men. They jabbed mockingly at him with their spears, causing slight cuts as he tried to defend himself. Then one of the Red Feathers stuck out an open hand and spoke.

Surprisingly, Tonik understood the words. It was the same language, but his accent was strange. "Come, give yourself to us. Give yourself to us!" said the man.

Tonik understood they wanted him to surrender. When he didn't respond, one of them speared harder at his side, opening a gash. This made Tonik lose his footing on the ledge. Leaning backward, he waved his arms wildly, trying to regain balance. He dropped his spear, but regained his stance on the ledge. Now he was unarmed, and the four men laughed at his brush with the cliff.

The warrior yelled again impatiently, "Give yourself to us!"

Tonik grabbed his side in pain as blood dripped down his side. His mind flashed to his childhood. He remembered his father's bravery in hunting and thought of all the men of his tribe—Kadam, Rooti, and even Pliny and Jin. Their heroics and defiance in the face of danger were an important part of their culture. Tonik was shaking now. His enemies enjoyed the sight of his fear, and it embarrassed him. He felt giving up would betray his people.

He looked over the edge at the river below. They were laughing hard now, gloating with victory over his capture. He squeezed his sinus and coughed up mucus. With a heave, he spat straight into the warrior's face. The man yelled in anger, raising his spear to strike, but Tonik had already turned and jumped.

* * *

Kadam stood defiantly around a dozen men. He beat his chest and yelled as adrenaline ran through his veins. He tried to goad an attack, but they stood their ground. A voice suddenly yelled out from behind the line of Red Feather warriors, "Kadam!"

The men parted way for the man who had yelled his name. Kadam saw a tall but thin warrior; his body painted with red and black stripes. "You are the one called as Kadam, yes?" He spoke Kadam's language, but it was more complicated, with sounds he was not used to, and his accent was strange.

"Yes, I am Kadam. Today I fight, and today I will die! I am a hunter!" Kadam announced proudly.

"A man does not always get what he wishes. Sometimes our wish turns to a curse, and what we hated and feared becomes our strength," Master said.

Kadam did not understand the meaning.

Master continued anyway. "You are a powerful warrior, and you have killed many of us. This is good. We need more warriors. Shall we have him prove his strength?" yelled Master to the warriors.

"Eagle fly, men fall. Eagle fly, men fall," the men chanted in low voices.

Master grabbed a club from one man and threw it at Kadam's feet as they chanted. He untied a similar club from around his waist; it was thin, with a bulbous head for striking. The warriors continued to chant as they formed a ring around them. "Very well, my eagles, let's see if this big bird can flap his wings."

Kadam did not understand the words but realized he was in a duel and the man had chosen weapons. This made him chuckle with confidence. "With this club, I shall smash your head, little man!"

"Eagle fly!" the men chanted louder.

Kadam grabbed the club quickly and was two paces ahead with such speed and ferocity that it impressed Master. Kadam two-handed the club, swinging with all his might. It was a swing that had bested many enemies, a swing with a force that no other man could equal, one that could kill with a single hit. But when Kadam followed through, it hit nothing.

Master ducked, and his feet swept to the side. The club missed his head by a hair. Kadam felt a whack to the back of his own head, and he went crashing down face-first into the dirt.

"Men fall!" the warriors cheered loudly.

"You are strong, Kadam. You think strength is always the way. Strength is only good at the right moment." Master said, enunciating every word as if speaking to a child. He wanted to make sure Kadam could understand his more complicated style of speech. His war club rested lazily upon his shoulder, and his back was turned to Kadam as if he were of no consequence.

"Eagle fly!" the warriors chanted.

Kadam rose to his feet and felt a knob on the back of his head already forming. With his opponent's back turned, he rushed in again, this time with an overhead strike so the tall man could not duck.

Master twisted on the balls of his feet faster than a jackal evading a lion's charge, and Kadam's club missed again, hitting the dirt. Master whipped his club with one hand across Kadam's face, sending him to the ground again.

"Men fall!" the warriors cheered again.

Kadam was on all fours and spit out a bloody piece of tooth. Fighting dizziness, he saw the flint knife on the ground and picked it up, switching the club to his left hand. He stood up a little slower and rushed in to attack again, swinging and stabbing with ferocity.

Incredibly, Master anticipated all of Kadam's moves. It was as if he were a cat, toying with his prey. He struck Kadam's knife hand with a flick of his club and it dropped to the ground.

"I would love to continue this lesson, but we have more little birds to catch today," Master said as he nodded to a warrior.

Kadam felt a bee sting his rear, and he looked back to find a miniature arrow in his cheek. He yanked it out and noticed the tip covered in a black substance. He threw it to the ground in anger. "You play with children's toys! Come, I wish to fight and die now!" He rushed forward again, swinging his club wildly.

Master continued to block and parry Kadam's weak swings with his club as if he were a child.

Kadam's feet began to feel heavy, and he had trouble lifting them.

"Men faaall," the warriors chanted.

Kadam's vision of the men and the trees twisted and melted together as he lost control of his eyes. "Huh?" Kadam grunted. His vision went black, but he stayed on his feet, stumbling around still swinging his club.

"He stays on his feet still!" said Master, impressed.

A club swept the back of Kadam's foot, and he fell onto his back with a crash, losing consciousness.

"Eagle fly, men fall!" the warriors chanted one last time.

"Bind this one twice. He has an auroch's strength! He will fly like an eagle or he will fall." Master looked to the other hunters who lay slain and shook his head in disappointment. "All this trouble and all we got was one big one. Make sure to bring me back the girl."

Master bent over Kadam's body and cut off the sabre-tooth canine tied around Kadam's neck. He held the trophy up and glanced at it curiously. *A powerful hunter indeed.*

"Master?" A Gondo-Var warrior was standing over Rooti's body, gesturing his fingers to his mouth.

"Very well," said Master.

The man's face lit up with glee as he realized he would not spend another night without fresh meat.

Chapter 6

At the end of the slope, Sira found herself among a maze of massive boulders that stood more than twice her height. Sharp white rocks littered the ground. In her haste, she had slipped on one, and it punctured her foot wrap. It was bleeding badly, slowing her down and leaving a bloody trail to follow.

Now that she was out of the forest, the sun beat down on her relentlessly. It was miraculous how quickly the chilly morning had turned hot. Exhausted and thirsty, Sira limped along, trying to keep calm.

She came upon a jagged and notched boulder, so she climbed up to get her bearings. The river was to her left, its white water raging over giant rocks that made it too dangerous to cross. To her right were more boulders that led to chalky white cliffs. Directly ahead rose a steep hill covered with broken loose rocks. It was her only way out.

From her periphery, she saw a blur of brown and orange and heard the echo of a rock sliding and falling. She must have frightened a deer or an impala. Shouts of excitement came from the men behind her. A group of three warriors had tracked her into the rocks and easily spotted her. They came running in between the large boulders. She cursed herself for climbing up here and putting herself in clear visibility; she should have known better. Warriors surrounded her boulder, cutting off any escape.

One man shouted in a strange accent, gesturing with his hand, "Come down, come down!"

Another one pulled out a gourd containing water, shaking it and holding it up to her in a fake gesture of kindness. She looked over the side of the boulder and saw a warrior with his bow drawn. She quickly ducked as an arrow whizzed past her head.

The man with the gourd shouted, "No! We want her alive!"

One of them climbed up the rock after her. She pulled back from the edge and waited. As he reached the top, she kicked hard at his face, snapping his nose. The man yelled and crashed onto the rocks below with blood gushing from his nostrils.

The other three laughed and jumped with excitement.

"Yah, she has spirit! She will give Father much pleasure! But first, she will give us pleasure!"

"I will tie her down and ride her hard!" the man with the broken nose cried.

She could barely understand the language, but realized they were trying to capture her. Her mind tried to suppress what they would do to her if they caught her. She looked at the next boulder close to hers and judged the distance. It was close enough for her to jump to, and from there, she could jump from boulder to boulder, staying above them. She took two steps back and launched herself. She landed squarely on top of the next boulder and screamed as she felt the sharp pain from the cut on her foot.

The Red Feather warrior with the broken nose climbed up the first boulder again to follow her, so she hopped to the next rock. Below, the two warriors were following and shouting, trying to hit her with stones. She ducked at a stone and almost lost her balance on the slanted rock face. The next closest rock was much higher, so she had to jump up to it and grab the top of the ledge with her hands. She felt a dull thud of a rock connecting to her back. The pain gave her renewed anger as she felt a rush of energy to pull herself onto the ledge.

"Argh!" she shrieked down at them with frustration.

The one with the broken nose was ready to jump up to the rock she was on. She untied the flint knife, slid back, and waited. He made the same mistake twice, only this time it would prove lethal. As he grabbed the lip of the rock, she stabbed his hand. It pierced clean through, and he screamed in pain. He fell back with the knife lodged in his hand. His head hit a rock with a sickening thud, and it burst open in a splatter of blood.

Fresh shouts of anger sounded from the men below as she jumped down to the next boulder. She kept doing this, staying out of their reach. She came upon a flat rock and was ready to jump again when she felt a hand grab her ankle.

They pulled down her from the rock, and she hit the ground akwardly.

"She is here! I got her!" the man cried joyfully.

She tried to get up, but he punched the side of her head, and she fell back onto the ground. "Come, Bulaf! Come, I have her! We will have fun now!" he said as he removed his leather skirt. "Bulaf?"

There was no answer.

"I will have you for myself first then," he said greedily as he grabbed himself with pleasure. He fumbled to hold her hands down as she struggled. As he got close, she lunged forward and bit down on his lip, tearing off a piece of flesh. Screaming in pain, he backed off, holding his torn and bloody lip.

She tried to rise to her feet, but he kicked her in the chest, and she fell back down to the ground, coughing in a cloud of fine white dust.

With blood dribbling down his chin, he looked down at her with menace and snarled. "I'm going to smash that pretty face before I stab you!"

She inhaled, steadying herself for a fight she knew she could not win. But the man suddenly froze. His mouth and eyes both opened with a look of dread. He did not even have the chance to turn when a giant creature crashed into him full force. It sent the man flying back five paces. A huge sabre-cat was on top of the man's body, pinning him down. He screamed and writhed on the ground in panic. But the sabre-cat was double the man's size, and his arms flailed at it uselessly. The giant cat bit straight down into the man's skull, its two huge fangs piercing his brain. The man's thrashing stopped, but his legs still twitched and jerked involuntarily.

Sira heard the crunching sound of his skull as she crawled backward in shock. She did not need to witness anymore, and she got up to run. Around the next boulder, another man lay face down with two holes in his head, apparently Bulaf. The man hadn't been given the chance to scream before the cat punctured his brain.

Sira limped along as fast as she could, favoring her

uninjured foot as she headed toward the slope.

The sabre-cat caught the scent of her, the same scent it remembered the day it lost its cub, and its anger rose. It rocked its head back and forth, causing the man's upper half to shake like a stick doll until he came loose from its fangs. With its dagger-like canines free, it bounded forward in a trot after Sira.

Sira fell to her hands and knees against the steep rocky slope. Sweat poured down her face and mixed with the white dust. The loose rock made it difficult to scale. She could hear the cat hiss below. She looked back as it leaped up, landing just beneath her. The weight of the cat was too much for the loose rock to support, and it slid back down to the bottom. Sira tried to push up the slope, but the rocks gave way and she slid down a few feet.

The cat leaped up at her again. One of its front paws landed by Sira's foot. It took a swipe at her leg, but she raised her leg at the last instant. The movement made the cat slide back down again. Sira turned back and continued to climb more carefully. Having learned from its mistake, the cat treaded slower, its razor-sharp claws extended to dig into the slope. But Sira had almost made it to the top and exhaled with relief.

She grabbed onto the lip to pull herself up, but the stratified rock was cracked. Under her weight, it broke free. The momentum made her lose footing, and she was sent sliding down into the cat. She flipped onto her back to defend herself. It tried to bite her leg, but she reared back and kicked the snarling creature in the face. This made the cat slide down the slope further. On her back, she desperately tried to scramble back up in a panic, but the rocks were even more slippery now.

The cat easily made its way back up to her. She tried to kick the cat again, but it was too close and caught her leg in its mouth. It bit down, and one of its massive canines sank deep into her right thigh. She screamed in agony and kicked the cat again with her other leg. The cat slid back down to the bottom, dragging Sira with her.

As she slid, she grabbed hold of a rock and struck at the

cat's head. The broken rock cut across the cat's eye, which was enough for it to release her leg. It hopped backward a pace, turned, then growled in anger, showing its massive fangs. Dropping into a pouncing position, Sira knew at that moment the cat was going to kill her.

Time seemed to slow down, and thoughts raced through her mind. She was not ready to die. She did not feel the same sort of bravery as the men had earlier. Although they faced danger daily, knowing death was always a possibility, she felt it wasn't her time.

From out of nowhere, a rock flew down from the sky, striking the cat hard on the side of its head. It shook and swayed with dizziness, and its yellow eyes wandered upwards in confusion.

Sira noticed the rock; it was so large!

The cat growled again and showed its fangs, but this time, it directed its anger toward the direction of the flung rock. Its nostrils flared as it sniffed, searching intently for the unseen threat. It took two more sniffs of the air, then gave a low-sounding growl. It looked at Sira one last time, then turned with reluctance and bolted off.

Blood came gushing out of her leg—too much blood! She felt her body already going into shock. She thought back to her mother, Tikara, who had tried to teach her how to heal wounds and treat the sick when she was young. But Sira was never interested, preferring to spend her time throwing spears and tracking small game with the boys. But she knew about the precious red liquid inside every person and how it was linked to life. Losing too much of it meant death. She put pressure on the hole in her leg, trying to stop the bleeding. She looked up to the ridge and into the sun.

"Help!" she screamed desperately. Feeling faint, the world around her spun. Her eyelids became heavy, and she fought the urge to close them. She fell back onto the dusty white rocks and licked her dry, cracked lips. Fine white dust particles entered her throat, making her cough.

Up on the ridge, a figure appeared. The silhouette of a man stood in front of the bright white sun. Even in the distance, she could see the thickness of his torso and the outline of his stout frame. He held a large rock in one hand and a spear in the other. She tried to cry out with her last bit of strength, but her mouth made no sound. Her eyes closed, and she could not get them to open again.

She felt a rough hand on her leg. Pressure was being placed on her thigh, near her pelvis. Her leg was being tied with something so tight it caused pain, but she did not have the strength to resist. She felt the wound being wrapped, and through her semi-conscious mind, realized she was being saved by someone. She was grateful, even if it was a Red feather.

The man had a pungent smell that she thought she had recognized from somewhere recently. She had a feeling of being lifted as easily as if she were a small child. Blurs of movement passed through her eyelids as she faded in and out of consciousness. Cool water washed over her head, and it dripped into her mouth. She swallowed automatically, all resistance within her gone. Then she was moving again, being carried away while she drifted into darkness.

Chapter 7

Tonik was drowning. The skin on his arms and legs stung and welted from contact with the water upon landing. His lungs burned as he choked on water. He had been so sure that he would not survive the fall that he almost forgot to swim as the water raged over him.

In an instant, his head came up, and he saw the sunny sky above him. He coughed and gagged out water as the current pushed him under again. He tried to open his eyes, but the water was murky, and he thrashed around desperately trying to get his head above water.

He bobbed up and caught his breath but saw he was heading toward more raging white water. His body crashed against a rock, and it knocked the air out of him. The river thrashed and twisted him around angrily. He sucked water again as he pushed up for the surface, coughing and barely getting enough air in his lungs. He fell over a short waterfall, and it pushed him under the surface again. His lungs burned, and he no longer had the strength to keep himself afloat.

Images of Sira struck his mind. She was running; she was bleeding and running. He thought about her beautiful smile and her light brown eyes, full of life. It was over; he had survived the fall, only to drown in the river. He was surprisingly at peace; his only regret was he would never see his love again.

Before everything went black, there were hands on him. They were slapping and beating his back; trying to make him breathe. He came to, coughing and heaving up water as air rushed back into his lungs. With his vision blurred, all he could see was the muddy bank of the river. He felt a pair of soft hands turning him over onto his back. They stroked his forehead and then gently slapped his face. *The Red Feathers must have caught me.*

He struggled to speak. "Just kill me," he sobbed weakly. But the hands shook him harder, and his head cleared.

The boy spoke in a familiar, feminine voice. A hand brushed the mud from his face, and the voice came through more clearly. "Tonik, Tonik, wake up. Can you hear me?"

Tonik opened his eyes to a squint, as if afraid to see what had happened. The sun was directly overhead, too bright to make out the face hovering above him. He heard the voice cry out, "You're alive!" Then the young man's face moved in front of the sun, and it came into focus. There, looking down at him with the biggest grin he had ever seen, was one of the twins, Pliny.

Pliny dragged Tonik farther onto the riverbank in some soft grass and allowed him a few minutes to rest. He dug up some thick clay and molded it onto Tonik's side to stop the bleeding of the stab wound.

"Jin...?" Tonik questioned.

Pliny responded enthusiastically, "He is still alive, Tonik. We led a group of Red Feathers away, but there were so many of them! Only some of them followed us; the others kept going after you. We were trapped and wanted to jump off the cliff like you, but we found a place to climb down. It was steep, and we had to go slow. You know how Jin is on high places," he said, flapping his arms dizzily. "We had to jump down into the water on the last part, so we can't go back that way. The Red Feathers saw us climbing, and they were throwing spears at us from above using a bent stick!" Pliny was up excitedly, mimicking the bow and arrow. "That's when we had to jump!"

"Slow down, Pliny," Tonik said. He grimaced at the pain on his side.

"How bad are you hurt, Tonik? Can you walk?"

"Yes, I think I can, but my whole body hurts," he said, looking at the welts from his landing in the water.

"Look, I broke my nail on the climb down," Pliny said in an attempt at consolation.

Tonik looked up at him, unimpressed.

"Sorry, Tonik."

"Sira!" Tonik suddenly said.

Pliny responded, "Jin went to find her, Tonik. We saw you jump and decided to split up, Jin to find Sira and me to chase you down the river. That was brave Tonik, jumping from the cliff like that. I will tell the others, or else they won't believe it."

Tonik thought about those words. Was he brave? Or was jumping from the cliff an easier prospect than facing four enemies? He wasn't sure.

Tonik shook his head somberly. "Pliny, the other men, Kadam and Rooti... the Red Feathers..." He lost his words.

"All of them?" Pliny asked.

Tonik did not respond, and Pliny dropped his head. They sat in the grass for several moments, allowing the tragedy to sink in.

"From dirt our bones, and our bones to dirt," said to himself in a whispered eulogy. "We will tell the others of their sacrifice. Let's move, Tonik. We are far from where you fell. The river pushed you quickly."

Pliny helped Tonik to his feet, and they moved into the thick grass. As they walked, Pliny handed him a handful of fruits he had found lining the riverbank. Tonik shoved one into his mouth ravenously, the sweet fruit juice running down his chin.

Tonik looked up from his meal gratefully, "Pliny, we are very lucky that you and Jin are still alive."

"Of course you are. But umm, Tonik, no more talking or noise from here on, and rub some of this mud on your body," Pliny said casually.

"Why?" asked Tonik.

"You know, the nose horns," Pliny responded.

"Nose horns! Wait, where, here?" Tonik asked worriedly.

"Nose horns, yes. That's what I said. They are all over here," Pliny responded matter-of-factly.

Tonik threw down the fruit and hastily rubbed more mud on himself, looking around the tall grass. He tried to inquire further about the woolly rhinoceros issue, but Pliny just hushed him and kept moving.

***

The elephant grass along the rushing river stood twice as high as a man. Its fluffy tops swayed with the wind rhythmically while the bottom stems sat thick and motionless. Creatures had trampled paths through it, and their dung had mixed with the muddy ground. New shoots of bright green grass grew up along the sides of the paths, prized grazing for woolly rhinos.

Pliny moved silently through, and Tonik followed several paces behind. It amazed him how the young man walked without making a sound, and he tried to follow his steps. This was a dangerous place to travel through. Rhinos are highly territorial and wary of humans; they won't hesitate to trample and gore any creature that threatens them. In this thick grass, you could almost walk right into one before seeing it. What made matters worse was this was a favored spot for mother rhinos to give birth, as they could hide the newborns in the grass from predators.

Pliny kept his keen eyes fixed on every corner. They could not see the river any longer, but could hear its roar and see the white mist rising over the tops of the grass. Pliny had run this way while chasing Tonik's body downstream and was now retracing his steps. Several times, Pliny had to hold up his hand for them to pause, and Tonik could hear shuffling through the grass and the smell of the rhinos' fresh dung.

They made their way to a spot in the river that narrowed between two big rock ledges, forcing the water to rush through. A massive tree had fallen and created a natural bridge over the angry waters. Pliny and Tonik squatted behind the grass, surveying the tree.

"This is the place Jin will cross. Red Feathers are on the other side searching for us. We must wait here," Pliny whispered.

After a long test of patience, four Red Feather warriors appeared on the other side. They pointed to the tree and spoke to each other, but Tonik could not hear because of the rushing water. They tested the strength of the fallen tree by pushing down on it with their feet. When it held firm, they began to cross.

Pliny signaled for them to move back into cover. "Where is Jin? He should have found Sira and been back by now," Pliny whispered.

The Red Feather warriors had now reached the grass and were investigating the ground. They raised their voices in excitement as they found Tonik's clumsy footprints in the grass. More shouts from the warriors as they split up and rushed into the green wall of stalks, one to the left and one to the right. The other two swing their spears in an arc, swatting a path through the high grass.

"We know you are here! Come out!" one warrior shouted.

Pliny and Tonik heard the shout and moved to the side, away from the voice. But a warrior came straight at them through the grass. They'd been flanked! They turned to run the opposite way, but after a few paces, another Red Feather warrior appeared in front of their path, his spear raised.

"Stop!" the man said in their language.

Two more men joined the other warriors. They had been outmaneuvered and surrounded.

"Come with us, or we will spear you again." The same warrior Tonik had faced on the cliff motioned with his spear to Tonik's side. "This time there is no cliff to jump off," he said in his strange accent.

* * *

Deeper in the grass, Jin had been waiting for Pliny. He could now hear the voices of the Red Feather warriors and understood Pliny and Tonik were caught. They were all unarmed, so trying to fight the Red Feathers would be futile. He tried to ignore the crunching sound of the grazing rhinos behind him when he suddenly smiled to himself at an idea.

He picked up a dried piece of rhino dung and carefully parted a wall of grass. A massive mother rhino and her calf were rolling frantically in the thick mud, trying to rid themselves of biting insects. The smell of their urine and scat mixed with the mud was heavy in the air.

Good, she is already in a bad mood. Jin aimed with the rock and threw it at the mother rhino as hard as he could. The rock-hard dung struck the rhino on its rear, just enough to startle her, and she jumped up to her feet in surprise. Jin grunted as if he was a rhino and shook the grass. The mother rhino turned to face the threat, and the baby rhino tucked back behind her. The mother dipped her head in anger at this intrusion and her nostrils widened and inhaled deeply, its giant horn as large as a man's arm. Jin gulped with fear, then thrashed the grass once more before turning to run. He whistled the bluebird song as he ran, hoping his partner would get the hint.

* * *

Pliny thought he was mistaken when he heard the frantic bluebird call. But as the second and third whistle came, growing closer each time, he knew it was his partner trying to tell him something.

"Get down, Tonik!" Pliny yelled as he tackled him to the side.

Together, they fell into the long grass. The timing was less than perfect, as Pliny did not know exactly how far Jin was, so they lay in the grass for several awkward moments.

Pointing their spears, the warriors shouted in frustration at them. "Get up!"

Before he had time to repeat the command, Jin came bounding through the grass with a nervous grin on his face. He immediately noted the scene and dived to the side of the mud where Pliny and Tonik lay.

The warriors jumped back, shouting with surprise. "Another one? All of you, get up now or die!"

But Jin ignored him and covered his head. The warriors, to their credit, at least understood something was wrong from the way the man had entered the scene, and they turned to face the direction from which Jin had come. A great crunching sound emanated from deeper in the grass. The warriors bunched together and raised their spears for what they thought was an incoming ambush.

By the time they saw the beast, it was too late. The rhino had spotted them, and their tall bodies painted in red ochre were an easy target. The mature mother rhino vented her rage in defense of her territory as she rammed into them at full speed. Two warriors flew up into the air and the giant horn speared another low in the stomach. The man's spear snapped in half against the creature's thick hide. The rhino huffed and grunted, shaking the man off her horn.

Tonik glanced up to his side; he was almost directly under the animal and dared not move an inch. One-step and the rhino could crush him, and if it saw them laying there, it would surely trample them. But it took no notice of the men lying motionless, its attention focused on the moving, screaming targets.

The lone warrior who was yet unscathed saw the carnage and turned to run, yelling in terror. The rhino dipped her head and chased after him through the grass.

Pliny grabbed Tonik immediately. "Now is our chance, Tonik! Run!"

With Jin leading, they ran off, away from the river and deeper into the grass. In the distance, they heard the grunting of the rhino and the cries of the man being trampled.

"You see! Nose horn!" Pliny said, smiling at Tonik.

"Nose horn could have killed us!" Tonik said, exasperated. Relieved, he punched Jin on the shoulder. "I will remember this; it will be a good story!"

The twins helped Tonik as he made a hobbling run through the grass. Once they were a safe distance away, Tonik's curiosity got the better of him. "Jin, wait! Did you find Sira?" he asked, grabbing Jin's shoulder.

Jin stopped at the question. He squatted in the grass, his face somber.

"Tell me, Jin! Where is she?" Tonik cried, still catching his breath.

"I tracked her into the big rocks. The Red Feathers chased her there... and it looked like they caught her." Tonik was ready to interrupt but Jin continued, "But the Red Feathers were killed by a big tooth!"

"A big tooth! Here?" Pliny questioned.

"Yes, the cat killed them both," Jin said, mimicking his fingers like fangs into his head. "Then it chased Sira to a slope. I found lots of her blood, too much. I did not have time to track the cat, as other Red Feathers were coming. But Tonik, her body was gone." Jin held his hands to his face and dropped his head in shame, as if he had failed.

Tonik fell to his knees in despair. He felt a wave of confusion and sadness that he could no longer control, and he screamed in rage as the emotion swept over him. The twins tried to hold him down to quiet him, but he brushed them off and sobbed in anger.

Pliny turned to Jin, wiping the tears from his eyes. "We have to keep moving, Jin. Can we make it to the Fishtooth following the river and staying hidden?"

"Yes, let us stay on this side under cover so it will be harder for them to track us."

After a few moments, the twins helped Tonik to his feet and supported him to walk. He had become silent and despondent. His despair seemed to make his injuries even more burdensome now. His spirit had left him, and the twins knew he would need all their help to make it back to the rest of the tribe.

Chapter 8

Raam and Tikara led the tribe for two days along the river, keeping ahead of the great auroch herd. At night, they slept out in the open, surrounded by fires. Underneath the cloudy white stripe of the Milky Way, millions of stars twinkled under the clear sky. Lions roared, and hyenas answered back with their yelping songs, communicating their territorial boundaries to each other.

On the third day, they came upon the auroch herd crossing. They eroded the riverbank from season after season of crossing on their way to the grasslands. The lower elevation brought less snow in the winter and made it easier for the auroch to meet their voracious grazing appetites.

Raam had high hopes they would spot the Fishtooth village soon. He imagined their hunters would also be in the area in anticipation of the aurochs' arrival. The day was cloudless, and from where they stood on the hill, Raam could see the outline of the vast blue horizon.

Raam remembered visiting this place as a boy. A severe drought had pushed the dwindling herd to the northwest, and it was the farthest his tribe had ever traveled. The two tribes had met on the hills near the coast by accident, but the meeting was a peaceful one. The great Fishtooth tribe had been welcoming, inviting them into their village, and feeding them for a few days while they traded together and rested.

Raam could barely remember the great village and its massive dwellings made from a mix of stone, mud, and wood. The Fishtooth village was an amazing sight for a nomadic tribe who always traveled light. The journey to this village as a man seemed much shorter than when he was a little boy, but no less significant.

As they came closer to the Great Sea, a group of people appeared in the distance. They were not approaching, but he could see they were moving.

He turned back and looked at the rest of his wearied tribe, eager to give them some encouragement. "It is them! It is Fishtooth! They are here, and we have found them! They have come to meet us!"

There were sounds of approval, and the clan's spirits rose. The thought of meeting with other friendly people brought them a great feeling of hope. They picked up their pace, young ones singing their favorite words and adults humming the bluebird tune.

As they got closer, Raam raised his hands above his head and waved them back and forth. This was a universal sign. It signaled a wish to meet in peace. When meeting strangers, it was protocol to make yourself seen and known to the other party or risk having your intentions misunderstood.

To Raam's dismay, the people did not respond. In fact, they made no movement that signaled to Raam that they had even noticed him. Raam counted ten figures, and they looked as if they were walking in circles.

He yelled out, trying to get their attention, but they paid no mind. Raam's group approached and stopped to gaze upon the odd behavior. They were much too thin, and both men and women wore ragged hides that hung off them carelessly. They were pacing in circles and gave no notice to Raam's group, even when they shouted to them.

Tikara held Raam's arm. "What is wrong with them?"

"Stay here and keep a lookout!" Raam said to the tribe. As he approached closer, he could hear their soft moans. The man in front of him was sickly pale, and a line of drool fell from the side of his mouth. He wore an elaborate shell necklace with several large sharp teeth, the emblem of his tribe.

"Fishtooth! Can you see me?" Raam cried.

The man looked up sluggishly, but did not respond.

Raam approached closer, grabbing the man's arm, "Fishtooth, what is wrong with you?"

The man let out a scream that was chortled, his lungs sounding clogged with mucus. He fell to the ground, holding his head in pain.

Tikara rushed forward to Raam's side.

"Tikara, stay back!"

Tikara got a good look at the man shaking on the ground, his gaunt frame and sickly yellow skin. Dark circles ran underneath his eyes and pustules circled his lips.

"They have a sickness!" Tikara yelled back in warning.

The tribe gasped in fear and withdrew to a safe distance. Raam and Tikara backed up. The group made a wide circle around the sick, watching them in surreal horror.

Diseases were one of the unknown terrors of their world. No one knew why or how they came, and they seemed to strike anytime, affecting the young and old alike. Raam had never seen such a sickness that could make people behave this way, and it made him shudder. He could not imagine why the Fishtooth would leave their people exposed like this. Shaken, they moved on in the direction of the coast in search of the Fishtooth village.

Chapter 9

Many centuries ago, near the current Fishtooth village, two spear fishers swam out into the blue water of the Great Sea. They were a strong and resourceful people, with caramel skin and light brown eyes. Their ancestors developed and adapted from a harsh desert climate.

The waters were calm and clear as the men swam out to the reef for the challenge. On low tide, the rock offshore reef came up shallow until it was waist-deep. It ran parallel to the coast for as far as the eye could see. Thousands of fish of all shapes and sizes circled the crystal-clear water. The reef was a holy place where men would go to gain honor.

It was guarded by the revered reef guardians, large gray beasts with sharp teeth. Whenever one speared a fish here, the reef guardians would come to its defense. Some days, the guardians would allow you to pass with your catch. Other days, you could not, and you would have to sacrifice it to the guardian, or you could not leave the reef in peace.

If one speared only a small fish, it was more likely the guardians would allow you passage. But bringing back a small fish brought little honor. The larger the fish, the more of a blessing you had with the guardians, and it was a symbol of good fortune for your family.

The leader of the village was favored by the guardians, having consistently brought back the largest fish each season. Today, the leader of the village was in high spirits. A younger man had challenged him, and he would again have to prove he was favored by the guardians by spearing a larger fish, guaranteeing another year of leadership.

In his ambition, he speared the heaviest, most massive fish he could find. The first spear throw only slightly disabled the big fish, and he had to spear it six times, chasing down the thrashing fish caught amongst the rocks. Pungent-smelling dark blood drifted out along the reef. He quickly tied the other end of the spear around his ankle. This would enable him to drag the fish at a distance on his swim back to shore.

If the guardians did not come for the fish, he would be

free to go. He had not got but a few lengths from the reef when he spotted the largest guardian he had ever seen; it was swimming directly under him. Surely, this great guardian had come to give the biggest blessing his people had ever seen. He surfaced quickly and let in a huge gulp of air, then he dived, all the way to the seafloor. Here he would wait for the guardian's return. If it did not return by the time the fisherman had to resurface, he was clear.

He caught a few flashes of the giant blue-gray beast as it circled. The fisherman's lungs began to burn; he could not stay down for much longer. The giant guardian started circling even closer now, eyeing his catch. With great regret, he untied the thread from his foot and let his fish go.

Guardian, as this is your reef, please accept this offering and leave me dishonored, but in peace.

He resurfaced, filling his lungs with the salty air. The immediate pain of a dozen sharp spears stabbed his leg. He was dragged violently beneath the surface. Instinctively, he grabbed at his leg to free it from the painful grip. He looked through the crystal water at the large guardian, whose teeth were lodged firmly into his leg as blood billowed out like smoke. He grabbed onto the snout of the guardian, trying to pry its mouth open; its eyes were white and turned into the back of its sockets.

Then he asked the guardian, "Why are you taking me, O' Great One? I gave you my catch. I have honored you. Was it not enough?"

Then the guardian opened its eyes. They were black and lifeless, with no compassion or understanding. The eyes gave away the true nature of the creature, dull and without honor. The eyes closed again. As it dragged him down, the fisherman had a sudden flash of insight, the kind that only comes to those who are in their final moments. He understood the guardians had never truly honored them. They did not give blessings; it was just dumb luck, luck as dumb as the black eyes of the creature who held him. In his greed, the fisherman had spilled a lot of blood, and it had called the biggest and most aggressive guardian to him. You decreased your odds if you spilled more blood, as smaller fish attracted little attention. That was the truth of it.

The fisherman's last thoughts were how foolish they had all been. If only he could live to tell the others, tell his family and village, their entire belief was based on a falsehood. As if any creature could care or honor what men did.

As saddening as it was, it was somehow refreshing to learn, as if a veil of lies had been lifted and he could finally see clearly for the first time in his life. Moments before he passed out, another creature appeared. It swam toward them with the speed of a thrown spear, and it swam in up and down movements, not side to side like that of other fish. The creature smashed into the side of the guardian with skill and deliberate force.

The fisherman heard a crunch of cartilage and ribs being smashed, and it freed him from the guardian's jaws. He swam up with the last of his strength, resurfacing just in time before blacking out. After a few moments of catching his breath, he noticed the new creature surface. It blew mist from a hole in its head. Quickly, he submerged to see whether it was going to attack him.

Then he saw it. The creature floated under a single beam of sunlight, which reflected through the water, giving it an aura. It gently swam up to the fisherman and turned its head to the side, smiling at him. Then it did something no other creature had ever done before. It looked him right in the eyes. The eyes were not dull and lifeless as the guardian's; they were bright and intelligent. They were the eyes of something wise, and they peered into his soul. It shook him.

The creature chirped and clicked playfully, obviously speaking to him, and he memorized the sounds. It circled and nodded its head up and down like that of a playful child. After several moments, it turned and swam away.

When the fisherman reached the shore, his family aided him as he limped out of the water with his bloody leg. The village shaman walked over and somberly pulled out a large guardian tooth from out of the fisherman's leg. The villagers gasped. Surely, this was a bad omen.

But the fisherman grabbed the tooth from the elder and stood up straight, seemingly oblivious to the injury and pain. With far-flung, dreamy eyes, the fisherman looked at everyone and proclaimed, "My people, I have had a vision while I was beneath the sea! It spoke to me and told me its name." He held the blood-smeared tooth of the great fish in one hand, then tossed it dismissively into the sand. "The reef has a new guardian, and its name is Samaki!"

Chapter 10

As they entered the Fishtooth village, Raam still had high hopes that he would find the large, powerful tribe he once knew. His hope was soon crushed. The village was full of the sick. Ailing bodies of men and women lay all around, some of them on the verge of death. They could hear coughing and wheezing coming from inside the dwellings, while others attended to their chores in a weak and sorry-looking state. There were massive triangular wooden drying racks that stood over two men high. These were used for drying and smoking great numbers of fish. But the racks lay mostly barren. The villagers stared at the visitors with blank expressions as they walked by.

Raam's tribe commented to each other in whispered voices, lamenting the sight of the human suffering that lay before them. Still, the village itself was impressive. The size of the structures was many times larger than the simple wood and hide tents of Raam's clan. The mud-brick technology mixed with the dry grass and sticks was something most had never seen before. Sculptures of a curled, smiling fish made of wood and whalebone of varying ages decorated the outside of the dwellings.

Raam marveled at the clever use of wood overlaid with mud and rock that was used for construction. Yet the construction itself was so simple and obvious, Raam wondered why more people had not used it. Although, if one were to build this, they could not move it. This type of dwelling was suitable for people who could rely on the sea for their sustenance all year round. It was not suitable for people of the hills, whose survival depended on the movement of the animals they consumed.

Raam approached an opening in the center of the village that held a large central fire pit, its contents reduced to smoking embers this time of day. A group of Fishtooth men formed together upon seeing Raam arrive. A series of surprised shouts ran through them before they could assemble and approach the visitors in greeting.

Raam held up one flat palm, signaling for his tribe to

stop as they approached. Then he held up both hands as a sign of peace.

A young man led the Fishtooth group, and he came up swiftly with his spear at the ready. "Who are you? Why have you come here?" Spit formed on the corners of his mouth as he spoke. He looked nervous with authority, and his eyes moved quickly, trying to size up Raam's group.

"Young man, there is no need for that." Raam pointed to the spear. "We have come here as friends; we need your help."

"We have nothing to trade! You will find nothing here! Do not think you will take anything from us!" he shouted.

"We are not here for trade. My father was a friend of Kessec. I am Raam, and we are old friends of the Fishtooth from beyond the hills." Raam pointed to the southeast. "I have not visited this village since I was a young boy."

The young man lowered his spear and stood up straighter. "Kessec died many winters ago. I have not heard this name in a long time. Kessec was my father's father. I am Jessec, and I am the leader of the Samaki now."

"But you are just a young man. You are the leader of this village? Where are the rest of your people? Have they all died of this sickness?" Raam asked.

Jessec grew angry at this exchange. "I am a man, and I say I am the leader of the Samaki! We are a strong tribe, and we will not give you anything!"

Raam could see he had miscalculated his choice of words and trodden upon the young man's ego. He also realized that he was referring to his tribe as the Samaki, and Fishtooth must have been the slang or even derogatory name given to them on account of the jewelry they wore.

Tikara stepped forward with a look of passive diplomacy and opened her hands in peace. "We have come from such a long way to meet the leader of the great Samaki. We see you now, and we ask for help. We need to rest. A great tribe of hunters is coming this way. They will follow us here, and you are all in danger."

"Great tribe of hunters coming, you say? Friends of Kessec, you say?"

"Yes, this tribe who wears Red Feathers is bigger than even the Samaki. They have killed many of us and pushed us here. They will do the same to you," Raam added.

Jessec looked back at the group and seemed to think for a moment before looking up to Raam. "Come. If you were a friend of Kessec, then you may rest with us. I will hear about this great tribe that you speak of."

Raam sighed with relief that the welcoming nature of the Samaki people he remembered still held. He turned and gave his tribe an optimistic nod of his head.

***

The rest of the afternoon, Raam spoke at length with the young leader of the tribe. Jessec explained how the sickness had taken to the tribe last spring and how quickly it had spread. It had not killed everyone it inflicted, but was especially harsh on the weak and elderly. Thankfully, many of the children never showed symptoms, and no recent cases had manifested in many days. Those who were currently sick would either waste away and join the tribe's burial place or slowly recover within two moon cycles.

Raam did his best to highlight the dangers that the oncoming Red Feathers represented, but was disappointed with Jessec's response.

Jessec brushed his hands aside with aloofness. "We are the strongest tribe. No one would dare attack us," he said impatiently.

Raam could see that between dealing with the sickness and managing the normal day-to-day difficulties, Jessec was overwhelmed and frustrated. He did not have the experience of age or the temperament to lead such a large tribe. Raam's warning of more disaster was the last thing Jessec wanted to hear. It was as if he was already at the limit of what he could handle.

Raam realized that although the Samaki were still large in numbers, they had lost many of the older generations to guide them. With the recent leaders falling to the disease, the young tribe members had turned to the next in line of the family for lack of leadership. But Jessec looked close to Tonik's age, and he had grown up with a somewhat privileged life, being as his father had been the previous tribe leader.

To Raam's disappointment, the Samaki were a tribe of lost young men and women, doing their best to recover.

As Raam left him to Jessec to ponder, he entered one of the large and recently vacated dwellings the Samaki had offered to them. Tikara had been waiting, and Raam looked around at the shelter, impressed by the design. A special mud that had dried and hardened covered even the floor of the dwelling. It kept the floor free from dampness.

"Does he see the picture of what you speak, Raam?" Tikara asked expectantly.

Raam sighed. "I do not think young Jessec can lead the Samaki, and I do not think he can see tomorrow enough to prepare for the Red Feathers."

"What will we do? You must get him to see!" she pleaded.

Raam had been thinking about this already and looked sympathetically at his partner. "I saw us coming to the Fishtooth... sorry, the Samaki... to join them. I was wrong. I now see that we have come to lead them."

"And what of Jessec?" Tikara asked.

"Either he and his people will follow us because they can see it is good, or we will wait for Kadam and the others, and we will force them to. Either way, all of us must be ready for the Red Feathers unless we plan on running forever."

Chapter 11

On the foothills of the mountain range, the Gondo-Var warriors regrouped at the junction of the river. The men stayed clear of Master as he was eager to take out his disappointment on the nearest person. The expedition had been a failure, with ten of his men dead. Although they had captured Kadam, he was a man so wild and savage, Master wondered if he could ever be tamed.

The people of Raam's tribe had proven brave and stubborn, fighting it out until the end rather than surrendering. It was a common trait of the hill people, and he wondered now whether these people were worth the effort.

Master awaited the return of Last Chance to hear the report about the rest of the tribe, and it was more bad news. Last Chance had tracked the auroch herd across the river but stopped once he found the sick Samaki out in the hills. The disease was something that the Gondo-Var tribe had experienced before. They had a right to be fearful. Like a silent hunter that could ambush you without notice, once it caught its prey, it could kill you, no matter how strong of a warrior you were. And no amount of running or hiding could escape it. The Gondo-Var shamans had many reasons as to what caused the disease, with remedies and potions to cure it, but Master was always skeptical of these. His practical experience told him the best solution was to stay away from it. Regrettably, he decided to stop hunting the rest of the tribe, at least for now.

Besides, all was not lost. At least one discovery had made Master's skin tingle with anticipation. His trackers had followed the dark-skinned girl and had come upon the grisly scene at the rocky slope. The discovery of big tooth kills was not the most surprising, it was that they had discovered evidence of one of the Others. Master insisted on seeing the partial footprint himself. Only when he saw the large man's wide prints did he truly believe it. It was the first sign of one of the elusive people they had seen in years.

Even more interesting was that it seemed the Other had possibly interacted with the girl. Although she had lost a lot of blood, there was no evidence that the Other had killed her.

The entire scene perplexed Master. *Why would one of the Others break custom and carelessly leave his tracks behind? What did he want with that girl?* Although Master knew the futility of trying to track one of these elusive men, perhaps the weight of the girl upon his shoulders would slow him down and make it harder for him to hide his spoor.

Master sent his best trackers upon them. It led higher into the mountains and he hoped the cliffs would be impassable, creating a trap. He could not hold his excitement to think that he would finally catch one of the Others and maybe force him to show where his kind was hiding. Father expected his war parties back by the next full moon, so he could not hold his men at the river junction for long. On the slight chance the trackers located the Others, they would return to camp with the good news and prepare reinforcements.

Master walked over to Kadam. The large man was still bound and lying on his back. He was awake now and very silent. A terrible scowl crossed his face. Master could not tell if it was from the pain of his blows or just the man's temperament, but he guessed the latter. Master looked down upon him. "I would like to cut your hands free; I enjoyed our last fight. You will have another chance. But first, you will meet Father, then you will eat and rest. I want you at full strength. If you complete the test, your life will begin again. A life in which a man of your strength will be honored. You may have any woman of your choice, more than one. Men will follow you, and you may hunt for the rest of your days."

* * *

Master's trackers were on the trail of the mysterious man as they climbed higher into the mountains. It amazed them at how he used the steep rocks and landscape in cunning ways to disappear, but the girl's blood left an easy trail to follow. At a certain elevation, the ground became covered in frost, which made following the man's spoor even easier.

As the trackers continued their way up, the sky turned an ominous white and the temperature dropped. The Gondo-Var warriors were completely unprepared for the biting cold of the icy wind. Their legs and feet were thinly covered to allow lighter and faster movement, but it made snow travel ineffective. Their feet were quickly becoming numb, but they knew the importance of this hunt and they pressed on, ignoring the pain.

They stopped by a broken bunch of frozen yellow flowers. The stems had been broken off in a hurry and stripped of their skin.

The lead tracker picked one up and sniffed, then tasted it. Its bitterness was sharp. He spit it out in disgust. "This man eats grass like a wild animal. We must be getting close."

They hurried up the steep slope, their view of the mountain now obscured by the low incoming clouds and thick snowfall. The wind increased as they ascended, and soon the snow was ankle-deep.

One tracker whined, "Our feet will become stoned and black if we continue!"

The lead tracker cut him off. "Master will cut off our feet anyway if we go back with nothing!" He motioned for them to keep moving.

Any normal man would have lost wind by now, but the trackers had amazing stamina through years of hunting. As the wind gained force and snow blew into their faces, their lips turned blue. However, they could see fresh drops of blood in the snow, and it motivated them forward. The slope became steeper as the trackers trudged through the fresh powder, which was now up to their knees.

The lead tracker stopped and hooted in delight. Pointing up the slope, he could barely see the outline of a cave opening through the snowstorm. Above the cave, the mountain steepened so that it was no longer passable. The cave opening was the only dark spot against the white that was quickly surrounding them.

Through chattering teeth, the lead tracker yelled to the others, "They have gone into the cave! We will have them now!"

As he looked up, the man's outline came into view. Standing still at the opening, he looked down upon them calmly. The man's confidence unnerved the lead tracker. He hesitated at the sight, pausing to catch a glimpse for the first time in his life at one of the mythical people, often talked about but rarely seen. A person who their Father was desperately trying to capture.

"I have you now," the tracker told himself, smiling, though he could no longer control his shivering body.

The sight of the man inspired their spirit. With eyes on their prey, they rushed forward up the steep slope with their last reserves of energy, eyes fixed on the strange man at the dark opening. They noticed the man now had a large rock in his hand, and he raised it at waist level. He spun around in a circle twice, gaining momentum before releasing the rock. It flew up the side of the steep slope at a great distance, disappearing into the white. Before returning to the cave, the man let out a shout so loud; it stopped them in their tracks. The yell had a lingering echo; the vibrations bouncing off the cliff sides as the trackers looked out into the white that surrounded them.

"Quick, he might call others for help!" cried the lead tracker.

With arms clenched around their chests from the cold, they shuffled up through the knee-high fresh powder. Getting to the cave now was a matter of survival. As they got closer, they heard a cracking sound in the distance farther up the slope – the sound of tree limbs being snapped and broken. A strange hiss filled the air, and they strained to look up through the white of the blizzard. As the lead tracker's eyes focused, he saw the entrance of the cave being enveloped in white. A wave of snow several men high was rushing down the slope toward them.

"Run!" the tracker yelled, but it was too late. The avalanche rushed over them, lifting them off their feet like insects. The wall of snow snapped entire trees in half and lifted the loose stone, hurling everything down the mountain with a force that only nature could achieve. Only in the spring would the men's broken bodies be exposed and thaw, allowing scavengers to pick their bones clean.

* * *

In the darkness, with the cave entrance covered under snow, Harq gently picked up the girl and treaded deeper into the cave. Many paths led to dead ends and deadly drops under the ancient mountain peak, but Harq knew all of them by heart. He chewed on the hard stem of the yellow flower and felt for the girl's mouth. She was still whimpering and shaking in a semi-conscious state. Harq lifted her head and spit the bitter liquid into her mouth to help ease her pain. He also swallowed some for good measure. After the storm, the mountains would be impassable until spring. This snow-covered tunnel was the only passage to the secret valley beyond. The avalanche had covered the entrance and any traces that led to it.

Chapter 12

The Gondo-Var warriors were on their way back to see Father. He would grow impatient if they did not return in time, so they made haste, moving at a speed and stamina that no other men in the world could match.

Kadam had proven to be much too powerful to keep on his feet, so they bound his hands and legs to a hefty wooden log. Some of the larger warriors took turns carrying him as he swung back and forth as if he were a slain animal. Kadam could not exactly keep track of which direction they had been moving, for he drifted in and out of consciousness. Every so often, they stopped to allow him to drink water from a deer bladder.

One night, the one they called Master plopped down a raw rabbit's leg on Kadam's chest. He had to wiggle and squirm to get the leg into his mouth without his hands and managed a few bites before it fell to the ground. The warriors sitting around the fire laughed at this. Kadam was too weak to insult or speak, and he wished for death. He would have preferred to die fighting than to be bound and dragged like an animal.

He counted five nights spent traveling with the Red Feather warriors before their direction abruptly turned and headed for the coast. The party followed one particularly fast-moving stream as it led into a dark copse of dense trees. Once they were deep enough into the wooded area, hushing sounds passed through the line of men until they all fell silent.

Echoes of rustling leaves and snapping twigs filled the air around the dense forest. It was as if a dozen animals had suddenly been agitated. There was a yelping noise, followed by a brief howl. The warriors whistled in their direction.

Through the tree line, Kadam could see the blurred outlines of wolves trotting back and forth with speed. They continued to make yelping sounds at the men, then cautiously came closer. They were much too close to Kadam's liking, and he wondered if he was to be fed to them. The shoulders of these large canines came up higher than waist level, and their heads were twice that of a man's. Even for a large hunting party, an entire wolf pack was a dangerous force to be reckoned with. But to his surprise, the wolves did not attack. They shimmied and whined at the men, keeping their distance.

The warriors unwound pieces of animal meat from their recent kills. Leftover rabbit carcasses and deer's legs were thrown out to them. They growled and snapped at each other as they rushed in for their free meal. Once the wolves were preoccupied with establishing their pecking order, the warriors quickly gathered back up and condensed the men into a tighter group.

It wasn't long before they arrived at a large rock formation on either side of the stream. The path narrowed between the boulders, forcing them to walk two by two on a well-worn path. Red Feather warriors appeared on the tops of each of the boulders. They carried the funny bent sticks that he had seen days earlier during their encounter. The men yelled down from atop the rocks, "Eagle Fly!" to which the men on the marching line triumphantly cheered, "Men Fall!" The rock walls continued on each side of the boulders, but they looked unnaturally placed, creating a defensive wall.

As they passed through the boulders and a winding path of dried thorn bushes, the area widened, and the Gondo-Var camp opened before them. The path was lined with mammoth skulls and tusks artfully set up to form an entrance. More mammoth tusks lined their camp than Kadam had ever seen in his life. A multitude of people encompassing a vast open camp materialized into view. He soon realized the party that had been chasing them was not the actual tribe; it was only one hunting party. This hunting party was only one of many in this massive tribe.

Kadam could see people performing all manner of tasks. Although none seem out of the ordinary from any other tribe, they seemed to work with more urgency and efficiency. A section of camp appeared to be solely for knapping stones and making weapons. He passed another area that looked as if it was only for cleaning and drying hides.

What Kadam did not realize was that the Gondo-Var tribe had discovered the efficiency of creating a specialized workforce. While in his tribe, everyone had to be adept at all survival skills, the Gondo-Var people became specialized in one task, perfecting and becoming efficient at it. One could be a maker of spears and arrowheads, for instance. Or if one showed an aptitude for hunting or tracking, that is what they performed, and nothing else. Everything else was provided to them in a complex social hierarchy that included an elite member class of war party leaders. Master was the leader of all the war parties, and the individual war chiefs reported to him. At the head of the tribe was their honored and worshipped leader- Father.

The war party led the captives to the rocky cliffs by the shore, to an open-faced cavern with a sandy floor. Kadam tried to see how tall the top of the cliff was, but it was so high that when he peered up, the sun shone into his eyes. He could only make out the faint outlines of giant black-winged birds circling the rocks above before the glare forced him to turn away. As the water crashed against the rocks in the cave, the sound was amplified, creating a thunderous roar.

Here, Kadam was dropped and unbound from the stick. They made him to sit on his knees alongside other strange men who were bound in the same manner. He rubbed his raw wrists and hands gingerly.

Above them, perched upon a great flat rock covered in various animal skins and mammoth tusks, Kadam saw the strangest man he had ever seen. The man was huge, but short in stature. His belly stuck out as if he were with a child. Both legs were as round as black logs and his face puffed out and sagged in a way so that you could not see his neck. It was the first time Kadam had ever seen an obese person.

A younger boy came running up with an open log and laid it upon the big man's lap. With his two stubby fingers, he reached in and plucked a large grub from out of the log. It was as long and wide as his finger, and he shoved it greedily into his mouth. He grabbed a thick ripe plum and bit into it, the red juice dribbling down his chin. Whilst still chewing, his hands went up, waving down at the warriors below.

One of the Gondo-Var warriors yelled enthusiastically, "Our Father! All lands and beasts are his. he is the owner of all people! He is the owner of everything as far as we can see and more! He is the Father of Eagles!"

Chanting ensued, "Eagle Fly! Eagle Fly! Eagle Fly..."

The one they called Father lifted his hand, and they became quiet. He spoke, his voice bellowing with a deep resonance and harshness. "Long ago, in a cave that looked like this, one of our people was captured by an enemy village," Father said, speaking slowly so they would understand. He had to pause at every other sentence as the rhythmic roar of the waves hit the cave wall. "He was a young man, thin and tall, but not very strong. The enemy village was going to cut out his heart while he watched, as a war sacrifice." The waves thundered the cave again.

"One warrior suggested that if the man climbed to the top of the cliff and plucked a red feather from the tail of the great eagle, they would allow him to live. The enemy men laughed in amusement, for it was an impossible climb. The young man would surely either fall to his death or have his head opened by the eagle's claws!" Father made his hand resemble a talon and made a slicing motion as the thunder of the waves hit again.

The men in the cave chanted, "Eagle Fly!"

"So, the young man climbed, and after many hours, he somehow made it to the top where the eagles' nests were. The eagles shrieked down upon him. The birds were as tall as him, and their claws were the length of his forearm." Father held up his arm and chopped his elbow, showing the size of the claw. "But the man was brave and held no fear. He spoke to the eagle as if speaking to a man, and he asked, 'Please, Great Flying One, can you give me one of your feathers?' Then the eagle flew up and circled overhead but did not attack him, for it had decided the man had no fear and deserved to live. With great difficulty, the man climbed down and presented the feather to those who wished to kill him. He stood proud, and said, 'You may kill me now,' The enemy chief was so impressed, he allowed the man to live.

In time, the young man became chief of the village, proving himself many times in battle. In our tribe, if one wants to become a true warrior, one must make the climb and retrieve the feather. Some of you, if you prove your worth, will be given that chance."

With that, Father reached over and plucked another juicy worm out of the log and waved his hand, signaling to take the prisoners away.

Kadam understood enough of the story despite the man's accent, and he laughed in defiance. He raised his head and looked directly at Father. "And you, Great Round One with your fat belly, I would like to see how you make that climb!" Kadam did not have time to wait for a reaction, he immediately felt a knock to the back of his head, and he fell over unconscious.

***

Kadam awoke at night by the sound of a crackling fire. The back of his head pounded with pain. He felt an animal skin being put to his mouth, and he jerked away. The wetness of his lips made him realize it was water, so he stuck out his mouth as someone poured for him. He drank greedily until he heard a familiar voice. "That is enough. You have not had enough water these past days. Too much will make you sick."

Kadam cautiously opened his eyes and saw Master standing over him with the waterskin. He turned his head away from the man and moved back.

"Ah, yes, still the rage inside. You must not lose that anger."

Master grabbed his arms and hoisted him up to a sitting position. Surprisingly, Kadam felt that his arms were free, so he immediately probed the back of his sore head. There were now two lumps, and he could feel a bit of dried blood.

Master took a place on the other side of the fire. They were in a cave recess against the rocky cliff. Mammoth bones and animal skins enclosed the entrance. Outside, through the billowing flaps of hanging hides, he could see the outline of shadows and flickering of firelight. He could hear the familiar sounds of men and women around their family night fires. In the distance, the sound of the waves hitting the rocks was now quiet; the sea must be resting now as well, he thought.

Kadam glanced back at Master, and a thought crossed his mind, but he quickly gave it up. He was too weak right now for a fight. His head was pounding with pain, and his wrists and ankles were swollen red from the bindings over the past few days. For the first time in his life, Kadam realized a brazen attack would not work in this situation. He relaxed his body slightly, resting his head gently back on the rock.

"Ah, yes, finally the big bear knows when he is beat," Master said with a smile.

"I cannot kill you now, but I will kill you soon," Kadam replied.

"Maybe one day, when your skills improve, you will be an adversary worthy enough."

"If you stopped using those tricks that you did, I could kill you easily."

Master laughed. "There are no tricks in battle, Kadam, only those who live and those who die. I can teach you to fight better, but not now. Now you are still an animal. You must first learn how to be a man."

Master called out some names toward the tent entrance. A few moments later, two young women came in carrying chunks of fatty meat in each hand. They sat next to Master and made skewers, then held them over the fire. The juicy steaks dripped with fat, which made the fire crackle.

The smell made Kadam's stomach growl like the big tooth he had killed. Master now wore the canine tooth around his neck.

Kadam thought back to that hunt, which was so recent but seemed somehow long ago. A yearning to go back to that moment hit him. When all he had to worry about was finding the next meal, sometimes gloriously so.

Master began eating along with the two young women. They giggled and fed him pieces of meat as they vied for his attention. Kadam wondered how these women could enjoy being with a man so terrifying.

When Master had finished, he took one of the half-eaten steaks and tossed it to Kadam. Kadam tore into it like a ravenous animal, and the girls giggled at the sight.

"Oh, look, he behaves like an animal," one girl said.

Master smiled. "If he is an animal, he will attack us in our sleep."

The girls oohed and awed at the thought, the sense of danger and suspense seeming to arouse them. Master then folded himself under a large fur, and both girls joined him underneath.

As Kadam continued eating, he could hear them making love. The first sounds were of giggles and squeals from foreplay. Then came Master's grunting sounds and the feminine whines of either pleasure or pain; which of the two, he could not tell. Kadam waited patiently for what seemed a very long time for one man until finally, all three went quiet. He waited a while longer until he heard the rhythmic breathing sounds of sleep.

Kadam got to his knees; he had to bend his head so that it did not hit the rock ceiling. He quickly scanned the area for a weapon. There were several small rocks in the side of the cave, perhaps big enough to crack open Master's head if he used enough force. He got up as quietly as he could and tried to tiptoe over to the rocks, but Kadam was never good at being quiet, and his feet and knees made cracking sounds as he walked.

He chose a rock and held it in his hand, looking over at the three bodies underneath the fur. He snuck over to where they lay and held the rock in his hand for a moment. He felt very uncomfortable trying to be sneaky; it didn't suit him. He suddenly remembered what Master had told him about being a man. *No, this is not how I want to kill this man.* Even if he accomplished it, he would be dead in moments trying to flee the camp.

He walked back over to his place by the fire and dropped the rock. He lay on his back and closed his eyes as exhaustion took him over. *I will have my chance.*

Under the fur, Master smiled and relaxed his grip on the club he had been holding between him and the girls.

Chapter 13

Legend tells of a wolf that lived long ago. She was the leader of her pack, the alpha female, with lustrous, long, black fur. With cunning and strength unmatched, her pack grew so large it soon outnumbered all the other animals. Her children had dark shiny fur, just like she did. But like all creatures, her strength and vigor waned with age.

One day, a younger group of she-wolves managed to beat her, and they took control of the pack. Humiliated, the wolf mother was expelled, doomed to die alone.

Instead of accepting her fate, she made a deal with the moon. She howled at it all night, with all the strength left in her, louder than any wolf ever had. The moon was so impressed by this display that it granted the wolf a wish. She wished to be transformed into another creature, for she no longer belonged with the wolves. She wished to build a new pack, one whose power and numbers could surpass those of the wolves themselves.

The moon granted her wish, and when she awoke the next day, she was a young woman, dark, strong, and more cunning than ever before. She once again built her pack, and she bore many children. Soon their numbers outgrew even those of the wolves. But although her kin looked like normal people, they behaved like wolves. These people become known as the wolf-people, cursed to battle each other like those of the wolf packs.

Dealing with the wolf people was like dealing with wolves, dangerous and unpredictable. It was impossible not to get caught in their never-ending power struggles, no matter which side you chose. The ancestors learned long ago that their only option to survive against the wolf people was to hide. But the wolf people quickly grew. In a few generations, they took over all the lands the people once occupied, pushing them farther north or into the mountains. Hiding and surviving on the fringes became their way of life as the wolf people continued to spread.

An elderly woman thought about this story as she gently stoked a small fire. She remembered the way her mother told it, in her simple language. The story was important to her and her people.

She blew hard into the fire embers, igniting the kindling. The cavern that held the fire was not spacious, but it was tall, with small cracks overhead to dissipate the smoke. Some smoke still lingered, and it gave the cavern a hazy appearance.

The noise of the crackling fire stirred the young, dark-skinned woman lying in the furs, and she moaned and tossed her head from side to side. The old woman stood over her, whispering soothing words. She placed her hand on the woman's forehead, and it was hot with fever.

The old woman quickly took out a mixture of leaves and herbs she had prepared in a water gourd warmed by the fire. She drizzled a few drops along the woman's leg, and the young woman stirred and moaned even louder. She continued to pour the liquid drop by drop for some time until it was finished. She formed some clay, patting it flat in her hands until she had the desired thickness and shape. She gently molded the clay over the bite wound. A nice hard scab had formed, and there was no ill smell to it.

Satisfied with her work, she sighed while looking down at the poor child. It was up to the spirits now. As she got up, she saw the young woman attempt to open her eyes and mumble some words that the old woman did not understand.

"Ton. Toni," she gasped.

The old woman lay her hand upon her head again and gently stroked it, and soon the young woman fell back asleep. The girl was gaining strength; she would survive, after all. It might have been easier if the girl had just died; it would have surely eased all the fears surrounding her.

The old woman felt a pang of guilt for this; her maternal instinct would never willingly let this happen. The old woman was the tribe's healer and medicine woman. Her adopted son, Harq, had brought the girl to her for that very reason. But the girl wasn't one of them! One of their own had brought this bad omen upon them here, in their hidden home in the mountains. The fear and sensation this had caused!

This beautiful girl with dark skin could very well be the she-wolf herself. Some of the young ones cried at night to fall asleep, thinking the she-wolf would come to get them in the night. The people were angry with Harq, confused about why he would bring the girl. Secretly, the old woman knew why, but it was something that could not be spoken.

With much on her mind, the old woman crept out of the cave, taking along her bundles of medicine.

***

Sira awoke in a state of shock. The world was a whirl of blurred vision, and it was a struggle to keep her eyes open. Any attempt at movement sent a spasm of pain into her injured thigh. Bits and pieces of the recent events slowly came together to form a picture in her mind, the faces of her attackers, and the snarling cat. Her head was so deep in fog it was hard to focus on her surroundings. Warm furs covered her skin, and the hollow sound of the air told her she was in a cave. For the moment, she felt safe enough to close her weary eyes and fall back into a deep sleep.

Fevered dreams filled Sira's nights, moments of semi-consciousness in which she could not distinguish whether she was asleep or awake. With time, the fogginess diminished, replaced by moments of clarity. In those moments, her stomach groaned with hunger, spurring her awake more often.

Sometimes, while she drifted in and out of sleep, she became aware of a presence within the cave, although she never could catch who it was. Someone must be taking care of her. She wondered if it was the same person who had rescued her from the big tooth. Whoever it was, they only seemed to enter while she was asleep.

A day came when finally gained the strength to sit up and investigate her surroundings with more lucidity. She was inside an oblong circular cave and saw remnants of dried grass and old coal ash littered on the floor. A dull white light entered one end of the cave- the entrance.

Desperate to get a glimpse of her surroundings, she

attempted to stand, supporting her weight on the side of the rock wall. There was a fresh shot of pain as she tried to put weight on her injured leg. She could barely stand. Before she could take a step, her strength failed, and she fell back on the fur with an exhalation.

Over the next few days, Sira spent her waking moments reminiscing about recent events. Being alone and isolated was worse than any of her physical pains. What was worse, she had failed her clan. They might have successfully distracted the Red Feather warriors, but she had led her group to their deaths. What was she thinking, trying to be a leader? Wallowing in self-loathing, she wished she had died with the others. Fighting back tears of frustration until her throat swelled was a daily occurrence.

As her strength slowly returned, so did her hunger, and she placed her hand over her roaring stomach as if this would calm it. She wondered when the mysterious caretaker would return.

Then one day it happened. She heard the faint shuffles of footsteps from the entrance of the cave.

Upon hearing this, she laid back down on her side pretending to be asleep, positioning her head so that she could get a peek at whoever was entering. Sira kept her eyes firmly shut and struggled to maintain a slow rhythmic breathing pattern, feigning she was asleep. She squinted one eye open as tightly as she could, trying to get a peek.

A shadowy figure hooded in fur stood over her. A cold hand covered her forehead, feeling her temperature. It took all her nerve not to react to the touch. Although the hand was rough, there was no mistaking it was a woman. It had a gentle caress, like a mother caring for her child.

The woman turned her back to Sira and bent over the fire, stoking it with twigs. The fire made the cave glow with orange light, and the woman turned to approach Sira, revealing her face. What Sira saw made her gasp with fear. She cried out and shuffled back, rising to a sitting position.

The old woman's face was contorted, human-like enough to pass for a person, but different enough to cause disbelief. The brow above her eyes and nose were too big, and her forehead sloped back at an odd angle. Her jaw and mouth were wide and square, and they jutted out as if inflated. But the old woman did not react to Sira's cries of fear. She held out her hands as a sign of peace, then made a hushing noise as if she were calming a baby. She bent down and picked up a water gourd, offering it to Sira.

Frightening as she was, Sira realized this must be the person who had cared for her, and the old woman had an aura of tranquility about her. Besides, if she had meant Sira harm, she could have done it while she was unconscious. Sira reached out, noticing she was trembling. She chugged the water rapidly without taking her eyes off the woman. She immediately reacted to the acidic bitterness. It had that traditional herbal plant flavor that medicines had, so she tried to hide her distaste. She handed back the gourd, saying "thank you," with a cracked voice.

The old woman did not respond. A million questions raged through Sira's mind, but first on the list was food.

"Food? Can I have food?"

The woman stared at her uncomprehendingly.

Sira touched her stomach and made a growling noise. Again, the woman did not understand. Sira put fingers to her mouth and made a chewing noise.

With that, the old woman let out a massive smile through her wolfish mouth, showing a row of rotten teeth, giving her a comical appearance. She set down some freshly dried meat and winter berries. Sira ravaged into it, clearly trying to show and show that she was starving.

The old woman just sat and watched, her eyes transfixed with curiosity and fascination. Sira thought it odd the way the old woman watched her; it was as if Sira herself was the strange-looking one.

When Sira was done eating, she had already lost her strength and was forced to lie back down. The old woman grabbed the furs and covered Sira as if she were a child. Sira lay back and watched her, her initial fear now replaced with a strange curiosity. She protested for more food, but the old woman let loose a flurry of words that Sira did not understand. She decided not to press it further. Nothing was right about this situation. She had to get out of this cave as soon as possible.

* * *

The next morning Sira awoke to find her body had gained some strength. This time, she could sit up with relative ease. The strange old woman had left a pile of red and dark blue berries next to her bed, so Sira plopped them into her mouth one at a time, savoring the sweet juice until they were finished. It only slightly quelled her hunger. She took her time in trying to stand this time.

The dried clay mud and herbs on her leg itched badly, but she thought better than to remove it. Painfully, and with great effort, she was able to take a hobbled step forward. She managed a few more steps, and as she rounded the curve of the rock, the cave entrance came into view. Two furs were hanging over the opening, which were secured with sticks and rocks. The furs gently flapped with the icy wind.

Hope swelled within her. She had to get out of this cave and find out where she was. She hobbled against the opening and pushed open the hanging fur hide. Immediately, she was blinded by the bright white surrounding her. As her eyes adjusted to the light, she gasped in horror. Around her, in the distance, as far as the eye could see, stood massive white mountain peaks. She was on a steep rocky ledge, high above the valley floor. The tips of the dark green pines were the only color against the white of the snow. The only exit was a thin icy path that wound its way down the ridge. With her injured leg and lack of strength, it would be impossible. She was more likely to slip and fall, sliding off the ridge and down into the rocks.

The wind did its best to dissuade her escape, biting her cheeks with tiny particles of snow. She cried out in despair, but her voice was barely audible against the howl of the wind. She cried out again her father's name in desperation and fell to the ground. The thought occurred to her to just lie here and let the cold take her away, but it stung her exposed skin, and she was tired of the pain. She thought of her father,

her family, and Tonik.

No. I must find a way out and get back to my clan. Dragging herself to her feet, she inhaled, calming her nerves. It would not serve her to panic. She went to the far side of the cave to relieve herself and hoped the old woman would return soon with more food. When she got back under the fur, she felt her fever rise again. She cried for several minutes, her body shivering before exhaustion once again took hold of her.

Chapter 14

"Kadam, Kadam! Come on, hurry, the best ones are higher in the tree!"

Young Sira, Tonik, and a few other kids from the tribe yelled down to Kadam, who was straddled atop the first branch of a large plum tree. Kadam was only two years older than Sira and Tonik, but was twice their size.

Kadam slowly stood up and grabbed the next available branch. Before pushing himself up, he glanced down and was overtaken by paralyzing fear. The ground seemed too far from where he stood, and his body froze. He tried to sit back down, but his legs wouldn't respond. All Kadam could focus on was the forest floor and their footprints at the base of the tree.

"Come on, up here, it's so good," Sira said with a mouthful of plum.

While still focused on the ground, Kadam yelled back up, "Why would I need to climb like you two rats when you can just throw them down to me?"

"Maybe he doesn't know how to climb," little Tonik said, barely able to pronounce the words.

The other kids laughed at this.

Kadam looked up and saw Sira many lengths higher than him, and the height made him dizzy. He grabbed the tree with both arms, hugging it for safety. Sira looked down upon him. Her big dark eyes shone bright, and she cracked her big, beautiful smile, the smile that melted the hearts of every young boy in the tribe.

Kadam's eyes met hers and his face was red, full of fear and embarrassment. He shook his head at her pleadingly.

Sira was about to yell with joy, the one time she had found something that Kadam was not better at, but something made her keep quiet. She looked down at him and nodded back, accepting his secret.

"Kadam, I think I can throw these plums farther than any of the boys up here. You can try to catch them from the ground and tell us who threw farther," she announced, coming up with the rules of a new game.

The other children's minds were immediately distracted by this new challenge.

Young Kadam slowly returned to the ground. His breathing was heavy, and his cheeks felt hot, but the momentary panic abated. It would be the last time Kadam ever attempted to climb a tree or get anywhere near high places. From then on, whenever the gang of boys went out on one of their hunts for rabbits and other small game, Kadam would never deny Sira's request to take part.

Growing up, Kadam had both respected and resented Sira. It wasn't just because she was the daughter of the clan leader, there was a genuine nobility that surrounded her. She was always above the petty childlike squabbles and competitions, and she often took the blame for others who found themselves in trouble. Sub-consciously, perhaps Kadam knew Sira had an innate intuition for leadership, qualities that he lacked. Being the strongest kid wasn't good enough, and that always bothered him. Whatever the case, Sira had never spoken to the other children about Kadam's weakness with heights.

* * *

At the Gondo-Var's camp inside the rocky fortress, the captured men had endured a grueling regimen throughout the winter. They forced men to work all day, lifting large rocks to reinforce their camp walls. They forced other workers to dig the earth with flat-ended stone spears. Under the first few layers of sand, the earth was black with tar. Workers gathered and hauled the sticky black substance to a large earthen mound where it was heated by fires and combined with birch bark to make lighting fuels and adhesives.

Every day, Kadam saw war parties of men and women leave through the entrance of the fort, returning a few days later. They would bring back a variety of items, either fresh meat and skins, birch wood, and sometimes new captives.

As the temperature grew colder and the snow fell, they sent fewer hunting parties out. The Gondo-Var tribe hunkered down in the cold of their shelters. Kadam could tell they were not as accustomed to the low temperatures as his people were. Except for all the strange new technology around him, the Gondo-Var tribe was not so much different from any other Kadam was used to. They cared for their families, danced and sang songs, painted on rocks, and sculpted wood objects. The ritual of singing and dancing was almost a nightly affair. The tribe used drums and instruments that harmoniously combined, entrancing people to dance and sway around a large central bonfire.

Kadam and a few other men had been selected and separated away from the rest of the captives. This more elite group was forced to line up every morning under a guard of Gondo-Var warriors supervised by Master. They were pitted against each other in wrestling matches. Master himself was present, coaching and teaching them skills in battle. If they refused to take part, they were beaten, then tied to a rock in the cold and denied food and water for an entire day.

One night, Kadam broke free and dashed through the twin-boulder entrance, only to feel a tiny arrow land in his backside. He dropped unconscious after a few dozen steps and woke up the next morning with the same head-splitting pain he remembered from his first encounter with the toxin.

He tried to escape by sea on another attempt, but Kadam was a man born on the hilly plains, and he swam clumsier than a bear chasing a deer upstream. With his hands still tied together, he splashed through the water awkwardly and was almost bashed into the rocks by the current before returning to land. He heaved out a belly full of saltwater and shivered with cold, much to the entertainment of some Gondo-Var guard patrols.

He did not take well to his sparring lessons with Master, refusing to listen or follow instructions. Instead, he predictably rushed toward his opponent, attacking brute strength and never-ending fury. Master was always a step ahead of him, and Kadam usually ended up on the ground with fresh bruises. Still, Kadam had great strength and could easily overpower any of the other captive men. He had potential as a warrior, so Master did not send him to work in the tar pits like the other captives.

One day, another short but stocky captive named Durok was able to knock Master to the ground using his legs to trip the man, a technique Master had been instructing them on. That night, Durok was rewarded with double rations of meat and given an auroch horn of fermented honey wine. Two young women visited him that night, and their howls of pleasure were loud enough so that the other men heard.

The following day, many of the captive men's attitudes had abruptly changed, and they took part now with more vigor.

This routine went on for more days than Kadam could count. Through time, a curious phenomenon happened to the captive men. They became willing participants instead of forced captives. Eventually, except for Kadam, the men's hands no longer needed binding before going to sleep.

Kidnapping was a curious phenomenon, and it was not an uncommon practice for tribes of the area, but usually, it was performed by single males, who would kidnap a female of another tribe to procure a mate. While the process was not exactly understood, eventually the kidnapped individual came to accept their fate, and they began to see their new tribe as allies, rather than captors. To each person, the process of acceptance was different, and physical size and strength had little correlation to it. For the ten captive warriors with Kadam, none could recall the exact moment in which their spirit of resistance had gone.

* * *

As the winter days lessened and the snows gradually melted, the captive men heard talk about the day of the climb. One evening under a full moon, there was a grand celebration in the camp. Tribe members drank fermented honey, and they stumbled around, fornicating in the open and dancing around a large fire. A mammoth was served, and the captive men were each allowed a generous piece of the liver.

Using rounded sticks, Gondo-Var men and women beat on drums made from hollow logs stretched over with crocodile hide. The repetitive beat created a rhythm that heightened their dancing and drunken frenzy. Having never witnessed drums of this size and quantity, Kadam was in awe. The sound itself was simple, but when a half dozen were played at the same time in harmony with one another, it created a hypnotic quality.

Gondo-Var warriors passed Kadam and the other captive men, sizing them up and arguing with each other. One man stopped at Kadam, his eyes studying him until he smiled with recognition. "Kadam? It is you!"

Kadam looked up at the man, and his face was a familiar one. It was one of his old clan members. "Yaykee?" Kadam questioned.

"Yes! It is I!" The man embraced Kadam, but he could not embrace him back because of his bonds.

"You disappeared the night they raided us. Your woman too," Kadam said, remembering the incident.

"Yes, they brought us here." The man looked embarrassed for a moment, then became defensive. "There was nothing we could do. They would kill us if we tried to escape. Here, at least, we are safe. I can hunt mammoths with the other men every day. And my woman is safe. She is with child!"

The man's betrayal disgusted Kadam, but he was in no position to judge, so he kept quiet.

Yaykee tried to change the subject. "It looks like they have chosen you to be an eagle warrior! They have it the best here, the Gondo-Var eagle warriors. They can have more than one woman and all the meat you could ever want. Everything is taken care of for them. I was in your position when I arrived, but I could not make it to the top of the cliff. Beware of the climb, Kadam. Stay in the middle of the cliff. It is the easier route." Yaykee smiled, looking at the other men milling about the captives. "These men are wagering on which captives will make it to the top and retrieve a feather. I will wager ten arrowheads that you will be one of them," he pronounced.

Kadam gave him a contemptuous look, so Yaykee bid him good luck and farewell.

The drums and dancing went on until early in the morning and only stopped when everyone had become too intoxicated or dropped from exhaustion.

* * *

Late the next morning, the captives were led to see Father in the cave overhang by the sea cliff. This time, Father got up from his rock throne and slowly stepped down to the sandy floor of the cave. Master walked over to him and kneeled. The two men exchanged words that Kadam could not hear. Master then rose to his feet and lifted his hand.

The drums of the Gondo-Var beat again, in the same rhythm as the night before. They then marched the captive warriors in a procession led by Father to the base of the white cliff.

From their nightly celebration, the Gondo-Var tribe came back to life. Children ran around the men and laughed at each other with excitement. Men and women slowly gathered lazily into a crowd behind the captive men as excitement grew. The cool air blew softly at the base of the cliff, but there were no clouds in the sky and the sun provided some unusual warmth to the late winter day.

Father walked to the middle of the group of men with Master by his side. He was covered in a cave lion skin, whose paws wrapped around his waist. The head of the lion formed a hood, with colorful stones placed in the lion's eyes. His legs were wrapped in wolf furs up to his knees and his chest was intricately painted with black and red dye for today's ceremony. Father looked up at the men, then raised his hands, gesturing for the tribe to quiet.

The drums and conversations were silenced. Only the thunderous sound of the waves beating against the cave could be heard.

Father then said, "You men, although you were born to a different mother and father, you are all my sons." Father pointed his chubby finger to each of the captive men, his wrists covered in bracelets comprising teeth from various creatures. "Each one of you will prove to me you are fit to be my warriors, my eagles. It is here where you will fly, like an eagle, or fall as a man. You will climb up this cliff, and you will retrieve a feather from the nest of the great bird. If you return with a feather, the spirit of the eagle will be with you. But take note, the eagles can smell your fear, and they will rip out the hearts of the unworthy. But if you fall, at least you will fall like a man."

Father looked up at the great peak of the cliff and the Gondo-Vars started chanting in a low voice, "Eagle fly, men fall, eagle fly, men fall."

Father continued, "Any warrior who does not make the climb, you may stand back now."

The captive men looked at each other and their surroundings, but no one moved. The men were now fully invested in proving their worth to their new tribe.

During his time with the Gondo-Var, Kadam had grown accustomed to their strange accents and could now understand them fully. He had the impulse to lunge straight at the big round man and break his neck, but something prevented him from giving in to the urge.

Father walked by the men and looked slowly around at the tribe. "Shall we see the eagles fly?"

The entire tribe let loose a frenzy of powerful screams and shouts with crazed expressions, pointing and waving their fists at the men lined up facing the cliff.

Kadam ignored the screams and focused on the white rocks above him. It was a sheer vertical face, but it offered many jagged rocks and steps to climb. Just as Yaykee had warned, the path in the middle looked easier, offering more cracks for foot and handholds. However, the route was not big enough for two men, and Kadam knew the other men would notice this, so he clenched his fists in anticipation. When he looked up, his cheeks flushed, and his breathing increased rapidly. Although it had been many years, he knew the telltale signs of his fear creeping its way through.

Master took his place next to Father. He also wore a wolf's fur, which crossed over his chest and one shoulder. He reached under the fur on his chest and pulled out the large canine of Kadam's sabre-tooth tied to a leather string. He held it up and smiled at Kadam, waving it back and forth in the air. Kadam held the man's gaze with a look that promised to get back his trophy.

Master raised his hands, looked up to the sky, and yelled, "Begin!"

* * *

The powerful birds that soared over the coast and plains of the area stood almost as tall as a man. The males were dark black with red-tipped wings. They were the largest creatures in the sky, and their aerial circling was always a clear sign to hunters that a kill was near. Along with scavenging, they preyed on deer, wolves, and other small mammals, even children. There were horror stories of young children being swooped up and flown away in the bird's powerful talons. In numbers, they were known to gang up and steal the fresh kills away from even the largest predators. The helpless chicks of the great raptors were fiercely defended by both the male and female, and any attempt to approach the nest was met with fierce aggression. These nests were found high on the coastal cliffs, out of reach of other predators.

All these characteristics were significant to the Gondo-Var tribe, and they revered the birds, building totems and statues in their camp to honor them. Even the name *Gondo-Var* was an iteration from their old language, roughly translating to "birdmen."

At the sound of Master's word, the men rushed forward to the cliff. Several men headed straight for the middle path, arriving at the same instant. Kadam grabbed the closest man and picked him up with two hands over his head, then turned and threw the man to the ground. The man landed on his back, bounced, and rolled at Master's feet. Another man tried to push Kadam away, but he grabbed the man by his hair and bashed his head against the side of the wall. The man fell backward, unconscious. A third man had climbed up a few steps, but Kadam jumped up and grabbed his foot, pulling the man down. He fell awkwardly and rolled over onto his side, holding his chest in pain.

A few Gondo-Var warriors ran over to Kadam with their spears raised, but Master shouted, "No, leave him! We must not interfere with the climb!"

The warriors backed off and let Kadam continue. The middle path was now clear to him. He took a deep breath and pushed himself up onto the rock face. There were bloodstains and bone fragments between the rocks from men who had fallen in the past. He grunted as he pulled up step by step, not daring to look down.

For the first few minutes, he made a good effort, but the higher he got, the more his breathing became erratic. His grip became slippery, and his hands trembled. He looked up and could see other men above him. Even though his path was easier, a few of them were already much farther ahead.

He heard the Gondo-Vars below; their voices had turned from incoherent screams to the chanting of names. A few voices were shouting for Durok. But, from the grisly beginning which took place at the start, there was no doubt about who their favorite was, and their voices chanted Kadam's name, reverberating along with the percussion of the drums up the cliff face.

Durok had found a place to cross over onto the middle path, and he now was climbing up even faster, directly above Kadam.

A flash of motion on Kadam's left proceeded the horrible yell of a man falling. Kadam dared not look down, but the Gondo-Vars yelled with excitement.

"Men faaaaaaall," they sang as the body thumped onto the ground below.

Kadam pushed up to grab the lip of the next rock with his right hand, but it gave way. The rock broke under his weight and he fell. Blindly, he reached out with his hands, and they made contact with a ledge. His legs dangled freely below him, and the crowd gasped in awe. He looked down and adjusted his hands to get a better hold as panic struck him. His legs scrambled up and around, trying to find a foothold. Once his feet felt something solid, he adjusted each hand so that he was holding on in a spread-eagle position.

He was hyperventilating, and his eyes darted back and forth, unable to focus on anything. He froze, fear taking control of his bodily functions. Below, people chanted his name louder, urging him on. It sounded more like a taunting than encouragement to him. The mighty hunter Kadam, slayer of auroch and mammoth, killer of a big tooth. A man who had bested many men in battle. The same man who was now stuck frozen on a rock.

He had a flashback of that day in the plum tree so many years ago. He could see the face of little Sira as clear as if it happened yesterday, the smell of the ripe fruit. She was looking down upon him, smiling. This time, she was teasing him. She pointed and laughed mockingly. Soon, the other children in the tree were looking down at him and laughing.

The sound of laughing morphed into the present, and he could hear the Gondo-Vars laughing at him from below. Their laughter caused a pain greater than any physical pain or humiliation Kadam had ever felt in his life.

"Stop laughing. Quiet! I will kill you!" Kadam yelled angrily.

The chanting of Kadam's name became louder still, but all Kadam could hear was taunting and laughter.

"I will kill all you!" he cried out, still frozen on the face of the cliff.

A sudden gust of cool breeze hit Kadam, and for a moment, it made him focus, like a slap to the face. From this height, he had a view of the great blue sea. It stretched as far as the eye could see. In any other circumstance, it would have been a stunning sight. Kadam's breathing gradually slowed as he looked out across the water. He was now lost; his mind had shut down, and he was out of options. He either had to let go or try to descend in disgrace.

Suddenly, the voices below went silent. Even the drums stopped beating. He heard a ghastly sound, like a mix between an injured baby boar and a crow. A shadow flew over him. One of the great black birds entered his vision and soared by him. It circled, then came straight toward him. Kadam braced himself for the impact, but at the last moment, it beat its giant wings twice, bringing the creature to a stall and landing on the ledge an arm's length above him. It spread its long wings, blocking out the sun. It shrieked down at Kadam with its ugly bald head and giant yellow-stained beak, so close he could smell the stench of its breath.

At first, Kadam flinched, leaning away from the bird. The tribe below watched in awe. Kadam looked up at the bird and yelled at it, an angry roar to shoo it away. The bird looked down at Kadam again and shrieked, and he wondered whether it was going to attack him.

"Come on then, come at me," he said, but the bird didn't move.

Below, the tribe had started chanting again, "Eagle fly! Eagle fly! Eagle fly!"

Kadam gazed at the bird again as it moved its head from side to side, studying him with each eye. It pulled back its wings, cocked its head to the side, and made a gentle clucking sound.

Kadam had never been much of a spiritual man; he had always considered the mystic rituals and supernatural stories to be a waste of time. He never gave much respect to the shamans or mystics in the tribe, who held such high social statuses with no physical prowess to back it up. But here on the cliff, something touched his soul.

As the crowd chanted his name, something snapped within Kadam. He had accepted that he would fall to his death. This was not the worst possible end; perhaps he should have died in the forest fighting alongside Rooti and Markka. Accepting his fate wiped his fears away, like fog after sunrays shone upon them. It emboldened him, to the extent that, as he looked down again, the familiar emotion of terror was completely gone. He had reached the depths and limit of his fear and had faced it down, banishing it forever.

He looked back up and saw several men climbing high above, but the height no longer made him dizzy. He looked up at the bird and smirked. "So that is what you want? Very well, watch as I climb to the top and pluck a feather right out of your mother's ugly ass!"

With his powerful arms, he pushed up hard and threw himself dangerously over the ledge, the lack of fear multiplying his strength.

The bird squawked and launched itself out of Kadam's way. It soared downward to gain speed and then caught a rising thermal, gaining altitude without even having to flap its giant wings. It circled Kadam, shrieking its horrible cry as if in acknowledgment of his triumph.

The people below, who had been completely enraptured by the spectacle, now roared with approval and began chanting his name again. Master yelled at the drummers to begin again. They had been so caught up watching the scene they had forgotten to play.

Kadam now climbed with ease, his pent-up emotions having been released. A wave of euphoria and adrenaline rushed through him. As he lifted himself quickly over a large outcrop of rock, the breeze hit his face and blew his hair back.

"Aghh!" he cried out with exhilaration.

He was gaining on the other men, who were slowly tiring. Men to his left were finding their path very difficult, as the rock steepened and there was no way of getting over to the middle. A few of them had given up and returned to the ground in disgrace.

Durok was the farthest ahead, and suddenly, Kadam heard a commotion of wings above him. Dozens of the giant birds had been disturbed, and they shrieked, launching themselves one by one off the cliff side. The men were so high now that the tribe's voices were barely audible; only the muffled drums could be heard as the sound bounced up the rock face. The magnificent birds soared in a wide circle above the men, and several of them swooped close to Durok's head as a warning.

As Durok continued up, another bird rushed by and shrieked at him, its giant claws only a hand's length away. With that, Durok became more careful, taking his time and moving from cover to cover. The sun's glare made it difficult to look up and keep watch over the attacking birds. Even the rocks themselves were covered in bird droppings, making them slippery.

Kadam heard more screams from above him. Two birds were attacking a man, and their talons latched onto his shoulders. The weight of the birds on him strained his arms to the breaking point. One bird pecked at the man's neck, opening a sizable gash. Blood gushed down the man's side. He couldn't fight off the attack, so the birds kept on him. Finally, he flailed both hands to rid himself of his attackers and fell off the ledge. The birds, still latched with their talons, fell with him until they released their claws and spread their wings, catching air and soaring away as his body fell down the cliff. The man climbing underneath him had nowhere to dodge, and they collided. The force knocked the second man off the ledge and now they fell together, heading for Kadam.

Kadam released his left hand and foot from the cliff face, shifting his weight completely onto his right side. He leaned out, his body hanging precariously to dodge the falling men. Their tangled bodies flew past him by a hair's width, grunting and screaming as they bashed against ledges.

Kadam did not bother to look down as he struggled to turn his body back around and grab back onto the ledge with both hands. The screams were suddenly silenced, and he could hear the faint cheers of the people below.

More birds were circling closer to him as he made his way up. Ahead, Durok had found a place where he could stand in the crack of a rock and take refuge from the bird's attacks. One of the other men who had been climbing to the left crossed over onto the middle path ahead of Kadam. He reached the same crack that Durok was seeking shelter in. The space was not big enough for the two of them, and they jostled for position. The man tried to squeeze in, but half of his body was exposed.

One bird glimpsed the struggle and folded its wings for a dive. Its sharp talons connected with the man's head, ripping off a piece of the man's scalp. He cried in agony as blood squirted out from an artery. The man lost his balance and reached his hands out for Durok to help.

Durok grabbed the man's arm, keeping him from

falling. The man cried up, urging Durok to pull him up.

Durok looked down at the man apologetically, "Thank you, brother, for you will keep the birds off me." Then he wedged the man's arm into a crack on the ledge by his feet. The full weight of the man came down to bear on his arm, now caught in the crack. He screamed in agony as his shoulder dislocated. He dangled from the side of the cliff, kicking and screaming, unable to free his arm as blood ran down from the gash in his head.

The birds saw the commotion and immediately swooped down onto him.

Durok used the distraction to turn and continue to climb to the top.

When Kadam finally reached the cracked ledge, the man had stopped moving. They had ripped his abdomen open and long tubes of intestines hung down the cliff face. Kadam watched as the birds fought over the man's guts in an aerial tug-of-war. While they were still distracted, Kadam made haste on his way to the top. He passed several of the great nests on the top section of the cliff. Many held large eggs, and some contained chicks only a few days old. None of them contained any of the great feathers.

It took some time for Kadam to finally reach the summit of the cliff. The birds now soared overhead but curiously did not attack. Perhaps they were willing to attack a man climbing on a ridge, but not bold enough once he was solid on two feet.

He found Durok sitting calmly, looking out over the horizon of blue water. Kadam could see he had arrived long before him, as his breathing was normal. He held a single black and red feather, which he twirled in his hand. Kadam made his way over to him and sat nearby, catching his breath.

"Finally, you have arrived. Looks like we are the only two. For a moment, in the beginning, I thought you had given up," Durok said to Kadam, still looking out over the sea.

"You should never doubt me. I am here. Now I just need to find a vulture's ass to pull out a feather."

"Oh, you mean one of these?" Durok held up the feather. "Don't bother, I have searched this entire peak. There is none left."

Kadam huffed. It was clear the man was teasing him. He got up and moved around the rocky top of the cliff. The summit was only the length of a few men wide, and it did not take long for Kadam to search every rock and crack, but he found no feather. He walked back over, looking down at Durok. "Well, I suppose I just have to take that one from you. I will not move rocks or dig holes for those shit bird people."

"You could do that, and we both know you are stronger. But I would take you down with me. How is it these people say? Men faaaaaall," Durok said, mocking the Gondo-Var's accent.

"Humph, well, I guess that is the chance I will take. Being in their war party is better than cleaning their shit," Kadam said as he prepared for a fight.

Durok sighed in agreement. "You are right about that. Sit for a moment, rest before we find out who will take the feather."

Kadam took a seat next to the man, and they sat in silence for several moments, gazing out into the endless blue expanse.

Durok broke the silence first. "Why do you do it then?"

"Do what?" Kadam replied.

"Why do you do what they say? Why not die fighting them instead? Why climb up here to get a feather? Do you wish to be one of them?" Durok asked seriously.

Kadam thought for a moment, but he was not sure that he knew the answer himself. "No, I do not wish to be a shit bird. It is Master... I wish to kill the one they call Master, but I could see a way to do it from where I was. I did not wish to die before killing him."

To Kadam's surprise, Durok smiled at the response. "Did these vultures make war against your tribe, as they did mine?" Durok asked solemnly.

"Yes, they did. We have lost many. We were once part of the great Auroch Tribe. We split from them before I can remember, and we became Raam's tribe," Kadam said with pride.

"Raam's tribe? I am of the Bear Clan. Several winters ago, we made a battle. Do you remember?"

Kadam had to think for a moment and then smiled. "Ah, yes! One of our men took a woman from the Bear Clan, and we made a battle over her. She was an ugly one, had the face of a pig! I couldn't understand why she was worth fighting for!" Kadam laughed and shook his head.

"She was my father's sister," Durok replied seriously. A moment of awkwardness hung in the air for a moment at Kadam's insult. The tension was broken when Durok replied, "Though she had the face of a pig!" and both men laughed.

"One of our men suffered a blow to the head; he was never the same after that battle. All for an ugly woman. What happened to them, anyway? Did my father's sister and your tribe brother... mate?"

"Oh, yes, many times! Four children... and all were ugly as pigs!" Kadam replied.

To that, both laughed again.

Kadam's smile faded as he looked down the ledge in contemplation. "But all of them were killed by those shit birds down below who call themselves eagle warriors. They don't even know the difference between eagles and rotten vultures."

Durok nodded his head in agreement and replied. "Remember those days of the past? The way we used to battle. There was an honor to it. The elders of the tribes always settled the battles, and we moved on. But these people, all they want is war and death. There is no honor. They took all my tribe. There is no one left. I also do not wish to join them. But where will I go? They have taken everything!"

Kadam nodded.

"So, I ask you. What will you do, Kadam? Will you now join them?"

Kadam thought about it for several moments before responding. "I am waiting for the right moment. I want to be sure I can kill as many as I can."

Durok's eyes lit up and his mood elevated, as if he had been hoping to hear this. He placed his hand underneath the leather strap that held his hide skirt and pulled out a second black and red feather, larger and more beautiful than his own. He held it out to the man sitting next to him.

As Kadam reached for it, Durok pulled it back. "I could give this to you, or I could throw it off the ledge. But I will give it to you, Kadam, if you promise me one thing."

"What is that, then?" Kadam replied suspiciously.

"Promise me that one day, we will see these shit-smelling vulture people burn to the ground."

At that, Kadam gave him a nod of acceptance and took the feather.

"Well, Kadam of Raam's tribe, let's get off this cliff before the birds gain any more courage. We cannot go back the way we came, obviously."

Kadam looked down. The tribe looked like ants from here, and they were moving out of the camp, through the entrance of boulders and veering to the right. Kadam followed the path with his eyes. The cliff they stood upon descended and curved down, eventually reaching the level which the tribe was marching to.

"There." Kadam pointed toward the path of the long cliff. "We must make our way down from there, and it looks like they are going there to meet us."

The two men made their way along the jagged clifftop as it slowly opened and descended. As they walked, they learned they had a great deal in common. Although they had never met, their tribes had come together many times over the past years to trade partnerships with eligible females and other items. Many of their customs were similar, and both were hunters of the auroch on the hilly plains.

They reached a point where the cliff curved away from the sea, and Kadam stopped. Straight ahead of him to the south, the terrain slowly descended to the coast.

Durok saw him stop and could read his expression. "Don't think about it, Kadam. They have hunting parties out everywhere. There is nowhere to run."

Kadam gazed out into the distance. "No, I will not leave this place until we have burned it. I will see Master's head on the end of a spear. But we will most likely die trying, and I wish I could have seen my people again. I even know where they have gone. To meet up with another larger tribe. Seeing how many warriors there are, I wish I could warn them."

Durok walked over and grabbed his shoulder. "I hope what you say is true. We could use more people in our fight. But first, let us join these vultures and gain their trust. We will wait for the right moment to strike."

Kadam nodded in somber agreement, and they headed down to meet their new tribe.

Chapter 15

During the coldest of the two winter months, Sira had been completely confined to the small cave. The ledge that led out was still too steep for her to descend with her weakened leg. Even if she could, the world outside was nothing but white snowy mountain peaks. She did not know the lay of the land and, in her condition, she would surely perish on her own.

Now that she was fully awake during the day, the old woman came more often, spending most of the day with her. Sira had overcome her initial fear and mistrust, realizing that the old woman was one of the Others. She had also grown accustomed to the creepiness of the woman's deformed face. Of all the imaginations Sira had ever held about the mysterious people, the old woman was much more humanlike than Sira had ever expected.

They were not the mysterious monsters everyone had imagined. In fact, Sira could not find one major difference in the woman's behavior, other than her language. The furs she wore, the way she started a fire and cooked, reminded Sira much of her mother. Verbal communication between the two women was difficult, and Sira had to rely on hand signals. The woman's language seemed very basic in comparison, with grunts and simple syllable sounds.

Sira could discern that the old woman's name was Needa. The "a" was pronounced more like a gruff or breathing sound from the back of the throat. Similarly, Needa learned Sira's name, but she could not pronounce the "r" sound, and it came out sounding like Seehaa.

During the nights and mornings, Needa left Sira alone in the cave. For someone who was used to sleeping with an entire clan nearby, it was torturous. Some days, Sira yelled out into the white mountains for Needa to come back, just so she could have company, but Needa only arrived late in the morning. Sira had begun talking to herself during the nights; she gave names to some of the rocks in the cave. Her spot in the cave's corner with the soft dirt was becoming too small to cover her daily waste.

The days were becoming less cold and the number of snows had slowly decreased. Sira spent more time limping back and forth around the cave, each day gaining strength on her injured leg. The hard scabs on her thigh had dried up, and in their place were two thick red scars where the cat had bitten down. Her muscles were slowly recovering from the atrophy, and she felt she would be ready to escape soon. She did not want to be around to find out what the Others wanted from her.

Each day, she cared less and less about her survival chances and more about getting back to her tribe. While initially she was fearful of her physical injuries, she now worried more about her emotional state. She spoke to herself more and more, and sometimes she laughed for no reason, other times broke down and cried. On some days, she could barely get out of her fur bed, her feelings of depression and isolation were too overwhelming.

One morning, Sira woke up and walked to the back of the cave to relieve herself; the smell of her old urine was now pungent. While she was still squatting, half-asleep, she heard birds singing at the entrance of the cave. It was the first time she had heard birds since she had arrived. She made her way to the entrance, and the bright sun hit her. It was still cold enough to freeze water, but the air had lost its bite. The clouds had broken and there was, for once, no wind. The steep path now had a small line that was free from ice, probably worn down by the old woman's steps.

Sira went back and gathered the fur from the cave. She used a length of tendon cord left by Needa to tie the rolled-up fur on her back. She looked out from the cave entrance once more. Below her, she saw a wooden rope bridge made of bark fibers and wood logs that stretched from once side of the ravine to the other. On the other side of the ravine, a clear path led down to the valley floor below.

Instead of trying to walk down, Sira sat on her backside and inched down the path slowly, the icy cold rocks stinging her unprotected thighs. Sira wondered how the old woman had made it up to the cave every day under these conditions. She reached the rope bridge and tested it by giving it a firm shake. The bridge swayed slightly, but it looked sturdy.

If it did not hold her weight, it was a long fall to the ground below. She stood up and grabbed both sides of the bridge with her hands and took the first step out onto the wooden plank. It was sturdy and held solid. With the next few steps, the bridge sagged more, and it slightly swayed more and more with each step. When Sira reached the middle of the bridge, she had to stop and steady herself and wait for it to stop swaying. She tried to focus on keeping her eyes ahead instead of looking down. She exhaled in relief when she reached the other side, not realizing her breathing had been so shallow.

Here, the path was less steep, and it wound down to the valley floor. She moved forward slowly until the path curved around the ravine wall. If she had not been paying close attention, she could have missed the sudden cave opening to her left. She heard loud voices and gasped, putting her back against the wall and out of sight. Again, she heard voices and the sound of laughter. The verbalizations sounded more like grunts and huffs rather than people talking. It was clearly more of Needa's people.

There was no other way down to the valley floor, and she was desperate not to spend another day alone in that cave. Without another thought, she skipped past the cave entrance, using her bad leg as a pivot, launching and landing with her sturdy leg.

Immediately, she heard a surprised grunt come from inside the cave. She cursed her luck for having been spotted, but she tried to ignore it as she limped, jogged as swiftly as she could down the trail. The pain in her thigh became easy to ignore as the adrenaline produced its effects. She had no plan other than to make it into the valley and find some cover to hide.

By the time she got to the bottom of the trail, she was winded, and her muscles burned. The lack of exercise and movement over the past months had taken its toll on her physical strength. The high-altitude air wasn't helping her either. She hobbled for the nearest line of brush. Several figures were making their way down the trail. She made it into the cover, crawling under a large pine tree whose low-lying branches touched the snow-covered ground.

She wished could have run further, perhaps try to cover her tracks, but there hadn't been time. Curling her legs up towards her, she hoped somehow no one would see her. It was only a few moments later that a pair of hands pulled the pine branches open. She kicked feebly at the hands, but was gripped tightly around the ankle and pulled as easily as a baby along a patch of ice. She thrashed onto her back in the snow, still trying to defend herself.

Three men of the Others looked down upon her, grunting their deep bellows. She gasped in terror at the sight. They were the ugliest men she had ever seen. Their faces held so much hair, more than she thought was possible. The beard was broken by their large protruding noses and thick eyebrows. Although they wore thick hides around their chests, their exposed arms were also covered with hair. Underneath, their skin was pale and sickly. They grabbed at her roughly, wringing her hands down while one tried to grab her feet. She tried to resist, but their strength was overwhelming. They were yelling and grunting in their language, and one of them pulled out a flint knife. Sira cried out in terror.

She heard another man's voice yelling from behind them. The other men stopped at the sound and let her go. They turned to face this new man, but Sira's vision of him was obscured. It sounded as if an argument was taking place between them because, although their language was different, she could easily discern the anger in their words.

The three men who had chased her were now standing up to the fourth man. They yelled at each other in their crude language, and they got in each other's faces. The macho display went on for over a minute, but when it was clear the fourth man would not back down, the three Others lost interest and walked away, clearly upset as they grunted and waved their hands.

The fourth man came closer to Sira, and she backed up instinctively. At this, he squatted down and held up his hands in peace. He approached with his palms out passively.

Amazingly, the man spoke in her language and pointed to her leg. "Not hurt?"

Sira sat up and put her hand on her leg, squeezing it gingerly. Although they had handled her as if catching a baby pig, they had not hurt her during the ordeal.

"Not hurt," he said this time, as if stating a fact. He stood up and offered his hand in assistance.

Sira steadied herself and stood up on her own. He backed up, his palms still up in a sign of peace. He waved them, gesturing her to follow. "Come. It is cold. Come eat food," the man said with his broken accent.

Sira got a smell of his body odor and recognized it as being the same as her rescuer from the big tooth.

Sira looked around at the endless maze of pine trees and ankle-deep snow. As if the wind had a mind to persuade her, it blew again, and her body shivered. Defeated, she slowly limped toward him. Logic had won, and she realized how stupid she had been to escape in her condition. At least she was out of that lonely cave. That had become worth risking her life over. Also, there was something very gentle and honest about this man. He moved in a very non-threatening way so that, inexplicably, Sira trusted him.

Instead of heading up the ledge to the cave to join the Others, the man led her to another small cave around the side of where the ledge began. Large bones and hide furs blocked the entrance. The interior was decorated with a diversity of antlers, skulls, and hides from the valley's animals.

It surprised her to find Needa inside this small dwelling, and the old woman held out her hands and smiled, speaking in her language. "Seeha, Seeha," she said, gesturing for Sira to sit near the small fire.

Needa took the rolled-up fur from Sira's back and laid it on the floor.

The man tried to repeat her name. "Seeha."

Sira corrected him, "See-Ra."

The man repeated. His pronunciation was much better than that of the woman's. "Harq," he said as he touched his chest. The R sound in his name was more of a guttural h sound.

"Harq," Sira repeated, pointing to him.

At that, the man smiled and pushed his hair back from his face. It was then that Sira got the first actual glimpse of him. His face was nowhere near as ugly as the rest of the Others. It was much softer and gentler. Although his brow protruded more than normal, and he had thick bushy eyebrows, Sira had seen normal men uglier than him. Perhaps she had been stuck in that cave too long. But her lack of social interaction had left her curious, so she inspected him again. His skin was a very light brown, and he carried a lot more hair than any normal man ought to. Although he was slightly shorter than Kadam, he was more muscular, with wide shoulders and thick legs. When he smiled, his face looked comical, and Sira could not help but smile at that. She hoped he wouldn't realize she was laughing at him instead of with him. But Harq kept up that goofy smile while he stood up and brought back meat to the fire.

Sira pointed. "Eat, yes, please. I'm hungry."

"Eat, yes! Hungwy?" Harq repeated as he handed her a cut of deer steak.

The old woman went on to make one of her herbal drinks for Sira as Harq continued to try to communicate. His vocabulary was like a four-year-old child, and he would often pause and think hard to remember certain words. Sira could only wonder where he had learned to speak in the first place. Did he kidnap women often?

A sudden fear entered her as she realized she did not know what the Others wanted from her. But again, something about Harq's soft smile and gentle way was reassuring, and she relaxed as he laughed when Sira spoke. He seemed thrilled to hear and remember words from her language.

Sira then pointed down to the wound on her leg and asked, "It was you, Harq. Harq saved me from the big tooth?"

Harq only grunted and changed the subject by pointing at the meat and asking, "Meat? Good, yes?"

Needa eventually left the cave, leaving her alone with

Harq. This made Sira nervous, but Harq mostly left her alone, going about his business back and forth out of the cave. He would return with fresh logs for the fire or with gourds full of freshwater. He was shy, keeping himself nervously busy with non-important items.

Sira noticed that every time she glanced out of the cave entrance, a few of the Other children tried to peek a glimpse of her. Their warped, elongated little faces were a miniature version of the adults. They all had long hair, making it difficult to tell the boys and girls apart. The children's tiptoeing to the entrance was so quiet she never even heard them approach, but once they caught her attention, they would shriek like wild animals and run away.

Harq had to constantly shoo both children and adults away from the entrance with grunting sounds. The Others held both a great curiosity and fear of her.

Throughout the rest of the day, Sira would approach the entrance of the cave to get a better look, but Harq would stop her. When she questioned this, he would say, "Sira, stay here. People afraid."

Sira began to realize that the Others were just as afraid of her as she was of them. Only when it was dark did Harq allow her out of the cave to relieve herself, and even then, Harq stood a close distance away. The way he stood guard over her made her feel uneasy, as if some wished to do her harm.

It was hard for her to sleep that night, and they stayed up late, asking each other questions as he tried his best to answer in his simple vocabulary. But conversing with her had improved his speech. It was as if words that had long been forgotten suddenly came it life within him. He seemed to be as curious as she was about where she came from and who her people were. He was patient with her until his eyes faded and all he could say was, "Sleep now, Sira," before passing out.

Sira discerned the Others were a small band comprising only a few families. They lived exclusively in this large mountain valley, which held plentiful game and was devoid of people such as herself. The valley comprised many small groups of Others, much like Harq's tribe. Steep snowy peaks protected them from the outside.

It was horrifying to think she could be stuck here for months, but at least she seemed to be out of immediate danger. Her odds of making it through this maze of mountains alone were slim, and she would have to somehow convince Harq to act as her guide once the weather was warmer. She also realized that until such time, her odds of survival would improve if she could win some trust with the rest of the tribe. These strange people would easily kill her if they saw her as a threat. She would have to show them she was not an enemy, and that she could take part and possibly even help. Overcoming her fear would certainly be a challenge, but overcoming theirs would be more so.

PART II – A New Kind of Hunt

Chapter 16

As the worst of winter subsided, and the sun hung in the sky each day a little longer, the temperate climate of the coastal Samaki village warmed. Inside one of the rock and mud shelters, Raam awoke and stretched his aching body. Aches and pains were all too common now, manifesting themselves as reminders that he was old and past his prime. After the return of Tonik and the twins bringing news of Sira's death, he felt even older than ever, his life force drained.

A part of his spirit had died with his daughter, and emptiness filled his heart. His task and purpose for joining and uniting his people in the Samaki village seemed a little less important. *What was left to fight for?*

He looked over at Tikara, noticing the subtle aging lines that had seemingly formed overnight around her eyes. She wept a lot, and Raam instinctively held her tight in comfort most nights. She never accepted her daughter's death. With no witness to Sira's body, she pleaded with them to go search for her, stating she knew Sira was still alive. Raam tried to reason with his partner; there was simply no way their daughter could be alive after what Jin had found.

He stepped out of the dark shelter and into the morning light as a fresh breeze blew in from the sea. The sickness in the Samaki village had stabilized; those who had survived had recovered. But they had lost so many. The tribe's burial site had almost doubled in size. The past few days had been unseasonably warm near the coast, and the frosty ground was now thawing. The graves had to be guarded to keep scavengers from digging the bodies up. Raam had convinced four volunteers to take turns guarding the graves at night by fire, despite Jessec's objections. Raam and Tikara brought gifts of food to the guards most evenings, and the men came to respect Raam for his insights and leadership.

Raam approached Jessec's shelter and went in without announcing, partly because he was his elder, and partly because he knew it irked the young man. Jessec was in an argument with his older sister, Laksha, the tribe's shaman.

She wore a beautifully thick cave bear fur and carried an intricately carved staff with the head of the smiling fish. Again, Raam marveled at the skill level of the Samaki artisans and the luxury of having a cave bearskin robe. When she noticed Raam, she bowed in greeting, but her smile was insincere.

Laksha turned back and scolded Jessec like a child, "We will discuss this when you return," then turned and stormed out of the shelter. The bone charms she wore around her neck rattled as she passed.

Jessec was preparing his hunting gear and did not bother to look up. "What is it you want this time, old man? Every day you bother me about what I must do or what I must not do. Make your request quickly, for today we are going on a hunt."

Raam was pleased to hear the impatience in his voice, expecting that Jessec would acquiesce easier to his suggestions. Raam inquired whether he may use the village artisans to help him make a Red Feather weapon that Pliny had witnessed being used.

Jessec agreed and waved him away, too preoccupied with the upcoming hunt to argue.

Raam was having difficulties dealing with Jessec, encountering opposition to his suggestions purely out of ego. Raam would have to gently persuade him into understanding, and finally, Jessec would give in, announcing whatever plan it was to the rest of the village as if it were his own.

Raam had no desire to be lauded or respected; he only wished that the village and his tribe recovered so that they could together face a greater threat. Since he had arrived in the Samaki village, he had made it a point to understand all he could about their technology. He had quickly learned and progressed to the point that he was even improving upon their designs.

Every day, the Samaki came to know and respect Raam's wisdom, and his people easily adapted to life in the village. The two tribes were a perfect match. Many men from Raam's tribe had died fighting the Gondo-Var, leaving mothers and children without men. Contrarily, many Samaki women and children had perished from disease, leaving men without a mate. The tribes had already found partnerships with each other, much to Jessec's apprehension.

Yet, Raam's one great worry was for Tonik; there was a confrontation building between him and Jessec from the day Tonik returned. Jessec could see the way Raam treated him, grooming and teaching him things as if preparing him to be a leader. Jessec was smart enough to understand that Tonik and Raam were a threat to his leadership, and Jessec tried his best to undermine and belittle Tonik every chance he got. What made matters worse was that Laksha had taken a liking to Tonik. Something infatuated her with the outsider, and she made no effort to hide her feelings. Tonik had not responded to her. It had been too soon since his loss of Sira. But Raam knew Tonik could not ignore her advances forever. All men's body's hunger the same, and one can only ignore the hunger for so long.

Laksha's position as a shaman gave her high social status. Pairing with her would instantly improve Tonik's social position. It saddened Raam to think of his daughter and their loss, but this was the reality of their lives now, and they had to move on.

* * *

Today was special for the Samaki because the great auroch herd had made its way to less than a quarter of a day's walking distance from the village. For people accustomed to catching and eating fish, an auroch hunt was special, something they had been looking forward to all year. Trackers had gone out earlier to sneak in downwind to spot any weak or old individuals that could be easily separated from the rest of the herd.

As Jessec and his chosen hunters gathered, Tonik met with Pliny and Jin to finish organizing their hunting gear and auroch hides, which would be used as a disguise. They could see Jessec and the other Samaki men looking in their direction, mumbling words, and laughter.

"You women won't hit anything with those bent shafts. Better you go back to throwing spears as the young ones do. And you will burn under those skins today," teased Jessec.

For larger game hunting, they used a weapon known as an atlatl. It consisted of a wooden handle and a nook to lodge the spear into. While the handle was being gripped, two fingers held the spear in place. The wooden handle acted like an extension of the arm, providing more leverage and allowing the spear to travel farther and faster.

Raam's old injured knee was now prohibiting him from hunting or spending long hours on his feet. As such, he spent more time with his hands, testing weapon designs. He had come up with a slightly curved wooden atlatl shaft instead of a straight one. It took many hours of practice, as the thrower had to adjust for the bend in the shaft. However, the curve gave even more leverage and velocity.

Although Tonik and the twins were invited on the hunt, Jessec relegated them to the back in a support position. From the plans Tonik overheard from Jessec, he could tell that the fishermen did not have as much experience hunting auroch as his tribe did. Wanting desperately to show up the arrogant young Samaki, Tonik decided they should try to break away from the group and take down a large male bull on their own.

Raam would have surely disagreed with this plan, as three men taking an auroch alone sounded like a good way to get trampled to death.

As the hunting party they set off, younger women had gathered outside the village. They waved and flirted with the men, wishing them luck on their hunt. They scowled and stuck out their tongues as the twins passed. The twins responded in kind.

As soon as the hunting party was far enough away from the village, Tonik called out to Jessec.

Annoyed, Jessec asked, "What do you women want? Already tired and wish to go back?"

"Why don't we see who can bring down the bigger auroch, me and the twins, or you and your men?" Tonik challenged.

The men roared with laughter, mocking the twins and mimicking Pliny's feminine voice.

"You three should wake up because you must be dreaming!" Jessec bellowed. "One man and two girls cannot even kill a small auroch. You will be trampled."

The men laughed again, and they turned to walk away.

"Challenge accepted then, Jessec?" Tonik questioned.

Jessec strode back in anger. "If you three wish to die, go ahead. It would make us all happy."

"It would not make your sister happy!" Pliny replied.

Jessec reached for Pliny to hit him, but Tonik stepped in front and blocked his path, and the two men stood nose to nose.

"Very well! Hunt auroch with these two women. I accept your challenge! And if you are still alive and shamed, I will get to challenge you, one of my choosing."

Tonik nodded in agreement, and Jessec smiled and turned back confidently. They heard the men laughing as they crested over the hill.

"Are you sure this plan will work, Jin?" Tonik asked.

"Well, it worked that one day when we were younger, but there were six of us," Jin replied. The twins then turned and walked off in another direction, leaving Tonik standing alone, shocked.

"Wait, six of you?" cried Tonik as he trotted to catch up.

***

Jessec's men met with their trackers at the tail end of the great auroch herd while remaining downwind. As they lay flat on the top of the hill, the trackers pointed to an animal near the end. It was limping slightly as it grazed. It certainly was not the biggest auroch in the herd, but it was of considerable size. With its injured leg, the ten of them could corral it quickly away from the rest of the herd. If all went well, they could even have it slaughtered and cut up, returning by nightfall. Besides, Jessec thought, there was no way the other three were going to take down any auroch on their own, much less one this big. All they had to do now was create a distraction and separate it from the herd.

Tonik and the twins were at the opposite end of the herd. They were so far that the aurochs at the other end looked like tiny insects in the distance. Their side was where the alpha males of the herd were located. The giant bulls constantly jockeyed for position as the cows came into oestrus.

The three of them had rubbed auroch scat over their bodies to hide their scent, and the auroch hides over their shoulders further camouflaged them. Pliny and Jin had expertly led them so close to the herd they could see white foam forming around the bull's mouths. They were on all fours, hunched close together under the hides.

Jin whispered to his side. "That white foam means it is mating time. The bulls will be very aggressive. Once Jessec's men startle the herd, the auroch will turn and head in that direction. We will try to get the attention of just one bull, distracting it from the others. We must go after the biggest and meanest bull we can find."

Tonik protested, "Jin, I agree I want to win this challenge but-"

Jin cut him off. "You will see, Tonik. My father used to say that for this plan to work, it has to be the biggest, most stubborn bull, one that will chase us forever."

Tonik wanted to add that this would not improve the situation, but stopped when he heard a rumble emanate from the ground. The herd had been agitated. Jessec and his men had begun the hunt.

In the distance, the three men could barely make out the insect-sized figures of Jessec's men attacking an auroch. The big bulls had not caught the scent of Jessec's men yet, but slowly the line of the herd moved like a wave as more and more aurochs became agitated.

Tonik felt his heart pump wildly as sweat ran down his dusty sides. It was a clear day, and the sun was now beating down upon them. It was heating up underneath the auroch hide, but Tonik dare not lift it over his head for fear of being seen. Instead, he peeked out of the side to see Jessec's men in the distance. They had already downed their beast of choice and were dragging the carcass back before the herd could mount a proper charge. But the aurochs did not seem brave enough to take on a group of ten men. They only followed them angrily. Once Jessec's men were far enough away from the herd, they would gut and slaughter the carcass into transportable pieces.

Tonik thought about how long it would take for them to do this, as the auroch would surely follow them for a great distance. It would take at least half of his men to defend the carcass from scavengers while the other half gutted and cleaned the carcass for hauling.

Jin whistled softly like a bluebird, so they looked over at him from under the hide. He pointed out the auroch of his choice. Tonik gulped at the sight. It was the biggest male he had ever seen. Its shoulder came up two hands higher than any of the other animals around it. The beast was hot and irritated, its aggression rising during oestrus and now from the disturbance of the herd. Its mouth was thick with foam and between its legs hung two massive swollen testicles. It grunted and mashed its head down in agitation as the other aurochs around him became unsettled. The lead bulls had now completely turned in the direction of Jessec's men, too far away to see what had happened but close enough to smell the intruders as the wind shifted direction every so often.

Jin gave a hand signal to Pliny to move to the left and for Tonik to move forward. Jin moved to the right, and they surrounded the bull. As the lead bulls trotted away, Jin broke cover and launched one of his atlatl darts in a high arc into the air. It was expertly thrown. At that distance, it would not cause serious damage, but it would surely get the bull's attention. The spear hit the bull high in his hindquarters, and it spun around in anger to face the threat. The other lead bulls were already running in the direction of Jessec's men, and they did not bother to look back when the big bull grunted in anger with a small spear sticking out its backside. They had successfully isolated it.

The bull shook its head in confusion at the sight of the men under the auroch hide and scent. Jin made the sound of the bluebird, and they all got up in a squatting position and trotted forward, careful to keep the hides covering over them. The bull noticed Jin first, and it grunted and thrashed its head down in aggression.

Tonik licked his parched lips as perspiration ran down his temple. With a closer view of the bull in front of him, he gasped slightly at the sight of it. Mounds of hard muscle pulsated under its thick hide. It was in the prime of its life and full spring rut.

As the bull turned to face Jin, Pliny popped out of the fur and let loose another dart. Thrown from less distance than the first, it lodged into the auroch's side, piercing its hide. The bull turned again, now toward Pliny. It lowered its head and charged, unaffected by the two small spears poking out of it. Pliny dropped back down to the grass, out of sight.

Tonik had prepped another spear into his atlatl. Once the bull presented his flank, he popped out of the fur and let loose one of his darts with full force. The sharp spear hit its mark, burying itself deep behind its front leg.

The sharp pain made the bull turn quickly, and Tonik was not quick enough to get back under the hide cover. Despite its poor eyesight, it glimpsed the human figure and now the ruse was up. He dropped his head and rushed toward Tonik in a full charge. Tonik dropped to the ground, getting below the grass line and out of sight. The bull snuffed in anger and again changed direction before reaching him.

Jin had popped up out of the hide once again, letting loose two of his darts. In its pain and fury, the bull veered and charged toward Jin.

Once Tonik realized he was safe, he popped his head up over the grass line and saw the bull bearing down on Jin. Pliny had already let loose a dart of his own, but it had only punctured the hind leg. The auroch was very close to Jin now. At this distance, it would no longer be distracted.

Tonik desperately tried to yell and wave his hands to get the bull's attention, but it was no use. Jin waited for the last moment to see which direction the beast would joust its horns. He spun the auroch hide to the side, giving the bull a target. The bull's horns missed him by a fingers' width, puncturing the hide, just as Jin dived to the side. Warm foam from the bull's mouth splattered onto his shoulder. Jin landed and rolled onto his back, getting up onto one knee. Quickly, he reloaded his atlatl with another spear and prepared for the bull to turn to him. But Tonik and Pliny had rushed forward, yelling and waving wildly. They were able to get the bull's attention. They let loose the last of their darts in haste, not all hitting their mark. The bull took a labored breath and once again charged toward Tonik and Pliny.

Both men fled at full speed, side by side. Jin used the opportunity to let fly his final spear. His dart hit true, finding its mark between the bull's two ribs.

As the two men ran, the bull gained ground on them. In just a few paces, they would find themselves trampled. Just before the bull reached them, Pliny pushed Tonik to the side, making him veer sharply. Pliny kept running dead ahead, and the bull followed him. He was the fastest runner of the three, and he grunted hard, willing his legs to move faster.

Once he realized he was in the clear, Tonik stopped and turned. He noticed the bull had finally lost speed, and it was heavily favoring one side. Jin's small spear must have hit deep, perhaps nicking a lung.

Pliny had the bull chase him in a wide circle, able to stay just ahead of the wounded animal. As he came around, all three met men back together now and ran side by side, keeping the bull behind them in a chase.

Tonik cried out through burning lungs, "Pliny, throw your last dart!"

"No, Tonik, if we kill him now, how will we get him back?"

"What... are we going... chase all the way back?" Tonik gasped between breaths.

"That's why my father used to say it must be the most stubborn bull!" Jin replied.

They ran on hard over the knoll of the hill and down the side. The semi-dry grass whipped their legs until sharp red lines appeared across their glistening thighs, salty sweat further irritating the cuts.

Tonik looked back and noticed blood had begun to spill from the bull's mouth. Although they had slowed slightly, there was no way he was going to keep this pace up back to the village. His heart felt as if was going to explode, and he had difficulty getting enough air. He felt himself slowing down, and Jin and Pliny were gaining ground ahead of him. Tonik dared not turn around and lose a precious step, but he felt himself slipping. His running slowed.

He looked back and fully expected to meet the auroch's horns. But the auroch had lost ground as well, running with a more labored effort. "Hey, it's slowing down," Tonik blurted.

Pliny and Jin then slowed down to meet Tonik. "Don't stop now, big ugly ass, come catch us!" Jin mocked.

The bull kept up the chase with stubborn determination, but it was reduced to a slow trot. The men now only had to jog to keep ahead of it. To Tonik's amazement, even with blood spilling from its mouth and nostrils, the bull kept coming at them. Jin was right. If it didn't collapse first, that stubborn bull was going to follow them all the way back to the village!

Tonik had never run so hard in his life. He looked down at his dusty body full of cuts and scrapes and couldn't tell who looked worse, him or the bull. As they got within sight of the village, some of the Samaki spotted what was happening. In a few moments, word had spread, and everyone had come out to watch the scene.

The three men's pace had been reduced to a slow jog as they got within earshot of the first shelter. The entire village ran out to meet the three men and the giant auroch, spears in hand ready to defend. But the bull now walked forward weakly, its sides riddled with darts, resembling a porcupine. It took a few last steps forward, then stopped; its breathing wheezed as it struggled to fill its one good lung with air.

People murmured and gasped at the spectacle; it was the biggest auroch anyone had ever seen. Many of them had never been so close to a bull while it still lived, and they surrounded it in fascination. The beast rocked dizzily on its feet, ready to fall over.

Pliny then approached the bull, skipping to it as if he were a young girl picking berries in a field. The bull shook its head at him in defiance one last time. Intense anger still burned in its bloodshot eyes. A thick strand of bloody mucus ran from its snout to the ground, pooling in the dusty earth.

Pliny bent over, and within a hand's reach, he came face to face with the auroch. He shouted for the benefit of the Samaki spectators. "Who are the best hunters in the village?"

As if in agreement, the auroch coughed one last time. It swayed, then its legs gave way under it, collapsing in a cloud of dust and blood. Pliny performed a dainty spin to face the villagers and raised his hands high into the air, fabulously.

The entire village erupted into a roar of approval. They rushed over to the three men and hoisted them onto their shoulders in cheers. Raam stood back and shook his head, half in disbelief, half in pride.

* * *

The meat from the bull was large enough so that everyone in the village at least got a morsel. To prepare for the feast, some women and children had spent the day foraging for spicy tubers that were grilled together with the meat. It added a spicy flavor and was one of the tribe's delicacies. Although the meat's taste was slightly tainted from all the stress and adrenaline the bull suffered before dying, no one complained. The meal, mixed with the fabulous story of the hunt, brought an air of festivity in the Samaki village.

It had been quite some time since either tribe had felt this level of happiness, and they naturally attributed some of this to the newcomers. After so many months of hardship, the people felt safe and full of hope for the first time. Pliny had discovered his knack for showmanship, and his stylish recounting of the hunt, together with the challenge against Jessec, had the entire tribe in laughter.

The sun had set by the time Jessec's men returned,

strolling cockish and triumphant with pieces of carcass swung over their backs. Entering the village, however, they were dismayed by everyone's attitude. Normally, an auroch kill received a hero's welcome.

Jessec called out to one of the younger boys, "Is this not a fine kill of auroch we have made?"

The boy shrugged his shoulders and replied casually, "Ahh, yah, but the twins' was bigger," and then ran off.

Jessec fumed at this. Once they got closer to the center of the village, they saw the boy had not been lying. There was a clear crowd around Tonik and the enormous bonfire. Already skinned and stretched out to dry was the largest auroch hide he had ever seen. It was almost twice the size of the one his men had killed. It had a beautiful shiny black color, and its species-defining, front-curved horns were each longer than a man's leg.

Jessec gestured for his men to drop their meat. Instead of facing embarrassment, he left his men and strode off to his shelter in disgust.

Tonik watched him go and smiled with self-satisfaction. Although it felt great, he knew he had just made a mortal enemy.

Jessec's men had no such pride; they approached the twins with adulation and wonder, desperate for details.

Laksha had inched her way beside Tonik ever since they had returned. She could not take her eyes off him, and although he did not notice, she stood beside him in a way that made it clear to every other woman in the village that he was her territory.

Pliny took notice of it and whispered to Tonik. "I think you better sleep somewhere else tonight. Jin and I wish to celebrate by..."

At that, Tonik immediately crunched his face and held up his hand, not wishing to hear any more details.

Laksha caught this exchange, and Pliny winked at her. She understood what he meant, and secretly she smiled and nodded   back   in   gratitude.

Chapter 17

When it was dark, and the Samaki had their fill of eating and celebrating, Laksha persuaded Tonik to bathe in the sea to wash the dirt and blood of the hunt from his body. They swam naked in the cold water under the stars, and she helped wash him clean. While Tonik was still cold and dripping wet with saltwater, Laksha offered him a new fur, a cave bear. The fur was a veritable treasure, rare and highly prized. He thanked her gratefully as she led him to her dwelling.

Tonik was too tired to protest. He was still high from the adrenaline of the day's events, the intoxicating effect of living in the moment and forgetting his past.

Laksha's dwelling was astonishing. The shelter was lined from floor to ceiling with all kinds of different animal hides. Small wood and bone carvings of people and animals hung down from the ceiling. In the middle of the dwelling stood a massive wood sculpture of the strange smiling fish with a bulbous head. One wall of the shelter had an indentation for a fire pit made with rocks and dried mud, which formed a tube to let out the smoke.

Laksha placed some dry lichen to the hot embers and added kindling to get the fire going. Soon the flames danced around the firepit, and the myriad of trinkets threw hundreds of dancing shadows around the walls and floor. They sat by the fire on yet another large bear fur, and Tonik wondered about the warriors who killed such a fierce creature.

"I have never seen anything like this," Tonik remarked.

"It was my Father's dwelling. Jessec did not want it for himself. He said it gave him bad dreams," replied Laksha, moving up close to him.

She prepared a pasty mix of plant leaves and began to gently rub it over the grass cuts on his thigh. He jerked slightly at the sting of it.

Laksha giggled. "The big auroch hunter, hurt by a few minor cuts?" Her hand moved over him sensually. She ran her fingers over the scarred claw marks on his shoulder and the stab wound on his side, admiring them. She asked many questions about his tribe, where they were from, and what they had been through.

Tonik retold the encounter and battle with the Red Feather warriors and spoke of his parents' death. He told her about his jump from the cliff and about the big tooth that took Sira.

Upon hearing Sira's name, Laksha changed the subject. "I've never seen anything like that today, what you did. That bull, it was beautiful. You were beautiful."

Tonik quivered as her hand moved higher up his leg. He wiped tears from his eyes, embarrassed to have such emotions in front of this female stranger.

She grabbed his head and looked into his eyes; her light green eyes were beautifully hypnotic. Laksha stood up over him and dropped her bearskin.

In the firelight, without the bulky fur, he finally could admire her figure. Except for Sira, she was the most beautiful woman he had ever seen. She had caramel skin and eyes green like the forest, a color Tonik had never seen on a person before. She lifted her hands and removed a small wooden fork from out of her hair, and shook her head. Her curly hair fell over her shoulders, and she was soft and sweet-smelling. Her status in the tribe removed her from any hard labor, so her skin was smooth and unblemished. She gave him half a smile, a sensual look as if she were expecting a delicious meal.

"Your brother does not tolerate me; I think after today even less so. Imagine if he knew I was here," Tonik cautioned.

"He cannot appreciate a good thing when he sees one, but don't worry about him. He cannot harm you if I say so. But he will challenge you, and you will have to accept if you intend to keep the respect that you have earned today."

"He cannot harm me if I say so? I thought he was the leader of the Samaki?"

Laksha laughed at that. "Don't you know who I am, Tonik?"

"Yes, Raam has told me you are the shaman of the Samaki, sister of Jessee, and daughter of the last leader of the Samaki."

She giggled again. "Oh, yes, Tonik, that is true, but I am more. Oh, so much more." Her voice slightly changed, sounding deeper. It gave Tonik a shiver.

She handed him a gourd of liquid. Tonik raised it to his mouth, but it smelled foul.

"Drink," she said. "It will bring visions, and you will be stronger for me."

Tonik took the empty gourd without further protest. Tonight, he felt invincible, and he drank the foul-tasting liquid in one gulp. Laksha got up and Tonik raised himself to his elbows to watch her. Her plump backside wobbled from side to side as she walked over to the statue of the strange fish. She straddled and sat upon it, rubbing the statue's head and smiling at Tonik. Tonik felt the room spin under the effect of the drink.

Laksha spoke about being a protector and guardian of the tribe, but Tonik was finding it difficult to follow. The hanging sculptures in the room came to life, flickering and vibrating at first, then weaving together in colorful trails. His body became weightless. Laksha and the statue swirled into one, and her laughter sounded inhuman. Her head morphed into the smiling fish shape on which she sat upon.

Tonik shook his head, trying to clear his vision. Laksha's body vibrated, and her skin shimmered like fish scales. Tonik shook his head again and closed his eyes tightly. He knew of the powerful hallucinogenic plants that shamans used to partake in visions, so he told himself it wasn't real.

Laksha straddled him, expertly guiding her flesh over his, and in a moment, he was inside of her. He opened his eyes, and she was the beautiful woman again, more beautiful than before. Her eyes glowed a bright green, and her breasts bounced up and down as she rode on top of him. The flesh of their bodies swirled in his vision, melting together so he could not tell where he began and she ended. She bounced on top of him harder and harder, and he felt pleasure he never had before. He came to a spasm quickly as he released.

She grabbed his neck and pulled him closer, his face in

her breasts. It was her turn, and he felt her body spasm as she cried out his name. Tonik fell back onto the fur, crashing into it as if from a high fall. The effect of the drink kept him spinning, in a semi-conscious state of euphoria as Laksha now lay beside him, her head on his chest.

He could not tell at what point he fell asleep, but suddenly he was swimming out into a crystal-blue sea. Beautiful fish swam all around him, and the sun was shining brightly. The beautiful blue sky and fluffy white clouds reflected off the water. Raam and the people of his tribe stood on the shore. They entered the water and swam out to meet him, and one by one, the Samaki swam out as well. Soon everyone was out in the water with him, holding each other's arms in one long chain and chanting in unison.

Then the sky grew dark, and the Red Feathers appeared on the shore. They were yelling their warlike cry and brandishing their spears. They also entered the water and swam out to meet them, their faces scowling in war rage. The blue water slowly turned red. Pieces of people, both his tribe and Red Feather warriors floated all around him. Arms, legs, and decapitated heads bumped against him in the foaming red water as he tried to keep his head above the surface.

Sira lay on the shore, alone and dying. He struggled to swim through the bloody water and human remains to reach her, but he was unnaturally slow. He called out to her, but she could not hear him. By the time he got to shore, it was too late; she was lying dead on the beach. His dream went black.

Chapter 18

The warming weather had melted the tundra snows outside the Gondo-Var camp. What was once frozen hard ground had become muddy and soft, pocketed with water holes yet to evaporate. The hardy elephant grasses exploded into life. It took only a few weeks before they had grown to be over two men high. The tall grasses provided excellent grazing and cover for mammoths and their calves.

Kadam took his place next to Durok, behind the last line of trees before the ground opened into the vast, grassy marsh. The gentle breeze made the red feather braided into Kadam's hair tickle his neck. Durok turned silently and pointed to his nose. Kadam followed his direction and inhaled deeply through his nostrils. Although they were invisible behind the grass, there was no mistaking the musty, earthy scent of mammoth dung. Kadam looked back and raised his two fingers in a curved fashion, making the hand signal for mammoth.

Behind him, the Gondo-Var hunting party divided into two groups. The first group, which consisted of twelve men, silently made their way through the tree line, staying downwind of their quarry. The first team would be the group that spooked the animals. The other group of twelve, which included Kadam and Durok, would apply a pincer move, using both bows and the atlatl spears to make the kill.

Kadam felt his impatience grow as he waited for the antler horn, the signal that a mammoth was on the move. He hated these quiet moments, which was why he always tried to stay busy. Quiet time alone forced him to be introspective. It brought back raw emotions. Anger and hatred toward the Gondo-Var tribe burned in his soul. The burning had become more subtle over time, like that of a smoldering ember rather than a scorching flame.

The other emotion was guilt. Guilt at having to accept his place, at least temporarily, among his enemies. Guilt that he had not died fighting them, but found himself entering deeper into their world.

He reassured himself he was waiting for the right

moment to strike, but as the days continued, the further that goal seemed to move. He often wondered if the end would justify his means. It was a difficult and painful subject to face, and he found it was easier to put it out of his mind if he kept occupied.

Luckily, hunting mammoth was never a routine the Gondo-Var broke from. The great mounds of meat from the animals could fill many bellies, and their cultivation of salt meant they could store and dry it when the weather was warmer. The tribe had grown so successful at hunting mammoths; they had to travel farther and farther away into the hills to spot them. The mammoths had become wary, and with their amazing sense of smell, it took long marches and clever planning to stay downwind.

When the antler horn finally blew, it didn't take long before Kadam heard the loud, angry trumpet of warning from the animal's trunk. An entire group of mammoths had been spooked and now were trudging toward them through the thick sea of grass.

Durok pointed, "That's them. Get into position!"

The twelve men jogged forward, swinging their spears in an arc to part the stalks of green grass aside as they took their places. They formed a wide U-shape, hollering and making noise as they did so. The mammoths would keep their distance from the voices, leading them straight to the bottom of the U-shape, in which laid the trap. Kadam and Durok waited on the other side of the trap, which was a large mud hole. The chest-high mud would slow down the mammoths long enough for the hunters to make their kill. They had refined this to an art. First, they would kill the large matriarch, then proceed with the other adults, finally finishing with the calves.

When the mammoths finally appeared through the grass, they had worked themselves up into such a panic that they did not stop at the sight of the mudhole and fell right into it. The archers immediately fired their poisoned arrows at the matriarch. The poison was not powerful enough to render such a large animal unconscious, but enough of them caused a strong torpid effect.

The mammoth flapped its ears out in aggression, trying to charge the men, but she was stuck in thick black mud. There were two other adult mammoths in the group and the third was a calf, around one year of age. They huddled together in defense, the one-year-old having to keep its trunk raised to breathe through the cold black mud.

As more hunters regrouped to the mudhole, they flanked around the mammoths, letting loose their atlatl spears into them. The spears pierced through the thick furry hides, although not deep enough. It would take time and many spears and arrows for the creatures to bleed out. One overconfident hunter entered the mud to hand spear the matriarch. Thinking the great creature had been sufficiently weakened, he got too close. The mammoth jerked upward and thrashed her head out to the side. One of the massive tusks hit the man in his side, lifting him and throwing him high into the air. The man was thrown back into the mud and grass. He would limp back to camp with a broken rib for his carelessness. The mammoth trumpeted again and lifted onto its hind legs, towering over the men below. Black mud dripped from its matted fur like raindrops.

Both Kadam and Durok seized the opportunity and jumped into the hole, getting as close as sanely possible. Just before the mammoth dropped back down, both men threw their spears into the underside of the mammoth's chest. The mammoth came down in a giant splash, splattering the gooey black substance all over them. She tried frantically to regain her footing, but her massive tusks became lodged in the mud, and the poison had weakened her.

The men now approached her without fear, stabbing the mammoth near its neck and side. As with all creatures, it fought and struggled valiantly for its life. It took many minutes and hundreds of stabs with their spears before the three mammoths were finally slain.

The mudhole had become a mix of red-stained mud, and it covered the men from head to toe. Unlike Kadam's old tribe, there was no cheering, no dancing, no celebration of happiness after hunting such an exceptional creature.

With the Gondo-Var, it seemed very routine, like an

everyday chore. The thrill and glory of hunting mammoth that Kadam had once felt were no longer there. In its place was loss and an undefined feeling of nostalgia. Like the mammoths themselves, his memories of those joyful hunts were slowly disappearing.

He reminded himself that this was still a mammoth after all. It was a substantial amount of meat, hide, bone, tusk, and other essential materials, which was a survival necessity. He whistled like a bluebird out of habit, then smiled and looked over at Durok. He was attempting to crawl his way out of the mudhole, looking very ungraceful as he did so. Kadam offered his arm and pulled the man out of his sticky predicament.

The other group of hunters that had originally spooked the mammoth had arrived with their tools. The laborious and dirty job of gutting and butchering the carcass would begin. Those who wore an eagle feather were spared this dirty chore. Their job of making the kill was complete. Kadam remembered all the hours spent hacking and cleaning out the stinking guts of various animals over the years. It was a rare moment that he enjoyed the Gondo-Var's hierarchy. Warriors who wore the red feather were exempt from most menial labor tasks. Kadam could participate in all the exciting parts of the hunt, with none of the tedious after work.

The men who got to work butchering the carcass were experts. Their butchering tools had become refined, using specialized blades depending on the task. A dozen of them could completely strip a mammoth carcass and have it tied up for hauling before scavengers even had the chance to arrive. This left the hunters free to track down even more prey. But these days, all they could find was one group of mammoths every few days, if they were lucky. Today they had traveled from sunrise until the sun was a quarter of the way back down before they had found this group.

Durok mentioned to Kadam that someday soon they might not find any mammoth at all. Kadam scoffed at this, not believing such a thing was possible.

On their way back to the camp, with a long line of men

hauling fresh meat behind them, they entered the forested area before the entrance. As always, the wolves were waiting for their free meal and began their chorus of yelps. The meat scraps were unloaded and thrown out, the men whistling and cheering to their favorite canids.

The man with intricate circular scarring on his cheeks was there to meet them—Last Chance. He called out to Kadam and Durok. Even though Master referred to the man by his new moniker, he did not like to be called this by anyone else.

He looked contemptuously at Kadam and Durok and pointed his finger. "Master wants to see you two. Leave this group now and hurry to him. Otherwise, he will be angry."

Kadam approached. "When Master asks you to put his spear in your mouth, do you hurry to fill it, Last Chance?"

Durok laughed out loud, for they both had little respect for the man.

"I can cut your neck while you sleep, big man, or maybe cut something else. Then what would your woman think of you?"

"While I sleep, yes, that is the only way you would ever have a chance, Last Chance, as even Nara can out wrestle you!"

Both men laughed again as they passed him, Kadam bumping shoulders with the smaller man, making him lose balance. No other man would dare speak to him this way, but there was little Last Chance was willing to do about it. Not only was Kadam twice his size, but both he and Durok had become respectable warriors in the tribe. In a world where social status was a prized commodity, there was no way he could assault a fellow eagle warrior without serious repercussion.

When the two men reached the overhang, they found Master waiting by the entrance with a few other men. Kadam noticed the notorious human trackers. They were the thin-framed men who could follow a man's spoor until the end of the earth and never tire. Durok called these men the real scourge, for it was they who sought and found new tribes to raid.

Master instructed them to follow and led them into Father's cave overhang. The tide was low, so without the thunderous sound of waves against the rocks, the cave lost some of its dramatic effects. Father had fallen asleep on his rock throne, his double chin scrunched against his chest as his head hung forward. He was drooling. Master and the other men stood at the bottom for many minutes. There was no attempt to wake him.

Finally, the old man awoke in a drunken daze. He spoke down to Master, "Ah-hum, finally you have come. Have you brought your best hunters?"

Master bowed slightly. "Yes, Father, they are here."

Father looked up at them and smiled. "My sons, my eagles, you are here because you are special. You have proven yourself for an important task. Perform this, and you will earn my blessing."

Kadam and Durok both glanced at each other warily.

Father cleared his throat, "I want you to find my long-lost sons, the gray hairy people of the mountains. I believe some of you know them as the Others. These people differ from us; they know of things that even we, the great Gondo-Var people, do not. Just one of these Other men is as strong of two of you." He purposefully pointed to Kadam. "But fear not, we Gondo-Var people know much. We have weapons they do not, and we are many. But you must find these Others; my lost sons. Bring me them back alive, especially a female."

Father leaned forward, looking at each of them, opening his eyes wide with excitement. "Go, my sons! Find them for me, and I will reward you for the rest of your lives."

Master bowed his head. "We will do as you wish, Father. Trust we will find these Others of which you speak." There was a slight intonation when Master referred to the Others, a hint of disrespect at the word. It was not enough to cause further discussion. "Father, with your permission, now that the snow has melted, we would like to send some trackers to seek the Samaki village. My scouts say they are a great tribe with the most beautiful women they have ever laid eyes on."

Kadam was not familiar with the term Samaki and was relieved to hear that they would not be in search of the Fishtooth village. Raam and the rest of his old tribe would at least be safe for a while.

"Good, our Gondo-Vars need more women. Send them and let me know what they see. But do not attack," Father instructed.

"Yes, Father," Master replied, again with a slight intonation of annoyance. He bowed, then turned and motioned for the men to exit the cave overhang.

Once they were far enough away, Master separated them into two groups and spoke under his breath in irritation. "I am tired of hearing about these Others. There are villages out there with proper women and real men, not those mountain spirits. I will not waste any more time on his dreams." He swore and spit on the ground in disgust. "This group, we are to track and find the Samaki. That day, my trackers retreated upon encountering people with a sickness. But winter has passed, and I am guessing the sickness has passed as well."

Master's group comprised almost everyone, which left Kadam and Durok with only one tracker, a tiny little old man with grey hair and wrinkled skin. "You two, you are the newest of the Gondo-Vars, so with that, I give you a job that I know you will fail. The mountains are five days away from here, four if you are fast. Go into them with the old man and see what you can find. There must be a passage through those mountains. Unless the Others can fly as well. If you find them, Father will give you three wives each. Remember," he said, pointing at Kadam. "You are a Gondo-Var warrior now. The only way you will stop being Gondo-Var is when you die. If you try to run from us, I will kill your unborn. I will make your woman mine and mount her hard every night. I will keep giving her young ones until the day her body fails from it," Master said, his calm voice belied its resolve.

The threat confused Kadam, as he had no woman awaiting the birth of a baby. Walking away, he muttered one last instruction. "Meet me at first light tomorrow at the entrance of the camp."

* * *

That night, there was more drumming and dancing by the fire. The smell of roasted meat was thick in the air. Durok, Kadam, and the other hunters were honored with pieces of the giant liver. Ever since the day of the climb, particularly Kadam's encounter with the giant bird, Kadam had become a popular figure within the Gondo-Var tribe. His defiant attitude and insults to everyone around him only seemed to add to his reputation. He was a snarling, resentful bear of a man, and they loved him for it.

His rough sexual prowess came to be known among the Gondo-Var women, and against Durok's advice, Kadam never denied them. Even the women belonging to other men would visit him at night once their partners had gone to sleep. He came to understand that this was normal among them. Unlike his old tribe, in which adultery meant a hefty fine in the form of goods paid to the man whose woman they mated, the Gondo-Var tribe paid little mind to it. Men and women fornicated freely, and some men had two wives, something the women of Kadam's old tribe would never have accepted.

Kadam's fornications ended once he met Nara. She was a fiery, dark-skinned woman warrior who liked to keep her hair cut short. She had also been a captive, although she had been taken as a small child and was fully conformed to Gondo-Var traditions. Once Kadam mated with Nara, the nightly visits from other women mysteriously and abruptly ended, although he suspected Nara had something to do with it. She was fierce, with a hunting prowess that matched or surpassed some men. Taller and heavier than many of the thin-framed Gondo-Var, her thick thighs and large muscular buttocks provided a sturdy athletic frame. Although many men had tried, none ever had the strength to satisfy her sexually. Quite a few men had ended up with twisted arms or bloodied faces in their unsolicited attempts.

Kadam and Nara had made a perfect match from the

moment they met. But unlike Kadam, she had fully accepted and loved her tribe, and this was a point of contention between them. Nara became angered whenever Kadam spoke ill of the Gondo-Var.

Nara came to sit next to Kadam, and she stared him down contemptuously. Kadam tried to hold her stern gaze, but it was stone cold, so he acquiesced and cut his portion of the liver in half and handed it to her. She smiled and with an exhalation of happiness and took a large bite out of the raw liver. Her brilliant smile revealing teeth already red with blood. Kadam could only smile at the sight of it. She was the first person in the world who could lighten up his legendary bad mood.

"Tomorrow you hunt again? Bring me back more liver?" she questioned as she bumped shoulders against him.

"No, it seems you will not have liver for a few days unless you make the kill yourself. I am going with Durok up into the mountains, on a hunt for something that we will never find," he said disappointedly.

"The Others?" she questioned.

"How did you know? Well, anyway, it doesn't matter. Those people do not exist; it is just a story we used to tell young ones. My old tribe used to speak of them almost every night, always the same story, but we have been to many places and I have never seen one."

"I hear they can move silently through the trees and can break a man's neck as if he were a bird." She looked at him seriously. "I need you to come back. Who will feed us liver?" she said, placing her hand on her belly.

"Why do you say us?" Kadam asked, puzzled.

She grabbed his hand and held it to her belly. It wasn't swollen, and he couldn't feel anything, but when she pushed in harder, he could feel there was a lump.

Kadam's face paled, and words failed him as his mouth opened in dread. "Is it? No, it cannot..." he stumbled.

She laughed merrily, clearly amused by his fumbling expression. "Of course it can, Kadam! The way you push your spear so deep into me every night, did you not know that is how babies are made?" She laughed again at the sight of his face.

Confusion rushed through Kadam. He suddenly lost his appetite and handed the liver to Nara.

"Oh, more for the young warrior who grows inside me. See, you are already a great father," she said.

But Kadam was still in shock, and his mind went into turmoil. Somehow, he always imagined being in this tribe as a temporary affair, one day crushing the leadership together with Durok and then fleeing back to his old tribe.

Nara's fierce loyalty to the Gondo-Var was a snag he had been avoiding. Her having his child now meant a further complication to his plans. He wondered how Master could have known about this. His mood now thoroughly soured, he got up and returned to his hide tent.

Kadam could not put his mind at ease and did not sleep well that night. In the morning, he was happy to leave the Gondo-Var fortress and his newfound troubles. They set out with Master and the other men at first light. With only leftover mammoth bones to offer the wolves, the snarling creatures followed behind them closely until they were out from underneath the trees.

"Why don't they just kill these beasts and be done with them? Why do they keep giving them meat?" Kadam asked.

Durok shrugged.

The old man who was their tracker turned and smiled. "It is so that if our enemies come, they first have to get through the wolves. Any group who tries to approach, the wolves will make an alarm. Clever, yes?" It was the first time they had heard the man speak, and to their surprise, his accent was not like the Gondo-Var, but more like their own.

The following morning, Master split up the group, and the little old man led Durok and Kadam toward the mountains. At the start of the journey, they mumbled to themselves about how this tiny old man would slow them down. To their surprise, they found they could hardly keep pace with him, and soon they had to demand that they stop for a break.

"What is your name, old man? Where are you from?" Durok asked, panting as he sat down.

"I am Poyop. Poyop was not born from them," he referred to himself in the third person, then he unwound the small bow and quiver of arrows from off his back and squatted. "Poyop came from a village very far from here, many moon's journey. The Gondo-Var warriors came to Poyop's village just like Durok and Kadam village. They killed many men, including Poyop's son. Many of Poyop's people were taken. The Gondo-Var camp was not here. It was near a great river that never ends. The Gondo-Var move camp after hunting all the people. Poyop was the best tracker in the tribe. Poyop made to track and not work digging black sand. Poyop now living with Gondo-Var for many winters."

"The best tracker of your tribe, you say? If you are so good, then why have they sent you with us on a hunt that will fail?" Durok scoffed.

"You think I track good for those vultures?" Poyop bellowed angrily. "Why? So that more sons can die like Poyop's? Poyop track, but only good enough so they don't send Poyop to dig black sand. They think Poyop don't track good, but they don't know, Poyop track better than all! Poyop can track fish through water!"

"That is good, Poyop. We are also not friends with these people. We also think they are vultures, not eagles," Durok said. His face lit up with insight. "We will be five days' journey or more away from camp. That is more than enough time for us to leave and never be caught. If Poyop is an excellent tracker like he says, we can seek another tribe, or even find your old tribe, Kadam, yes?"

"No!" Kadam blurted quickly. "We made a promise that day on the cliff, remember?" he added.

"Yes, but we have lived with them now through the winter, hunted with them, fought with them, seen how many they are. How do you think we must fight them? Alone? We need to find other tribes, ones that can join us," Durok explained.

"I won't leave until I kill Master," replied Kadam.

Durok stood up angrily. "No, that is not why. It is because of Nara! I saw you last night, with your hand on her belly. She is with a young one! That is why you will go back! I told you not to mount those vulture women. Now you will have a vulture of your own!"

"Close your mouth, Durok! Or I will close it for you," responded Kadam angrily, standing up and meeting the man's gaze.

"And what if we find your old tribesmen? Will you tell them you are a vulture now?" Durok asked.

With a burst of violence, Kadam shoved Durok to the ground. He went down hard, throwing up a small dust cloud. He coughed and rolled up onto his knees. As he looked at Kadam, he shook his head and gave a mocking chuckle.

"A promise, Durok, you and I will see the end of Master and those shit birds. Remember that."

"Very well, Kadam, I am a man of my word. And I also understand you are now stuck. She is quite a woman, after all. I want to know if you will truly turn against them when the time is right?" Durok asked.

"I will keep the promise that I made. One day when we are ready, I will fight against the Gondo-Var, not with them."

Durok looked down at the scratch on his arm from his fall. "I hope for our lives you are telling the truth! We can speak of this later. Right now, our task is to find these Others." Durok got up and dusted the dirt from his hide clothing. "Master claims they must be hidden in the mountains. It is the only place they have not yet searched. They have hunted everywhere else and have never seen one."

"That is because they do not exist," said Kadam, sounding annoyed.

"Oh, the wide feet exist," Poyop corrected. "Poyop's tribe have seen their tracks, found their abandoned camps, we did. My tribe called them wide feet. They are heavy men with big feet. Master is right, they now live in the mountains, far away from men. Poyop will find them. Poyop can track fish   through   water!"

Chapter 19

Sira stood over the little red deer while Harq squatted near its head. The creature had stopped thrashing, but it continued to breathe harshly, gurgling blood from its mouth. It fought valiantly for every breath, such as all wild creatures do. Harq placed his hand over the deer's head, and Sira sighed and braced himself for Harq's little speech. Over the months they had spent hunting together, she had grown accustomed to Harq's tradition. But she still didn't understand it.

"Thank you for giving us your life. You will feed us. You will feed our family. Your life gives us life," Harq recited. Sira had never quite grasped the purpose of Harq's words after every kill. But she suspected it was like her own people's ritual. She whispered the hymn she had been taught since she was a little girl. "From dirt our bones, and our bones to dirt."

Harq removed his obsidian flint knife, and Sira helped to hold the deer's head still. The black knife easily sliced through the artery running down its neck. Sira learned of the black rocks during her time here in the valley. Harq's people used obsidian in all their tools, even spearheads. Sira had never seen a substance like it.

Black as the night sky, but near translucent once chipped into thin pieces, obsidian shards were so sharp a gentle brush could shave the hair off of one's skin. The downside was that they were extremely brittle, and it took a real practiced hand to knap them into proper flakes without shattering. Harq had tried to explain that in battle, once you had stabbed your enemy, you could twist the knife or spear, breaking off the point. This would leave a piece of the rock lodged in your opponent. It caused immense damage and pain, and if the piece wasn't removed, one could die later by the fever.

Sira remembered this as she looked at the black tip of her spear in wonder and awe of the new substance. Then she looked back down at the deer. Too much blood had drained, and its heart had finally come to rest. Instead of the cheerful banter that Sira was used to after a kill, Harq was solemn, never speaking while butchering a carcass.

It was again just one of the many ways in which they differed. Although many mysteries surrounding these new people, she had to admit that they were very efficient hunters. Harq's way of hunting seemed to rely on a great deal of patience and stealth. He could lie still in a position of ambush for hours on end, just waiting for his quarry to pass by. He also preferred hunting in silence.

This way of hunting had been excruciatingly difficult for Sira at the beginning; she simply didn't have the same amount of patience. Throughout the months' Sira had spent stranded in this valley, she had used the time following him, learning his methods and habits in how he moved quietly throughout the forest. Through his limited conversation, she sensed that this way of living was born out of a need to stay hidden from others, other people like herself, most likely. It was as if they had been forced to live a life in the shadows to survive.

Here, even though they were protected in this remote mountain valley, they still lived as if under threat. One could almost walk right by their camps and never knew they existed.

Her time with Harq improved the feeling of loneliness and isolation of being away from her tribe. She had learned from him, and he had an almost limitless supply of patience for her questions. Despite their differences and Sira's yearning to reunite with her family, she genuinely enjoyed his company.

And he was extremely protective of her. He never let his guard down for a minute. From the time he awoke until he went to sleep, it seemed he was in a constant state of alert.

As if to prove this point, Harq abruptly stopped cutting the hindquarters of the deer and popped his head up. His large eyebrows raised, and he lifted his nose to the sky, inhaling through his wide nostrils. He did this so often that Sira now ignored it. But this time, he held up his hand for Sira to remain quiet.

Sira held her ear to the wind, trying to hear whatever

spooked him.

"Sira, come, you take one leg, I take one leg. Leave the rest, we go now," he whispered.

His tone of concern made the hair on the back of Sira's neck spike. She no longer questioned his sense of danger. He had always been right, hearing or smelling something in the wind before she could.

They did not even wait for the blood to drain out fully from the hind legs before tying the hooves around their shoulders with cords made from the dried tendon. Harq threw some of the precious organs into a hide sack. Warm blood dripped onto the back of her calf as they made haste through the thick pines and away from the kill.

Behind her, she heard the unmistakable sounds of men and deep voices at their kill site. Harq moved more swiftly now. All attempts at a silent getaway were forgotten. They ran hard through the light snow. The voices were still behind them and following. It was the unmistakable vocal sounds of the Others. The idea of meeting a more hostile version of these men had been on Sira's mind every day since she had arrived in this valley.

The men behind them never stopped their pursuit, following them back to the cliffs of Harq's clan. Harq called out in his language, something she had never heard before. It sounded more like barking than a word, but it had the required effect.

In several brief moments, every man had responded to the warning call. They scrambled out of the craggy caves of the cliff; weapons held in anticipation.

Before Harq could explain, the men who were pursuing broke out from the trees. Sira noticed there were at least a dozen of them, big ugly men armed with spears and primitive atlatls. The intruders yelled out something of a challenge, and Harq's responded with their own. That caused the men of the two tribes to rush together.

The women rushed back toward the caves, lifting their babies and young children in their arms. Sira retreated as well, but kept her eyes locked on the grisly battle scene in front of her. One man from Harq's tribe already lay on the ground, holding his bloody chest in pain. The men fought brutally, with little regard for their safety, as they rushed headfirst into each other. As it roused more and more men from the village into battle, it became clear that the attackers were becoming outnumbered, but they were fierce, swinging makeshift clubs tipped with jawbone or antler points. Their fighting was interrupted when a massive sonic boom exploded in the distance.

The snow around Sira's feet vibrated, and she looked up to see the trees swaying as if caught by the wind, yet she felt no movement in the air. Although it was a clear day, a thunderclap struck the air with such force she could feel its vibrations. The force of it threw Sira to the ground in fear.

The men abruptly drew back from one another, searching the air in fear. The thunder echoed throughout the valley, followed by more rumbling, like that of rolling thunder. Sira felt the ground shift under her, then vibrate. The men searched the air until they found the source of the explosion.

Sira's gaze followed as she got up slowly. Off in the distance, the highest peak in the valley was billowing with black smoke, as if a great fire had been started.

The attackers fell back, motioning to the smoking mountain and chattering something in their language. Great, bushy eyebrows raised in alarm, enhancing their already enlarged brows. Whatever the attackers were trying to convey, the men of the village were too high on adrenaline to respond. They simply barked back at the attackers, howling with threatening sounds.

It amazed Sira the sound these men could make. From having spent so much time with such quiet people, to hear them suddenly shout with so much force was jarring.

It took several more shouting matches back and forth until the attackers lost interest and retreated into the forest, their eyes transfixed on the column of smoke, which was increasing in size by the second. Some men of the village followed in pursuit, not to re-engage, but to make sure they made an honest retreat.

Sira ran over to Harq, who had a slight cut on his upper

arm where a spear had glanced at him. She touched his arm gently, but he didn't move; his eyes were still fixed on the tree line. Several others noticed the two of them together, and they strode angrily over to Harq, barking at him. Harq immediately put himself between her and the men. One of them approached Harq and bumped against his chest.

Although Sira considered Harq to be strong, the other man's collision sent Harq stumbling back two steps. He recovered, and immediately stood his ground. Another man rushed forward toward Harq. Again, their chests collided, sending Harq back with another step. Harq stepped up again, waiting for the next challenge.

This continued at least a dozen times, each time a man backing up Harq and Sira until they had almost reached the entrance of Harq's dwelling. Sira could make out their slurs toward her. "Wolf woman!" and "Leave!"

Eventually, the men grew tired of challenging, and the chest-bumping ceased. Only then did Harq turn his back and return to his cave with Sira. Sira finally understood what had provoked the Others to attack. It was her.

Back in the cave-dwelling, she gathered her things.

"Sira, what do you do? Where you go?"

"I cannot stay here, Harq. It is too dangerous for me, and you. I am bringing danger to your clan. I know those men attacked us because of me."

Harq looked down and shook his head. He did not argue. She was right. "We must go. I bring you here, I must take you back," he decided.

Sira sighed in relief, hoping he would come to this decision.

"But the cave, the snow you told me about. Will we be able to make it out?" she asked.

Harq shrugged. "If there is snow in the cave, we dig out," he said. The look on his face did not inspire confidence, but she no longer had a choice. This clan of Others had only tolerated her presence when they realized she wasn't a threat. Now that she was discovered by another group, no doubt the word would soon spread. These people had a deep mistrust of her kind and, for good reason. She was enemy number one in their eyes, and they would tolerate her presence no more.

In Harq's cave-dwelling, Sira stoked the fire, regretting the violence that had taken place today. She felt somehow at fault. *There I go again, taking responsibility for everyone around me. No, I wasn't asked to be brought here. It wasn't my fault.*

She wondered if her parents and fellow tribesman would believe her story of meeting these people. This was not the way she had envisioned meeting them, although, under any other circumstances, it would have just been a childhood fantasy. A part of her felt annoyed that the Others discriminated so vehemently against her, but she did not know their history.

She wished she could express to them that her people were not all bad. There were many with open minds and loving spirits. Those who were willing to accept and love all people no matter how they looked. Sira did not want to leave under such bad terms and decided to try to make peace. She stood up and went over to the rocks where the pieces of deer meat were laid out. She picked up the liver and heart, the two most prized organs. Harq looked at her quizzically.

"Take those two legs. We are going up to share a meal," she said.

"Sira..." he protested, but she was already walking toward the entrance.

Needa seemed to understand exactly what she meant and gave a big, comical grin. She pointed up in the cave's direction and grunted to Harq.

Harq sighed, shaking his head. Without further discussion, he slid the obsidian flint knife into the back of his hide skirt just in case, then he grabbed both deer's legs and rushed out to catch up.

Sira stood awkwardly at the entrance to the large cave. She held a heart in one hand, and a liver in the other as if presenting it. The men in the cave stood up, and a few of them barked in a warning. Whatever activities or conversations were taking place before Sira arrived were immediately cut short as every eye fell to her. There were at least twenty of them, a mixture of men, women, and children. They were all dead silent, and the two children who had been hand painting on the cave wall scurried away toward their parents near the fire.

Two men got up and started toward her aggressively, making the barking noises in their language. She suddenly felt very foolish at her attempt at making peace. She was just about to retreat before Harq entered with his hands raised. He grunted in his language, "Peace... Peace," and the two men stopped before reaching her. They barked and huffed again, waving their hands, gesturing for them to leave.

Harq took Sira by the shoulder, pulling her back when suddenly one of the older women toward the back of the cave grunted. The two angry men reluctantly backed up, and the older woman continued to argue with them until they retreated to their seats around the fire. The older woman walked forward and took Sira by the wrists, leading her close to where they sat. She took both the liver and heart, grunting something in her language and smiling. Then she gestured for Sira to take a spot around their fire.

As she sat, the Other women made space away from her in fear. The older woman turned back to Sira, speaking in her language. Sira could not understand.

"She accepts your peace offer," Harq said, doing his best to translate the ancient phrase.

Needa had also entered the cave, and she spoke with the older woman, bowing and putting their heads together in greeting.

"Who is she?" asked Sira.

Harq searched for the words. "She is the eldest of our tribe," he explained.

"Is she the leader?" she asked.

"No leader. Clan no have leader. She is eldest, she keeps our ways and keeps peace," Harq tried to explain, but it would have been difficult even if he had the sufficient vocabulary.

A younger woman rose to help the older one, and they cut the liver and heart into pieces, skewering it with cooking sticks to roast over the fire. They shared the meat around in equal parts and then sat silently while they ate, watching Sira with a mix of curiosity and fear.

"Is it always this quiet?" Sira whispered to Harq.

"Yes... um, no," he responded.

Finally, one man could not contain himself any longer and angry words burst from his mouth. "What does she want here? Why don't she go away, leave us alone!"

Harq argued back, while Sira again held her hands up in peace. She asked Harq to translate her words. "I came from a tribe out in the hills. A larger tribe attacked us. They killed many of us and stole many women and children from us," she said and waited for Harq's translation.

Some of them hushed and made wooing sounds, shaking their heads.

"I will leave soon, back to my people," she explained.

At this, one man stood up and barked his warning sounds again. "She will lead the wolf people to us! They will come to us again! Maybe it is her that made the fire mountain angry!" he yelled down to the others.

They all became agitated by this, and some women hissed angrily.

Harq translated for Sira.

"I am not like those people. Those wolf people, as you call them. We are peaceful. I only wish to return to my family. I will not speak of you or your home to anyone. Your valley will be safe, I promise you that," she pleaded to them.

The man responded, speaking down to the others, "She can lie! How do we know?"

"One of you saved my life." She patted Harq on the back. "I owe him a life debt. I could never do anything to harm him or his family," she explained.

This seemed to settle down the man, and Sira was grateful this was one thing their cultures had in common.

Harq spoke to his clan. "It is true what you say. The wolf people are dangerous. But there are good people among them. I have seen them. I wished to show you this, and I could not leave her to die. It is a bad omen!"

They murmured in agreement as Sira chewed on a piece of the heart. It was chewy and undercooked, but not wishing to be rude, she ate it nonetheless. One of the little girls, who Sira judged to be around two or three years old, approached her without fear. Her mother called out desperately for her to come back as if she were about to fall off a cliff. Sira winked at the girl, and the girl laughed. She reached up and grabbed one of Sira's black hair locks, squeezing it curiously. In return, Sira lifted two fingers' worth of the girl's stringy red hair. It felt like fiber as she twisted it between her fingers. The entire tribe of the Others watched intently as their two worlds collided. The girl, oblivious to the surreal moment, grabbed Sira's cheeks and nose as if testing to see if they were real. Sira squeezed the little girl's narrow nose, and she snorted with laughter.

The little girl's mother called for her again, this time with less apprehension.

The little girl turned to her mother and said, "She is ugly, Momma!"

This made some of them laugh. Sira had not understood the child's words and pressed Harq to translate. When he refused, it made the remark funnier, and the entire tribe joined in on the joke. Another woman chatted something to Sira, and again, she looked to Harq for a translation, but he shook his head uncomfortably. The woman didn't let up, and now a few more women joined in the chatter. Their amusement seemed to grow the more Harq looked uncomfortable.

"Well, what is it? What do they want to know?" Sira asked.

Harq sighed, defeated. "They want to know if we..." He lost the words and moved his hands uncomfortably. "If we... love together," he said, looking embarrassed.

"What?" Sira asked in surprise, shaking her head.

"I told them no, but they don't believe. They want to hear you," Harq said.

Sira looked up at the women, who were now giggling like silly children. "No, no way. I mean, No! We did not," Sira said, shaking her head. But the women kept up their chatter.

"They ask why. I tell them we are different. You would

only love another wolf people, not one of us," Harq explained.

Sira nodded in agreement, then thought of a counter. "What about you?" She pointed at all the women, saying "you" in their language. "You make love with Harq," she said, pointing to him.

"Sira!" Harq objected. This made the women squeal. Their faces were plastered with a look of disgust.

"They say I am too ugly to mate. I say they are more ugly."

Sira looked at some of the other brutes sitting around the fire and then looked back to Harq. There was clearly a big difference between them.

She leaned over to him and whispered, "I don't think you are ugly, Harq. I think you are handsome."

He looked up suspiciously at her.

"For an Other," she added.

* * *

Harq awoke Sira just before daylight. The fire was down to embers, so Sira could only make out Harq's silhouette in the dim cave. He stoked the fire and added more wood, and soon the cave lit with an orange glow. Black shadows danced and mixed with the firelight as Harq moved to gather the items he had prepared for travel the night before. He wrapped some cooked meat into a hide skin and tied two spears to his back. His flint knife was wrapped tight around his waist with some fibrous cord.

Needa aided Sira in dressing her in thick furs and was only satisfied when she could cover her entire body so that none of her skin was visible. Sira assumed they would travel through freezing temperatures, such as the tops of mountains, hence all the cover.

Needa offered her hands, and Sira took hold. Her cold, knobby fingers grasped Sira's tightly as she closed her eyes, whispering some words of encouragement in her language.

By the time they left the cave, the dull yellow glow of the sun was lighting up the valley. An adolescent boy was the only one outside the cave shelters, his furs wrapped around him tight. Sira guessed he was heading out on a solo hunting trip.

Seeing them, he approached Harq and held out his hands. Again, the boy closed his eyes and whispered the same words as Needa.

Harq roughly rubbed the top of his head and told the boy, "Good hunt."

The boy nodded and continued, smiling at Sira with that wide, elongated jaw she was now accustomed to.

"What is it they are saying?" she asked Harq.

"They wish us safe travel," responded Harq. "We go out of mountains, very dangerous."

"Why did you go outside the mountains, Harq?" Sira asked as they walked along briskly.

Harq pondered the question and inhaled, then exhaled deeply. She loved when he sighed like this. It was at least one very manlike trait in his otherwise stoic personality. After several moments she thought he would never answer, but then responded thoughtfully, "Harq want to see other people. Not just my people."

Sira thought about the way Harq's clan treated him like an outsider and the women who called him ugly last night. It was a puzzle she had not pieced together.

Then Harq said something unexpected. "Needa not my mother. Mother die when I young. Needa take me. Help me grow. Needa..." He paused to think of the words. "Needa Harq mother sister."

Sira asked an obvious question. "Where is Harq's father?"

At this, Harq frowned slightly, shaking his head as if he didn't know.

Sira thought for a moment. "Is Harq's father dead too?"

Harq shook his head, then looked at Sira with consternation. "Harq's father... is wolf people." He lowered his head as if this was a great shame. When Sira said nothing, he looked up to her with a mix of hope and relief, as if speaking about this long-held secret felt good to get off his chest.

Sira looked at him, shocked. Was it possible Harq's father was one of her kind, and his mother one of his? The idea of it seemed repulsive to her, unnatural, and she squinted her eyes and frowned, thinking about how it could have been possible.

He caught the look on her face, and his shoulders dropped in disappointment. Had he expected a different reaction? He turned to continue their journey. "Come, we go. Long way to go."

Sira immediately felt embarrassed for having reacted the way she did. They continued silently, and this new revelation was stuck in her mind the entire morning. When they stopped to eat, shearing off pieces of dried meat, she could not take her eyes from him. Her curiosity peaked.

Harq said nothing and ignored her stare. Many things now made sense to her. His looks for one thing. He was nowhere near as ugly as the rest of his kind. Although his body was stout and muscular, she now noticed it was somewhere between her kind and his, and Sira now saw him through fresh eyes. He mainly stood out because of his lighter skin, reddish hair, and thick beard. But these were superficial, and underneath, he was mostly a normal man.

The revelation also answered the question as to why the rest of his village treated him like such an outcast. He had no woman or children of his own, and he had passed the age he could take a mate long ago, even by their standards. She thought back to that day he had rescued her. The Red Feather men had been chasing her, not to mention the big tooth. It must have been a significant risk to him, and she suddenly wondered if his rescue had not been by accident. She wasn't blind to her female intuition, and although his ways were so much more subtle than her own kind, she couldn't help but notice the way he looked at her. In all honesty, she found his form of affection to be both indirect and profoundly deep at the same time. He was always there for her, protecting her and caring without ever asking for anything in return. There was something unconditional about his fondness, whereas men from her kind were forceful and impatient, Harq was entirely the opposite. He was a rock of stability. She almost laughed out loud at the thought. All her life she had wondered about these mysterious people. When she finally met one, it was out of fondness for her.

* * *

Their journey led them on a steep ascent as they left the valley back toward the mountains. By mid-day, they arrived at a junction between two high cliffs. The morning had been foggy and overcast, hiding the effects of the erupting volcano. Now that the fog had passed, Sira could see that much of what she had thought was low-lying clouds were smoke and ash. The mountain was spewing out a giant column, rising into the heavens and stretching out as far as the eye could see.

Sira's wonder at the scene was interrupted by Harq.

"Sira, cover," Harq whispered. She pulled the fur over herself, making sure none of her skin was visible.

"Come," Harq gestured as they cautiously approached the ravine. He untied the deer's leg and dropped it to the ground. He gave a barking sound, then waited.

The ice-cold mountain wind gave a slight howl sound as it passed through the two cliff sides. It was the only audible sound in the dead stillness. Sira felt grateful for the extra layer of fur, and she pulled it tight over her face. From a sliver of an opening covering her face, she caught a movement from the cliff as men were exiting the cave openings, looking down upon them from narrow cliff ledges. It was very similar to Harq's own cliff side home.

The men looked almost indistinguishable from one another. If it wasn't for the slight differences in hair colors, it would have been difficult to tell individuals apart.

One man pushed over a woven fiber ladder, then climbed down. It looked as if it were the only way to the ground, offering them a very protected and defensive position. The man approached slowly and stopped in front of the deer leg. He grunted a few times, and Harq responded with a grunt of his own. Then he pointed up at the smoke column, grunting angrily and stomping his foot against the ground.

Harq shook his head, grunting back at the man.

The man then smiled, turning instantly from a dangerous-looking adversary to a comical-looking friend. He picked up the deer leg, continuing to huff and grunt as he did so. Then he looked up at the other men on the ledge. They were nervously shaking and pointing their spears toward the gigantic column of smoke in the air. The man with the deer leg howled back up at the other men on the ledge, and Sira could catch both the words, "Harq" and "go." They shouted back down, pointing their spears down the ravine.

Harq took Sira by the arms and moved forward cautiously. Sira kept her face lowered so that their view from above would not allow them to see her face. It was then she realized that the covering of fur had been primarily to hide her from the Others as much as to keep warm. She was thankful for both reasons.

The howling and grunting of the Others continued as they walked between the two narrow ledges. It was an agreement of trust, as they were completely defenseless if the Others attacked them from above. But no attack came, and as they walked farther down, the ravine narrowed, and the ground descended until the men's voices were only echoes.

The trail eventually came to a dead end.

"Well, now what?" she asked.

She did not need a response, as she noticed Harq was removing a pile of large stones that were placed against the V shape of the cliff. The stones revealed the entrance to the cave passage. Once inside, Harq insisted they replace the stones to cover the entrance, and this took some work and finesse to get the stones aligned so that it completely covered back up the hole. There was very little light inside, and Sira now removed the fur from over her head.

"How are we going to see?" Sira asked.

"No see," Harq responded. "Follow," he added as he took Sira's hand in his own. Then he stepped forward and Sira had no other choice. Hand in hand, they stepped into the darkness.

Chapter 20

Tikara sat on the floor of her dwelling near the fire. The smoked fish that was to be her breakfast lay on a flat river stone, keeping warm by the fire. It was untouched. She was staring blankly into the dancing flames and had another bout of anxiety. When these came, it was as if she could feel her daughter next to her. The feeling was gut-wrenching, and a mix of sadness and guilt overtook her again as her head sunk and tears formed again in her eyes.

Raam had tried his best to console her, urging her to move on, to look to the future, to not give in to sadness. At first, she had truly tried to follow his advice. But as the days wore on and her sadness continued, she realized there must be something else mixed into her emotions.

A strange sensation nagged her, and it wasn't simply grief. The feeling grew every day, building upon itself and growing into a giant tangle of emotion. Now, as she stared into the fire, the tangle unraveled. A memory came back to her. A memory she had not thought about in many years, but now, for some reason, it had found its way back into her mind, almost as clear as the day it happened. She gasped!

Her trance was broken, and she stood up quickly, the stone tipping over into the fire and the fish sliding off into the ash of the fire pit. She paid it no mind as she ran full force to the entrance of the dwelling and out the door. She ran between the dwellings, yelling like a madwoman.

"Raam! Raam!" she yelled in excitement, bordering on panic.

People in the village stood by and stared as they watched her run.

"Raam!" she yelled again as she got to the end of the village, now completely out of breath.

Raam was within earshot now. He was with Pliny and Jin, and they were working on their final version of a working bow based on Pliny's description of the weapon. They were very excited to have it working and frustrated now to be interrupted, but the sound of Tikara's voice gave Raam great concern.

He rushed over to her, holding her by the arms as she caught her breath.

Tikara had been in such a rush to find her husband, she hadn't given much thought to how she was going to explain herself. She focused on catching her breath while she searched for a way to explain what she had felt.

Raam could see the mental turmoil of his long-time partner. "Come, sit here, Tikara. Take your time, tell me what is wrong," he said patiently.

They sat on the grass with their legs folded. Pliny and Jin's curiosity was too great, and they stood over Raam's shoulder. Raam gestured them away, but Tikara stopped him.

"No, it's good. It is good they are here. Let them hear me." She took one last deep breath, calmly describing her feelings. "Raam, do you remember the day Sira fell from the tree? When she was young?"

Raam looked up, thinking back. "When her foot became swollen? And she couldn't walk on it for a few days?"

"Yes! Yes! Oh, good, you remember," Tikara said. "Think back to how we found her. She was alone, remember?"

"Yes, yes, I remember, Tikara." Raam was slowly losing his patience.

"No, you don't remember, Raam!" she said in frustration, then steadied herself. "How did we know she was hurt and alone? I felt something, remember? I felt something was wrong. I came to you, and I said, 'We must go find Sira, something is wrong,'" Tikara said, now becoming more excited.

"Hmmm. Yes, that is true. I remember," said Raam, unsure where this story was heading.

"I feel that now, Raam!" She looked into her partner's eyes.

These past months, she had been adamant about Sira, and Raam had become weary of it. He had not wanted to keep being reminded of his beloved daughter. But right now, something touched his soul. Maybe it was the look in Tikara's eyes, but something nagged at him, and he realized all this time he had been feeling it as well, only he had chosen to ignore it. He shook his head in disbelief.

"But we went over this. Jin saw the tracks, the blood. It's not possible, is it?"

Tikara cut him off by grabbing his head and lifting it to meet his eyes. "I know you feel it, too. Don't ignore it! Sira is alive, can't you feel it?" she asked one last time.

Finally, for the first time, Raam was sure too, and he embraced Tikara as fresh tears poured from her face.

Raam sent Pliny and Jin to the dwelling of Laksha to summon Tonik. Since the day of the auroch hunt, he had been living with her permanently. He rarely saw or spoke to any of his old tribesmen. Raam should have felt happy for the young man. Partnering with the sister of the tribe leader was an excellent position for him, yet something about Laksha made Raam uneasy, particularly the stories he had heard about her shamanism.

When Tonik finally arrived with the twins, Raam's worries increased. He looked disheveled as if he was not getting good sleep, and the whites of his eyes were red and glassy.

"Yes? You wanted to see me?" Tonik asked Raam unemotionally.

"Yes, come, Tonik, sit down with us, eat, and let us talk. It has been many days since we have spoken." Raam gestured to the floor around the fire.

"I have no time to sit and eat, neither am I hungry," Tonik responded.

Raam immediately distinguished his word choice; it was in the style of the Samaki, not their own. "I see," responded Raam. "Very well, but I will sit, because I am getting old, and my knee is aching." He sat down near Tikara.

Pliny and Jin followed suit and squatted by the fire.

"Tonik, Tikara, and I feel strongly that Sira might be alive. I cannot explain, but it is something we can feel," Raam explained.

Tikara took his hand, giving him strength.

"And? Just because you feel it does not make it true,"

Tonik responded coldly.

Tikara sighed, but Raam steadied her.

"Yes, you are right, Tonik. We could be wrong. That is true. But it is also true that Jin could be wrong," Raam said, looking at Jin.

Jin took the cue. "I did not see her body. There was so much blood, and I saw the tracks of the big tooth. But I did not see any sign that the Red Feathers had taken her."

There was a pause as if they were waiting for Tonik to respond, but he remained quiet, his face showing signs of impatience.

Raam continued, "We believe we must go back and look for her. We must be sure. You were a great friend to her; we would like you to go with Pliny and Jin—"

Raam had not finished his sentence before Tonik burst into mad laughter.

"You think I am a fool?" Tonik asked.

"Fool? No, Tonik. I am asking because you were her friend, because she is our daughter, and—"

Tonik interrupted again, "Your daughter is dead, Raam!" he shouted down at him.

Tikara flinched and gasped at his tone. They had never heard Tonik speak this way to anyone, especially to Raam; it was unlike him.

"Dead!" Tonik shouted again, looking directly at Tikara. "Even if she lived, the Red Feathers have taken her, and what do you propose to do? Steal her back from them?"

Raam stood up, facing Tonik. "Jin saw Red Feather tracks, but none that showed they had taken her. Don't you think it is worth looking for her?" he asked, raising his voice.

"You are wasting your time! I won't join you. I have more important things to do now." Tonik's gaze looked distant.

"What is more important than our clan? Our family!" Raam yelled and grabbed him by the arm.

"My family is dead! Killed by the Red Feathers," Tonik said, jerking his arm from Raam's grasp. "The Samaki is my family now. You told me yourself, we must look toward tomorrow! Not the past! You said we must lead the Samaki against the Red Feathers. Well, here I am. Laksha and I can take control of this tribe Raam. We have a plan. Isn't this what you wanted?"

Tonik was now shouting angrily. His bloodshot eyes looked crazed and wild. He was uncharacteristically smiling, and it led Raam to an ominous feeling that Tonik was not quite acting himself.

Raam gripped him, peering closely into his eyes. "Not like this! Not like this, Tonik, I did not want to lose you as well!" he said, gripping the young man's shoulders hard, trying to get through to him.

Tonik pushed Raam to the ground. He fell over onto Tikara, and she yelled as his weight came down on her.

Jin was on his feet, his spear pointed to Tonik. "Tonik, stop!" he yelled at him.

Pliny helped Tikara and Raam sit up. They were unhurt, but the violent act had shocked them.

Tonik stood over them angrily, his aggressive stance showing he would react at the slightest provocation. Pliny picked up his spear as well, pointing it at Tonik defensively.

Tonik looked at them, then relaxed. He laughed at the twins, who took up arms against him. "Hmph. So, this is how it is then? Do what you wish, Raam, but leave me out of it. You were once our leader; you could see tomorrow in ways we couldn't. Maybe that time has passed," he said solemnly as he turned to walk out.

"And who will be the one to lead them, Tonik? You? How do you propose to take that away from Jessec? Or will Laksha do that for you as well?" asked Raam.

Tonik stopped at the entrance of the door, his back toward them.

Tikara pleaded with him. "She is Jessec's brother. You must not trust her, Tonik,"

Tonik made as if to turn but stopped himself. Then he shook his head in frustration and left the dwelling.

Pliny hugged Tikara, trying to comfort her. "Don't worry, Tikara. Jin and I will go alone."

"No, I will join you," Raam said.

Pliny looked at Jin warily.

"Raam, Pliny, and I will be faster on our own. Besides, the Samaki need you. The rest of our families need you here as well," Jin said.

Raam sighed, feeling another sharp pain in his knee as he plopped back down on the ground next to his wife. "Very well, Jin. You two will go. Find our daughter, but be careful. We don't wish to lose either of you," he said as he closed his eyes in contemplation.

***

The next morning, Pliny and Jin were shocked to find that it was snowing, even though the air was not cold. The snow itself was not white but gray. It was only when they touched it and held it to their nose that they realized it was not frozen water. Before they left on their journey, they found Raam outside his dwelling, studying the ash that was falling around them.

"What is it?" Pliny asked, holding out his hand and capturing it in his palm.

"Somewhere, there must be a great fire," Raam said, looking up. "But I have never heard of fire so great that it could cause this. You two must travel carefully. I have made more arrows for your bow."

They had come up with a separate name for the weapon and the little spears that it shot. "If you find Sira, bring her back safely to us. She might be the only one who can get through to Tonik. Laksha will see her as a threat, so we will have to prepare for that fact. Something is wrong with Tonik. I saw it in his eyes yesterday. It is the work of Laksha, I'm sure of that."

"Be careful here, Raam," Pliny said.

The twins sneaked out of the village and back toward the grassy hills. The ash obscured the view of the distant mountains, and the twins worried they would not be able to find their way and end up wandering the hills aimlessly.

After two days of travel, to their luck, the ash subsided, and the mountains once again came into view. They had done well to stay on course. The source of the ash cloud revealed itself, coming from behind the mountain ridge itself.

"That must be the biggest fire anyone has ever seen," remarked Pliny.

"It seems the mountain itself is on fire," added Jin.

They looked at each other again in nervous apprehension, but pressed on. The revelation only hurried their pace as they traveled faster than they ever had, pushing their stamina to the limit. They made it to the location of the river in half the time they did months ago when they had traveled with Tonik.

Pliny studied the giant maze of boulders and the steep slope of loose rock. "I don't get it, Jin. I can't see this picture. Where could she have gone? The only way she could have got out is if the Red Feathers took her back the way she came in," he said, pointing back to the slope of the mountain.

Jin shook his head. "I told you, they didn't take her back that way. I saw no sign of that."

"You didn't have time to see. They were chasing us. The only other way would be up that slope, but we know she didn't go up that because that is where the big tooth attacked her."

Jin's head shot up. "That's it!" he said and kissed Pliny on his head. He ran back over to the loose slope of rock. "That's it, Pliny. She went this way!"

"But how? There's no way she could crawl up that. You said she had lost too much blood," Pliny reminded him.

"Yes, there is no way she could have," Jin agreed.

"So?" Pliny asked, looking frustrated.

"Someone carried her out," Jin said.

"What? Who? Who could carry her up that?" Pliny looked up the slope in wonder.

"Someone very strong," said Jin. "Someone strong enough to scare away a big tooth, and then carry Sira up that slope,"

Pliny looked around again. "Over that slope just leads to the river. How could they have gone through both us and the Red Feathers without being seen?"

"Because they didn't go that way, they went up there," Jin said, pointing to the white tops of the mountains range. "And that's where we are going."

* * *

Travel up the slope was made easier because of a large swath of the brush that had been cleared. Even large trees had broken in half, and the twins could only guess what had caused such destruction.

Under every bit of shade, the last vestiges of winter snow still clung to the ground, holding out until the sun finally warmed the surroundings enough so that soon the mountainside would be covered in fresh grass.

The giant ash column was closer now. It rose high above them, then drifted out toward the horizon in the coast's direction. They continued to climb up, searching for some human signs. If people regularly traveled through here, there would inevitably be some tracks, or signs, even a well-used game trail. Pliny and Jin found none of these, and their frustration heightened when they reached a point where the mountain face transformed into a sheer vertical cliff, over a hundred feet high. They both agreed that no person could scale such a cliff. They doubled back, this time crisscrossing the slope, hoping to find a clue.

* * *

Sira had already tripped a few times over the rocky ground of the dark tunnel, but Harq's tight grip always saved her from falling to the ground. They came to one section, and she felt the air temperature drop, and there was a hollow sound in her ears, as if the chamber of the cave was now larger.

Harq stopped and pulled Sira closer to him. "Sira, stay close, hold on."

His voice had an immediate echo, confirming the cave had widened. They walked forward steadily, and Sira heard the air hiss around her. Every few steps, a fluttered movement flew over her head, becoming more frequent. The faint but unmistakable squeaking sound of bats echoed in the darkness. As soon as she understood what was flying around her, a creature landed on her head, its tiny claws digging into her hair.

She screamed, and with her free hand, struggled to knock the creature free. It had clung tightly to her frizzy locks, and in a panic, she struggled to grab it. Feeling the hairy little creature, the bat screeched as she threw it off in disgust. In the commotion, her weak leg stumbled on a loose rock and she stepped out to steady herself with her left foot, only there was no ground beneath it.

Her left leg fell into nothing, and her still weakened right leg gave way as she fell onto her knee. The momentum made her slide off into a hole. Harq still had her by the hand, and she screamed again, fighting to get her other hand up to him. Both legs were now dangling in the air, with nothing solid beneath them. She struggled to get her feet onto the rock side.

Harq lifted her with one hand as easily as a child and, wrapping his other hand around her waist, he placed her back onto the ledge beside him.

She caught her breath, keeping very close to him. "Why didn't you tell me? You could have warned me not to step that way!"

"I tell Sira, stay close."

When they continued, Sira placed her right hand on Harq's shoulder for good measure. They moved forward for many paces before the air suddenly changed again.

"We passed a big hole," Harq said, the echo no longer audible in his voice. He lifted Sira's hand and brought her to his side.

She felt the wall to her left and realized they were in a much smaller chamber again. Side by side they made their way forward, this time the ground sloping upward.

"We are close," Harq said.

Sira looked up, and sure enough, a slight point of light was now visible through the darkness. The point of light grew as they made their way up, and rays of light illuminated the ground, finally allowing for some visibility. Sira had to squint as they got close to the entrance.

"Hole to cave open. No snow?" Harq said to himself in surprise.

"Maybe winter ended early. That is good, right?"

"Hmm, too early. Wolf people can find the cave. They will come back here," he said, concerned.

They had to squint as they exited the cave entrance, the brightness of the day blinding them after having spent hours adjusted to the dark. Through the blinding light, Sira saw a figure appear at the entrance. Before she could cry out, it jumped onto Harq's back. Another man rushed forward at the same time with a spear, but Harq dodged it, catching the spear in one hand and easily wrenching it out of the attacker's hands. Harq grabbed the man by the throat and lifted him off his feet with one hand.

Sira rushed forward and tried to pull the man off Harq's back, but he had his arm wrapped around Harq's neck in a chokehold. Harq reached back with his free hand and pried the man off. Now he held both men in the air by their necks, choking them. They thrashed out with their legs, trying to kick at him, but Harq was unconcerned as their feet bounced off his chest.

Sira strained to see them, her eyes rapidly trying to adjust to the brightness. Then she heard a voice of surprise, and it was very familiar.

"Si... ra," he strained through the chokehold.

Sira squinted, and as her eyes adjusted to the light, the attacker's face came into focus. "Pliny?" she questioned.

"Yeeesss," he struggled out.

"Pliny! It's you!" She rushed forward, slapping Harq on his arms and shoulders. "Let them go, Harq. It's okay, they are from my tribe!"

Harq released both, and they fell to the floor in a heap, coughing and gagging as they caught their breath.

Sira rushed to the ground and embraced them both. "Pliny, Jin, you're alive! We all thought you were dead!"

"We thought you were dead too," Pliny said, holding Sira tightly.

"Sira," Jin said, backing up and away from Harq with a look of dread.

Pliny caught a better glimpse of the man they had attacked, and his jaw dropped as he gasped, "Whoa!"

Sira had been so happy to see the two she had forgotten about Harq. "Oh, I guess I need to explain," she said, standing up and placing her hand on Harq's shoulder to reassure them. "This is Harq. He is the one who saved me from the big tooth. Harq, this is Pliny, and this is Jin." She pointed to each of them. "They are from my clan. They are good people."

"Is he... is he a..." Pliny mumbled, still staring at Harq as if he was witnessing a ghost.

"Yes, he is," Sira responded, smiling. "Sort of," she added, and Harq raised an eyebrow at her.

The twins stood frozen, except for the rubbing of their sore necks.

"Is Tonik alive?" she asked.

Hearing the question snapped them out of their trance. "Yes! Yes, he is. They are at the Samaki village with Raam and Tikara," Pliny responded.

"Samaki village? I thought they were going to meet the Fishtooth?" Sira asked.

"Yes, it is the same. The Samaki is a fish creature that lives in the Great Sea. They believe it is their protector, and they build gigantic statues of it in the village. Fishtooth is what people from the outside call them," Pliny explained.

Sira sighed and dropped to her knees. Her months filled with the agony of not knowing what happened was released, and she sobbed. It was a mix of happiness and exhaustion, and Pliny immediately knelt to comfort her. Sira was the strongest woman Pliny ever knew, and it was the first time he had ever seen such emotion from her.

After a moment, she collected herself, then got back up to her feet. "Come, take me back to my family."

Before leaving the cave, Harq insisted they do their best to cover up the entrance. There weren't enough rocks in the area. In the end, they covered about half of the entrance before giving up.

Before turning to head back down, there was a rumbling sound, and again, the ground vibrated under their feet. It only lasted for a few seconds, but it was enough to make Pliny jump.

"What was that!" he yelled in fear as he steadied himself, looking up toward the mountain.

"Fire mountain," Harq said calmly.

"Must be some fire. Look at all the smoke it makes. I've never seen a fire so big." Jin said as he pointed up at the sky.

Harq shook his head at that. "No, not fire on mountain. Fire mountain."

They shook their heads in confusion, and Harq gave one of his distinctive sighs of frustration. Sira knew Harq simply didn't have the words to describe in their language, and she felt pity for him.

"Fire... in ground. Come out mountain. Make rocks go on fire," he said, pointing up at the ash cloud, trying to explain to men from another land who had never witnessed a volcanic eruption before. "Fire will burn, then stop. Mountain will close again. One day, fire mountain come again. Fire mountain angry when wolf people come!"

Sira thought better than to press the subject and thought about the volcano painting she saw in the cave in Harq's village. Her thoughts quickly returned to reuniting with her family, so she pressed them forward as they made their way down the mountain slope.

Sira kept them occupied with questions about the new Samaki tribe. She showed Pliny her scar where the big tooth had bitten her leg. It had healed over, but left a nasty mark. Her right leg was slightly skinnier than her left, but she explained it was getting stronger each day.

Pliny gave his best encouragement. "Your legs were too perfect before, much too beautiful for a warrior. It's an improvement," he decided, pointing at the scar. Then he looked back at Harq. "Are we to take him into the village as well?"

Sira shot back immediately, "Why not? He saved me! Our tribe has always taken in strangers who do not have a tribe of their own."

"It is not our tribe anymore, Sira," he said sombrely. "Things have changed. The Samaki tribe is different. They bicker and fight among themselves all the time. There is a young leader, Jessec, but he is not very good. He does not see tomorrow well enough to lead such a large tribe." Pliny thought about the next part of his story cautiously. "Raam had wanted Tonik to challenge him, then we could finally get the Samaki village ready for battle against the Red Feathers. It seems Tonik might do that after all."

"Well, that is good, right? What is this challenge, a duel? A hunt?" Sira asked.

"I do not know. But Tonik has partnered with Jessec's sister. She is a shaman and a healer, but Raam says he does not trust her. Before we left, he..." Pliny thought carefully. "He was not acting himself, and it seems he is more loyal to Laksha than to us now."

Sira was quiet for a few paces, thinking to herself. She felt a small pang of jealousy. But then again, could she blame him for wanting to get on with his life? "Mated with a shaman, it didn't take him long, I see," she said coldly.

"We all thought you were dead, Sira," Pliny said in comfort. "Except Tikara. She said she could feel you were alive. We thought she might just be dreaming, but she was right! She is why we came to look for you. I would like to think we are good trackers, but we got very lucky when you two came out of that cave. We figured that was the only way you could have gone, but Jin and I sat around all day trying to get the courage to go inside."

Sira looked back at Harq again, thinking about what they would do once they arrived at the village. There was no way Harq would trust her kind enough to enter a large village, and she had no way of knowing how the people would react to him. Deep down, she knew they would have to part ways, and her sadness at the thought surprised her. With so many dangers around, she felt safer with him by her side. But whether it was just that, she wasn't sure.

Jin interrupted her thoughts when he suddenly stopped and motioned for them to remain quiet. At first, they thought perhaps there was danger, and Jin took out the bow he had been wearing over his shoulder. He nocked an arrow into the bowstring and then pulled it back, aiming.

Sira had seen this weapon before, the day Kadam and the other men had fought and been killed by the Red Feather warriors. She tried to follow where the arrow went, but it was so fast she could hardly keep her eyes on it. It hit the ground with a soft thud, and Jin hit his hand against the side of his leg in frustration as the hare bounded away.

Behind him, they heard laughter coming from Harq. He walked forward and took the bow away from Jin without asking, inspecting it before handing it back to him, still chuckling.

"That was the Red Feather weapon I saw that day they attacked us, right?" she asked.

"Yes, we have been trying to make one of our own with Raam. This is the fifth one we have made. It works, but it's very hard to hit what you want," Pliny explained and closed one eye, pretending to aim.

"Well, if you see another hare, let's use the spear or bola. Unless we are going to eat grass tonight!" Sira joked with   him.

Chapter 21

At the Samaki village, the apprehension surrounding the ash fall increased as it continued to rain down. People spoke of a bad omen, a sign of some terrible disaster to come. Raam preyed on this, fomenting it into a sign that they must again prepare the village with defenses to be ready for an incoming attack.

This was in direct contrast to Jessec's message. He and Laksha said that the ashfall was a sign of favor to them. Laksha explained that because the dull gray ash was the same color as their guardian's skin, it must be a sign of protection. However, neither Laksha nor Jessec could calm the nerves of the Samaki men, who realized that the auroch herds had disappeared immediately after the arrival of the ash.

* * *

Jessec pulled hard on the crude wooden pole mast, leaning back as the raft chopped through the swell of the sea. A group of six rafts went out to the reef to spearfish early in the morning, and they had very little to show for it. While the newcomers were adept at hunting on the hilly plains, they were useless at fishing, and many of them couldn't swim very well. The ash fall seemed to have scared away the game from the hills, so the men of the Samaki tribe had to fully rely on their fishing abilities. But even the fish seemed to be scarce, and it wasn't long before the few fish they caught had attracted the reef sharks, effectively ending their day early.

As the men rowed the raft onto shore, Jessec jumped off and ordered the men to tie up the raft, and summoned the women to clean the fish. Frustration took over him, for he knew today's meager catch would be met by more complaints from the hungry people in the village.

Angrily, he strode directly to Laksha's dwelling. He pushed aside the hide covers to the door without announcing his presence. There, in the bed of furs, Laksha lay straddled on top of a man. Behind her was another man, and they were both thrusting into her. Sweat covered her body, and she groaned with pleasure, laughing and throwing her head back.

"I am glad you are enjoying yourself while we are out trying to find food," Jessec announced.

Laksha moaned with displeasure, her shoulders dropping in frustration at the interruption. She pushed back the man behind her and got off the man lying on his back. "You may go. Await outside and do not let anyone in," she commanded and waved the two men away.

"Yes, my shaman," they said in unison. Both men got up, revealing their nakedness. Their large muscular bodies gleamed with sweat, and they walked off the bed of furs, their large erections still showing. They walked around Jessec with no shame.

Laksha threw a fur over her shoulders and sat at the foot of her fur bed, composing herself after all the exertion. After both men tied their hide skirts around their waists, they left the dwelling to stand guard on either side of the entrance.

Jessec shook his head. "Is there any wish that these two will not do for you?"

"Oh, brother, don't be jealous. We have many enemies now, you know. We must keep our friends close."

"Every day, we will have more enemies. The people do not trust us anymore. There is no game to hunt, even the fish are few, and this ash continues to shit on us from the sky!" Jessec said irritably.

Laksha could see the frustration in her brother and sighed. "Come, sit." She gestured for him on the bed next to her.

"Where is Tonik?" he asked.

"He is out scouting in the hills; I don't think he will be back now. Anyway, my boys outside won't let him in," she assured him.

Jessec walked over and plopped down on the fur next to her. She opened her arms, and he rested his head on her plump breast. She gently stroked his head and shushed him as if he were a child.

"What will we do, sister?" he said with concern.

"We must get rid of those outsiders," she said in a calming voice. "They turn our people against us," she added with a twinge of aggravation.

"How will we do that? There are many, and they have mated with our people," Jessec asked.

"We won't need to get rid of all them, just those few who are trouble. After that, the rest will follow with us."

"What of Tonik? We must get rid of him, too. And that old man, Raam. He goes against everything we say."

"Don't worry about that. I will fix everything," she said reassuringly. Then she held his head up to hers. "After that auroch hunt, there are many who like Tonik. You must get him to challenge you for leadership, then he must die," she said, and her menacing tone gave even her brother the shivers.

"I cannot just kill him. The people would not accept that," Jessec countered.

"You will not kill him. I will arrange for that. But you must choose to challenge him the old way!" she said.

"The guardian's passage?" Jessec asked, his eyes widening.

"Yes. I will give you something to strengthen you, and I will give him one of my toxins. Once he goes out into the sea, he will not return." She smiled devilishly. "You will return with a fish, and you will tell of a vision of the guardian. There will be no one else to challenge us." She kissed him full on the mouth and placed his head back on her breast.

"He is strong, isn't he?" Jessec asked.

"Yes, men of the hills are strong, but see how easily he has bent to my magic? Don't worry, my brother, rest," she said. "Do you remember when Mother was alive? How she used to tend to you?"

Jessec shook his head, remembering his beloved Mother. Then she held up one of her plump breasts, placing it in his mouth. Instinctively, he suckled it, just as he had before his mother had become too sick to provide it anymore. To his surprise, milk squirted into his mouth, and he wondered how she could have done so with no child present. But then again, there were many mysteries about his shaman sister that he did not understand. His body relaxed as he took in the warm liquid.

* * *

Later in the day, Tonik and his hunting party arrived back into the village. Heads held low, and bodies covered in ash, they made for a sorry sight for the villagers who watched their return. They had found no game in the hills, and the relentless ash had covered all spoors. They had wandered through the dry hills, watching as it blanketed the grass in a dull grey.

Tonik bathed the ash from his body in the sea, then headed straight to Laksha's dwelling. Time away from her made him anxious, and after a full day, his head ached. Her potions always eased his pains and cleared his head, and she always obliged him for it when he asked. For Tonik, Laksha was more than a woman; she had become his purpose in life. Her endless depth of knowledge and powerful presence gave her an enchanting aura and a strong sexual presence. She never tired nor denied his sexual appetite, and she performed acts on him that Tonik had never dreamed of. He could not get enough of her, and his appetite for her grew more each day, until even an hour away from her seemed like an eternity. He needed her now more than ever.

Her two guards were not at the entrance, as they sometimes were, so he entered and found her at the foot of the fur bed. Her hair looked uncharacteristically disheveled, and she was crying. Tools of her craft and pieces of her charms lay on the floor, broken into pieces.

"Tonik!" she sobbed as he entered.

"Laksha! What is wrong?" He rushed to her side.

Laksha kept her head held low to the floor, sobbing and too upset to speak.

"Please, tell me, what is wrong? Who has broken these things?"

"Please, Tonik. He is my brother. I do not wish him harm, but, oh, the terrible things he said," she whimpered.

He stood up and clenched his fists in anger. "Jessec," he whispered in contempt. "I do not care if he is your brother. If he hurts you, I will kill him!" Tonik raged as he smashed his fists against his thighs. "Ah!" he winced as a shot of pain throbbed through his head.

"Oh, Tonik. My warrior. You are in pain. Here, wait," Laksha said in concern as she went over to the fire and removed the horn filled with her potion. She had been keeping it warm, awaiting his return. "Here, drink this. It will help," she said as he took it from her.

The familiar wave of euphoria came rushing back to Tonik, alleviating his headache, and giving him a renewal of strength.

She opened her fur and pushed her naked body against his. Her soft breasts and the hair between her legs rubbed against him, giving him goosebumps as the effect of the drug took hold. "You must be clever about this, Tonik. You cannot kill him. You must take his position!"

"How must I do that? He was the son of the leader. Many still follow and listen to him."

"You must challenge him! Challenge him in our ways! That is the only way the Samaki people will respect you."

Tonik held up his head, confidence building, then dropped it again, looking down at the dark green potion left inside the empty horn. "I cannot beat him at the Samaki challenge. I cannot swim like him."

"I will give him something so that he will fail!" Laksha responded.

Tonik thought about that but shook his head. "Even if I win? I know nothing of how to lead the Samaki people. I am a hunter of the hills, but I am not like Raam. I do not see tomorrow as he can," he said, sounding deflated.

At the mention of Raam's name, Laksha stepped back from Tonik in anger. "You are more a man than Raam!" she said so violently that it surprised him. Then her face softened again. "You do not need to see tomorrow; I will do that for you. I will be your guide, but the Samaki people will think it comes from you. A female shaman cannot be the leader of the Samaki. It is a bad omen; the people would never allow it. You will lead them in my place, and we can be together forever. If you do not, Jessec will never accept us."

She gently rubbed between his legs, stroking him. He lifted the horn and emptied its contents into his mouth with one last gulp. The politics of Tonik's old tribe had been much simpler, and he cared little for the power struggles of the Samaki. But to have Laksha with him forever was something he could risk his life for, something he would kill for.

"I want to give you a young one, Laksha," Tonik suddenly blurted out.

The sudden statement threw her off guard for a split second, and she paused. She knew very well that was impossible. The number of toxins she had ingested in her life to become a shaman had not only destroyed her insides, but made her immune to them. She smiled nonetheless and put her arms around him. "Yes, Tonik. I will give you many young ones. You must challenge Jessec first. I will make it so that once my poor brother enters the sea, he will never return." She rested her head upon his shoulders. He couldn't see her malicious smile.

***

The next morning, talk of the challenge went through the village like wildfire. Many had been predicting the showdown between these two rival men for some time. There was a growing rift between Raam's people and their supporters versus those loyal to Jessec. Many were relieved the challenge had come. It meant there would be no violence, no civil war. They would settle the matter in a cherished ancient custom that the people respected.

The memory of their prosperous village was a shattered remnant of what once was. Disease had worn them down, and no sooner had they recovered from it, than a new and more sinister threat had come down from the sky. Never had the people been so hopeful for change, and somehow, they believed that their very existence hinged on the outcome of this challenge. Whoever won would have the blessing of the guardian, whose wisdom would transcend through him and lead their village to a new era of prosperity.

The two men stood on the shore, the entire village behind them. Raam had to push his way through the throng of people; his bad knee had reduced his walk to a limp. Laksha was in front of her wooden Samaki statue, which had taken six men to carry down to the beach from her dwelling. She was on her knees, and in her hands, she held a long silverfish, chanting as she held it up toward the statue in tribute.

Both men were side by side, each holding a fishing spear and a length of fiber cord.

Raam finally made his way toward Tonik, whispering from behind him. "Tonik, what are you doing?"

Tonik turned his head halfway, whispering back, "What does it look like? I am ending this. I will have control of the Samaki village, and then we may lead them."

"Tonik, not this way! He is a fisherman, he has grown up in the sea, you cannot beat him!" Raam whispered, but Tonik ignored him. "Do you even know what awaits you in those waters? You are not prepared!" Raam whispered a little too loudly.

Jessec looked over, grimacing at the sight of Raam.

"I know what I am doing," Tonik said confidently as he looked at Laksha.

She took a bite from the raw fish, then chanted again. Finally, she turned and faced Jessec. She offered the fish, and he took a bite from it, chewing and swallowing. Then she went to Tonik and held it out to him. He took a bite. The pungent odor and taste made him gag, but he chewed and swallowed it.

She stood back in front of the statue and held her hands up to the sky. "People of Samaki village, today we are here to see which one of these men shall be blessed by the guardians!" Then Laksha addressed the two men. "You have until the sun reaches directly over the reef. If it passes and you are not back here, you fail. You must fish only from the reef, and you must bring the fish back to shore. You may not interfere with each other. Whoever brings back the largest fish brings the blessing of the Samaki and all the rights to the leadership of the Samaki people. The loser must abdicate his position and may never challenge the other until the end of their days. Turn to the Samaki people and accept that you wish to continue."

Jessec turned first. "I, Jessec, son of Kessec and rightful leader of the Samaki people, accept these terms and wish to continue!" he yelled to the crowd.

Most of the village roared with approval, and Jessec puffed at the sound, turning and smiling confidently at Tonik.

Laksha had helped prepare Tonik's words, making him practice and repeating them. "I am Tonik, a great hunter from the hills. My tribe came to the Samaki people when we were in need. We have found among you a new life, and I believe the guardian has sent me to you. He was with me when I hunted the great auroch. He will be with me when I enter the sea, and he will be with me when I exit. The guardian will greet me today in the sea, and I will receive his blessing on behalf of the Samaki people!" Confidence filled his words, so much so that the people couldn't help but believe it. The village cheered, and even those in favor of Jessec couldn't help but get caught up in the moment.

"Very well," said Laksha as she held up her hands to calm the crowd. "As shaman of the Samaki, I shall lay my blessing upon each of you." She picked up an auroch's horn that had been half-buried in the sand next to the statue. "The first, for my new partner, the hunter of the hills, and the challenger, Tonik." She handed him the auroch horn, and he sipped the bitter liquid.

"The next, for the son of Kessec, defender of the Samaki people and my brother, Jessec!" she chanted, handing him a different horn of the same size.

He gulped it, and Tonik studied the reaction, wondering if he could see any effect.

"It is known I love both men, so I shall drink from each horn and wish them good luck." She drank the remaining contents of each horn.

Suspicion immediately gripped Tonik and Jessec. Both

were promised that the other would be poisoned, so they wondered how it was Laksha could drink from both horns if that were so. They glanced over at each other questionably, trying to read for any signs.

The challenge began when Laksha turned toward the sea and lifted her hands. The entire village roared and cheered with excitement.

Tonik's bare feet dug into the sand and he hurled himself into the ice-cold sea. To his surprise, he had reached the water first, as Jessec had jogged to the water, conserving his energy for the swim.

When he was just a boy, Tonik had learned to swim in the rivers and streams that intertwined the hills where he grew up. Sira's insistence on learning and practicing was why he had learned in the first place. The fact that young Sira was the first in their group who could swim clear across the river only spurred the boys to conquer this feat themselves.

But as Tonik swam through the choppy sea, it was obvious that swimming in the slow-moving river was much different from the sea. The current was gently pulling him toward Jessec, and he had to fight to stay on course. Jessec's strokes were long and smooth, and his arms stroked over his head in a rhythmic pattern. Tonik felt stiff and clumsy in comparison. The cord of his spear was attached to his ankle, and it dragged behind him. It caused little resistance, as the Samaki had refined them to be hydrodynamic.

His arms and legs were burning by the time the rocks came into view. The tip of the reef disappeared and reappeared as the sea swell ebbed and flowed over it.

When Tonik finally reached rocks, he took several moments to catch his breath before lifting himself onto it. The reef under his feet was a grey-blue, with green plants swirling and bobbing with the current. Between the spaces and cracks within the rocks, he could see fish of various sizes and colors darting away as he came into view above them.

He looked to his right at Jessec, who was on the seaside of the reef's edge. He had already been on the hunt well before Tonik had arrived. Watching him, Tonik realized the best strategy was to spook the fish from out of the rocks, and then spear it once it was clear of the reef. It seemed easy enough, but the rocks were both slippery and sharp. He could just as easily lose balance and injure himself, which would probably end his chances.

Big fish were consistently breaking off from the rocks upon sight of him, but they presented themselves only for a second before disappearing into the deep blue. Frustratingly, the fish always appeared whenever Tonik was moving, which was precisely when he didn't have sufficient footing upon the rocks to throw the spear. When he found stable footing and stopped, so did the fish.

He looked over at Jessec again, but he saw no signs of frustration; he was patiently making his way along the reef, but at a certain point, he turned and walked back the same way he had started.

Tonik thought about this, but it didn't make sense. Once you scared the fish from the rocks, what was the point of going back? Curiously, he turned to look back at where he had started; the pieces of plants and algae he had previously kicked up had already settled. Several paces back, he saw the flash of a fish returning to its hiding spot in the reef.

Tonik smiled to himself. That spark of joy once the hunter learns its prey's weakness. Tonik realized he should have been memorizing the places on the rock that gave him secure footing, then he could move faster and be ready once a fish appeared.

He checked the spear tip. Instead of one point, it was splintered and separated into four smaller points, adding more surface area to the spear. It was not so much different from the spears the women and children in Tonik's tribe had used in the rivers, only of higher craftsmanship. He hefted the spear in his hand, testing its balance point.

Now, remembering his previous steps, he placed his foot on the rock just as a fish cleared the rock face. His fast-twitch arm muscles let loose the spear, and it hit the water, ending up directly where he had aimed. The fish, however, continued to swim away.

Realizing that he had completely missed, he pulled back the fiber cord to retrieve the spear, cursing to himself. In the many years since the last time he spearfished, he had forgotten one of its most crucial techniques. The light and water played a trick on the hunter's eyes, and one had to aim lower than the actual target to hit the mark.

Tonik continued to search, and every so often, he found a fish big enough to warrant a throw, but the fish was too fast, or his aim was off because of the refraction of the water. When he returned to the area where he had started, a large fish broke out from the rocks.

In his excitement, he let loose the spear without having solidly planted his feet. He lost his balance as his leg slipped into a crevasse. He felt a sharp pain in his calf and pulled it out to see a thin red line running down his calf muscle. Small lines of blood trickled out down his leg, mixing with the saltwater. It was a minor cut, but he still cursed his foolishness. It could have been much worse.

He grabbed the cord tied around his ankle, reeling back his spear. The cord jerked in his hand. He pulled on the cord again and felt the immediate weight of it. *I must have speared a fish!* He firmed his stance upon the rocks to reel it in. The cord pulled hard again, and he almost lost his balance as the fish tried to wriggle free. As it got close, he could see it was a big one.

As the fish got close to the surface, it caught sight of him and thrashed wildly. Before he had the chance to grab its tail, it broke free of the spear, swimming awkwardly back out to sea. But it was mortally injured. It only made it a few paces from the reef before it surfaced, belly up and thrashing.

Tonik dived headfirst into the water in pursuit. The current had pulled the fish farther away from the reef, and Tonik swam hard to catch it. Between breaths, he saw a gray fin surface above the water ahead of him. Something pulled his fish underwater, and he lost sight of it.

Tonik held his breath, then submerged. The visibility of the clear water was excellent, and even from this distance, he could see the big gray fish, at least three times the size of the fish he had speared. Its jagged teeth tore into his fish aggressively, circling as it chewed. The speed and size of the predator fish frightened Tonik. He had never seen a fish so large, and Tonik's instinct told him it was dangerous. It was entirely conceivable that it could attack him next.

He retreated to the safety of the reef. Upon hoisting himself back onto the rocks, he noticed another gray predator. It had circled around his exact exit point. The creature had been following him. The thought sent a shiver of fear through Tonik, which was exacerbated by the ice-cold water.

Tonik put the gray fish out of his mind and returned to his task, finding the rocks he had started from. He was facing Jessec now and watched as his spear arm went up high, then shot downward with a smooth throw. Jessec reeled in his spear until his catch was upon the rocks. Even from this distance, Tonik could tell he had speared a great fish.

Tonik looked up at the sky; the sun was rapidly rising to his spot on the reef, signaling the end of the hunt. He shook his head as he regained focus and felt another surge of energy from Laksha's potion. He thought about Laksha's promise about Jessec not returning from this challenge. It didn't seem like it inhibited Jessec, but he trusted her, and it gave him renewed strength to forget the cold water and cut on his leg.

A few moments later, his focus paid off. Just as he gained another stable foothold, another giant fish broke from the rocks. But this time, Tonik had been expecting it. He threw his spear, this time adjusting for the water refractions. It sliced into the water and speared the fish squarely in the middle of its body. As he reeled in his cord, he bent down as the fish got near the rocks. He did not allow it time to start its thrashing before grabbing its tail with both hands. It was so heavy he had to fall backward onto the rocks, fish in hand.

Once safely lodged in the reef, he stood up to assess the fish. It was hard to tell whether it was larger than Jessec's, but it was certainly bigger than any river fish he had ever seen. Brown and white, its mouth gaped open and closed and

Tonik thought he could probably fit his entire head inside. He got to work, breaking one of the spear's points, and attaching the cord to it. He threaded the cord through the mouth of the big fish and out the side of its head, finding an opening between its gills. He tied the other end of the cord around his ankle.

Remembering how exhausting it was to swim to the reef, he vowed to take his time on the way back. With the weight of the fish, the swim would be even more difficult. Jessec was already a quarter of the way back to shore, his fish in tow.

To Tonik's luck, his fish had bloated with air and was floating on the surface. The weight of it wouldn't be dragging him down. He had not gone but a few paces before he heard Jessec in the water. He was shouting something incoherent from his distance. As Tonik got closer, he found he was gaining rapidly on Jessec, who was now being dragged by the current toward Tonik's path. Tonik tried to pick up his pace. Whatever trick Jessec was playing, he did not want to meet the man in the water, where Jessec had an advantage.

"Help!" Jessec cried out. He was now thrashing and struggling to keep his head up.

The villagers on the shore could not hear him from this distance, and they looked on curiously as Jessec waved his hands in the air. Jessec was now only a few lengths out from Tonik and in a panicked state.

Tonik, still thinking it could be a trick, changed direction, heading against the current to swim around him. The moment Jessec heard Tonik in the water behind him, he turned, and Tonik could see the wild-eyed expression on his face. "Help!" he cried out. "Help! I can't move my legs!"

Tonik tried to swim away from the man, but Jessec was swimming with the current, while Tonik was swimming against it. Jessec was on a collision course with him. With no spear, he had no way of defending himself. He thought about the rules, of not interfering, but it would make no difference if Tonik was dead.

As Jessec swam up to him, gasping for breath, his arms

desperately grabbed at Tonik's shoulders for support. "You did this to me!" he yelled at him. "Laksha did this to me!" he yelled again.

Tonik could no longer support the weight of him, and they both submerged. Tonik kicked at Jessec, pushing him away. At that moment, looking down, he could see Jessec's legs. They were as straight and stiff as tree limbs. Although his arms and torso thrashed about, his legs never moved. Tonik realized it was not a trick. Laksha's promise was working.

Tonik punched and fought to free himself. But Jessec was fighting for his life and received Tonik's blows to the face without letting go. Jessec got his arms around Tonik's neck. Realizing it was useless to fight at the surface, Tonik inhaled a deep breath and submerged again with Jessec still holding onto him. Under the water, Tonik placed both feet upon Jessec, pushing to free his hold.

Without warning, the water turned red. Blood surrounded Tonik's vision as it billowed up through the water. Tonik searched out into the clear blue, trying to discover the source. A gray body appeared to his left. It flashed by, then came up from under them. Its mouth opened, revealing a line of teeth resembling spear tips. It bit down on Jessec's foot, above the ankle. The fish thrashed its head, and Jessec was pushed from side to side, still desperately holding onto Tonik. When the fish finally broke free, Jessec's foot had been ripped clean off.

Paralyzed, Jessec did not feel any pain, and maintained his grip on Tonik. More blood filled the water around the men, obscuring Tonik's vision of the surrounding sea. He did his best to keep his eyes on the fish as it circled behind, but he could not turn his head while Jessec still held him. If he didn't free himself soon, he would run out of breath.

Suddenly, the fish rammed hard against his backside, sending him up and out of Jessec's grip. Just before he reached the shimmering blue and white surface, Jessec grabbed his ankle. He looked down to see the man swirling in a mixture of crimson and azure. Tonik tried kicking at Jessec's head, but the man took the blows despite the pain.

His grip was one of desperate survival.

The gray fish circled back, but this time, it went straight to Jessec's torso, sinking its teeth into his side. He immediately released his grip, and Tonik fought his way to for the last few inches to the surface. He came up and exhaled hard, gasping for breath as the blood rushed back into his head.

Too terrified to look back, Tonik frantically swam toward shore. It was only once he was a few lengths ahead did he dare to look back. Jessec was now surrounded by a circling group of gray fish. They took turns at him, tearing him to bits. The terrified opened-mouth expression on his face was still present, although there was no life behind it.

Tonik swam on, hoping the man's body would satiate their appetite long enough to ignore him. His lungs burned, and he felt as if his legs were going to give up. But as he looked up, he could now make out Laksha on the shore. Her curvaceous body was clear even at this distance. She held her hands out to him as if pulling him toward her. Tonik realized she was all his now. Laksha, the Samaki village, it was all his, and again, he felt a surge of energy as made his way   to   shore.

Chapter 22

As the sun set over the water, the Samaki bonfire raged. The effect of the ashfall heightened the orange and yellow sky. The colors reflected off the water, creating a beautiful backdrop for the customary celebration that takes place after a challenge has been completed.

A new guardian spirit had arrived at the village, and he had manifested himself into a young man who they would now respect as their leader, with their shaman as his spiritual guide.

There was no sadness or mourning over the loss of Jessec. The people believed the man's spirit would return to the sea and into the body of a Samaki, who would continue to protect their village. The rituals and beliefs were not Tonik's own, and he cared little for them, but the sudden respect and admiration that had been bestowed upon him by the villagers was exhilarating.

Laksha had coached him into recounting how a vision of a Samaki had led him to safety, choosing to save him over Jessec. Although it was not true, he did not care. The effect had solidified his position as being truly blessed by their deity.

The villagers came one at a time to pay their respects. There was no congratulation from either Raam or Tikara, and they sat across the fire, silently watching with suspicion. This annoyed Tonik, fouling the great mood he had been enjoying. He had accomplished everything Raam had set out for them. Even so, his old leader did not give him the respect he thought he deserved. His former clan had never appreciated him as he was now. Even the woman he had once loved had not loved him back in the same way, at least not in the way Laksha did.

He took another gulp of the auroch horn Laksha had given him until the negative thoughts subsided. His vision blurred as the villagers and fire in front of him mixed into a trail of colors. Laksha sat behind him, watching the scene with satisfaction until a scout ran up and quietly whispered in her ear. Tonik was so caught up in the effects of the drink and distracted by the villagers dancing by the fire, he didn't notice when she slipped out with her two guards.

* * *

On the hills not far from the Samaki village, the fading twilight allowed Master and his trackers to crawl up onto a ridge within sight of the village. Master turned his head back and waved his hand in a motion to come forward, a fine cloud of gray ash lifting as he did so.

"Last Chance, look here, I need your eyes."

Last Chance held his hands over his eyes, blocking the orange and violet colors of the setting sun from his vision.

"There are many," Last Chance whispered to Master. "Many women, many men. They dance!"

"How many war parties will we need?" asked Master.

Last Chance took several moments looking again through his hands at the village. The dancing figures around the bonfire at the center of the village threw hundreds of shadows that flickered off the dwellings, and their voices sang through the night air.

Last Chance looked back at Master and reluctantly told him his opinion. "There is no chance to ambush them," he said, examining the surrounding hills. "They might have scouts posted outside the village, so a surprise attack will have little effect. They are many, and they will defend their homes. If we have enough warriors, we can surround the entire village. With the sea at their backs, they will have nowhere to run." With hesitation, he added. "We will need all the war parties, Master. We will need everyone."

Last Chance half expected to be slapped or insulted at the thought of sending all the war parties, but Master paused for a moment, looking down at the enormous village on the coast.

"For once, you are correct. We cannot surprise them, so we will attack in daylight. Just the sight of how many Gondo-Var warriors we have will create fear. It might even force them to surrender immediately."

Last Chance exhaled in relief as Master motioned his

group to back down from the ridge of the hill. They would waste no time in returning to Father to start the battle preparations. They did not want to alert the village lookouts to their presence, so they did not light any torches. Instead, they would make their way through the fading light, using Last Chance's excellent vision to backtrack their spoor.

Last Chance led the men around a corner of a steep hill when, from out of the dark, a torch exploded to life. Surprised, Last Chance staggered back, regrouping with his scouts, who raised their spears in defense. A short figure stood in front of them, wearing the fur of a bear. Part of the bear's jaws and teeth were still present in the hood, giving the figure a menacing appearance in the torchlight's shadow. Behind the figure stood two giant men on either side with spears and shields, but they were not a non-threatening, neutral stance.

The Gondo-Vars dropped low and were ready to attack, but Master stepped forward and held up his hand.

The one with the bear mask spoke, and it surprised the men to hear a woman's voice. "I know who you are, warriors of the red feather. And I know what you want."

Master smiled at this very unexpected visitation and sized up the individual speaking to him. She had appeared from nowhere, lighting a torch instantaneously. That, combined with her demeanor and style of dress, hinted to Master who he was dealing with. He stepped forward, a hair outside her guard's striking range. "If you know what I want, then I have a better question. What do you want... shaman?" Master asked, adapting his accent to match hers.

The figure paused before responding, "I want to give you what you want."

Master smiled again. "The entire village? Every stone of those beautiful dwellings?"

"Don't play with me, Warrior," she said brusquely. "You don't want the village. People like you can't sit still for more than a moon cycle. You only want the people in it."

"You see tomorrow well, shaman. Tell me why we shouldn't just kill you now and take all your people when we return," he said, taking yet another step closer.

There was no sign of emotion in the figure's voice as she responded. "Because I could burn us all right now, here in this field of ash."

She pointed her torch of flame to the side where Last Chance was standing and threw a handful of dust at him. The dust flew through the flame and the torch roared into a fireball. Last Chance and the others raised their arms, falling back at the sight.

"Witchcraft!" Last Chance whined as he backed away in fear.

Master had not flinched. He had watched as the flame lit up the face underneath the fur of the bear hood; her bright green eyes and beautiful face revealing itself for an instant.

Master raised his forearm to his mouth and gently blew off a tiny piece of spark that was smoldering on his skin. He showed no sign of pain. Unblinking, he responded drily. "Impressive, shaman, but your magic will not save you. You will have to do better than that."

"Then I tell you this, warrior, my people will die defending their village. I will give them something so that they will not feel fear. We will kill many of you before we die. You will not take us alive," she said.

Master paused as he thought about this outcome, then smiled. "Again, I am impressed, shaman. You have a gift to see tomorrow well." Master was genuinely intrigued now by the woman behind the bear mask. "What do you offer, then?"

"Half of the people, of my choosing. I will get them to surrender without a fight, and you will name me as their protector on your behalf," she offered.

It wasn't enough, and Master stepped toward her. He did not take his eyes off her, even as her guards dropped their shields and readied their spears. Holding his gaze, she held up her hand, calming the guards. "What else?" he said with a wicked smile.

"Our craftsmen are the best. We will provide your warriors with weapons," she offered.

He stepped forward one last time, and now the shadow of the hood could not hide her face from his stare. His initial glance had been correct; she was the most beautiful woman he had ever seen. Gently, with no sudden movement, he carefully pulled the hood over her head. Her long curly hair fell to her shoulders, and she held his gaze with her bright green eyes as cool as a snake.

Finally, she understood what he meant. Before her stood the leader of a great tribe of warriors. She had heard many stories and rumors surrounding them. The fact that he was an enemy meant nothing, his power excited her, and she could feel it radiating from him. The thought of being with such a man and then twisting him to fall under her control was a delicious temptation, and she licked her lips.

She moved forward and kissed him, slipping her tongue in his mouth and slithering it around like a serpent. She hardly felt any reaction from the cold man, but upon her touch, she felt him inhale slightly. Like an insect being caught on a spider's web, it was all the signal she needed to spry the trap, and she grabbed both his hands and slid them through the bear fur.

He grabbed each of her perfectly rounded cheeks of soft buttocks and squeezed them roughly, spreading them open. Her skin was as soft as a baby's, and she smelled of flowers. She exhaled in pleasure, faintly but purposefully as she bit down on his lip, just enough to cause a single drop of blood.

He didn't flinch at this, instead, pushing her closer. His manhood was so large the tip of it pressed against the top of her belly. At the feel of it, she exhaled again in pleasure, this time genuinely. She pushed her head back, looking into his eyes again. They were just as cool and calm as they had been a few moments ago.

"You may have as much of me as you want... if you accept my terms," she whispered seductively.

"Very well. I accept, shaman," he said, bowing his head as if giving respect to a worthy adversary, still clenching her soft cheeks in his hands. "When we arrive back in a few days, you will deliver half of the people of your village, a mix of men and women, without a fight, and we will name you as their leader on our behalf," he repeated.

Her expression changed, becoming softer and more

feminine as she smiled back at him. Placing a hand gently on his chest, she said in a hefty voice, "then let us seal the bargain." She handed the torch to one of her guards, then squirmed out of his grasp, lowering to her knees. Lifting his hide skirt, she grabbed him with both hands. She gripped him tight, moving her hands back and forth roughly. He grunted with pleasure and smiled down at her. Then she used her lips and tongue to massage him. This time, her magic impressed him. There, surrounded by the gray hills of ash, and under the torchlight held by her loyal guards, she pleasured him to a climax as the men watched on and applauded.

* * *

Tonik awoke in the morning, having not remembered returning to his dwelling. He did not even remember at what point he had left the celebration. His head was still whirring and spinning, and he felt Laksha's warm soft body against his. He looked over and noticed she was still asleep, a slight smile of happiness on her face as she breathed rhythmically. He did not remember her returning to the dwelling either.

He shook his head at the confusion of having lost his memory. With his head now clear, it felt strange that he had forgotten so much about last night's events. He got up and wrapped himself with his bear fur and headed outside.

The ash had not stopped its falling as the villagers had hoped it would from last night's celebration. He felt personally responsible in a way, almost believing the Samaki idea that his ascension as their new guardian would have put a stop to it.

He walked on without direction, heading somewhere to relieve his full bladder. His head throbbed once again, robbing him of his concentration and inner thoughts. While he walked, trying to focus and process all that had occurred over the previous day, he found himself standing outside of Raam's dwelling. He had no intention of visiting him but had somehow instinctively ended up here as if a force had guided him.

He thought about turning back, then sighed. He knew he would have to confront his old clan leader at some point. He would have to make peace. Raam would have already awakened, as the older man habitually rose at first light.

He walked over and knocked on the wooden poles between the stretched hides but there was no answer. "Raam, it is I, Tonik." He did not have any reasonable explanation for visiting so early. "I only wish to speak with you, Raam." Tonik did his best to place authority in his voice; he was the new leader of the tribe, after all.

The hide flap opened, and to Tonik's surprise, he found one of Laksha's bodyguards. He hadn't expected Tonik and stood at the door awkwardly. Tonik peeked inside. "Where is Raam?" he demanded.

The guard opened the door fully and inside he saw the second of Laksha's bodyguards. He was picking up Raam's belongings and furs from off the floor. The second guard looked around and shrugged his arms. "We do not know where they are. We came this morning to ask the old man for spears he had promised to make us, but they are not here."

Tonik looked suspiciously at them. "So, what are you doing with their things?"

The guard walked over to the door. "We only came looking for what was promised to us. We cannot find them anywhere in the village, so we came back here to look. If you find them, tell them we want our spears," the large man said as he walked out of the dwelling. Then the two-headed back toward the village center, looking back and whispering to each other.

Tonik immediately felt a sense of dread, but shook his head at the thought. After all, it was not uncommon for both Raam and Tikara to rise very early to gather plants, herbs, or rock flakes. It was likely they were foraging somewhere outside the village.

Still, he was angered by the idea of those two men going through Raam's belongings without permission, a punishable offense. His head throbbed again, so he put the issue out of his mind. He would have to remember to bring it up   later   with   Laksha.

Chapter 23

Kadam, Durok, and Poyop had traced back the steps in which he had been on the run from the Gondo-Var many moons ago. The rocky forest plateau was just as calm as it was the last time he was here, and Kadam stopped when he got to the area where he had first fought Master.

He picked around the area as Durok and Poyop allowed him a moment of reflection. Pinecones and cedar leaves littered the ground as Kadam kicked through them. Something white caught his eye in the dirt, and Kadam knelt and brushed the dirt and dried pine needles away from the object. He stood up and held a necklace with the teeth of various animals on it. It was Rooti's necklace. Kadam blew away the rest of the dirt and then tied it around his neck.

Durok and Poyop stood quietly, watching him. Durok motioned to say something, perhaps ask a question, but Poyop grabbed his arm, stopping him.

"This is where the vultures killed his tribesman and took him captive," whispered Poyop.

"How do you know this, Poyop?" asked Durok.

"I was here that day. I helped track them that day." Poyop held his head low, shaking it with regret.

Durok dropped his head with tragic memories.

"Will we stand here, crying like women, or are we tracking?" Kadam suddenly said to them, his facial expression changing from that of a crestfallen warrior to a determined hunter.

Poyop was the first to respond, returning to the business of tracking. "Your tribe mate and the dark-skinned woman, they were chased by vultures, down into the big rocks." Poyop pointed with his walking cane. "None of them returned," he said. "Let us see if Poyop can track where the wide foot has gone."

* * *

The three men looked up toward the great column of smoke that rose and stretched out to the horizon.

"Have you ever seen such a fire so great to cause that?" asked Durok ominously.

Kadam could only shrug in wonder at the sight.

Poyop ignored them, picking his way through the dirt. He was seeing and readings things that were only visible to him. He grumbled, becoming frustrated.

"Do the tracks stop?" Durok asked, looking down.

"Hid them, he did," remarked Poyop, laughing excitedly to himself. "He is a clever one, the one with the wide foot. See the smooth dirt here and there. But here, the dirt has been moved. Covered his tracks he did."

Kadam huffed, "So why do we care? Look ahead. There is nothing but white mountains. Unless they can fly, there is no way anyone can walk over that. Even if they did, there is no end to those mountains. They go on forever, and you will get lost and freeze to death."

Poyop had not been listening and was already ahead of them, jogging through up the steep slope.

"Curse this! We are wasting our time," Kadam blurted.

"I don't like the look of that smoke," Durok said, pointing up at the giant ash column. "Something bad is happening there. That is not the smoke from a normal fire. But let us follow this old man and see what it brings us."

Kadam was convinced they were heading to a dead-end into the vertical cliffs, so he did not attempt to catch the two men ahead of him. It is only when he heard the excited cheers of Poyop far up ahead did he give any interest. Durok soon reached the same spot and whistled down to Kadam, waving his hands for him to hurry. Kadam trudged on, and by the time he reached the two men, he was breathing heavily; the cold ground was starting to seep through his foot wraps.

"Look, Kadam!" Durok said with excitement.

Kadam looked at the small entrance of the cave, half-covered in stone, slightly obscuring the view of the entrance. "You two made me climb all this way for a cave?" Kadam said breathlessly.

"Poyop says this is the way they came from; it might go all the way through to the other side!" Durok exclaimed.

Kadam looked at the giant mountain ahead of them with obvious skepticism. "So, why don't the two of you go inside and find out?" Kadam asked sardonically.

"We need the black mud torches of the vultures! Then we can see our way through!" explained Poyop.

"You see, Kadam, we have not found one of the Others, but we have found their tracks. They are either living in this cave or it leads to where they are!" Durok exclaimed.

Kadam sighed and reluctantly peered into the cave. It descended endlessly into the dark, and there was a good amount of airflow blowing out from it, meaning it must be deep.

"Others are there. Poyop is sure!" the old man exclaimed.

"Well, we are not going in there with just the three of us, and as he says, we would need many torches to find our way through. There could be an ambush in there waiting for us, and what if those Others can see in the dark?" Durok wondered.

"Agreed. We will need reinforcements. That fat vulture Father may even want to come here; most likely he will send many men. Perhaps in these mountains is where we can make our move against them," Kadam said. "It is days of travel to get back. Come, let us get off this mountain and find something to hunt back in the forest before we starve to death. And my feet are cold."

Both men mumbled in agreement. Before they had reached the bottom of the mountain base, a deep rumbling sound erupted behind them. They all turned toward the column of smoke as it continued its slow rise into the sky. The rumbling slowly diminished until it was barely audible. The men looked at each other in concern but said nothing, eager to put a great distance between them and the smoking mountain.

Chapter 24

Sira and Harq were being led by Pliny and Jin, and they had made camp in a small forested area well outside the Samaki village. It sat hidden in a short valley of two hills. A freshwater stream ran through. As always, any reliable source of fresh water created an oasis of green in the hilly plains. Pliny and Jin had discovered the patch one morning during one of their scouting trips.

Their final days' journey had re-entered them into the ash fall, and their bodies were covered in the fine dust. Upon finding the stream, Sira and the twins immediately stripped for a bath.

When Harq did not join, Sira ran out of the stream naked and tried to pull him in. "You are going to bathe today; we cannot take your smell any longer!"

It took all three of them and a lot of pulling and cajoling to get Harq to strip off his hide and get in the water. Pliny gave Sira a handful of special leaves he had crushed and worked into a lather. The substance cleaned and softened one's hair and left it with a pleasant odor. She dropped them into Harq's hands, but he stared down at them blankly.

"Oh, come, don't your people ever bathe?" asked Sira.

"From the smell of him, I would say they don't!" exclaimed Pliny.

Harq gave the young man a stone-cold look, which was enough to make Pliny back away.

"Here, let me show you," Sira said, taking the leaves from him. "Turn around and put your head back."

Harq stood stiffly and looked warily at the leaves.

"Come on, it doesn't hurt," she said and grabbed his shoulders, turning him around. She worked the leaves into his coarse hair as the dirt and filth came free. He had a colony of lice, so Sira massaged the lather deep into his scalp until the little bugs went limp and washed away.

Harq's eyes rolled back into his head in euphoria. Although his people were known to bathe, they did so seldom, and it was usually a quick affair. Harq had rarely had the pleasure of a woman's touch at his former village.

The lather tingled his scalp, and the smell of the herbs was relaxing and pleasant.

Once she was finished, she abruptly dunked Harq's head underwater, and he came up in a gasp of surprise. She laughed and grabbed him again, pulling his hair back to rinse the lather from it. She was surprised to find his hair had straightened slightly, some locks coming apart under the effect of the plant. She turned him back around and worked the herbs into his beard now, washing away the dirt. With his hair wet and slicked back, he had a much softer appearance. Being uncomfortable in the water, he had revealed a more fragile side to himself, and Sira couldn't help but smile. Her eyes raised to his, and for a second, they caught his own. His gaze was always far flung, and even up close, they seemed to look out into the distance. For a moment, they caught her.

She was the first to break away, looking back down at the leaves in her hands. She held up the green jumble to him, gesturing for him to take them.

"Do the rest yourself!" she said, splashing some water at him playfully. She turned and found that Pliny and Jin had been watching so intently they forgot to react when she turned to face them. "What are you two staring at?" she chided.

They immediately broke free of their trance and mumbled and giggled in unison, "Nothing!" and continued bathing.

* * *

With their hair still drying, the four of them lay flat on the ridge of a hill outside the trees, scouting the village in the distance. They would have to carefully plan their next move.

Harq had no trouble with his own decision, preferring to stay back alone. He neither cared nor sought the company of their kind and understood very well the temperament of men. Most likely, the villagers would chase him away out of fear, or worse yet, resort to violence.

"My father will know what to do. He is a good man, and he can see tomorrow better than anyone I know. I will bring him here, and then we will decide what to do," Sira said to him.

Harq only nodded curtly. "No place for me there, Sira," he said, eyes fixed to the distance. "That village, so big," he said, stating the obvious.

"Yes, but that is good. We must have many so we can fight against the Red Feather people."

Harq shook his head. "Not enough. Many wolf people in that village, but Red Feather wolf people are more."

"At least together, we have a chance. We can fight them and send them back to where they came from," Sira said angrily.

Harq shook his head again. "Sira no understand. There is no end to the wolf people who come. We must keep going, look for better ground, away from them." He pointed north.

Sira sighed. "You might be right. But please, at least give me one day. Wait for me here. Let me go down and bring my father. Then we can discuss what we will do once I return."

She was not sure he would still be there once she got back, having completed his promise to bring her back to safety. As Sira and the twins started to leave, she turned suddenly and embraced him tightly. Her arms wrapped around his neck and she whispered, "Thank you."

His arms came up and embraced her as well, although awkwardly. "I wait for you here, Sira, one day only."

She smiled at him, then turned with the twins and headed for the village.

The falling ash worsened the closer they got to the village. The onshore breeze met the descending air from the mountains, pushing the ash down heavily onto the coast. It blocked the sun so effectively, daylight was reduced to a dull, grey glow. Under it, one could not even tell what time of day it was. Much like snow, it dampened sound, creating a silent, grim, and lifeless feel to the once vibrant hills. Every step they made kicked up a small fine cloud of ash.

Sira was eager to get to the coast and wash the foul substance from her skin, but the twins insisted on making a wide loop and entering the opposite end of the village. After the long journey she had been through, her weak leg was throbbing with exhaustion.

"Why are we entering this way? It seems as if we are going to sneak in."

The twins said very little, and when she inquired, Pliny only responded cryptically, "we are just being safe."

They headed directly for Raam's dwelling, which was one of the last structures at the far end of the village. Although several men took notice of Sira, huffing with approval as she walked by, most of the villagers were out and about in their daily routine and the three newcomers aroused very little attention.

They made haste to Raam's dwelling, and Sira could not hold back her emotions any longer; her eyes were already crying with joy, and her throat had become a hard lump. She wondered if she would have the strength to even speak as she burst through the hide door of the dwelling. But the emotion suddenly crashed as she stood face to face with two strangers.

It was an elderly couple, but not her mother and father. The man stood up in surprise and had a thick Samaki accent. "Yes, what is it, young lady?"

"Oh, I am sorry. I apologize, this must be the wrong dwelling," she said as she walked out.

Pliny and Jin had been waiting outside, allowing the family some privacy at their reunion. Their faces turned to confusion as she stepped back out.

"What is it? Are they not home?" Jin asked.

"No, it is not them! This is not their dwelling," she answered.

"That's impossible. This *is* his dwelling," Pliny said in confusion.

The female occupant stepped out and held Sira by her shoulders. She looked into Sira's eyes, investigating her face.

"Who are you? Where are Raam and Tikara?" Jin asked her.

"Are you Sira?" the lady asked.

Sira nodded her head with affirmation.

"You look like your father. You have his eyes," she said.

Sira smiled, but she could not keep the emotions from overflowing as tears rolled down her cheek. "Please tell me where he is."

"I am sorry, my child. Raam and Tikara disappeared several nights ago. They left all their belongings. We were told we should move into their dwelling yesterday, as they have been accused of abandoning the tribe."

"What? That cannot be right! Raam spoke nothing of this to us. And they were anxiously awaiting our return!" Pliny cried.

Sira slumped against the dwelling for fear she would collapse into a mix of exhaustion and crushed hope. Pliny and Jin took her by each of her arms, and the elderly woman ushered them inside to sit and rest. The elderly man abruptly left the dwelling. He only nodded his head briefly in greeting before heading out in a hurry. The woman helped Sira to sit by the fire, then prepared a hot drink by placing heated stones into a horn of liquid.

Pliny and Jin looked around the dwelling. Raam's stone tools and half-finished weapons were neatly hung about exactly as he had left them. With suspicions now on high alert, the twins sat warily, keeping their eyes on the entrance. But they accepted the hot refreshment with graciousness.

The older woman introduced herself as Zabee. She explained it had been a great surprise to everyone that her parents had abandoned the village. Not long after, Laksha had offered the couple this dwelling, as their own was old and damaged. They thought it strange to move into another one's dwelling so quickly, with all their belongings still present, but the couple was desperate to move, and so accepted.

"Laksha!" Pliny whispered angrily to himself.

"Wait, the same shaman that you said Tonik has partnered with?" Sira asked Pliny.

The old woman lifted her eyes at the name. "Oh, you have met our new village leader?"

The three of them looked at each other incredulously,

and Sira could see Pliny and Jin might know more than they were revealing.

Pliny asked the old woman to recount the story of what had happened while they were gone, and the woman told the story of the challenge, celebration, and ascension of their new guardian, Tonik.

Pliny was the first to speak. "Zabee, if you knew Raam, you know he is a good man. Please, I ask that you do not speak of our visit here today. We must hide. I do not trust the shaman."

"I am not going to sit here and hide! I want answers. I want to know what happened to my parents! I will find Tonik and wring it out of him!" Sira said loudly.

"Sira, please!" Pliny said. "You don't know Laksha. She's dangerous, and Tonik is not himself. He seems to follow her every move. Raam did not trust her either. I believe she might have something to do with your parents' disappearance. If she finds out who you are, I don't know what she could do to you."

"It is true, Sira. Let us go out and investigate first. We will try to speak to Tonik. We will tell him you are alive, but not here in the village. Let us see what his reaction is to this news," Jin added as he finished sipping the horn.

"Will you keep Sira safe here for a while? While she regains her strength?" Pliny asked the woman.

"Very well. She may stay here for as long as she needs," said Zabee.

"Jin, let's go. Tonik is still our friend. We must try to speak with him away from Laksha," Pliny said.

Sira tried to get up to protest, but she fell back down to the floor. Perhaps it was the exhaustion, but she suddenly felt weak.

"You are tired, Sira. Stay here. We will be back soon," promised Pliny.

The twins stepped out of the dwelling and were immediately surrounded by two large men armed with shields and spears at the ready. Laksha stood between them, and the elderly man who had left the dwelling when they arrived was behind her. His head hung low in shame.

Laksha turned back to look at him. "Thank you, Habab. You will be rewarded as promised."

He quickly went inside, evading eye contact with the twins as he passed.

"Welcome back to Samaki village, friends of Tonik. I have been waiting for your return," Laksha said with a smile.

"Let us pass. We would like to speak with Tonik," Pliny said.

"Tonik is out on the raft with the other men, fishing so that he may feed us," she said, emphasizing the word *men*, insinuating that they were less. "Unlike you two, who are sneaking around my village."

"And these two? Why are they not trying to feed the village?" asked Pliny, pointing at the two guards.

"You are a clever little one, aren't you?" she replied. "But you know what the problem is with you people from the hills? You are like wild animals. You will never learn how to live in a village like ours."

The hide of the dwelling opened, and Habab helped Sira outside. She had an arm around his neck, propping her up. She looked unstable, and her head rolled as if she were about to go unconscious.

"What have you done?" Jin barked at Laksha, but no sooner did the words come out when he lost control of his body. He became dizzy and stumbled into Pliny. Feeling the effects of the drug, Pliny could not hold him up, and they both fell to the ground, holding their stomachs in pain.

Laksha motioned to a guard, and he walked over to the twins, disarming their spears and bow. She motioned for the other guard, and he approached Sira, propping her head up to face Laksha. Laksha sized the woman up from head to toe, and upon seeing the scar on her right thigh, she smiled.

"So, you must be the long-lost love?" Laksha questioned as she gripped Sira's chin, holding it up to look her into her eyes. Sira strained to focus, but her vision of the woman was a blurry mess. "No wonder Tonik could not stop speaking about you. A fierce and beautiful warrior indeed!"

Laksha got closer, wrapping her arms around Sira's neck. She kissed her full on the lips, and Sira did not have the strength to fight back, only managing a frustrated groan as she felt the woman's tongue sliding against her lips. Then, cheek to cheek, she whispered in Sira's ear. "He doesn't speak about you anymore. He has forgotten you. I killed your parents as well, buried them alive after they drank my poison. Soon I will give you and all your friends to the Gondo-Var. The men will use you a hundred times a day until your body fails."

She kissed her cheek again, then stepped back. Sira should have lost consciousness by now, but her anger fought her eyes from closing, and her face scowled.

Laksha laughed, taking great pleasure in her suffering. Then she turned to one of her guards. "Take them to the dwelling we have prepared."

Those were the last words Sira heard before passing out.

* * *

The raft jerked and swayed as the two men on opposite sides tried to reel in a fish. Tonik lost his balance and fell into the sea with a splash. The other three men on the raft burst into laughter. Tonik's lack of balance was a constant entertainment to the fishermen, who had grown up their entire lives fishing from the log rafts.

Tonik burst his head through the water immediately, growling at the men who laughed at his expense. "Get me up quick! Before those gray beasts arrive!" he screamed.

This made the men laugh more as they gave him a hand and pulled him back onto the raft. Once they could see Tonik was truly angry and embarrassed, they tried to subdue their laughter, remembering Tonik was the new guardian of the village, and mocking him was a sign of disrespect.

Luckily, they had not lost the catch, and they struggled to drag the big fish onto the raft. From out of the deep blue, a grey and white flash appeared, and it bit down on the tail end of the fish, still only halfway out of the water. The men yelled as they steadied themselves, pulling back harder. They had caught no fish today, and they were not about to lose this one. The fish came free, and it flopped onto the wooden poles of the raft, the bottom of its tail bitten off.

Tonik watched as the blood mixed with seawater and falling ash, creating a milky red liquid that pooled between the tightly bound logs of the raft. One man came up and bashed the head of the fish with a club, abruptly ending its flopping. Tonik sighed as he thought about the entire days' worth of work for only one fish. There seemed to be an endless number of the gray predators circling, but very little else.

Feeling defeated, they rowed the raft away from the reef and back to shore using the flattened logs. The normal jovial banter from fishermen upon returning home was absent today.

Tonik arrived back at shore but could not tell the time of day. The sky was nothing but overcast. He felt exhausted and dehydrated, as he had finished both his water gourds halfway through the morning.

A young boy who helped beach the raft onto shore peppered him with questions, inquiring where all the fish and animals had gone. Tonik tried his best to console the boy, but inside, he could not shake his anxiety. Many of the villagers would turn to him for answers. His head ached as he headed up the pathway into the village. He knew he would feel better once reunited with Laksha. She would start a fire and prepare him one of her soothing drinks. They would make love after she rubbed his shoulder. She would give him back his strength.

* * *

Down the path from Laksha and Tonik's dwelling, out of earshot, another dwelling that had been reserved for the shaman was being guarded by two men. Inside lay Sira and the twins, bound with thick fibers. Coarse leather strips were tied around heads and their mouths were gagged with pieces of hide. The villagers knew better than to try to enter one of the shaman's dwellings, or even question it, even if they heard the muffled sounds that came within.

Chapter 25

A stout man knelt before Father, staring at the floor. The man's legs were covered in black soot from the knee down, and he wore only a small loincloth.

"Repeat!" Father called down angrily.

"It is finished, Father. The black sand is finished!" the man said, terrified.

Father beat his hands on the lion fur that lay across the rock face. He looked around as if the answer would come to him, but it didn't. "Dig deeper," he yelled at the man.

The man screeched at the command and gave a mumbled response, "Ye...yes, Father!" He ran out of the cave with haste.

Over the past week, the sea tide had steadily risen, encroaching its way farther and farther up into their camp. Last night during high tide, the cliff cave had filled with knee-deep water before subsiding at low tide. Father had ordered that the miners dig as much black sand as they could from the pit, knowing at some point they were going to have to move. It was of no real concern to him; they were a nomadic people after all. They could gather their entire belongings and leave at a day's notice. They created a new fortress every few years, once the mammoth became scarce, or there were no more people to capture in the area. Hunting and making war was their way. Without it, they lacked purpose.

The black tar used for adhesives and fires was so useful, Father would demand they dig up the rest of it before the sea swallowed it up. It, along with all their possessions, including the captured vultures and their eggs, would be transported to a new location. Of course, they never made a move without knowing where they were going first, and scouts had reported several locations that could suffice their needs.

The threshold for making a camp was surprisingly low, but they favored an area that could be fortified against attack, preferably against a large cliff, so that a new colony of their beloved birds could make nests.

One of Father's wives skipped forward to him, and he watched as her small breasts bounced up and down as she made her way to his rock throne. "Master is here, Father," she whispered.

He reached out and gently stroked her plump cheek, then smiled at her as he looked down at her breasts. She giggled at this and then squirmed away. He watched her small, tight bottom longingly. He could not wait until she had her first blood, signifying her womanhood and her readiness to mate.

Master strode into the overhang with several of his scouts and bowed beneath the large man. "Ah, my favorite son, you have returned with good news?"

"Yes, my Father, we have scouted the village on the coast. There was a grand celebration taking place. I believe whatever sickness that was there is gone now," Master explained.

Father was still looking over at his young wife waiting in the sun at the entrance to the overhang.

Master tried to regain his attention. "It is the largest village I have ever seen, Father, with a great number of women for us to bring to you."

One of Father's eyebrows finally raised at the sound of this. "Very well. How many warriors will you need?"

Master paused at this, preparing for a shocking response he was sure to come. "All of them, Father."

"All of them?" Father now turned his attention fully to Master, amused. "What do you mean, all of them? Who will hunt or stay back to protect our camp?"

Master looked around at the signs of the recent high tide, knowing well this camp was soon going to be flooded with the rising water. He needed all the warriors to make his plan of capturing Samaki village work, so he took a dare. "I believe it is there where we can make our new camp before the sea rises and swallows this one forever." He expected Father to be angered, but the big man had watched the sea rise every day and understood there was no better moment for a move.

"We have hunted many mammoths, and we have

captured many men. The time has come to move," Father announced. Then he stood and held up his hands. "Let us prepare for the fly away!" The overhang echoed his voice so that it spilled out into the open air.

A few tribesmen, including his young wife, heard the announcement.

"Fly away celebration! Fly away celebration!" the voices outside chanted.

Slowly, the chanting passed through the camp contagiously, until all movement and work had stopped. The chanting would start preparations for the move.

Father sat down and smiled. Their time in this place had ended, and the thought of moving and conquering new lands set his blood pumping with excitement. He looked over again to his young wife, who was dancing in the sun chanting, and his heart soared.

"And what of the Others? Tell me good news from the trackers," asked Father.

Master bit his lip as he thought about Kadam. He wasn't fully sure if the wild man would abandon them, even under the threat he had given before he left. "No news yet, Father, but we expect them back soon. They had to travel farther than us to the mountains, but I expect them back tomorrow. They will find us gone, but I expect it won't take long for them to catch us," said Master.

Even for that old fool, Poyop, Master thought to himself.

Father sighed and looked back at Master again. "All the warriors, you say? Must be a worthy enemy. We have not faced a tribe like this in a long time." Father smiled nostalgically. "Before you leave to ready the Gondo-Var for battle, tell me more about this place." Father gestured Master to come closer.

Master would be forced to embellish his view of the village and knew Father might be disappointed once they arrived, but that worry would be days from now.

* * *

At first light, the Gondo-Var tribe was already on the march out from their fortress. Master looked back at the thousands of rocks that had made the wall, thinking of all the wasted hours of labor and manpower it had taken to complete it. It would now be abandoned, and the process of fortification would begin again once they arrived at their new home.

Hundreds of captives carried the entirety of the Gondo-Var warriors' belongings with them as they left. Weapons, furs, tusks, wooden poles for shelters, and many hides were wrapped and carried on their backs or dragged in wooden travois in any way possible. The warriors set a brutal pace, but the people of this tribe had incredible stamina and could travel all day before tiring.

* * *

It was well after midday when Kadam returned with Durok and Poyop. The three men had arrived at the empty fortress, and Poyop saw signs of the fly away celebration, so they made haste to catch up to the march. The three men had been harassed by the ravenous wolf pack that had been following a distance behind the tribe. The wolves yelped and snapped at them, circling around but luckily never attacking.

When they finally reached the rear end of the marching tribe, Kadam relayed his message to the first young scout he could find. The young scout rightly guessed it was very important news, so he dodged through the column of people like a cat to reach Father's litter. He skipped the normal chain of command of reporting through Master, wanting to deliver the good news himself.

Not long after, Master heard the blow of antler horns, and the entire tribe came to a stop. Hundreds of men, women, and children who had been in a steady rhythm of movement came to a complete and very disciplined stop. By the sound of the horns, Master knew something important had taken place, and he ran back through the line of warriors, knocking several over, desperately trying to reach Father and offer his council before the old man made some drastic decision. Master wanted nothing ruining his plan to take Samaki village and have his second chance with Laksha.

He finally made his way to Father's litter, which had been placed on the ground. To Master's dismay, he found Kadam and the other two men already there, and he cursed himself for having moved so far to the front. He noticed Father was smiling with pleasure.

"What is it, Kadam, what do you report?" Master shot his words like spears.

Father lifted his hand and answered the question for him. "They have found a passage into the mountains. They believe it is where the Others are hiding!"

"How do you know this? Did you see any of them?" Master asked accusingly, still thinking he could discredit this discovery.

Father shot Master a glance, annoyed by the question. "He has found one of their tracks, and they lead to a cave that might lead through to the other side of the mountain," Father said, repeating the discovery more to himself than to the benefit of his subordinate. "We are to split up the force at once. Sound the horns to regroup! I will take half of the Gondo-Var to find my long-lost sons in the mountains, and Master will take the Samaki village!"

Master approached Father closer and knelt before him. "Father, please."

"Yes, my son? What is troubling you?"

"The Samaki, they are many," Master said, trying to remain calm. "We need all the warriors to take the village! I beg of you, let us conquer the village first. Then we may send a party of scouts to confirm this... this cave passage story," he pleaded, holding his hands up in reason.

Father held up his hands, signifying for everyone to listen.

"My sons and daughters! Are we not the warriors of Gondo-Var, the sons of eagles?" he yelled out.

The crowd of people hummed and whooped in agreement.

"Do men not fall by our Gondo-Var warriors?" he yelled.

"Eagle fly! Men fall!" they chanted.

"This man here, my favorite son, believes that half of our forces are not strong enough to take down one village of simple fishermen!" Father exclaimed.

A chorus of gruffs and mumbles of disapproval was directed toward Master.

"Do you agree with him?" Father yelled.

An even louder chorus of disapproval swept through the warriors, and they scowled and hissed at Master, this being a rare time they could do this and live to get away with it.

Master kept his head down and continued to kneel, but his fists were clenched in anger and embarrassment. The logic of his battle strategy was sound, but he had made a fatal mistake in suggesting that the Gondo-Var warriors were less than capable of anything.

"Will you fly with the Eagles, my son, or fall like a man?" Father asked him.

Master clenched his teeth but slowly stood up, bowing to Father. "I will fly like an eagle, my Father," he said, with just enough irritation in his voice to pass.

Father announced triumphantly, "go then, and conquer the Samaki tribe, for no amount of men, can stand in the way of us!" Then he gave a hand signal.

The men near Father blew a tune into the hollow longhorns. There were no words needed, the rhythmic sound of the horns was all the signal the Gondo-Var warriors needed, and they split the war parties into two groups. The men performed this with military precision, each knowing what group they belonged to.

The entire tribe began to chant again, "Eagle fly, men fall!" as they lifted Father and the wooden litter off the ground. Father motioned for Kadam and Durok to join his group. Poyop would join Master. That way, Poyop could guide Master's war parties to the hidden cave entrance after raiding the Samaki village.

PART III – Into the Fire

Chapter 26

Master's force arrived in the hills outside the Samaki village six days after splitting from the rest of the tribe. The journey had taken double the time as when Master had journeyed there the first time. The hills were a sea of grey ash, devoid of any life, and his men had almost starved on the journey. They had relied on their dried meat rations, but when that ran out, they were forced to dig up varmints from out of the ground. The warriors spoke of bad omens and were on the verge of mutiny. It was only through Master's promises of the bounty that lay ahead that he was able to keep them from turning against each other.

It was morning when a Samaki scout had spotted the Gondo-Var force. The entire village was roused by the lookout's emergency call, and they answered by hooting and yelling into each other's dwellings, gathering their weapons in response.

For many of them, it was the first time they had ever had to respond to such a call, as their village had never been raided in their lifetimes.

Tonik prepared his spear and shield as he walked out of the dwelling. Laksha was already outside, and he looked to her for reassurance. She said nothing, but her calmness was steady, and that eased his tension. They joined the men and headed outside the village facing the hills, forming a defensive line where the lookout was still hooting his emergency call. All the Samaki men bore shields and spears. The crude wooden shield, despite making spear-throwing awkward, had proven itself to be invaluable in battle.

As Tonik and Laksha joined the middle of the line of Samaki men, she turned and summoned Zabee. She arrived with other women, all carrying bowls made from the tops of hollowed skulls. Over the last hill behind the village, the men could see the ash and dust cloud that was kicked up by the oncoming force.

"What is coming, Shaman? Is it the invaders that Raam warned us about?" one man asked Laksha.

"Do not fear. The Samaki spirit will protect us. Here,

take two small sips of this. It will give you the strength to fight, and you will not feel pain," she said as she passed the skull. The man smiled and sipped, then passed it to the man next to him. Zabee and the other women handed Laksha's skulls to the men, and they all sipped, one by one, and then passed it to the next man in line. As the rumor spread, it became more exaggerated. *Our shaman has made us a potion to make us invincible!* They chanted, and they felt a surge of confidence to face the upcoming threat that appeared on the top of the hill.

***

As Master topped the last hill before the village, it was no surprise they found the Samaki amassed outside in defense. The women and children were hidden away in the dwellings. With Master having only half of the Gondo-Var war parties, the frightening effect he had been hoping to achieve came up short.

The Samaki men were too many to count, but with his keen eye for battle, Master reckoned that the odds were slightly against him. What was worse, they were attacking men who were fighting to protect their homes, while his men were on the verge of starvation. He did not even have enough men to surround the village, leaving a good chance for his quarry to either escape or flank him. This was not the battle he had planned. He preferred making surprise attacks that caused panic and fear. The purpose of these endeavors was to capture people, killing them defeated the purpose.

He cursed as he remembered the promise Laksha had given him. There was no sign this village was going to surrender, and he now faced a bloody battle in which many men would be injured or killed. He tried to improve his mood by fantasizing about all the horrible yet pleasurable things he would do to Laksha if they were victorious. Then he put these thoughts out of his head to concentrate. He looked down the lines of his men, waiting for them to position into the well-practiced attack formation.

Some of the Samaki men watched as their enemy

gathered on the hill. Many hoped they would retreat once they realized how many they were. The remnants of Raam's tribe had no such illusions, and their fear of the men who stood before them was not unnoticed by the others. Any attempt at a retreat or negotiation was shattered once they heard the war drums.

Young boys had run out in front of the Gondo-Var's line; it took two boys to carry each drum and another to beat it with rounded sticks. The loud rhythmic playing began, and it instantly created a threatening sound as the percussion bounced its way down the side of the hill and into the village.

In response, the Samaki men of the village cheered and yelled, rousing themselves, creating a threatening sound equal to that of the drums.

Master raised his hand, and a few dozen men now came forward to the front of the line. They held bows in their hands and bunches of arrows in the other. They did not use hide quivers to hold the arrows during battle, instead; they held them in a bunch with their free hand for quick access. He allowed the drums to play for several moments longer, and once he was satisfied that the defenders would not make the first move, he signaled the archers forward. The archers descended the hill until they were halfway and then stopped. They stretched the length of the defensive line of Samaki warriors, although they were spread out widely.

The Samaki men noticed the bow weapon, as they had watched Raam and the twins attempt to create their own. New technology was something that traveled like wildfire among people, but Raam had never perfected the weapon. To the Samaki, it was never more than a small game hunting gimmick. They could not have anticipated its effectiveness in the hands of a skilled and practiced archer.

Master raised another hand, and his warriors started to hoot and howl down at the Samaki defenders, showing their backsides and taunting them. The effect served its purpose, angering the Samaki men. They did not have any practiced discipline of warfare, as there had never been the need for it.

As soon as one man began to charge up the hill, the rest

of them followed. The archers, however, were dead calm as they held their ground and nocked their first arrows. Once the charging men were in range, they let loose at will. The Samaki warriors had never faced such an accurate long-range weapon, and many did not bother to lift their wooden shields for protection as the arrows rained down. The men looked incredulous as their brothers fell next to them and, realizing the threat, raised their shields over their heads as they continued forward. The archers were able to let loose two more volleys of arrows, and at closer range, they did more damage.

This did little to thin the numbers of the Samaki warriors charging up the hill, and soon the archers had to retreat. The Samaki men were incensed by this maneuver; they had never faced an enemy that had an actual strategy in battle. They figured their enemy was scared, and the chase spurred them on harder and gave them more confidence.

The Samaki warriors had passed halfway up the hill when the first of them fell. The men were so focused on the charge; they did not notice that something was going horribly wrong with their fellow men. More and more of them slowed to a walk, stumbling dizzily or falling over for no apparent reason. It only took several more moments before most of the Samaki men were either struggling to move forward or lay upon the ground completely incapacitated. They had not yet made it three-quarters to the top of the hill before every single one of them was no longer on their feet.

Master looked down in fascination at the curious spectacle. He could see no obvious cause as to why his enemy had fallen, but many of them were behaving as if they were intoxicated. Master wondered if it was a ruse. Some men were rolling on the ground groaning or vomiting, desperately trying to get back up, only to stumble back onto the ground. A sliver of fear caught him, and he looked at his men to see if any of them showed the same signs, but they all stood firm, watching with morbid curiosity as their enemy fell before them.

Master waited until the last of the Samaki warriors had

fallen before turning to give his men instructions. They were to proceed with caution and bind all the warriors' hands and feet. They were to only attack if they encountered resistance. Any man caught harming the Samaki men would be executed.

Master could see the dismay and disappointment in his men. They were bloodthirsty warriors who had marched for days, psyching themselves up for battle, only to be denied the opportunity for a fight. Even Master himself felt a bit of pity that he would not be given the chance to bash a man's skull, but the day was young. Perhaps the opportunity would present itself later.

Tonik looked up at the horror that had occurred on the hill, then looked to Laksha for an answer, but she gave him none. She had held Tonik back during the charge, and he stood together with her guards as the rest of the men had charged forward.

"Did you do this?" Tonik asked her, his face stricken with horror at the scene.

"Tonik, I know you will not understand, but you do not see tomorrow. The only chance our village has is to make peace. They will take some of our people, yes, but then we can start again. We will no longer need to live in fear of these people," she said, rubbing his cheek.

Tonik was not convinced. His enemy, the same ones who had killed his parents and brought so much death and destruction to his tribe, stood before him now, and he would never have the chance at vengeance. He growled in anger. "You cannot stop them from coming! Maybe they will go away today, but tomorrow they will be back. They will keep coming until we are finished! And we will be weaker when they return!"

Laksha removed her hand from his face, then gave him a sharp look. "I will take care of them." She looked back up the hill in nervous anticipation toward Master, who was now making his way down the hill.

It took a great deal of effort to bind all the Samaki men and carry them back into the center of the village. They were thrown together in a pile, some of them still groaning and vomiting up their stomach contents as their bodies attempted to purge the poison they had been given.

The work of carrying all the men had robbed more of the enthusiasm from the Gondo-Var warriors as they surveyed the Samaki village. The normal anarchy of looting and raping that normally followed a battle was forbidden by Master. This caused serious discontentment. They had conquered another tribe, and by their custom, it was their right to take whatever women and valuables they could find. Instead, they were ordered to create an enormous bonfire and gather all the food.

As the bonfire grew, the Gondo-Var warriors became more and more disgruntled, until many disobeyed Master's orders. They entered the dwellings, looking for women to take as spoils of war. The morale plummeted further when they found that the Samaki village did not have enough food to feed everyone. As the sun went down, there would be no dance around the fire to celebrate their victory, and Master had to extinguish a few squabbles between his warriors.

Tonik had been hiding in Laksha's dwelling, which Master ensured would be protected in honor of her loyalty. Laksha had given Tonik a drink to calm his nerves. His hate and anger had been burning too strongly, and she knew he would do something foolish if she did not sedate him. With an extra dose, he drifted into a dream-like state. She left him on the pile of furs and set out to confront Master, her body already excited with the expectation.

* * *

"This was you're doing, wasn't it, Shaman?" Master asked Laksha, pointing to the Samaki men who were now slowly awakening from the effects of the drug.

"Remember, half of them, as promised," she responded. "And I will choose who goes and who stays. I do not remember your men having their way with our women or stealing all our food as part of the bargain," she said irritably.

Her words bit at him, as he was aware that many of his

men had ignored his order. But his men were quite literally on the verge of mutiny, and he understood their frustration of being denied their spoils. He did not allow his emotions to show through and remained calm and firm as he faced Laksha.

"Shaman, I do not understand. This village is Gondo-Var now. You are Gondo-Var. But you have delivered as promised, and for that, you will be rewarded. Our deal remains." He inhaled and looked around at the village, and Laksha thought she caught a look of disappointment in the man. "I will tell you the truth. I had no intention of honoring our deal. Father is at this moment on a search for a new home for us. And I had hoped it would be here." Laksha was ready to protest, but he interrupted her. "But now I see, this grey shit that rains down upon you is slowly strangling the land. In the morning, we will take our captives, and we will leave you here to waste away in this ash."

Laksha ignored his warnings and smiled. "Very well, I accept. I also offer you a special gift, as part of our bargain," she said, taking him by the hand. Laksha led Master down the path through the village, passing her dwelling and stopping at another nearby. It was under her guards' watch, and she waved the guards aside as they stepped in. On the soft ground laying bound and gagged were two young men and a woman. The dwelling smelled of urine.

"Do you recognize any of them?" she asked, but Master could not. "How about her?" Laksha said, pointing to Sira, who was mumbling angrily through her gag. "She led a few of your warriors down by a river, where she not only escaped them but a big tooth as well."

Master smiled, remembering his first encounter with Kadam. "Hmmm, I remember now. How did you know about this?"

She ignored the question and kicked Sira in the back, causing her to roar in anger behind the fibrous gag.

"Maybe she would make for a fine play wife for Father," Master said.

Sira scooted her way over to Laksha, trying to kick her, but Laksha stepped back, shaking her head.

"These hill people are too wild, too difficult to tame. We have come across many of them since we entered this land," Master explained, looking down at them. "She will never accept her place. Probably bite the old man's snake clean off if she had the chance. No, we will put her to work with the others. These pitiful creatures are the gift?" Master looked at Laksha in disappointment.

"Gift? Oh, no. I want you to take them and make them work until they die a suffering death." She smiled as if the idea was something wonderful.

"We have plenty of suffering to offer," Master promised.

"Now, I will present my gift," Laksha said, looking at him seductively. "But not here. It smells like the piss of these animals." She turned and took Master by the hand, leading him out of the dwelling.

As the Gondo-Var warriors sat around the great bonfire, they consumed all the reserves of smoked fish until there was nothing left. Laksha was with Master in a dwelling her guards had prepared for them. It would take hours before he was finished with her. For the first time, Laksha had met someone who could satiate her lust.

Meanwhile, Tonik lay upon his furs. He had partially awoken from the effect of the drug and was drowning in a mix of emotions. His anger and guilt tugged him into a dark place, but the euphoric effects of the drug prevented him from manifesting his emotions into any action or coherent state of mind. Instead, he lay in a fetal position, grabbing the furs and sobbing.

"They will be gone tomorrow. Tomorrow everything will be as it was. Laksha and I will lead the village, and it will be like nothing ever happened," he whispered before falling back asleep.

* * *

As the sun rose, Master roused his men early. There was no food left, and with nothing to hunt, he decided not to waste any more time. Father would be waiting for him. After the embarrassment he had suffered in the hills, he was eager to get back. The great number of captive Samaki would surely solidify Master as the top war leader once again in Father's eyes. It irked Master that he still vied for the man's attention, and he no longer held it to the same level of esteem.

The Samaki warriors had recovered from the effects of the drug, and they were furious at the invasion of their village. They had no notion of what a captive was, as they had never experienced this phenomenon. They could not understand what awaited them, and they still had not figured out that they had been betrayed by their shaman.

Master allowed the women of the village to give the captives water. While it seemed an act of sympathy, it was a strategy. He used this ploy to discover which women belonged to which man. He did not want those women as captives, as enemy men and women partnered together were always more troublesome. Instead, he left the women of the captured men and rounded up the women of the men who would be left behind. Separated from their families, it would more effectively break their spirits.

Cries of anguish filled the entire village, and Laksha looked over at them coldly. The idea of forcing an entire group of people into subjugated control had never crossed her mind. It was so devious and evil, but even as she watched it happening to her own, she marveled at how brilliant it was. Without dissension among individuals, a leader could command the people any way they chose. There was no limit to the things one could accomplish if one could so fully command others. Laksha had once again underestimated the enemy that lay before her, and she found herself envious of the power they controlled.

The Gondo-Var warriors organized themselves into a column to begin their march. The captives were bound with fiber ropes around their necks and hands and then tied to each other. Master performed one last feat that would solidify the future of Laksha as leader of the Samaki village. He summoned everyone to address them.

"You no longer belong to Samaki village!" he yelled at

them using their colloquial accent. "You belong to our Father! If any of you think that you could escape, or wish revenge, just remember, we hold powerful magic over you! Do you see what happened when you tried to attack us? We made you fall on the hill; we can do this again. Your shaman's magic couldn't save you, and it will not now. This village belongs to us now! In our place, we will allow the shaman, Laksha, to lead. Let no man challenge this! If so, we will return for the rest of you!"

A hushed silence fell over the Samaki. They had no other evidence to challenge this idea, and the thought that their shaman could have betrayed them was out of the question.

Laksha listened and again was impressed by Master's manipulation. The captives would fear Master and the magic that he held over them, magic that turned healthy men into unconscious and helpless worms.

As the marching column of Gondo-Var began to move, Laksha had her guards bring Sira and the twins to Master, making sure Tonik was still in his dwelling. They were added to the long line of bound men and women.

Laksha approached Sira, who was no longer gagged. "Have a pleasant journey, Warrior. I will make sure Tonik is well taken care of, as I'm sure Master will make sure you are well taken care of." She smiled viciously and laughed.

Sira did not want to give the woman any more pleasure by reacting and instead held a cold, hard stare. "I promise you, I will be back, and I will kill you myself." She wanted to continue to stare her down, to show she was not afraid, but the line was marching forward, and her neck and hands were pulled forward by the rope.

Master stopped to speak with Laksha one last time. "This place is wasting away, Shaman. Come, join us. Join our tribe. You would be loved. Our people could use your magic." Secretly, the real reason was that he did not wish to part with her beauty. He even thought about capturing her for himself. But if he did that, he knew her appeal and mystique would be gone, and that was part of her allure.

"What would I be there? Your woman?" she asked.

"There I would be just another shaman. Here, I am the leader!" she said, her eyes shining with the new thought.

"Very well, keep a place for me. I will return one day, with or without my war party," he said.

"I will be waiting, Warrior," she smiled back and bowed.

Chapter 27

Harq was not surprised when Sira did not return the next day. She had been reunited with her people and her family. What further use did she have of him? He was not one of her kind. She could never love him. He felt embarrassed and foolish to think anything otherwise. Yet an inner voice echoed from somewhere deep inside, anchoring him, urging him to stay.

Whatever it was, he had not left the next morning but lingered instead, fraught with indecision. He witnessed the arrival of the wolf people and knew the village was in great danger. With a feeling of helplessness, he watched the attack on the Samaki village from afar. Part of him ached with grief at the destruction and loss of life, but this feeling was overwritten with cold detachment. He had to remind himself that these were their ways. It was like trying to stop a bird from singing, or a lion from hunting.

Wolf people, as his aunt had warned him against. It gave credit to everything the woman had taught him growing up. Men were the enemy, and the only safe option was to stay out of their way. Reason told him this was true; he had witnessed it with his own eyes. But there was another side to Harq, one his aunt never spoke about. It was the side inextricably drawn to people, especially the opposite sex. No amount of reason could extinguish it, and his need only deepened with time.

Growing up in the mountains, Harq and his people had often come across glacier walls of dark ice. In a certain light, the ice created a perfect mirror. Children of Harq's village loved making funny faces into it, and even adults found it both amusing and profound to glimpse one's self. It was nothing more than a gimmick, something that garnered a few brief moments of entertainment. But young Harq would stare at himself for long periods. He knew he differed from everyone else, but it was an easy fact to forget. He could keep his differences hidden away, forgotten. But there was no hiding from his reflection. The ice exposed his slightly darker skin tone, his short flat nose, his smaller jawline. It displayed his odd traits back to him, as if in ridicule. Soon he stopped looking at his reflection, believing the ice was lying, perhaps playing cruel tricks on him. Only when he was older did his aunt tell him the truth, that the reflection in the ice had been right all along.

He squatted near the inlet of the stream, a place where the water settled, reflecting like glass the canopy of green foliage above it. Cupping his hands in the icy stream, he brought water to his mouth. Before he got up, he noticed the image of his face coalescing as the water stilled. He touched his reddish-brown beard, then rubbed his hands through his curly long hair. The reflection squinted back at him as he narrowed his wide eyebrows. He had always counted himself among one of his people, no matter what the reflection told. Looking at it now, he realized he wasn't so different from the wolf people. Who was this man looking back at him? Was it the image on the water? Or something else, something inside that the reflection couldn't show. Perhaps it was both, and neither of those things. He slapped the pool with his hand in frustration. The water rippled, breaking the image of his face. He stood up and made his way to the top of the hill, looking out at the Samaki village.

His time with Sira had quenched a loneliness that he never knew existed. Emptiness replaced that now, a void that he could feel in the pit of this stomach. His isolation was more obvious than it had ever been in his life.

The man inside Harq roiled, urging to be set free. It told him to rush down into that village and see her again. It told him to be reckless. If she was in trouble, he had to save her, even if it meant his own life.

He inhaled deeply, quieting the man inside. Drawing upon the inner strength and calm that he had inherited from his mother's people, Harq sat, watched, and waited patiently.

* * *

On their way to the mountain range, Master and the Gondo-Var found themselves blocked by a vast marsh. The melting snows had gorged the river, flooding its banks.

Cursing his luck, Master trudged forward with his column of captives, losing another two days' worth of travel before Poyop could find a solid path through the ever-expanding water level. On the third day, they finally had entered the foothills of the mountains and the beginning of the forest.

The Gondo-Var scouts spread out in all directions away from the traveling column, making certain there were no dangers in their path. Compared to Harq, the Gondo-Var scouts were like noisy, clumsy brutes. Tracking them while remaining unseen required little effort.

As he looked into the pitiful people bound together, he could not stop the surge of hatred storming in his gut. He had heard stories of wolf people capturing each other before, but he still could not believe it, even seeing it unfold with his own eyes. What purpose did this serve? The enigmatic cruelty bothered Harq until he became furious. If he could rescue Sira, he resolved to travel very far away from this land, to find some place where the wolf people did not exist. He shook his head to rid himself of these thoughts and focused on scanning the column of marching captives, searching for Sira's dark athletic profile.

At the very end of the column and to Harq's relief, he glimpsed her unmistakable shoulder-length hair locks. She looked thinner and weaker than before they had left the mountains, but she kept her head held high. Her eyes were searching out in the distance, scanning the trees and cracks of the rocky terrain. Harq wondered for a moment if she was searching for him. He wished he could signal to her, but it was impossible to do so without alerting the entire force of men.

* * *

Harq waited until dark before sneaking closer to the captive group. The warriors and captives were now bunched together, forming a great circle. Brimming with overconfidence, they put little effort into guarding or posting lookouts. They had camped right in the middle of a heavily forested area that offered cover for Harq to approach.

It was obvious they had no fear of being attacked. No one could challenge such a force, and any predator would have steered clear of such a mass of humanity. Harq would use this to his advantage.

Before the light had faded completely, Harq kept his eyes on Sira, remembering her exact location. Perhaps because of her intuition, Sira had forced the man she was tied together with toward the outside of the circle. When they finally laid down on the hard ground to rest for the night, the edge of the forest lay a stone's throw away.

Harq waited patiently from his hiding spot behind a dark green holly bush, counting the number of lookouts who passed every so often. The light of the crescent moon shifted in and out from the shifting movements of the scattered clouds.

As the temperature cooled, a thick fog formed, reducing visibility to a few paces. A lookout appeared from out of the haze; he walked around the captives and opened his mouth wide. For one terrifying moment, Harq expected the shout of an alarm. It turned out to be a lazy yawn. Harq waited until the lookout had disappeared into the thick of the fog, then crept out from the hollies. Placing each foot strategically, he stalked forward like a cat. After the exhaustive pace the Gondo-Vars had set over the past few days, the only sounds were a chorus of snores that echoed in the misty night. His obsidian flint knife was ready in his hand as he stepped over a captive man and woman. Although Harq had the nerves of a lion, he had never been around so many men before in his life. His heartbeat thumped so hard he wondered if it would wake someone up. The palm that held the flint knife was clammy with sweat.

A twig snapped to his right. He dropped to a squatting position and strained to look out through the dark fog. A figure was making his way directly to his position—a scout! He quickly dropped to his stomach as the young man walked forward. If Harq was spotted, the young man would shriek his alarm. In seconds, the entire force would be aroused. If that happened, there would be no time to save Sira, and they would henceforth raise their defenses.

He pressed his face against the dirt, trying to remain low. The man's footsteps got closer until, finally, the young man's silhouette stood against the moonlit sky. He stopped, investigated the ground, then bent down and picked something up from another young man who was fast asleep. It was the man's knife, and he held it in his hand, swishing it through the air. He made a faint mumble of satisfaction, then took out his inferior flint knife and placed it near the sleeping man in an unsolicited trade. He turned and walked back in the direction he had come. Somehow, in the brown dirt, he had not seen Harq's figure.

As Harq was about to rise, the young boy facing him suddenly awoke. His eyes eased open to a sleepy squint, then shot wide as he noticed Harq's face. Harq froze stiffly, staring back at the boy, knowing in seconds there would be the scream of fear. Unexpectedly, and with a look of bewilderment, the boy closed his eyes again and rested his head back down. It took several moments before the boy's mind caught up with him, and he opened his eyes again, gasping in fear. His fear subsided once he looked around and found the hairy man had disappeared. He turned his head back down onto his fur and sighed in relief, hoping the scary-looking man would not appear in his dreams again.

Harq almost stumbled as he made haste away from the startled young man. When he reached Sira, he gently placed his hand on her arm. This was not enough to wake her, so he shook her gently. She awoke from her exhausted sleep with a gasp, and Harq was afraid the noise would wake up those around her, but there were so many snores in the night air that no one noticed. Her eyes widened with surprise, then happiness, and she smiled with relief. If she was expecting a smile back, he didn't oblige. He was characteristically stoic. In response to her smile, he simply showed her the knife. With immediate understanding, she turned on her belly to expose her bound hands. Harq placed the knife between them. Although the plant fiber ropes were extremely strong at weight-bearing, the razor-sharp obsidian cut through easily. Next was the rope wrapped around her neck. It was so tight; he could not get the knife between it and her skin without cutting her. He opted to cut the cord between her and the man she was bound to. It would be enough to escape. As he cut through it, the release of tension in the rope jerked the man's neck slightly, and he mumbled and turned as if he were about to wake up.

In a fit of exhaustion, the man rolled onto his back, shifting his position in the dirt before resuming his snoring. Together, they turned and tiptoed their way back toward the trees. Once they were well behind cover, they embraced.

"Where are the other two?" Harq asked, referring to Pliny and Jin.

Sira tried clearing her voice. It still sounded dry and cracked. "I do not know. I have not seen them since we left. They split us up... They could be anywhere. Do you think you can find them?"

"No, I only watch for you. You lay down near trees. I no watch other two. Almost get caught coming to you," Harq explained.

"We can't leave them!" she pleaded.

Harq sighed—he knew she would say that. "We follow, we wait. We see where they go. Come. Find water."

Sira walked behind Harq as he led her deeper into the forest. She was starving, and her initial burst of adrenaline from the rescue was drained. Laksha's guards had fed her very little, and she had just endured a grueling three-day march. She stumbled and felt the welling up of tears and a great lump formed in her throat.

"Harq..." she whimpered.

Before her legs gave out, Harq turned and caught her in his arms. Weighing lighter than usual, he could almost sense her weakened spirit. He held her in his arms as gently as a child. Sira wrapped her arms around his neck, resting her head on his chest. He held her close to him while navigating over fallen trees and ducking below low-hanging branches. He did not have the verbal ability to soothe her, and he would not know what to say even if he did. As he became a ghost in the forest, he clenched her tighter than ever. No words could have soothed her. Instead, she reciprocated his hold, her arms squeezing around his wide shoulders. His hold on her felt as steady as the ground itself. It felt like no force on earth could tear her away, and it was exactly what she needed.

* * *

In the morning, already well past the first light, the warriors had to kick and prod the captives with the butts of their spears to get them to rise. Even the warriors themselves were getting up later and later, their energy becoming sapped throughout their journey. One woman was too exhausted to stand, even when they beat her.

Finally, several of the warriors cut her loose from the bonds and a scuffle broke out as the warriors argued, pushing and shoving each other. Master came down to investigate the squabble and the men immediately went quiet.

Master chose two of them, and the duo laughed happily, sneering at their peers who were not chosen. The two men dragged the woman off into the line of trees. The captives could hear her feeble cries for some time before they finally went silent. Before Master headed back to the front of the column, a scout called out behind him.

"Master! Master!" he said excitedly. Master turned to look, and in the young man's hands were strips of fiber rope. "Someone has broken his bonds and escaped!" he exclaimed.

Master stormed back down to the column to investigate. He pointed his spear underneath the chin of the man who had been tied up to the missing person, pushing the spear so hard the flint point drew a drop of blood. "Who was tied up with you?"

The man looked nervously at Master. "I... I did not know her name!"

Master pushed harder on the spear, causing it to cut deeper as the man cried in pain. "Who!" he yelled louder.

"I... do not know her. She is not from our village! Please! I was asleep. She was gone when I awoke!" cried the man.

Master lowered the spear and looked up and down the line of captives for the dark-skinned girl Laksha had given him. He found both Pliny and Jin still bound, but she was gone.

"The dark warrior girl, she escapes again," he whispered out loud. "Let me see those ropes," he called over to the lookout. He held them up close, feeling the fiber ends with his fingers. "These have not been broken. They have been cut. Cut by something very sharp," he marveled as he looked at the ends of the fibers. Then he looked back down at the young scout. Master had no patience, and with the blunt end of his spear, he knocked the man on top of his head enough to gain his attention.

"So? Tell me where the tracks lead. How many trackers have we sent?" Master asked impatiently.

The boy looked around as if he was now beyond his element until, finally, another older tracker came to his rescue. "Master, we could only follow the tracks into the forest. From there..." The man gulped hard, waiting for a terrible reaction he knew would come.

"The tracks disappear?" Master asked.

The tracker looked surprised. "Yes, Master. It is as if they flew away like a bird!"

"Yes, it is the second time she has done this. Impressive, don't you think?"

The tracker did not know the answer, but nodded in agreement.

"I think a little too impressive," Master said as he looked again at the distant ridgeline of the mountains. "Someone or something is helping this girl, and I would like to find out what it is."

"Should we send scouts farther down in their direction?" asked the tracker.

"I have tried that before; it did not work out very well for them. I won't waste any more time and effort on that girl now. I need to get Father's new children back before we all starve to death!" *The more time I am away from Father, the more time those wretched other war party leaders will whisper into his ear and gaining his favor.* Master raised his hand, signaling the drums and the start of the day's march.

* * *

When Sira awoke to a bright morning, the sun was already three hand-lengths above the horizon. She had slept late. Harq was squatting by a small fire, roasting a squirrel. She almost didn't recognize him. He had pulled and tied his long stringy hair back with a small cord of fiber, imitating the way men of her kind did. His face was free of hair, and under his chin, there were tiny red spots, the result of him having shaved his beard with the obsidian knife. He was clean, and Sira could no longer smell his body odor. She even caught the slight scent of the herbs she had used to wash him several days ago, and she realized he must have bathed himself.

She wished to study him longer, so she remained quiet. She heard running water and glanced over to see a small creek nearby. Parts of the leafy herbs lay in a used pile by a rock. She smiled at the thought that perhaps he had done this for her benefit. Whatever the reason, with his hair pulled back, and his face clean and shaven, Sira suddenly thought that he was rather handsome. She could no longer hold her surprise and accidentally let out a giggle of laughter.

The laugh took him by surprise, and he stood up, staring at her awkwardly. He could not tell if she was laughing at his attempt to change his appearance, and for a second, he thought she might laugh at his expense. He frowned and said nothing, handing her a gourd filled with water. She took it eagerly and drank the entire contents as she watched him tear off a squirrel leg. He handed it to her, and she smiled gratefully, still too hungover from sleep to speak. Before she could take a bite, she suddenly remembered the fire and pointed with worry.

"The fire, won't they see us?" she croaked in a harsh voice.

Harq held up his hand, calming her. "Men are gone. Left early. They no see the fire now."

Sira relaxed again and took a bite of meat off the

squirrel's leg. She was so famished that she did not wait for it to cool, so she chewed with her mouth open, inhaling the air to cool the burning meat.

Harq was watching, and now it was his turn. He chuckled at her in his deep voice. "Sira like squirrel very much," he said with his wide grin.

It wasn't until Sira had picked the little bone clean of meat that she noticed Harq had been finding her amusing. She smiled back and threw the bone at him, causing him to duck his head and laugh.

"Stop laughing, I'm starved. Give me another piece!" she ordered. Harq tore off the other hind leg and handed it to her. "Harq happy. Sira alive with Harq."

She stopped chewing and looked up at him. It was a rare moment when Harq expressed emotion, so she smiled back fondly. "It is the second time you have saved my life, Harq."

"Sira, not like wolf people. She is different."

She lifted herself gingerly, picking up Harq's fur that he had loaned her for the night. As soon as she took a step, she realized how stiff and weak her body was; the events of the past days had taken their toll.

Harq stood up in response. He helped her sit back down, then squatted next to her as she sat with the fur wrapped around her shoulders. He looked over at her, then moved closer.

These were the moments where she enjoyed Harq's style. Unlike other men, who would have made an abrupt move by now, he did so subtly. It was as if he were trying to capture a butterfly. Instead of grabbing it and crushing its wings, he held out his hand, following it until it came to land on his hand on its own. She looked over and gave him a welcoming smile. This made him move closer and sit next to her.

She threw half of the fur around his neck so their bodies could warm up faster together. She leaned on his shoulder for support and continued eating the squirrel leg.

She did not feel awkward being this close to him. It wasn't as if she was mating with him. She was simply sharing a fur with a man who had saved her life twice. A man who had bravely risked his own life for hers. A man that who seemed to care for her... she stopped herself. She pushed the thoughts from her mind. Yet she could not stop her curiosity, and she turned again to examine his face. She couldn't help but smile.

He stopped fidgeting with the fire and turned to look at her. She reached out and rubbed his face, then ran her hand through his hair. Harq waited for her quip or some clever remark to make fun of him, but none came.

"No hair. I like it!" she commented finally. She looked at him affectionately. "Why do you save me, Harq?"

Harq turned from her gaze, looking back into the fire. She knew speaking made him uncomfortable, but she was different. Females of her kind relied so much on communication. It was the foundation of their relationships. She realized how much difference there was between them, yet those differences seem to melt away when they were together. Perhaps she was too exhausted from her ordeals and wasn't thinking clearly, or maybe the past few days had made her go mad.

She tried to listen to her inner voice telling her no, but her hand seemed to have a mind of its own. She grabbed the far side of his face, pulling it toward her. Carefully, as if she did not know what his reaction would be, she kissed him gently on his lips. It was clear he did not know how to kiss, and he sat there stiffly. She kissed him again. It was both the worst and the best kiss of her life. There was something forbidden about it, and it heightened the arousal. She turned back and rested her head on his shoulder and continued eating. Now she *had* made the situation awkward. But then he wrapped her arm around her, pulling her closer. Her head now resting on his chest. Like magic, he had taken the awkwardness away again.

* * *

After breakfast, Sira took the opportunity to bathe in the small creek, washing away the dirt and ash that had collected on her march out from the Samaki village. It did not take long for her skin to dry, as the late spring day was warming up. They collected their small items, and Harq had been busy fashioning a spear for Sira. It did not have an obsidian tip, and it was made in haste by whatever materials Harq had found on the move, still, it was better than traveling unarmed.

They left their camp back through the forest until they returned to the tracks of the Gondo-Var. Harq was especially cautious and opted to remain half a day's length behind them. After discovering a prisoner had escaped, the tribe will be on higher alert for the rest of the journey.

"Where are they going?" asked Sira as she stooped down to look at the footprints.

"They no go to wolf people village, they go up to the mountain," he said.

"But that direction, it leads to the mountain cliffs. There is no way around. Unless... what if they found the cave?" she gasped.

"We must hurry," he said, trying his best not to sound concerned.

Harq was patient with Sira as they traveled, forcing her to take stops and rest her legs, despite her protest. He was not worried he would lose their tracks, as the tribe they followed left such a huge mark on the land. Weeks could go by and he could still track them. The day was even warmer than usual, the humidity high.

Sira and Harq looked to the distance and could see a great thunderhead cloud manifesting in the distance, heading their way. As the sun descended, and the clouds rolled in, Harq picked another spot to camp out under a dense thicket of trees. They wandered out together, digging up tubers and collecting berries to eat before it was too dark.

Because of the looming dark clouds, they had instinctively chosen a spot under a dense canopy. No sooner had they settled to eat, a great thunder rumbled in the distance. The hot humidity of the day finally broke as the first splatters of raindrops struck the leaves above them. The air smelled fresh as the geosmin lifted from the ground and the plant oils washed away. The sky flashed with lightning in the distance, lighting up the darkening sky in a brief instant.

They had both been silent the entire day, even by Harq's standards. Ever since their kiss yesterday, there was a growing pressure building between them, just like the thunderstorm above them. At some point, it would have to break.

"I believe it is time for another bath," she said to him, smiling.

"Bath? No river here to-" then he realized she meant the rain.

Sira got up first, removing the hides from around her waist and chest.

Harq froze as he watched her. His mouth fell open, half full of blackberries. He had seen her naked before, but this time, it was intentionally done for him. Sira walked out from under the patch of trees and into the open, under the falling rain. Thunder clapped again.

Sira lifted her arms and let the cool droplets bounce off her skin, cleansing her body of sweat and oil. Now that they were completely free from the falling ash, the fresh air and sweet rain were a blessing.

Sira spun around in the rain with her arms out, laughing and lifting her head to the sky, allowing the raindrops to soak her face. Every few moments, her naked body was lit up brightly as the lightning flashed overhead. Perhaps it was all the trauma and stress from the recent events in her life. All the pain and loss, her clan, her parents, everything. It was too much to bear. She just wanted to feel good, just for one moment.

She stopped spinning and turned to face him. Blowing rainwater from her lips, she stretched out her arms to him. She was no longer laughing or smiling, and her usual girlish playfulness was gone.

Harq stood up and undressed, then walked out into the rain toward her. He stopped and watched as the water droplets ran down her breasts.

She studied the stoutness of his body, his large chest, and the six chiseled muscles of his abdomen. Between his legs, he was just like any man, perhaps even more so. He was both different and beautiful. She looked up, and their eyes met. His normally timid nature was gone. He pulled her close to him. They embraced each other and kissed. Harq mimicked the movements of her lips, doing a much better job of it this time. With arms hugging his neck, she wrapped one leg around his waist and pushed him closer. Then she hopped up into his arms. As the rain poured down upon them, she worked her pelvis over him. She allowed him to enter her slowly. He held her tight as she rocked back and forth. Every spasm of the forbidden pleasure was heightening to a crescendo that would soon burst. Free, wild, and temporarily unconcerned for the future, they made love as hard as the thunder that boomed above them.

Chapter 28

Harq was a little boy again. Screams from his mother rang to him as he was dragged away by men, wolf people. A dark-skinned man had to be held down by four others, such was his anger. When the screams were silenced, the man cried out and fell to the ground in anguish.

Harq felt the kick to his back. He woke up in a blinding white of snow, shivering with fear under a small fur. Abandoned, alone, and freezing to death. He saw the faces of his people; they picked him up and carried him off.

Sira was awakened by Harq's gasp as he was shaken from his nightmare. It was morning, and Sira found she had fallen asleep on his chest. She wiped the drool from her lips and looked at him affectionately, batting her eyelashes and giving him her signature half-smile. She caressed his cheek in solace. She knew very well of nightmares as she suffered from them as well. But last night, she had slept calmly in his arms. She blinked, and tears ran down her cheeks. Tears for her parents, who she could not save in time.

Unlike her personality, which held an eternal sense of urgency, Harq was surrounded by an aura of patient and stoic resilience. It's not that he didn't feel emotion. She could see the intensity of it burning behind his eyes. He just seemed to have a better command of it. He was more aloof to the world around him, but that didn't make him any less aware. And the serene way he viewed life was contagious to her. Their personalities clashed, but not detrimentally. Being in his presence gave her a sense of balance and peace.

Lying here with him seemed to erase her troubles. For a selfish moment, she imagined the two of them running away together, far from the Gondo-Var and Samaki village. Perhaps somewhere they could seek a life with new people. She allowed the fantasy to play out for several minutes, but then shook herself back into the moment.

Pliny and Jin were more than family to her. She would never leave them to those monsters, no matter what the risk. She had been their leader; they were her clan, her responsibility. Thoughts of the twins forced Sira up, and her previous weakness turned to a stony resolve. She looked down to Harq, and he held her gaze. She felt a pang of guilt. Her clan was not his burden. She thought about trying to send him away, somewhere safe, but it would have been futile. She needed him, and he was bound to her now. He would follow her anywhere, even into death. No words were ever needed with Harq. He could read her expression. That was always enough for him. He stood up, and they collected their things.

They traveled in silence as the forest thinned. The cliffs of the mountain range came into view in the distance. Harq made sure they stayed a course that was higher in elevation than the Gondo-Var. It was easier to remain out of sight. The going was slow, as steep sections of rock stood in their way. He climbed up like a mountain goat, completely at home in this terrain. She smiled, knowing he was taking his time on account of her slower pace.

Sira had a few casual young lovers in her lifetime, but they were nothing more than an exploration of her growing sexuality. The young men in her life were either a disappointment, too competitive, or too possessive. Worse were the ones who had tried to control or dominate her— they didn't last long.

As they approached a steep section, Harq assisted her from behind, pushing her up the rock face. She turned and offered her hand. He could have hoisted himself up easily enough, but he took her hand in assistance. It made his ascent easier. She thought about the men of her clan. They would have never accepted her help in that situation. But there was no bravado from Harq, no pride to stand in the way of reason. He was practical, focused. There was a palpable connection between them as they took turns assisting one another up the steep terrain.

Sira contemplated what her clan would think once they knew she had mated and partnered with an Other. But after all the tragedy that had befallen them, this point seemed trivial now. Besides, there might not be a clan left.

Now that they were up on a ridge, they had a clearer view of the gigantic column of grey ash behind the mountain peaks. It did not show any signs of abating as it rose into the cloudless, infinite azure. Its ugly color stained the otherwise beautiful sky.

Harq's caution of taking the higher, more difficult path had proven wise. In the distance, they could see small fires in the hands of the Gondo-Var figures investigating the cave entrance.

"Torches," Sira whispered. "They have torches! Will they make it through?"

Harq shrugged, but his face portrayed concern. They waited patiently as the marching column and all the captives had disappeared, single file, into the cavern.

"Come, we follow," Harq said.

Near the entrance, a howl rang out from down the slope. It was so close it made Sira jump back in surprise. "Wolves! And so close?" She asked in wonder. The sound made her grip her spear and move into the entrance with apprehension.

"Wolf people," responded, shaking his head.

"It looks as if they were right behind those Red feather people. Were they following them?"

"Yes, wolves... wolf people," he said.

"Wait, is that why you call them wolf people?"

Harq looked back, and his far-flung gaze suddenly fixed on one canine as it appeared from around an outcropping of rock. "Yes... and no," Harq responded.

The wolf yapped and them, bobbing its head. Then it lay down on its haunches. It was so close they could see its grey and white fur sway in the mountain breeze. Harq studied the wolf for a moment. He couldn't put into words the entire mythos of how Sira's people had come to be. How her kind had descended from these creatures, and how they now shared a kinship. "Long story," he said. As Sira backed into the cave, she heard the wolves whine in protest.

The second time through the tunnel was not as terrifying. Sira knew what to expect, and kept her body glued to the left side of the cave wall. She did her best to ignore the unsettled bats as they flew around her head. Luckily, none flew into her hair this time. She imagined the difficulty of the bound captives trying to navigate through, but then again, the Red feathers had torches. With sufficient lighting, the tunnel was probably a cinch to navigate.

Arriving at the V-shaped opening, they noticed the rocks that covered the hole were strewn about the ground. There was no doubt they had made it through. Harq sniffed the air cautiously.

They kept their ears focused for any clues and movements in the ravine, but it was eerily silent. The silence was finally broken by the echoes of cawing crows. Before the slaughter came into sight, the putrefied smell hit them first. Sira gagged. The dead, bloated corpses of the Others lay strewn about the bottom of the ravine. Vultures and crows flew about the bodies, gorging themselves.

Around them, wooden poles had been shoved into the ground, each one piked with a severed head. A gruesome forest of decomposing faces. Sira covered her mouth and averted her eyes in horror. When she blinked, tears rolled down her cheeks.

Harq walked up to the head, shooing away a raven that had been pecking into one of its empty eye sockets. The heads were decomposed too badly to make out the individual faces, but there was no doubt it was the same small tribe of Others that guarded the entrance of the ravine.

Harq clenched his fists in anger and disgust, trying not to internalize the catastrophe that lay before them. He turned and took Sira by the hand. As they walked through the column of decapitated heads, Sira hid her face against Harq's shoulder and away from the nightmarish scene. Once they were out of the ravine and under cover of the forest, they stopped to process what they had seen.

"How could they have done this so quickly?" Sira asked.

"They no do this. Bodies days old. They are not the first wolf people to come," Harq said.

Sira thought about it. "Yes, you're right, other Red Feathers must have come through first. That is how they knew where the cave entrance was! They walked right to it as if they had a guide! They could have come here many days ago!"

"Yes, they came, and they killed," Harq said with a simmering ferocity.

Sira straightened with worry. "Harq! Your village! We have to warn them!"

Harq only nodded. This thought had already been on his mind since they had arrived. As they walked, the tracks of the Gondo-Var split, some leading toward the mountain on fire and others toward Harq's village.

As the familiar cliffs of Harq's people came into sight, they could see no movement in or around the cave entrances. Sira placed her hand upon Harq's shoulder, trying to steady him as they scanned the area. A duo of ravens cawed as they flew out from the main cave entrance. It made their hearts sink. Sira walked behind Harq as they approached, giving him space for the horror she fully expected to find.

Inside, the members of Harq's village were piled in a heap of corpses. Harq entered the cave, shoulders and head slouched in a sign of defeat. His spear slipped out of his hand and fell to the ground. It was so quiet the wood shaft made an echo as it rattled on the stone floor. Sira held her hand over her mouth in horror, sobbing as she walked behind him. She wanted to avert her eyes, but they were morbidly stuck on the pile of dead bodies as she came to terms with the atrocity. At the bottom of the pile, she noticed the red stringy hair from a tiny corpse of a body. She also saw Needa, her body, lying unceremoniously in a pool of blood.

Sira gasped and turned away; she could look no more. She turned and stood at the cave entrance, then began to sob.

The cries of anguish from Harq carried on in the hollow cave as he grieved. Sira watched the mountain smoking in the distance. She looked over at the red ochre cave painting by someone in Harq's tribe. It was a representation of the flat-topped smoking volcano in the distance, but it had been smeared over with blood. The image would stay with her forever.

When Harq returned, he said nothing. With red eyes swollen with tears of pain, he handed her a new spear. She held up the razor-sharp obsidian tip and watched it glint under the fading orange glow of the setting sun.

Harq's great jawline was clenched tight with determination. He spoke with purpose. "We go to fire mountain." Any doubts Harq had harbored about tracking down the Gondo-Var warriors were now gone. It was about revenge now. Together, they set off in the direction of the smoking mountain.

Chapter 29

Master and the Gondo-Var were in awe of the lush green land they had discovered in the valley. It was a veritable Eden, filled with edible plants and game that behaved as if they had never encountered men before. After traveling through the ash barren hills, it was a paradise.

At night, they feasted on meat from a family of wild boar and various species of deer. Even the captives were given enough rations to satiate their bellies. Tracks from Father's portion of the Gondo-Var led up towards the base of the flat-topped mountain, and Master wondered about the logic of heading toward such a fearful sight.

They found more bodies along their way, slain corpses of the Others. There was no evidence of large battles with these strange hairy men. There were skirmishes, which seemed to end with slaughter. The men often stopped to study the strange-shaped faces and hairy stout bodies that now lay slain and decomposing. To see the mysterious men massacred with such ease reduced the fear that had surrounded them, and it soon became clear that these people must be inferior to their own. They kept a careful lookout for an ambush from the Others, but they encountered no resistance on their way to the mountain.

* * *

Master strode into the makeshift camp that the Gondo-Var were rapidly constructing. It sat against a black cliff, below the final summit which led to the massive ash cloud.

Master studied the colors in the column of smoke. This was the source of the ash that was rapidly filling the hills surrounding the Samaki village. The higher altitude and mountain air current swept the smoke and ash high into the air and toward the Great Sea. There, the offshore wind collided with it, pushing it down onto the coastal hills.

As Master studied the mountain, a great rumbling came from within the earth. The ground shook beneath his feet, and the sound echoed through the valley. He looked back to the mountain and saw several black rocks loosen and tumble down the cliff. They shattered into hundreds of shards as they hit the rocky ground below. Although he had never been in an earthquake or seen a volcano, it was obvious to Master there was something very dangerous about this place. He questioned the logic of Father bringing them here.

Father was facing the black cliff at the base of the mountain, his arms extended outward. He turned when Master approached; his face glowed with a brilliant smile of reverence.

"Father," Master called to him and knelt. "We have raided the Samaki village. We captured many men and women, along with fine weapons and other items of value."

Father looked down upon Master as if he were a child who had accomplished something of minor importance.

"I must report that the smoke from this mountain has fallen upon the hills and the village. I do not believe it would be in a condition for us to make our fortress," Master reported.

"Fortress?" Father asked inquisitively, and then chuckled. "My son, we are no longer looking for a new fortress! We have found one!" he exclaimed, holding out his hands, signaling their current position.

Master looked up at the ominous black cliff, and then higher to the rising column of smoke. "Here, Father?" he asked dubiously.

"Yes! Have you seen the amount of game we have in this valley? Look up at these cliffs! It is the perfect location for our eagles to grow and for our new warriors to make the climb. A cliff of fire!" he said with enthusiasm. "The Others are here too; did you see them? There are many more just waiting for us to capture, I am sure of it!"

Master looked around again at their surroundings, his face frowning with dismay.

Father took notice and waved his chubby hand, gesturing to come forward. "Come, my son. I have something to show you!" He led him toward the cliff, behind his entourage of tents. "Look, there they are. Can you believe it? My long-lost people of the mountains, I have them at last," he said dreamily.

Master looked down upon the dozen young female Other captives who were bound together. They all looked alike to him, with large noses and mouths that protruded outward. Their foreheads were large and sloped back, and their hair was long and stringy. Some of them had dark hair, but others were a lighter brown. One of them had reddish-colored hair, which Master had never seen on a person.

"Ah, you see this one! Fire Hair, I call her! She will be the first to bear me a child!" Father exclaimed with excitement.

Master could not hold back the disgust on his face. "Child? You wish to mate with... with one of these creatures?"

Father paid no attention to Master's transgression. His eyes were still busy studying the bound women. "Our blood, and theirs, combined! Our skills, our cunning, combined with their strength! I will try again, and so will all of us. We will all take one to mate!" Father's eyebrows lifted in excitement.

Master looked back at the women with slight horror. He could not imagine mating with something so ugly, and the thought of the other warriors in the tribe making babies with them made him nauseous. "What do you mean, try again?"

Father sighed, walking over to the woman with red hair, reaching out and stroking it softly. The woman hissed at him like a wildcat, then cowed in fear as the other bound women hissed at him in her defense. "I once mated with one, a long time ago. I was just a young man, lost in the woods. She stalked me, found me. She was curious about me, as I was with her. I mated with her, even though we could not understand each other. She led me back in the direction of our tribe. I might have wandered those mountains forever if she hadn't helped me. I went back to her, and we visited each other secretly. When she gave birth to my son..." Father paused with emotion. "They took them from me. But I do not weep, for it hardened me, set me on a path to be the fiercest warrior. Set me on my path to becoming Father of the Gondo-Var."

Father paused as he looked up and reflected on the memory. "I will make another, more!" he concluded, smiling down at the captive women.

"You intend for us, all of us, to mate with these creatures, to have young ones with them?" Master asked again, needing to hear the absurdity of the old man one more time to make sure he understood. "I have brought many women from Samaki village. Some of them are the most beautiful I have ever seen. They are yours to choose from, yet here you are, Father, flirting with these beasts," Master said with careful protest.

Laksha's face appeared in his mind, her beauty like a heavenly vision, which stood in such stark comparison to the women in front of him.

"Useless women of a fishing village, bah! I am disappointed you do not see the tomorrow of Gondo-Var, but it is what I expected. I had high hopes for you, my son. You think for yourself, for your own glory, not for the tribe. That is why you will not lead the Gondo-Var when I am gone," Father said solemnly.

Master's face went blush as the words sank in. There was no warrior more cunning and qualified to lead the Gondo-Var than him. After all his years of leading Father's war parties, all the success that could be contributed to him, no man or woman was more deserving to lead the tribe. To have this honor taken away so over something as frivolous as a group of ugly women was outrageous.

Master clenched his fists, steadying himself. "Who, Father, might I ask? Will you give this great honor to, if not me?" he asked, his inner rage on the verge of losing control.

"The son that I lost," he said. "If I cannot find him, I will make another with one of them." He pointed to the women. "With my blood together with theirs, I will make the greatest warriors and leaders we have ever seen," he said prophetically.

Master looked down at the hideous-looking once more and then back at Father. He had been harboring doubts about Father's leadership, but nothing could have prepared him for this. *He has sunken into madness, and he will take all of us down with him if he is not stopped.*

Master decided to take leave. There would be no further use groveling before a madman. "Very well, Father, as your son and leader of the Gondo-Var warriors, I will do as you request," he said drily and bowed. He was certain Father could read his insincerity, but he was past the point of caring.

As if he were shooing a fly, Father waved his hand in dismissal. He did not bother to look at Master, and his mouth was upturned in a frown of disappointment. Master left him with the Other women as he turned away from the black cliff. As he walked out, there was another rumble from the mountain, and the ground jolted below his feet. The vibrations made him stumble, and he had to step firm to regain his balance.

It startled him, which was something not easily accomplished. The vibrations frightened someone else, and he spun back around to find Father's young wife. She had been hiding behind a low bush, secretly watching as Father interacted with the Other women. The rumble and vibrations made her cry out and fall onto her backside. She got up quickly to compose herself when she noticed him.

"Oh! Master, apologies. I was just... just going to see..." she tried to think of an excuse to justify her eavesdropping.

Master saw the look of grief upon her face, and he immediately understood why. "It is alright, little one." He was surprised at his sympathetic reaction to the young wife. Maybe her predicament was not entirely different from his. They had both loved and worshipped a man who was now turning his back on them, a leader who had become so obsessed with these new and exotic people he had forgotten to attend to his own.

His sympathy soon dried, and his normal vindictive self returned. "It seems you will share Father's fur at night not only with his wives but with a gang of those women as well! I know from many accounts that he likes to see his women partake in love with each other while he watches. How lovely and thrilling it will be for him to watch you and those women together making every kind of sexual act."

She looked over at the women and frowned in horror at the thought. She placed both hands over her mouth and sobbed. Master left her there and walked away. His mood slightly improved.

* * *

From the moment Father had declared the base of the black cliff their new home, the tribe immediately entered a flurry of activity. Both men and women had their roles, and they got to work with great efficiency. Women had already scouted the area for edible food and game trails and assisted in the set-up of the tents and shelters. Men cleared brush and small trees with their flint axes, then piled them up to form a temporary perimeter wall.

People stiffened as Master passed by. People who were taking a break from work swiftly picked up their pace in his presence. Despite this, Master noticed a change in their attitudes. They held his gaze longer than usual, and he heard murmurs behind his back as he passed. Since the chiding by Father on the hills several days ago, his respect had diminished. He was especially surprised by the lack of acknowledgment of his recent Samaki captives. The sheer number of them, especially women, should have been a cause for celebration. It was as if this spoil of war had gone out of fashion, the war parties realizing that capturing the Others brought more veneration from Father.

Master wondered if the Gondo-Var warriors had already learned that he was no longer in line to become the next Father of the tribe. The old man might have leaked this information out already to undermine him. As if in response, he heard someone shout "Iban-elek!" behind him.

Master spun around in a whirl. Several of the men laughed in the distance, but there were too many people to know where it had come. He had not heard his real name uttered in many years. It was meant as slander, his real name bringing him down to the position of a normal warrior.

Like a hawk searching for its prey, he scanned the scattered groups of people as they went about their work.

The coward would not show himself, so he huffed in contempt and continued his inspection.

* * *

Kadam and Nara had chosen a spot for their tent as far away from the black cliff of the mountain as possible. Although many were prophesying the burning mountain as a great omen, Kadam was wary. He did not care for the look of the black rocks. He did not like the strange rumblings and shaking of the ground, and he did not like the look of the Others they had come across.

Kadam had been present in the fighting inside the ravine. The men they had faced were exceptionally strong, but they lacked the Gondo-Var warriors' tactics in battle, not to mention their bows and sleeping toxin. It did not take long for the mountain men to fall to the arrows.

He did marvel at the black rocks attached to their spears. The first time he handled the substance he had cut his hand, ignorant to how sharp it was. He had found a small chunk of the black rock in one of the Others' caverns and brought it back with him. Now he sat around his fire, attempting to knap off a flake.

Nara was hanging wooden branches and hides over their shelter to extend the size of their tent. Her feminine instincts were already in nesting mode.

Kadam cursed as a potentially nice-sized flake shattered in two at his final blow on the chunk of rock. The black rock itself was easy to break, but they tended to shatter once they got down to smaller pieces. He cut his finger on a flake, and when red droplets appeared on his hand, he threw the rock hammer down in frustration. He was so focused on the task; he had not seen Durok approach.

"Better let me handle that, I'll have us a handful of spearheads before nightfall," Durok boasted.

Kadam kicked the rocks with slight annoyance on the ground in Durok's direction. Durok got to work, while Kadam looked out into the throng of activity.

"Have you seen the new captured women Master has

brought?" Kadam asked.

"Oh! Yes, I have," Durok said enthusiastically. He said nothing else, not wanting to give Kadam any more ammunition.

"Have you ever seen women like that?" Kadam asked, probing.

"No, I have not," Durok responded drily.

"They look as if they have never worked a day. So soft, as if the only task they had known was to stay inside and pleasure their men," Kadam said, trying to lure the other man.

"Doesn't sound like the kind of woman I would want," responded Durok.

"Humph," Kadam grunted. "Just as well, I plan to mount all of them. I guess you really wouldn't stand a chance, being so ugly."

Durok still did not take the bait but instead gasped an "ah-ha!" as he held up a point of the obsidian, almost in the perfect shape of an arrowhead. "And that was just my first try!"

"Good, when I am off hunting, you can stay here, making spearheads with the women," Kadam jibed.

"So, is that your plan? To continue to fight and capture these strange mountain people?" Durok whispered, making sure Nara could not hear.

Kadam sighed; he knew his friend would lead the conversation in this direction. He still did not have a concise plan on how he would kill Master and get his revenge without sacrificing Nara and the child she now carried.

The silence went on for a few moments before Durok broke the awkwardness. "I know it is not a simple task we have. I just hope you will take the chance when it comes, brother."

He got up and smiled at Nara. She smiled back and bowed in greeting before he walked away.

No sooner had Kadam picked up the obsidian rock, when another unexpected visitor. This one had made no sound, and Kadam did not notice his presence until he spoke.

"Kadam, the rising star of Father's great Gondo-Var

warriors!" Master said with a touch of cynicism.

Kadam looked up, startled by the man's sudden appearance. "It is you," Kadam said flatly, turning his head away from the man.

Master looked at Nara, and she bowed her head in respect. Master chose his next words carefully. "This tribe we have is the greatest I have ever known. I have never come across any more powerful, and I have seen many. Do you agree?" Master asked Kadam, who kept knapping the rock.

"Powerful, because you are many, and you have weapons that others do not," Kadam responded bluntly as he snapped off a piece.

Master smiled. The wry attempt at answering the question without offending the tribe belied Kadam's true feelings, which was just what Master had been counting on. "Come, let us walk alone, Kadam," he said, eyeing Nara.

With a hiss of displeasure, Kadam stopped banging the rock, then held out his hands, signaling Master to lead the way. Master led them away from the men building the perimeter wall until they were out of earshot.

"Many of you were not born into this tribe as I was. We have traveled very far from the land I remember as a boy, finding new beasts and men to conquer," Master explained, although he knew Kadam would not understand the word "conquer."

"I was young when Father took leadership of the tribe. Do you know how he accomplished this?" Master asked.

Kadam shrugged, showing he neither knew nor cared.

Master continued anyway, "He speared the leader through his heart in a challenge."

Kadam tried to look disinterested, but his eyebrows raised slightly.

"I have failed in this respect. I have missed my chance to do so," explained Master.

Kadam turned to Master and squinted in confusion, for the first time reacting with something other than contempt or indifference. "Are you telling me... you wish you had killed him?"

"I try not to think much about mistakes, or the past. It does no good. But I would like to correct one."

Kadam tilted his head.

Master sighed and let it sink in for a moment. "This is not your tribe, Kadam. You only want to see me dead. To see all of us dead. But for whatever reason, you do not. I can see it in your eyes, the anger." Master changed his expression, looking stern and resolute. "Take your chance then. Get your revenge. Cut the head off from the snake and kill it!"

"What?"

"Cut the head off of the snake, Kadam. Kill Father! I will not stop you! The other war party leaders will not stand in your way either!" Master exclaimed again.

Kadam took a step back. It seemed the man was being sincere, but Kadam was not about to fall into one of Master's traps. His mind raced for a moment, and he fantasied about the act. "They would kill me without hesitation."

Master shook his head in disagreement. "These people worship power, strength. They worship Father because they think he has it. Just as they think you have it. Whether or not you care, the warriors like you, Kadam. They respect you. Ever since that day of the climb, when you spoke with the eagle. They have seen your great strength and hunting in battle. They would follow you. All you have to do is take it!"

Kadam chuckled at this. The proposition was so farfetched it was laughable, but he entertained Master for the sport of it. "If it is so easy, why don't you do it? You are the one they call Master, leader of the war parties. I would think they would follow you instead."

Master turned to the side, lost in thought for a moment while he watched the men and women busy working in the distance. He considered his next words. "Many of the men and women in this tribe were ripped from their families by my hand, just like you were. And just like you, they would find any excuse to cut me down. There is great hatred simmering in this tribe. I am afraid it will burst soon. It is better to break the blister before in festers. You might not love the Gondo-Var, but I can tell you, your old tribe is finished. You are Gondo-Var now, you cannot change that. Take control of this tribe and live out your days in peace with Nara and your young one. Forsake this mad plan of Father to mix our blood with that of the Others. Name me as leader of the war parties. That is all I live for, anyway. Without battle, I am nothing."

"What do you mean, my old tribe is finished? How do you know this?" Kadam asked.

Master looked back at him quizzically. "Did you not see us return from the Samaki village with the captives? The shaman of the Samaki gave us half of the tribe, most of them comprising your old clan. I suspect she was happy to be rid of them, as wild as they are. The ones who remained are wasting away in the ash."

Kadam's mind suddenly clicked, as if two pieces of a puzzle had come together. "You mean the Fishtooth? That is the Samaki village?"

Master laughed mockingly, enjoying his revelation.

Kadam looked back anxiously toward the tribe, attempting to see farther into the line of captives.

"There is nothing left but to embrace us, Kadam. We are not your enemy. Your enemy is Father, for he is the one who ordered us to perform the raid on your tribe. We were only doing what we were told," Master explained.

Kadam's fists clenched, and his cheeks flushed. "You enjoyed it, all of it. You enjoyed killing my brothers and our families!" he raged.

Master shrugged. "Do you fault the lion for enjoying its kill? Or the hyena for stealing it? They cannot help it; it is their nature. I am a warrior; it is my nature."

Master reached back and untied the cord from around his neck. From under his hide shirt, he pulled out Kadam's sabre-tooth canine. "Here, this is yours. You have earned it back."

Kadam was about to reach for it, then stopped. He placed his hand on Rooti's necklace made of animal teeth, remembering that day. "You cannot give me what is already mine. One day, I will take it back."

Master smiled. This time it was threatening. "Very well.

Just think about my offer. You will never get a better chance. I can only imagine what your old tribemates will think of you once they see you."

He had heard enough. Turning his back on Master, he made for the captives.

* * *

Kadam walked through the miserable-looking people sitting on the ground, still bound by fiber ropes. A Gondo-Var warrior was pacing down the line, giving them the same speech Kadam had heard on that first day they had captured him.

It did not take long before a few people started to recognize him. "Kadam?" one said in half recognition.

"Look, it is Kadam! He is alive!" said another voice.

"Kadam is a Gondo-Var?" asked someone else.

Kadam said nothing; his emotions were roiling in a mix of guilt. At the end of the line of captives, he found Pliny. He was bound tight and his head was hung low, staring down at the dirt. Kadam squatted down in front of him. "Pliny," he said.

Pliny lifted his head weakly. His eyes focused on his face, and they slowly lit up. "Kadam! Kadam, is that you? You are alive! How did you find us? Wait, are you free?"

A slight breeze blew the red feather out onto the side of Kadam's neck. Pliny looked at it, and it took a moment to register. "Kadam! No!" he exclaimed.

Kadam raised his hand to silence him. "It is true, I became one of them. But believe me, my heart is still with you," he whispered. He wanted to explain more, but another Gondo-Var warrior was passing them, suspiciously watching Kadam speaking to one of the captives. Although it was unusual, the warrior knew Kadam and thought it wise not to enter an altercation with the big man.

Pliny looked up at him with confusion. He wanted to say something, perhaps an insult, but he was too exhausted, so he dropped his head back down.

Kadam waited until the warrior had walked far enough

before grabbing Pliny's chin and lifting it. "Little brother, I will get you out of here. I will not let you suffer through what I have. Who else is alive? Who else is here?"

Pliny summoned his strength and began naming some of their other tribemates. Jin was among them, but Sira had escaped. Kadam still had many questions, but he did not want to press the young man, so he allowed him to rest. Kadam walked down to the other end of the captives until he found Jin. He tried to approach, but a Gondo-Var intervened.

"Better leave this one alone, he's a sneaky one," said the warrior.

Jin looked in better condition but had a fresh bruise under his eye. *Jin would never go along easily.*

Jin glared up at him in contempt; no doubt the young man had already formed a traitorous opinion of him. Kadam held his gaze and then rubbed the red feather with his thumb and forefinger. He pursed his lips together and made the song of the bluebird. The warrior looked questioningly at Kadam, so he turned to walk away. Kadam hoped the signal to Jin would be enough.

* * *

Once evening fell, Kadam went to consult Durok about his encounter with Master. He found him knapping the black rock by the fire. Durok had learned by trial and error a much better technique for shaping the spearheads. He had already fashioned a hefty-looking spear for Kadam with the razor-sharp stone at its tip. Kadam was grateful and knocked his friend on his shoulder, smiling upon receiving it.

"I think a good spear is exactly what we need tonight," said Kadam.

Durok could hear the tone and stopped his task to look up, waiting for Kadam to come out with the details.

Kadam explained the conversation with Master and the proposal he had offered him. Kadam expected Durok to jump at this recent development, as he was usually the more impatient of the two when it came to the opportunity for revenge.

"I do not trust Master," said Durok, shaking his head. "You think he will simply let you kill Father to become the leader of this tribe? And you believe he will follow you and remain content to be your war leader?"

"If what he says is true, if the tribe names me leader after I kill Father, it will not matter what Master thinks or does. If he tries something, we will fight him together. Master told me one true thing. The people fear him, but they do not love him. They will turn against him if they have the chance," Kadam said. It sounded as if he were trying to convince himself.

"And if it does not work? Even if we can kill Father's guards, what if his brothers and followers want revenge?" Durok asked.

Kadam shrugged as if he had thought about this. "It is not the way of these people; they worship the strong. But you are right, some people might want revenge."

"And then?" Durok followed up.

"And then... the people of my tribe who are here now being held captive will see me. They will know I did not betray them. I will die fighting these shit birds, as I should have done long ago." Kadam said soberly.

"And what of Nara?" Durok asked.

Kadam sighed. "I do not know. Perhaps my son will be born without a father. But that is better than having a father who has no honor."

Durok accepted his reasoning and understood the risk his friend was taking. He shook his head in respect and laid his hand on Kadam's shoulder. "If that is the case, brother, then I can only say I would be honored to die by your side." He held out his arm to Kadam, and they embraced each other's forearms.

"Come," said Kadam. "Let us plan out our attack."

* * *

Kadam and Durok waited until the moon rose behind the giant smoke column. Without the moonlight, they could move unseen about the camp without raising suspicion. The first plan involved creating a diversion by freeing some of the captive prisoners of Kadam's tribe. They were still bound together with the fiber ropes, but no warriors were guarding them. They had been given a belly full of food and surrounded by small campfires to keep from freezing. Most were fast asleep.

"They are so confident. They leave them unguarded," Durok whispered to Kadam as they approached the captives.

"Where would they go even if they escaped? They are probably too scared to go back through this valley of strange men on their own," Kadam whispered back.

Kadam passed many of his old tribemates, and his heart was filled with regret that they would not have time to free all of them. He did not bother freeing the binds of the captives he did not know, as he couldn't risk them making noise and waking the Gondo-Var, who were sleeping in nearby tents.

Kadam found Jin and was not surprised that the young man was already awake. Kadam used his new spear and placed it between the fiber rope. He sawed at it, and it took only a few motions before the rope was cut in half.

Without a word, Jin motioned for the extra spear Kadam held in his other hand. Jin took it and got to work sawing off the rope around his neck, careful not to cut himself with the razor-sharp tip. The man who had been bound to Jin stirred but did not wake up.

Kadam motioned to the direction of Pliny, and Durok handed him a second spear. Kadam held up his palm, signaling that Jin should go alone. Jin answered back using their hunting signs, asking why Kadam and Durok would not join him. Kadam responded negatively by shaking his head, then gave the hunting sign of a kill. Jin paused, then nodded his head in understanding. Jin still questioned his loyalty and studied his old tribemate carefully for any signs of treachery. As if Kadam was reading his mind, he held out his arm.

Jin paused to look down at it, then offered his own. They embraced each other by the forearm, and then Kadam pointed in the direction the twins should go out of the village.

Jin looked and nodded, then watched for several moments as Kadam disappeared into the night.

Jin kept low and made his way down through the captives. He could not see any guards, but he was not about to take any chances. When he found his partner, he gently held his hand on his head. Pliny awoke and smiled with relief, while Jin cut through his bindings. He handed Pliny the second spear and pointed to his neck. In a few moments, they were free, making haste from the light of the fires.

"Pliny? Jin? Is that you?" They heard a voice call out from behind them.

The twins spun around and saw one of their old female tribe members. She had been awake and noticed them escaping.

Pliny and Jin both ducked down to the ground and gave her the sign to be quiet.

The woman, whether she understood them or not, blurted out desperately. "Pliny, it is I, Kera. Please, get me out."

With that, several other captives around her started to wake up.

Pliny took a step forward, but Jin caught his arm.

"We can't leave them!" Pliny pleaded.

Kera noticed the hesitation in the twins, and she grew more desperate. "Please! Do not leave me here. Take me with you!" she shouted.

Pliny rushed forward toward her, deciding it was better to set her free quickly before she made any more noise. But in his heart, he knew it was more than that. He started sawing on her hands and got them free and then told her to be still and quiet.

By now, several captives around them had awoken and were watching the escape attempt. The sounds of people coming awake with excitement were causing too much commotion, and Pliny knew at any moment a guard would be awakened. He tried to cut through the rope on Kera's neck, but she would not sit still, growing impatient and pulling on the rope with her hands.

"Be still or I won't be able to cut through!" he

whispered in frustration.

Several of the other captives were now whispering to each other, calling on Pliny to free them. Their combined voices grew in volume in the still of the night.

Before he could finish cutting her free, he heard the whistle of the bluebird from behind him and immediately knew it was trouble. He ducked down next to Kera and glanced up.

Sure enough, a guard had appeared on the other side of the captives, looking up and down, trying to investigate what was going on.

"Quickly, quickly, they are coming!" one captive shouted.

The young warrior had enough sense to smell trouble, and he immediately emitted a high-pitched yodeling. It was loud and clear enough for every Gondo-Var in the vicinity to hear, and they would not waste time in reacting.

Pliny cursed at his failure, and now worried his escape was in serious threat. He waited until the warrior, who was sounding the alarm, to turn his head before he dashed.

Kera immediately cried out, "No! Don't leave me! Come back, Pliny!"

The Gondo-Var warrior's head snapped in that direction, and just barely caught sight of Pliny as he disappeared out of the light of the torches. The guard let loose another high-pitched howl, louder this time. In seconds, there were six warriors gathered near the captives and more arriving at the call. The guard pointed in the direction Pliny had gone, and they set off after them.

* * *

Kadam and Durok snuck their way over to the section of the camp that held Father and his wives. Kadam studied the tents until he saw the large one in the center. It was here that Father would be sleeping with whichever wife he fancied for the night. They had not yet made it to the entrance of the tent before the alarm had sounded.

"Have they been warned about us?" Durok asked.

"No, that is their alarm warning for escapes. I heard it the same night I tried to escape before I was shot by the sleeping arrow," Kadam recounted.

They crouched behind one of the wife's tents and watched as some of Father's private guards rushed out in the direction of the captives.

"This distraction is good. Look, there are only two guards left, and they won't be expecting our attack," Durok said.

Kadam nodded, and both men stood up, walking casually over to Father's tent.

The two guards stood stiffly at their approach. "What do you want? The alarm is that way," said one of them.

The battle-tested men did not hesitate and simultaneously struck both guards with their spears, aiming for the necks to prohibit them from crying out. The sharp points went straight through the esophagus and out through the back of their necks, cutting through spinal cord tissue. With their spears still stuck in the guards' throats, they pushed them to the ground. The bodies twitched and fought, and one of them tried to cry out but could only manage a muffled, blood-filled gurgle.

Kadam exhaled deeply as he removed his spear from the now-still body. Adrenaline rushed through his system, and he could hear his heartbeat in his eardrums. Although he had killed before, this one felt different. Killing in self-defense, or in the defense of his tribe, had been easy. But he had just committed premeditated murder to a man who had been no immediate threat to him. He felt a rush of an unexpected guilt build up inside of him, and he felt like retching.

Durok could sense the slight hesitation and whispered, "Go, do it! I will wait here and hold off anyone who attempts to enter."

At the words, Kadam did his best to shake off his anxiety and pushed open the hide flap to Father's tent. The large tent was constructed of logs stuck into the ground and raised at an angle. At the top, the logs leaned upon a central pillar that had been dug into the ground in the center. It must have taken many hides to cover the entire tent, and the space was large enough to accommodate a medium-sized fire. The fire was still crackling, with enough light for Kadam to make out the people inside.

Father had awakened and sat comfortably cross-legged on a bear fur. One of his wives was lying next to him, and on his other side, a young female of the Others with striking long red hair. Her legs and feet were bound, and she lay naked on her back. She was sobbing and shaking, her body in a state of shock.

Father's wife shuffled back at the presence of Kadam entering. She might have seen the look on his face and sensed the danger, even if Father had not.

"What is it, my son? What have you to report?" Father asked.

Kadam stepped forward now with a spear in hand, closer than any warrior should approach him.

Father, through his confidence, still had trouble registering the threat, but Kadam looked down at him with murder in his eyes. He shuffled backward on all fours. "Wait, stop!" he yelled desperately.

Kadam should have ended the man before he made too much noise, but he hesitated. It was one thing to kill an armed guard; it was completely different to kill an unarmed old man.

Father tried to back up even more, but his back hit the side of the tent and he threw up his hands in mercy. "Please, please, my son! I am Father, what are you doing?"

Father's wife now scurried out of the tent, screaming and yelling for help.

Durok poked his head inside the hide entrance flap. "Kadam, you must hurry!"

Kadam raised his spear in response, and the old man held up his arms defensively, still crying and pleading. *Just one thrust. Just kill this one man and I can bring vengeance on this tribe. This is the tribe that has taken everything from me!*

But Kadam stood frozen. If he was going to kill the man, he would have done it by now; he had enough experience in killing to realize this. He stared down at Father, who was crying pitifully. He was no longer the great leader of his enemy tribe, just a helpless, fat old man. Kadam hissed in frustration as he lowered his spear.

He stepped over to the Other, cutting the bindings of her arms and legs. He helped her to her feet amidst the girl's uncontrollable trembling. He lifted the great bear fur from the floor and wrapped it around her. Then he thrust the spear shaft into her hands. She stood staring at him with shock and confusion.

Kadam mimicked the thrusting of the spear at Father and tapped the spear in her hands. Her face turned from confusion to alarm, then to anger as she squeezed the spear shaft in her hands.

Father looked up at her. "My child, my sweet mother, no!"

She did not understand his words, and it wouldn't have changed the outcome.

Kadam pushed her forward, urging her on. Father had violated her, and the pain and humiliation were just as fresh in her mind as the blood that ran down her leg. She screamed an inhuman sound, then thrust the spear into his chest. She had never killed before, and her mad spear thrust missed his heart, puncturing a lung.

Father cried out, and his hands tried to grab the shaft of the spear. The young woman had been made strong by her level of rage. She easily yanked the spear out of his grip, then stabbed him again and again, screaming with murderous violence. He whimpered and whined with each stab wound until his body fell silent and limp. She kept on screaming and stabbing him uncontrollably until Kadam grabbed her from behind. She kicked and screamed wildly even as her bright red hair flew into his face. But he held her until her angry screams turned to sobs.

He wrenched the spear from her hands and set her down, then motioned for her to leave the tent. She didn't waste a moment, fleeing like a wild animal escaping a trap.

Durok entered and looked down at the bloody scene. There was no sign of joy or sense of triumph from either of them. They nodded solemnly at each other.

"It is done, by your hand. That is what I will say until the end of my days," Durok promised him.

"I think that end might be today, my friend," Kadam commented   as   they   exited   the   tent.

Chapter 30

The quiet night had come to life outside the forest of the Gondo-Vars' camp, and Harq had been alerted first. His characteristic head motions swayed back and forth as he calculated the distance and location of the sounds. Sira and Harq knew they had been getting close to the camp and were planning on sneaking in and scouting it out as much as they could.

The sound they heard first was the high-pitched yodel. They did not need to be versed in the signals of the Gondo-Var to guess it was an alarm, but they did not know what kind.

Harq grabbed Sira by the arm as they moved to find better cover. He had no reason to suspect the alarm was on their account, but given a choice, Harq would always err on the side of caution. He found a nice depression in the ground near a tree. Its exposed roots rose out of the ground at an awkward angle, offering cover and a view through them.

"What could it be?" Sira whispered as the sounds of the tribe came to life.

But Harq did not reply and kept his head cocked to the side, investigating every sound and voice with his ears. The voices seemed to run parallel to them, deeper into the forest, and Harq could now make out a few of the words being shouted.

"Someone escape and wolf people chase them. Come, let us find them first," Harq said, as he rushed forward.

The blocked moonlight made the forest unusually dark, and one misstep could twist an ankle, or worse. Any injury would put them in a very dangerous situation.

Harq twisted and turned around the trees, keeping his ears locked on the sound of the voices so he could determine what direction they were heading. Finally, he stopped, holding up his hand and tilting his head to listen.

Sure enough, they caught the faint sounds of footsteps through the brush- they were close. Harq changed direction, following parallel to the sounds. They could now hear the voices of the Gondo-Var warriors in pursuit behind them.

Sira looked back and could see the dim light of their tar-covered torches through the shadows of the dark trees.

As they made their way forward, the forest and brush condensed into an impassable thicket. Only one game trail led through it, and Harq found the fresh tracks laid by the two men they were following. They followed the game trail as it twisted and turned around the fallen trees and thorn brush. The trail opened into a large meadow of tall grass. Searching the tall grass in the dark would be impossible, and he no longer heard any more footsteps of the two men. "They are in there, people who escape," Harq said, pointing into the dark meadow grass.

"What are we doing?" Sira whispered to him.

"People escape, maybe friends of Sira," he whispered back.

Sira thought about that; it was both a big assumption and risk. Then she remembered the bluebird song and put her lips together to whistle. Before she could blow out, she was roughly pulled by Harq as they entered the grass.

"They come!" he whispered, motioning toward the pursuing warriors.

They ducked into the shoulder-high grass, trying not to disturb the stalks and make easy tracks. When they had entered deep enough, they squatted down.

Sira put her lips together and this time, blew out her best version of the bluebird song. The bird did not sing at night, and Sira was not adept enough to make a perfect mimic of the whistle. It would be obvious to the Gondo-Var warriors that it was not a real bird whistle. Harq looked at her disapprovingly. But immediately behind them, only a few paces, they returned the whistle, then another. She knew that distinctive whistle by heart.

"It is Pliny and Jin!" she whispered to Harq in excitement.

They walked deeper into the grass in the whistle's direction. A few moments later, through a curtain of grass, the twins appeared. They embraced each other tightly and Sira exhaled a great relief. Their reunion was cut short as the voices of the warriors had also entered the grass.

Harq concentrated on the sounds and then held up three fingers, signaling how many warriors there were.

"You two, make a sound for them to follow," he whispered to the Pliny and Jin.

The twins understood they should create a distraction. They ran forward, stomping down on the grass as they went. Their stomping caused a large ground-dwelling owl to fly up and screech at them.

The Gondo-Var warriors immediately caught the movement and sound and rushed forward in their direction. As they passed Harq's position, he circled, coming up from behind them. Sira followed closely, despite Harq's signal for her to wait. She wasn't going to let him take on three armed warriors single-handedly, no matter how strong he was.

They caught up to the three men, who spun around once they heard their steps. Both Harq and Sira speared the men high in the chest, aiming for the heart. The men cried in agony while the third swung into an attack. He struck forward with his spear at Harq, but Harq anticipated the man's movement and dodged to the side.

Stuck between both Harq and Sira, the man realized they outnumbered him, and kept his spear moving back and forth from Sira to Harq, trying to expect who would be the first to attack him. The warrior had seen these strange mountain people in hand-to-hand combat and decided the woman would be the easier target of the two. If he could disable her, it might make enough of a distraction for his retreat and call for reinforcements. He rushed forward toward her, but it was the wrong move.

Harq launched his spear in an instant, and it landed on the man's lower back. The sudden pain made the man stumble his attack toward Sira, and she was able to dodge. As he stumbled to secure his footing, she thrust her spear into his side, and he cried out again. The warrior gripped the spear from her hand and pulled it out. Amazingly, the man was still on his feet, wild-eyed. He pulled out the spear from behind his back and stood his ground, a spear in each hand.

Harq approached just out of spear range, but the man swung threateningly, keeping his distance. He stepped forward toward Sira, thrusting again, but she hopped back quickly.

"Come, let us die together," the warrior spit out fiercely. His legs bent down in preparation for one last attack, but in that instant, a spear flew out from the dark and landed cleanly in the man's stomach. Jin broke out from the grass and the man grimaced once again in pain. He tried to pull the spear from his stomach, but the pain was too great, and he fell to his knees.

All three approached the man now as his strength left him. Harq grabbed the spear from the man's hand, twisting it free. The dying man's face held a confused look, and his last moments were spent wondering how one of the Others could be working together with one of his kind. Harq kicked the man down to the ground onto his back.

"Let him suffer in pain. He deserves it. They all do," Sira said vengefully.

The man coughed out his few last breaths.

After taking back their spears, they regrouped near the edge of the meadow. "Pliny... Jin... I knew you two would escape. You always find a way!" Sira exclaimed.

"How in all the fires did you find us?" cried Pliny.

Sira simply pointed to Harq.

"Ah, of course. Anyway, we didn't escape this time. It was Kadam. He set us free," said Pliny.

"Kadam? Kadam is alive? Where is he?" she asked.

Pliny looked over at Jin, both men a bit uncertain of how to answer. "Kadam is a Red Feather," Jin said plainly.

Sira gasped, taken aback.

"Gondo-Var is what they call themselves," Pliny corrected.

Sira remembered some of an ancient language, passed through generations, that Raam had taught her. Gondo was the word for man. Var was an eagle.

Pliny continued, trying to defend his old clansman. "But Kadam freed Jin, and he promised me his heart was still with us."

Sira thought about it for a moment, doing her best to justify a man who was once considered the most loyal to the tribe. "Perhaps they gave him no choice, and he was just waiting for the right time to attack."

"Why did you come back here? You were free!" Pliny asked.

Sira sighed before answering. "I am tired of running away from them. We tried to warn Harq's people, but it was too late! And of course, I couldn't leave you two. Those men are too ugly for your tastes," she teased.

"So, we are rescued. What do we do now?" Pliny asked.

Sira thought about the rest of her old clan; once again, the thought of running away crossed her mind. The four of them would be enough to survive, at least until winter. They could travel somewhere very far, meet new people, and join a more amicable tribe. But thinking about the cave of bodies, and the little girl with the red hair, her anger rose again.

In a voice of stoic resolve reminiscent of Harq, she said, "we get close, we wait. We follow them. We rescue more. We do whatever we can."

Then she balanced her spear back upon her shoulder and stepped forward down the trail.

The twins glanced at each other and gulped. They looked expectantly to Harq, as if it was his job to dissuade her.

He shrugged his shoulders. "Where Sira go, I follow," he said and walked forward quickly to catch up with her.

Chapter 31

Outside Father's tent stood Master, along with Last Chance and a few other of his loyal warriors. The night wind had shifted, and the moon had risen higher, passing over the column of smoke and illuminating the camp in a pale white light. Both men did not attempt to flee. It would have been futile at this point even if they tried.

Instead, they had stood their ground as the Gondo-Var warriors gathered. One of them had a bow drawn and aimed at Kadam.

Kadam could not tell if Master had been roused from Father's fleeing wives, or whether he had been already expecting them, but he guessed the latter.

Master's wicked smile broadened when he noticed the bloody spears in the men's hands, and the two guards who lay motionless in a pool of blood. "I cannot believe you have done it. You are brave, I will tell you that. Foolish, but brave."

Last Chance approached the men cautiously. "What have you done?" he hissed angrily.

Kadam stepped aside. "Go in and see for yourself."

Last Chance brushed by, wary of the two men as he stepped inside the tent. There was a pause for a few moments, then a shrill cry rose out from inside. Last Chance came rushing out with a crazed expression on his face, stumbling to his knees. He picked himself up and ran forward. This time he took a deep breath and cried out an alarm.

"You do not mean to honor our deal, do you?" asked Kadam.

"Brave, but foolish," Master repeated as he stepped forward. He whispered so that the others would not hear. "But I must thank you for what you have done. I will promise that your deaths be swift and that you are buried as warriors, instead of being eaten. Your woman and child will not be harmed. You have earned that much."

"Hmph, we have seen how you keep your promises," Durok said with contempt.

Kadam did not feel any fear, only a sense of relief. A weight of guilt he had been carrying around suddenly fell off, and he could not remember the last time he felt so peaceful. It was a pity that after freeing himself from this great burden, his life would now end. He thought about his tribe and especially of Raam. For the first time in a very long time, Kadam had done something he felt his former tribe leader would have been proud of, and it gave him a sense of contentment.

If the camp had not already been roused by the first alarm, it now entered a state of pandemonium as the news spread. Every warrior and able-bodied member amassed in front of Father's tents. There was a sense of disbelief, and it was only when Master ordered the men to drag out Father's body that the loss sank in.

Men howled in pain and rage, and women fell to their knees, wailing in tears, some cutting their arms with flint knives to show their anguish. It was not long before the cries of anger became those of revenge toward the perpetrators. They stood with their arms out, pointing at the men and hissing.

Master stood with several warriors, blocking them from attacking. It was too much for him to have it end so quickly. He held up his hands, calming the tribe. He would have to go about this calmly and strategically if he was to take control of the tribe.

All Kadam could see in every direction was a wall of angry Gondo-Var faces. He looked over to Durok, who was glancing back and forth anxiously. He was not taking his imminent death as easily as Kadam. Although it was Durok who first proposed the plan to destroy the Gondo-Var that day on top of the cliff, Kadam could not help feeling responsible for the man's fate.

In good humor, he stepped over and punched his friend on his shoulder.

Durok snapped out of his mental hole when he saw Kadam's relaxed and confident smile. "Surely, two men have never before faced such odds. I shall take this half, and you can take that half," Kadam said, cutting an imaginary line between the Gondo-Var with his spear. "Let's see who can finish first."

Durok wanted to laugh, but all he could muster was a quick sigh and a half-smile. "You would never win; you are too slow. You know that."

Master had finally accomplished hushing the tribe's laments, except for the few sounds of sobs and cries; at least now he could make himself heard. "Eagles! Children of Father!" he yelled. "Our Father has been murdered!"

A fresh round of yells and cries of anger swept through the crowd, and Master waved his arms down to settle them again. "We know it is these men who have killed him!" Master pointed to Kadam and Durok, and the people's suspicions were confirmed as they taunted the men. "As the leader of Father's war parties, I will take leadership of the tribe! I am announcing that all of you shall from today and forever shall become my children!" he yelled out into the crowd.

Many cheered, but many kept silent, and a few from behind howled in discontent, although they were not brave enough to show themselves.

Durok reached over and punched Kadam in the shoulder. "Now is your chance. Take possession."

"What?" asked Kadam, confused.

"Declare yourself Father. Challenge him!" Durok exclaimed.

Kadam had been so busy, lost in the thought of dying, he had completely forgotten about getting even with his nemesis. He looked back and forth over the people. Many were looking in disgust at Master. The thought of him becoming their Father was not a pleasant option. He stepped forward and summoned his voice. "Gondo-Var! I am Kadam. You all know me! I was not born with you! But like many of you, this man took from my tribe me!" He pointed to Master.

Master snapped his head over to Kadam, surprised that he had the confidence to speak.

"But I made the climb. The great eagle visited me. I am one of you now!" he yelled.

"You have killed our Father!" several people yelled from the crowd.

"Yes, I killed him. It is true. I walked into his tent, and I challenged him. He could not defeat me! He pleaded like a woman!" he shouted out.

The crowd roared with even more ferocity at this, calling for his head.

"Is this not a powerful tribe?" Kadam yelled. "Are we not to take what is weak? Are we not to be led by the strong?"

The crowd was now unsure whether to boo at these words, but their momentum had already taken them there, and they could not help but disapprove of everything he had to say. Kadam then took his logic to the next step. "I was told by this man that I should kill Father, so that he may become the new Father of the Eagles!"

Master stared menacingly at Kadam, and he shook his head in disgust for this sorry attempt to save himself.

"Is this the man you will choose as your Father? I challenge him! I say, let the strongest man win!" Kadam called out, pointing his spear at Master.

Now the angry sounds of the Gondo-Var became muddled, as Master's internal enemies suddenly realized the implication of this challenge.

A voice from the edge of the crowd shouted out, "Challenge! Challenge! Let us see who the better man is!" To that, there was a mix of shouts and approvals. Kadam looked over and saw it was Yaykee, his old tribe member captured long ago.

"Eagle fly! men fall, eagle fly, men fall!" Yaykee chanted, even while men around him pushed and shoved for him to be quiet. Slowly, more and more people chanted, and although they were few, it was enough to hear over the shouts of anger, and it threw the Gondo-Var into disarray, as disagreements slowly broke out within.

Because Father had no biological sons, the assumption was that the leader of the war parties would assume his place. But Master was the one man many in the tribe loved to hate. The man's brutal tactics and long history of abducting captives meant there were plenty of ancient grudges to resurface. The idea of Master taking over was distasteful enough for many to overlook Kadam's crime.

The crowd of Gondo-Var shifted and split apart, as people within the tribe argued and jostled with each other. Master tried once again to withhold order, but those who were against him howled and booed, causing more disruption.

Yaykee rushed out to the middle of the circle, turning to face the tribe. "Kadam has challenged Master! He must answer the challenge. Let us settle this matter here and now!"

The Gondo-Var had cooled their anger at this. A fair challenge was a just way to conclude the disagreement. More and more of them chanted for a challenge. Yaykee held up his hands again. "People, listen, we must not let this man become Father. He is a brutal man, and we will all suffer under him!" Yaykee pointed his finger accusingly. Master had heard enough; he could no longer control his anger at this arrogant outburst. He rushed over to Yaykee; whose back was turned to him. Master thrust his flint knife into the man's back, and Yaykee cried out.

"Shut up, you fool!" Master growled, throwing him down.

Yaykee fell, the flint knife still lodged in his kidney. Those who were on the fence about Master as a leader now changed sides at this cowardly act. They booed in anger as several men rushed forward to Yaykee's aid.

Durok took the opportunity to stoke the fire. "You see! He murders for no reason. Murderer!"

The words were helpful but not necessary; the crowd was no longer in control and had turned on each other. Disputes between warriors and war party leaders had broken out all over. A revolt had begun.

Kadam rushed forward as the people started to scatter, looking to engage with Master, but a flood of men blocked him.

"Kadam! Let us go!" Durok shouted. Durok had ducked between the tents, gesturing to him to make a break for the cliff.

Kadam turned to Master, who was ducking and slicing his way through oncoming attacks. Kadam ducked below as a warrior swung at his head, then countered by spearing his attacker. More were watching him, looking for an opportunity to strike. There was no way he would make it to Master through the angry, dispersing crowd. He turned and met Durok and together they fled through the lines of Father's tents. Every few paces, they encountered a crazed warrior looking to avenge Father's death. Several arrows whizzed by Kadam's head, and this made them hasten their retreat toward the cliff.

Master was being overwhelmed by a mutiny of his warriors. He shouted for Last Chance and several others still loyal to him, and together they formed a defensive circle.

"They have gone to the cliffs! We cannot let them live!" Master yelled as he motioned for his guards to retreat.

The sight of a well-formed guard led by Last Chance and Master thwarted any more attacks, but a few well-placed arrows found their mark, downing some warriors before Master arrived at the cliff.

Looking up, Master could barely make out the two silhouettes of Kadam and Durok as they climbed above them. Master looked back toward the tents. The entire camp now was fully engaged in a civil war. Old rivalries came to a boil, and war party leaders fought each other for position. Those loyal to Master still outnumbered the rebels, but with a tribe of so many, the fight could easily continue until early morning. Master knew he had to kill Kadam to squash the revolt in its entirely.

"Come, there is no escape for them up there," Master said to Last Chance as he grabbed the rock face. Last Chance looked up at the ominous black mountain and gulped in fear before he took hold of the rocks and hoisted himself up.

Chapter 32

The camp Sira and Harq had spied earlier did not look the same as the one they were approaching.

"What happened? Is it the captives?" she asked.

"I do not believe so. We could not free anymore before they came after us. I do not understand," Pliny said, confused.

"We need a closer look!" Sira looked to Harq as if it were his responsibility.

Harq sighed, then scanned the immediate area. "Follow close, stay low," he directed.

As they got closer, the sounds of chaos filled the air. Warriors raided tents, sending women and children fleeing in terror. Some were cut down by warriors with the same crazed look upon their faces that Sira remembered from her first encounter with them. Gangs of warriors torched tents of rival war parties and murdered those who stood against them. Each violent act only fuelled more bloodlust, as the families and friends of the slain sought revenge. Even from afar, they could see a massacre taking place the likes of which they had never seen.

"What is going on? They are killing each other!" asked Sira as she looked on in perverse fear.

"Wolf people," responded Harq, shaking his head. "When wolf leader dies, wolves fight to be the new leader. Wolf people are all same."

"Maybe we will be lucky, and everyone will kill each other," Pliny said.

Sira thought about what Harq said and responded, "These people are not like us. We would never kill each other like animals."

Harq looked doubtfully at her.

"Look, with all this fighting, no one is guarding the captives. I think we could make it to them," she said. She did not wait for a response and was the first to break cover, trotting low and trying to keep to the shadows, heading for the campfires around the captives.

Harq hissed in frustration as he watched her go, already

too late to stop her.

Pliny looked back at him. "Oh, well, where she goes, you follow, right?" he said mockingly.

Harq huffed one of his sighs, then broke out of cover after her.

The Gondo-Var tribe was too preoccupied fighting each other to be concerned over the fate of the captives, and Sira reached them without resistance. One by one, the four of them began to cut the captives free from their ropes. As more Samaki warriors were freed, they were able to wrestle some Gondo-Var to the ground, disarming them. The number of freed captives grew quickly until it reached a point where even the Gondo-Var warriors could not ignore it any longer.

Sira shouted over to Harq, who by now was receiving a large sum of attention as surprised and terrified glances. The twins had to stick close on either side of him, calming the nerves of their Samaki allies. Sira looked around; if they fled now, they could rescue many captives including some of her old tribe members. But she thought of Kadam, and that inner voice tugged at her again, touching that guilty spot in her conscious.

"Pliny, Jin! Take the captives. We will meet you near the cave!" she yelled to them.

Both twins wanted to protest, but Sira had already run farther into the camp, with Harq closely behind.

"She did it again!" Pliny cursed with anger.

"Come on, let's get these people out of here while we still can. Sira can take care of herself," Jin commented.

As more shelters burned by the hands of angry warriors, the fires lit up the camp. As if the fire was fuelled by the tribe's sense of rage, it grew, the dry ground and brush adding fuel to it. Someone soon engulfed a dead tree, and it sizzled and cracked as the dry limbs broke apart. A single spark from one of the broken limbs flew up into the night air. It whipped back and forth in the rising heat, then dropped gently on top of the massive perimeter wall. Consisting of deadwood and broken branches, the perimeter became the perfect host for the spark, and it grew into a massive wall of flames.

The outskirts of the Gondo-Var camp were now deserted except for some women and children who were hiding away from the light of the torches. They paid little mind to Sira and Harq as they passed through, although Harq received plenty of frightened stares.

Eventually, the ground to their right began to rise, as the edge of the black cliff rose toward the mountain. Sira did her best to whistle the sound of the bluebird every few paces in hopes of reaching Kadam, but the call went unanswered. With the fighting in camp to their left and the cliff to their right, they were heading for a dead end.

Behind them, they heard the screams of women and war cries of men as they clashed together in battle. They could no longer retreat the way they came, so they carried along down the cliff wall, staying underneath its dark shadow. They reached another group of captives who had been left in the dark, still bound to each other.

A young female Other with striking long red hair was trying to cut the bonds of the women. The spear tip was broken and rendered dull, but she was sawing frantically at it. She had only made it halfway through the thick fiber rope before Harq announced himself. She chattered about something in their language, and Harq got to work sawing the fibers, freeing all of them.

"Tell them they must run. They must get far away from this camp." Sira said to Harq.

Harq repeated in his language. In turn, the ladies chattered something back at him.

"They say they have nowhere to go. They wish to help us," Harq said.

"They cannot help us. They will be killed, so will we, unless we find Kadam."

The girl with the red hair tilted her head to the side. "Kaa... dam?" she asked.

Sira looked at her, surprised. "Kadam," she repeated, then held out her hands, motioning the size of a big man. "Kadam," she said again, imitating his deep voice.

The girl smiled. "Kaaadam, Kaadam," she said in

understanding.

"Where, Kadam?" asked Harq in their language.

The girl looked up and pointed. There, high above in the cliffs, they could see a few tiny figures against the night sky.

"Well, it doesn't look like we have much choice now. It is our only way out," Sira commented.

They allowed the captives to climb up first. Sira was worried that they would slow their progress but was immediately contradicted when she saw how fast the women climbed. Of course, Sira thought to herself, remembering the steep ravines and cliffs these people called their home.

The black craggy rocks of the mountain were firm, and under the moonlight, they had little trouble making their way up. Sira did her best to keep up, but the captive women were way ahead of her. At some point, the ground became less steep until finally they could walk up the slope.

They soon found themselves on a flat plateau, with the last climb to the summit now visible. Harq noted their surroundings. A small mountain goat trail led around the plateau and back down to the tree line, far away from the Gondo-Var camp.

"They must have gone that way!" Sira said, looking down the path.

The women did not wait for them and were already running down the trail.

Harq searched the dusty ground; he saw men's tracks, but none leading down the trail. He looked up toward the summit; the black face would make it hard to see anyone climbing up. He held his hands over his brow, shielding the moon and starlight from his eyes. Halfway up the steep climb to the summit, he made out the tiny movement of human figures. "They go up there. Into the fire mountain. He is leading men up there," he said.

Sira let out an enormous sigh. "And here I thought Kadam was always afraid of heights. Come on, let's go help them."

* * *

Kadam and Durok were close to the summit and the source of the rising ash. Instead of growing cooler as they rose in elevation, the air became hot around them. A curious orange glow appeared in the air, and both men understood that it must be the source of the great fire.

Looking back, Kadam could barely make out the men below as they climbed up in pursuit. He had no plan other than to find a suitable place away from the Gondo-Var, where they could ambush the men. But the perfect spot for this had not presented itself yet. Far below them in the distance, the Gondo-Var camp was burning as the fire took hold of more scrub and trees, now raging out of control.

Kadam smiled at the memory of his original promise to Durok. Events had aligned in their favor, and their promise was coming true. This gave Kadam a new sense of confidence as he hoisted himself over the top of the ridge summit. He noticed the rocks were hot to the touch.

As both men stood upon the summit, the heat hit their bodies intensely, more so than the hottest summer day. The air smelled of sulfur and smoke. Kadam took a deep breath, and it caused him to gag. They were on a flat ridge of a large circular crater. They could not see to the opposite side, as the rising smoke and ash blocked their view. As they walked forward toward the inner edge, they found the source of the heat. Far below them in the crater, a massive sea of liquid fire glowed angrily as it bubbled and churned, spitting flaming chunks of molten rock halfway up the crater. The lava chunks splashed in a shower of sparks as they hit the rocky sides of the crater wall. Intense heat rose and made them shield their faces and squint their eyes.

"Have you ever seen such a fire?" Durok asked. "Surely the fire spirit itself must dwell down there!"

There was no time to dawdle, as both men knew their pursuers would reach the top soon. Master was a deadly adversary that even alone would pose a threat to the two men, and he had at least two others with him. This was their final stand.

"Come, let us slow their climb," Durok said as he

rushed forward toward the ledge. He picked up a sizeable rock and spotted three men below climbing their way up. Master looked up to see Durok throw the first stone down upon him. He overshot the throw and it whizzed past his head.

"Split up!" Master yelled to the other two, and the other men climbed out to either side.

Kadam and Durok both did their best to rain down as many rocks as they could, but the stones were small. Those that hit their mark did minor damage as the warriors held up their arms in protection. Kadam found one sizeable stone, and he peeked out at the men climbing their way up. Below him, Last Chance was climbing rapidly, almost at the top of the ledge. He had taken his attention away from Kadam for a moment to secure his footing, and Kadam seized the moment. He hurled the rock as hard as he could, grunting as his arm released it.

The sound made Last Chance look up, and the black stone was the last thing he saw before the rock smashed into his head, right between his eyes. The blow made him lose balance, and he lost his footing. He bounced down the ledge, sliding and rolling until coming to a stop at a lip of rock.

Durok had waited for Master to grab onto the final ledge and attempted to stab the man's hand. Master moved his hand out of the way of the oncoming spear, transferring his weight quickly to his other hand. The obsidian tip connected to the rock, shattering the tip. With cat-like grace, Master pushed up with his legs and freehand. He used the upward momentum to land a punch into Durok's face, sending him backward.

In a flash, Master was up on the ridge, assessing the situation. His other Gondo-Var warrior was right behind him, now standing up on the summit. Ahead, Kadam was heading back to have them. Master motioned for this warrior to flank his side, preparing themselves for a fight. The hot air and orange glow had surprised him for a moment, and he glanced over, careful not to take his eyes off the two men who might take a chance at a spear throw.

"Here we are, Kadam," Master yelled over the sound of

the hissing lava. "Your moment has finally come. Just look at what you have caused below," he said, motioning down to the burning camp. "But for all your bravery, your strength, there is still one problem. You still must kill me!"

He dropped into his fighting stance and removed his club from the leather loop around his waist.

Kadam stood at Durok's side. The two men knew how dangerous Master was, and they would need to plan and work together to beat him.

"I will distract Master for as long as I can. Try and kill the other man quickly so you may come to my aid," Kadam whispered.

Durok nodded in agreement as they gauged the distance between each other. The air shimmered and waved between them in an optical illusion as the heat of the crater spilled out.

Durok and Kadam spread out, forcing the other two men to engage them one on one. Durok's opponent made the first move, rushing in and making a forward thrust with his spear. Durok dodged to the side, but the man regained his stance before Durok could counter. He was nimble, and adept with his spear. Master had obviously trained him.

Durok was ready for his second attack, this time allowing the spear to come within millimeters of his head as he countered with a downward slash. Durok's spear rasped against the man's chest, creating a superficial wound across his pectoral muscle. With Durok's broken spear tip, he was at a serious disadvantage, but the chipped obsidian was still sharp enough to cut through skin and flesh. The cut made the warrior back up and reposition himself as both men circled each other, just out of range of each other's spears.

Master advanced slowly toward Kadam, while Kadam retreated backward, waiting for an opening in Master's defense. He would have to make a move soon, as Master was deliberately pushing him toward the inner edge of the crater. Kadam had been in this position many times before, which included their first encounter, along with their training bouts. His anxious and furious attacks had never been effective.

But Kadam had learned a lot over the past months. He

had lost much of the zealousness and overconfidence and had learned the value of patience and strategy. Instead of rushing forward, relying on his brute strength, Kadam would take his time, waiting for an opening. Strength was on his side, although speed and technique were not. His spear was more deadly and had superior reach to Master's club, but the advantage was an illusion. Master could dodge and duck and be upon you in a flash, rendering your weapon useless.

If he could get close enough... If I could get a hold of him, crush him, perhaps even throw him over... Kadam's thoughts were interrupted as Master suddenly dashed forward.

Kadam stepped back and steadied himself, watching Master close the distance between them. A simple spear-thrust would be too predictable. Once Master was in range, Kadam swung, holding the end of his spear with both hands. He started the swing high, but as he did so, he dropped his legs, lowering the spear's arc of attack at the last moment.

Master stayed focused on Kadam as he rushed forward, ignoring his spear, and instead, following the direction of his eyes. The second Kadam's eyes dropped; Master read the intent. He hopped up, bringing his legs out from under him.

Time slowed as Kadam watched Master's legs fly up in anticipation. The man was fast, but not quite fast enough, and part of the spear's shaft knocked hard against Master's left ankle. It was not enough to knock him out of the air, nor enough to thwart Master's attack. But when Master's feet landed back on the ground, a pain shot through his left ankle as the full weight of his body came back down upon it. It caused his club swing to falter and lose a few centimeters of reach.

What would have been a knockout blow to Kadam's forehead instead smashed into the bridge of his nose. Kadam heard the crunch of cartilage as it shattered into pieces. His head flew back and blood gushed from his nostrils. The momentum caused the two men to crash together.

Kadam fought to keep his head from going black and ignored the pain as he worked his arm around Master's neck, pulling him down to the ground. Master broke the hold and rolled away, shuffling up to his feet. Master felt another jolt of pain as he attempted to put weight back onto his left foot. Kadam rolled back and got up on one knee. He expected the next attack, and instinctively two-handed the spear horizontally over his head in a block. The overhead swing of Master's club contacted the shaft of Kadam's spear, snapping it in half.

The follow-through of the swing put Master in an awkward position, allowing Kadam to grab the club with one hand. He pulled Master closer to him, once again wrapping his arm around the man's neck to get him into a headlock— exactly where he wanted him. Master once again proved himself too cunning, and wedged his wrist between his neck and Kadam's arm.

Kadam could not choke him out with Master's wrist blocking, so he dragged him in the crater's direction. Master struggled back with all his strength, and Kadam grimaced with each step, dragging the man along the rocks. He was only a few steps from the edge when Master kicked forward in the same direction, throwing Kadam off balance.

Master placed his leg between Kadam's, and they fell together toward the crater edge. Kadam landed face down and reached out with both hands to catch the ledge of the rock. His head was over the side, and he glimpsed the bright lava below. The heat hit his face so hard it made his eyes water, and he flipped onto his back to prepare for the next attack. Master had picked up the sharp end of Kadam's broken spear, and he thrust down. Kadam caught the shaft with both hands just in time; the tip of the obsidian point was a finger's width from his throat.

Master had the advantage of being on top, and using his leverage, he pushed down, inching the spear tip closer to his Adam's apple. Kadam did not have the strength to stop the thrust and knew the next push from Master would send the point into his neck. But something made him break off.

Master spun around to find Durok heading toward him in a charge. His hands held the spear of the other warrior he had killed. One of Durok's eyes was shut under a red slash of blood, the sacrifice of his victory.

Master dropped to a low stance just before Durok thrust forward. He attempted to avoid the spear and grab it by the shaft, but Durok had shifted at the last moment, and the flint tip hit Master low in the side of his pelvis. He fell back with Durok on top of him.

Using Durok's momentum, Master placed his foot on Durok's stomach and pushed him upward as they rolled back. Durok had no way of stopping the momentum as Master used the man's force against him. Durok flew high into the air, over Master and Kadam. He saw himself fly over the edge. The intense heat and choking smoke consumed his senses as he fell downward.

The last thing Durok heard was Kadam's shout of anguish before he hit the lava. He was knocked unconscious as he slammed into the thick substance, his body slowly engulfed in flames.

Kadam rolled away and came back to his feet. He spit out the metallic taste of blood out and rounded again toward Master. The piercing blow that landed on Master's pelvis caused him to favor one side. Kadam rushed him, and this time Master could not react quick enough. He gripped Master into a bear hug, lifting him clear off his feet. Squeezing with all his might, he heard a crack of a rib, followed by a grunt of pain.

Master reared back and slammed his forehead into Kadam's face, further breaking the bones and cartilage of Kadam's nose. Kadam tried to squeeze harder, but Master butted his head, again and again, hitting the ridge of his eyes and forehead. Kadam became dizzy and felt his vision blur. Finally, his arms lost their strength and Master fell out of his grip. Master stepped back and, winding back his leg, kicked Kadam's chest, sending him flying over the crater's edge.

Master fell to the ground, holding his side in pain. It hurt to breathe, but his face held a wicked smile of delight and relief. He looked down at the gushing stab wound on his pelvis; and he clenched his hand over it to stifle the bleeding. He was banged up pretty good, more than he ever had been in his life, but he would recover. He would have loved to watch Kadam fall into the lava, but there was not time.

Instead, he got onto his hands and knees and steadied himself.

He had to get back as fast as possible and cauterize this wound before he lost too much blood. More importantly, he had to get the Gondo-Var back under control as soon as possible. As he stood up, two more figures appeared on the ledge. At first, he thought it was some of his Gondo-Var warriors, and he smiled at the thought of some help. But as the figures appeared in the moonlight, he recognized the dark-skinned girl. The one who had escaped. Another man appeared by her side, one of the Others.

"Where is Kadam!" she screamed at him in anger.

He smiled, knowing he could play her anger to his advantage. He paused before responding, looking around for a weapon. He found his club on the ground, several paces behind him, and he lifted his finger, motioning over the cliff. "I have thrown him over into the fire. Do you wish to join?"

It was all the information Sira needed, and she rushed forward with her spear.

"Sira!" Harq shouted before moving after her.

Master waited until she was close enough before turning and diving into a roll, grabbing his club as he did so. The movement caused another great shot of pain in his broken rib, but he ignored it. He came up and turned on his knee in one fluid motion, blocking her spear thrust. He rose to his feet and spun, knocking her on the back of her head with the club. She went down hard on her stomach, holding the back of her head in pain.

Harq followed with his spear, but the thrust was too predictable, and Master's club smacked down onto Harq's wrist, forcing Harq to drop the weapon. But Master was slowed by his injuries, and his attempt to swing the club at Harq's head was weak.

Harq ducked the swing and grabbed the man by his neck, squeezing tightly and lifting him off his feet. Master's legs dangled and danced around like a child as Harq headed for the inner edge of the crater. Master kicked at him, but the blows bounced harmlessly off Harq's muscular chest. Master swung his club down at his head, but Harq caught it with his free hand, twisting it away in one movement and tossing it down as if it were a play toy.

The pressure against Master's throat choked his airway, and he felt his face go hot. His mind raced as he thought of a way to break free. He placed both feet against Harq's chest. With both legs, he pushed back as hard as he could while using both hands to twist Harq's index finger. The grip around his neck finally broke free, and he fell to the ground with a gasp of air, while Harq fell backward a few steps.

Master scurried back on all fours toward the edge of the crater, grabbing his club. He had never faced an opponent of such strength. Harq was patient, approaching Master calmly. For the first time, Master felt fear of another man. At the ledge, he found Kadam's broken spear tip and grabbed it as he stood up. He twirled his club with his right hand, and in his left hand, he kept the spear tip hidden behind his back.

Master rallied his confidence and smiled back at the man. "That's right! Come on, closer... closer, you ape," he taunted.

Harq reached out to grab Master, but Master had read his movement perfectly. He ducked, swinging his club against the side of his head. The blow put Harq down to one knee, his head dizzy. Master struck with the spear tip, but Harq caught his wrist before it pierced his neck. Master beat down with his club as Harq tried to defend with his free arm, but the vicious club caused intense pain with each blow. The point of the spear pushed closer as Master pushed with all his might, now using two hands; the spear point slowly touched the skin on Harq's neck.

Master smiled again and widened his stance. He braced himself to push harder as the spear started to puncture through the skin. But that was as far as he got. Master felt a presence behind him, but before he could react, it was too late. Two hands wrapped around his neck and hurled him backward. He struggled against the grip, but it was solid, and he knew at once who held him as they fell over the ledge.

Harq reached out as the two men fell over, grabbing onto Kadam's forearm, which was wrapped around Master's neck.

"Kadam!" Sira yelled in surprise as she rose to her feet.

Harq reached out with his other hand, grabbing Kadam's arm. He was holding both men, who were now leaning out over the edge. Harq could see the sweat of perspiration on Kadam's face from the heat. Below them, a lava bubble expanded up into a sphere, then exploded, sending the heavy liquid halfway up toward them as if in anticipation of its next meal.

Master looked up at Harq in desperation, now hoping he would save his life by pulling them up. Master's eyebrows raised as he got a good look at the man. Although his face was contorted, and his skin was pale, there was no doubt who he resembled, and Master almost smiled at the irony.

Kadam pushed back with his legs against the ledge, trying to throw them over as Harq's feet slid closer to the lip of the crater. He looked down at Kadam. "Let go, grab ledge!" he said to him in a strained face. But there was no way Kadam could save himself and let go of Master at the same time.

Harq tried to pull them back, but slid further. The front of his feet slid over the ledge. His toes could feel the heat of lava below, even through the leather wraps.

Harq glanced at Kadam to protest, but was caught by the man's expression. A peaceful calm had settled over it, and he smiled up at Harq.

"Let us go," Kadam whispered. "Let us go..."

The ball of Harq's lead foot had reached the edge of the crater, and he no longer had the grip to hold on. Together, the three men went over the edge. Harq let go at the last second, twisting in mid-air and grabbing the rock ledge. He could hear Sira's scream above the sound of the hissing lava. Master scrambled as he fell, trying to get loose of Kadam's grip. He managed to turn and face him and saw a glorious smile across the man's face.

"You lose," Kadam said as he ripped the sabre-tooth canine from Master's chest. An instant later, their bodies smashed into the hard liquid.

Sira was up and running toward the edge of the crater. She found Harq holding on, trying to get a foothold to pull himself up. She grabbed his hand, and together they pushed up. Once he was safe, she fell onto the edge, looking down toward the lava. She had to shield her face with her hand against the rising heat, and she choked on the acidic air.

Kadam and Master had burst into flames as their bodies were slowly being submerged into the dense liquid. Kadam's figure was on his back, his arms spread out open. She watched his burning body slowly sink, then disappear. The heat to her face became unbearable, and she had to turn away. She grabbed Harq, and they embraced each other.

As if the mountain had responded to something bad it had ingested, it rumbled again. There was a loud crunching sound of rocks being split apart. Cracks appeared underneath them as the ground separated.

"Come, Sira! Hurry," Harq shouted as he helped her up.

The ground shook again violently, throwing them off their feet. Behind them, a section of the crater's edge fell off, crumbling down the crater into the lava. The crater hissed and smoked as the rocks fell into the superheated liquid. Harq once again helped Sira to her feet, and they ran hand in hand, stumbling as the crater shifted beneath them.

As Sira neared the outer edge, another explosion threw her down. She rolled and fell over the outer edge. Harq dove out for her, catching her wrist as she fell over the cliff. He held her steady while she reached out for a handhold onto the rocks.

Yet another explosion shook the ground again, and a giant lava bubble burst from inside the crater, sending the sizzling hot liquid into the air. Lava droplets splashed down around them, and a small splatter landed on Harq's back, burning his skin.

Sira finally found a secure hold with her hands and feet, so Harq threw himself over the ledge just as more lava sprayed the ground. He fell over awkwardly but caught hold of the ledge and steadied himself, grimacing at the pain of the burn on his back.

They made their way down in a flurry of stumbles and rolls, slipping and sliding as the entire mountain boomed and shook. Reaching the plateau, they veered sharply upon finding the goat path. They dodged from side to side as liquid lava and rock shrapnel rained down from above. The goat trail winded and twisted its way through the plateau, the bovids always finding the path of least resistance. It soon led them away from the destructive side of the roiling summit and into the forest. From here, they could watch from a safe distance as boiling lava melted the summit of the mountain in half.

* * *

The Gondo-Var camp was still engulfed in uncontrollable flames. The internal battles had only ended once they saw the mountain blow apart. Families gathered their children and their most precious belongings to flee the flames. Despite a few skirmishes on the outskirts, it was clear which direction the fight had turned, with those loyal to Master succeeding in the end and taking control.

As the mountain rumbled and exploded, the crater that lay behind their camp above the black cliff crumbled apart. The crater revealed its internal orange contents as it rolled its way down the slope. Their camp lay directly under the path of the lava flow, consuming everything. There would be no need to bury the victims of their internal fighting. The rocks and lava had done so.

* * *

"Kadam! ...Kadam!" Nara screamed into the night. Her face felt the heat of the fire on the perimeter wall, and the hissing steam muted her voice. Even if her man had somehow survived, she doubted he would live through the night.

Her few belongings were wrapped in hide, and she picked them up and threw it over her shoulder with a chord of a tendon. She gripped her spear in one hand and the leather knife scabbard in the other. Her spear was already bloodied from one of Master's sycophants who had tried to attack her.

Away from the flames, she regrouped with some fellow warriors at the edge of the forest, watching as the slow-moving lava swallowed the rest of their camp. Eventually, the lava crawled its way to the perimeter of the camp, engulfing and extinguishing the wall of flames. Survivors moaned and cried with lament as the orange liquid burned everything they knew and loved. Nara licked her lips at the salty tears running down her face. It was an unfamiliar taste. In fact, it was the first time she ever remembered crying. She held her hands over her belly. A rage boiled inside of her, but she knew not where to direct it. After all, it was her own man who had killed Father and betrayed the tribe, sending them into this violent chaos.

Her thoughts were interrupted as the warriors began to chant, "eagle fly, men fall, eagle fly, men fall!" Nara looked over to find the man with the circular scars, the one they called Last Chance. There was a wound between his eyes, and blood had crusted around it. He brandished his spear in the air, calling for support to ascend as the new leader of the Gondo-Var. Nara knew the man well and despised him. *No, it cannot be this man. It should have been Kadam.*

"Is there anyone who challenges me? Let him show himself now!" Last Chance yelled out to the warriors.

Many Gondo-Var warriors shuffled and glanced at one another anxiously. He might not be the shining example of a leader, but he was Master's right-hand man, a man who had occupied a high rank in the tribe.

"Anyone who does not wish to see me ascend, challenge me now, or forever remain loyal!"

"I challenge you!" a female voice rang out.

The voices were hushed to silence as they parted to make room for the challenger. A chorus of muffled shocks and whispers erupted upon seeing Nara, a bloody spear in her hands and at the ready.

Last Chance balked. "Bah! You cannot challenge! You cannot become Father of this tribe!"

"No, I can be its Mother!"

Last Chance grimaced, stepping forward to meet her. He tried to hide his anxiety. The woman was no pushover, and she had already outwrestled him once, the day he tried to mount her without her permission. "Come then, it is fitting the woman of a traitor be cut down, here and now."

Nara threw down her spear and roll of hide. She unsheathed her flint knife from its leather scabbard. "Spears are for the weak. Face me like a man."

Last Chance recoiled in surprise. She might have the advantage at close combat, but he couldn't back down. He unsheathed his knife, finding the right position and balance in his palm. Without further discussion, he rushed toward her.

Nara met his run, and they clashed together. Both managed to grab each other's wrists before impact. They clashed together, chest to chest. Last Chance had a slight advantage in arm strength, and he used it to push his knife toward her chest. Her legs were stronger, so they stood together, evenly matched. She pushed him back a step, but when she did so, her hand gave way, and his knife inched closer. The lean muscles of his shoulders and arms strained as he pressed. His upper body was simply too powerful.

Last Chance smiled. His sharpened teeth and scarred face made a devilish sight. His knifepoint was now tickling her skin, just above the point of her hide shirt. Locked eye to eye, he spoke victoriously. "Eagle fly, men fall."

Nara smiled. "Men fall," she whispered. Guiding his hand down with the last of her strength, she released her grip. The flint knife punctured the hide shirt and entered her chest. She growled in fury. The moment of victory made Last Chance release his grip on the knife—a fatal mistake.

Nara grabbed his neck, pulling him closer. Her eyes met his, and she repeated. "*Men* fall..."

Last Chance felt the stab in his solar plexus, just beneath his ribs. He heard the snap of the obsidian tip break off as she twisted it. His mouth opened in surprise as he stepped back. The hole below his ribs gushed a fountain of blood, and he dropped to his knees.

Nara carefully pulled up her hide shirt, exposing the flint knife stuck inside her. Cupping her large breast in one hand, she pulled the knife from it, grimacing in pain. Blood flowed down her side in rivulets. It was a grievous injury, but it wasn't fatal. She pressed the hide shirt tightly against the wound, slowing the bleeding. One breast sufficed to feed a baby, anyway.

"Eagle fly, men fall!" She yelled in triumph, lifting the bloody knife into the air.

The Gondo-Var stood motionless and in awe. Their night of violence had ended with one final, bloody match, and it was a woman who had been victorious. It was a sign, and the females were the very first to shout her name. It did not take long for the other warriors to join in the chant—*Nara!*

As she looked out into the sea of survivors and blazing fires in the distance, something awakened inside of her. Old loyalties, tribal grudges, and rival war parties would remain a challenge to them, but she would quell that. She would see past it to a new future. And from the ashes of this volcano, the   Gondo-Var   would   rise   again.

Chapter 33

Sira and Harq found the twins near the entrance to the cave ravine, as agreed. They had rescued two dozen captives on their escape from the camp. They were a mix of their old clan members and Samaki villagers. As expected, the Other women had disappeared like ghosts as soon as they entered the forest.

They led the escapees into the dark cavern, chaining their arms together so that they could cross safely. The rumbling sounds of the volcano echoed in the distance.

At the exit of the cave, Harq and Sira ordered everyone to keep a tight group, as they were wary of the wolf pack. But there was no sign of the wolves. They had given up on their former benefactors, returning to the wild.

Only once they were down the slope and into the forest did they dare stop to rest. By now, the first glimmer of morning light started to appear, a sliver of orange emanating from behind the mountain range. They made a camp while men and women foraged for edible items, others took the opportunity to rest. They might have felt some sort of relief or gratitude to have been freed but losing so much had dampened any feelings of happiness.

Without direction, they naturally turned to the heroic woman who had risked her own life to free them, and Sira led them north. She followed Harq's advice, sticking to the rocky terrain to keep their tracks to a minimum.

They all agreed they should put a great distance between themselves and the remnants of the Gondo-Var tribe. The column of smoke behind them had calmed overnight, as if the terrible fire inside the mountain had finally cooled and subsided.

As if on cue, more signs of life returned to the forest. Butterflies bloomed around them, their yellow wings sparkling in the sunshine. Bluebirds danced in the air, diving in for a meal and gorging on insects.

Sira did her best to imitate the whistle of the little bird, and the twins joined in. Each did their best attempt, and they named Jin the clear winner. Then they heard the bird whistle from behind them. They turned to see Harq, his lips pursed together. It was indistinguishable from a wild bluebird.

"Looks like you still have a lot to learn," Sira said to Jin, pointing to Harq and laughing.

Eventually, the group came upon the same stream where Harq had taken Sira after her rescue. The group sighed in relief as they splashed their feet into the refreshing stream and scooped the clear water into their mouths. It did not take long before most of them had stripped down and entered the water for a bath.

Harq had found the yellow flower, and he taught Sira how to grind it up with a few drops of water. She made a salve with it and stroked it into the red lava burn on his back. He felt her sigh, so he turned and wrapped her in his arms. Her head fell to his shoulder, and he felt the warm droplets of tears fall onto his skin.

They were resting on the bank of the stream in silence for quite some time before the twins came bounding down toward them, grinning like silly children. In Jin's hand was a dead hare, with an arrow still sticking through its torso. He held it up triumphantly and asked, "Who's hungry?"

Sira smiled weakly, and the twins could read her mood.

Pliny sat next to her, bumping his elbow against hers playfully in an attempt to lighten her mood. "What's on your mind, big sister?"

Sira looked up at the sky. "We have lost everything, haven't we? Our families, friends, our clan."

Pliny threw his arm around her. "We still have each other. Look at the group we have. We can survive through next winter with all of us working together, right?"

Sira shook her head. "The Samaki wish to return to their village. I have tried to warn them that their shaman is dangerous, but they will not listen. Even if they believe me, they wish to return to their families, and I do not blame them. If they go, few of us will remain, hardly enough for our clan."

"Agh, let them go. We can make it on our own. I am sure we will find good people, far from here," Pliny said hopefully.

"Who would let *him* in?" Sira said, motioning to Harq. "People are afraid of him. They won't understand."

"Well, we all accept him. Who knows, maybe there is a place where people like him and us live together! Although I hope they talk more than him, otherwise nights by the fires will be long and dark," he said.

Sira smiled at this, shaking her head. "People would never accept him," she repeated.

Pliny sighed. "Well, what if we could find more people like him?"

"Good luck with that. Look how well hidden his people were!" she reminded him.

Pliny nodded and could offer no other suggestion, so he kissed her cheek. "I'm sure you will see something for us tomorrow. You always do. Let us live day by day for now. We will rest and get stronger while we wait for our opportunity."

Sira smiled at him. "You sound like my Father! One day, you will be a great leader."

This made him laugh as he rose to his feet, facing the two men who were busy skinning the rabbit. "So, we go north, Harq. What do you say about that?"

"Hmph," grunted Harq as he peeled back the fur of the rabbit.

Sira thought about fleeing north, far from the Samaki and Gondo-Var. It should have made her feel better, but it didn't. There was something on her mind, unresolved. What was it that was pulling her toward the Samaki village?

Tonik! Sira suddenly stood up quickly. "No!" she said, more loudly and forcefully than she had meant to.

The men stopped at this, looking up at her for an explanation.

She looked down at them, shaking her head. She had to pause for a moment to gather her thoughts. "We cannot just run away. Do you remember what I told you all? I am not running away anymore."

"Sure, Sira. But we are not running away. Are we?" Pliny asked quizzically.

"Yes, we are... I mean, I am. I am running away from

Tonik." She sighed and looked down. "I don't know what he has done, but I am sure that witch Laksha has something to do with it. I know she was involved with the Gondo-Var, and that is why they did not capture the entire village. We have to convince these Samaki to help us take their village back when the time comes! We have to save him."

Jin huffed in protest. "It didn't seem like he wanted to be saved that last time we saw him."

She squatted down to their level, looking at them sympathetically. "I know the last thing we all want to do is go back into a fight. But we have to try! Besides, I made a promise to that shaman that I would kill her. I wouldn't want her to think I'm a liar," she grinned. "I will never be able to live in peace if I run now."

Pliny placed a hand on her shoulder, and they all looked at each other earnestly. They had heard this speech before. There would be no use trying to dissuade her.

"I am not asking any of you to join me. I understand if you wish to move on," Sira said to the twins.

This annoyed them, and they scoffed. "Have we ever turned you down before?" Pliny asked. "Sira, you saved us. All of us. Of course, we will join you. But we must hide first. We must rest. We must get stronger and make a plan of attack."

Sira nodded in agreement. All of them were exhausted. They would offer no threat in the state they were in.

Harq was butchering the rabbit when they all looked over at him. He had been listening to the entire conversation but showed no emotion or signs that he cared.

"Well? What do you have to say about this?" Pliny asked him impatiently.

Harq stopped and pointed at Sira, and with his stereotypical stoic nature, he said, "Where Sira go-"

"Yes, yes, where Sira go, you follow," Pliny said and rolled his eyes.

They all laughed at this, and Harq stared blankly, not understanding the joke. This made them laugh even harder.

S. A. ADAMS

STAY TUNED FOR THE SEQUEL – JOIN THE EMAIL LIST! NO SPAM, I PROMISE. BUT YOU WILL RECEIVE A DISCOUNT OR A FREE ADVANCED READER COPY!
https://saadamsauthor.me/contact-2/

PLEASE FOLLOW ME ON AMAZON AT:
https://www.amazon.com/S-A-Adams/e/B08HM2BDTK/

IF YOU LIKED THE BOOK – PLEASE KINDLY LEAVE A REVIEW! REVIEWS HELP US STRUGGLING SELF-PUBLISHED AUTHOR'S A GREAT DEAL, AND WE GREATLY APPRECIATE THEM!
https://www.amazon.com/gp/product/B08HKFB2LY

Printed in Great Britain
by Amazon

25485402R00169